LORD OF LONDON TOWN

TILLIE COLE

COPYRIGHT

actual events or locales is purely coincidental. The characters and names are products of the author's imagination and used fictitiously.

The publisher and author acknowledge the trademark status and trademark ownership of all trademarks, service marks and word marks mentioned in this book.

"Hell is empty and all the devils are here."

- William Shakespeare

LORD OF LONDON TOWN BRITISH SLANG & TERMS

(Note: many of these slang words/terms have multiple uses in British slang. The ones stated below are used in the context of this novel)

Arse — buttocks. *"He fell on his arse."* Can also be used as an insult. *"You arse!"*

Away with the fairies — not all there. A little crazy. Dreamlike state. *"She was away with the fairies."*

Barmy — slightly crazy. Odd. Strange. *"You're barmy, mate."*

Bird — girl or young woman. *"That bird's hot."*

Bloke — man. *"He's a big bloke."*

Bloody — mild expletive. *"Bloody hell!"*

Bobby/Bobbies — a police officer/the police. *"Call the bobbies."*

Bollocks — testicles. *"She kicked me in my bollocks."* Can also be used to call out a lie. *"That's total bollocks!"*

Bonkers — insane. *"You're bonkers!"*

Boot — trunk of a vehicle. *"I put my suitcase in the boot."*

Booze — alcohol. *"Bring some booze to the party."*

Cabbie — taxi-cab driver. *"I paid the cabbie."*

Cig — cigarette. *"Pass me a cig."*

Clapped eyes — to see or look at someone or something. *"I clapped eyes on her."*

Cockney — a native of East London. *"He spoke with a Cockney accent."*

Dodgy — something wrong or illegal. *"That looked dodgy."*

Fannying — messing around. *"Stop fannying about with your phone."*

Fella — man or boy. *"Little fella."*

Firm — British-based organised criminal gang/syndicate. *"They're part of the notorious Adley Firm."*

Flannel — washcloth. *"I washed my face with a flannel."*

Flat — apartment. *"My flat was on the fifth floor."*

Gaffer — boss. *"Talk to the gaffer."*

Gear — drugs. *"They had the best gear in England."*

Geezer — man (generally old in age). *"He was a proper geezer."*

Gobshite — loud-mouthed person who talks a lot, but nothing of real worth. *"He's a proper gobshite."*

Graft — hard work. *"That was hard graft."*

Half-arsed — to do something to a poor standard. *"That was a half-arsed attempt."*

Hard — tough. *"He was hard as nails."*

Hen do — bachelorette party. *"It's my hen do on Saturday."*

Jumper — sweatshirt. *"He was wearing a red jumper."*

Knackered — extremely tired. *"I'm bloody knackered!"*

Knickers — female undergarments. *"Her knickers were lace."*

Legless — extremely drunk. *"He was legless!"*

Lift — elevator. *"We took the lift upstairs."*

Mate — friend. *"My best mate."* Can also be used in a negative term toward someone who has annoyed you. *"Mate, back the hell off."*

Mobile (phone) — cell phone. *"I answered my mobile."*

Numpty — a derogatory term meaning 'stupid'. *"He was a bloody numpty."*

Old Bill — police. *"Here come the Old Bill."*

Pigs — a derogatory term for the police force. *"Here come the pigs!"*

Pissed — drunk. *"He was completely pissed."*

Pissed off — angry. *"You pissed her off."*

Plank — mildly offensive term meaning 'stupid' or 'idiot'. *"Shut up, you plank."*

Prick — a derogatory term meaning 'stupid'. *"Stop being a prick!"*

Secondary school — High school. *"I'm at secondary school."*

Shag — to have sex. *"Fancy a shag?"*

Sixth Form — non-compulsory final two years of high school. *"We went to the same Sixth Form."*

Slapper — offensive term for a woman with loose morals. *"She was a total slapper."*

The Big Smoke — a large city, especially London. *"We headed back to The Big Smoke."*

Tosser — mildly offensive term. *"You tosser!"*

Trap — mouth. *"Shut your trap!"*

Trolleyed — drunk/intoxicated with alcohol. *"They were completely trolleyed."*

Trousers — pants. *"He wore black trousers."*

Twat — a derogatory term meaning 'stupid' or 'obnoxious'. *"He was a twat."*

Wanker — mildly offensive term. *"You bloody wanker."*

PROLOGUE

ARTHUR

Aged thirteen

I stared into the fire.

The flames grew higher and higher, crawling up the stone chimney. I felt the blistering heat on my forehead and cheeks, felt my eyebrows begin to singe. I leaned in even closer. I wanted to know what it felt like when the flames licked my skin.

I wanted to know what *they* had felt when they were trapped, when the fire had burned them alive. I reached out my hand, my fingers moving closer to the flames. Their dance was reflected in my glasses. All I could see was an aura of orange and red and yellow. My skin started to burn as my fingertips almost touched the flame. I smelled my arm hair burning. I moved closer and closer, almost touching it—

"Arthur!" Someone pulled on my shoulder, wrenching me back into the ancient wingback chair. "What the fuck, son?" My dad crouched before me. I looked into his eyes but could still see the flames beckoning me closer from the corner of my eye. "What the hell were you doing?" He took hold of my upper arms, then my throbbing hand. It was bright red where the flames had got too close. "Christ, Arthur! Look at the bloody state of your hand!"

"I wanted to know what they felt," I said, staring at my red and bubbled skin. Dad got up and walked into the kitchen. When he came back, he was holding a bag of frozen peas. He pressed it to my palm. It hurt like a bitch, but I wouldn't tell him that. I didn't care if it hurt.

I *wanted* it to hurt.

"Keep that pressed on there," Dad said, then moved to the bucket of water beside the fire and threw it on the raging flames. The fire instantly died down until it hissed as it lost its breath and black smoke raced up the chimney. I watched the blackness rush away. But the darkness in my heart and head never went away.

I saw our country cottage in my mind. Our family cottage when all that was left was burnt bricks and charred wood ... and only the teeth of my mum and little sister. Bodies burnt to nothing. Fire had eaten their flesh like a demon from the depths of hell.

Dad crouched down again and held my chin. I met his eyes. "I know it's hard, son. You lost your mum, you lost Pearl." I thought of Mum and Pearl. Pearl annoyed me. Always a shadow behind me and my friends. Always wanting to be in my room, in my fucking life. She was only a year younger than me, but she was still my little sister. I always protected her. In our life, I had to. But I hadn't protected her in the end. When she needed me most.

When I closed my eyes, I pictured her holding on to Mum in the middle of the living room in the cottage, the fire knocking the door down to get them, to consume them, to fucking burn them alive. I could hear their screams in my ears. Could hear Pearl calling for me to save her.

I'd failed her. Her and Mum.

"If you'd gone with them, I would've lost you too, son." My dad's voice was tight, low. He never showed emotion—he was an ice box when it came to his feelings. He was hard and brutal. Never spoke about love and shit. But when he mentioned Mum and Pearl, I heard the slight crack. Even though he hardly ever talked about them, I knew he missed them too.

His hand moved from my chin to the back of my head. He pulled me to his chest. He smelled of tobacco and mint. Dad had kept me from going to the cottage a month ago. He'd had business here in town. I'd just turned thirteen. He'd wanted me with him; my time had come to be shown the family business.

I could still feel the knife in my hand. Feel my fingers wrapped around its handle as I stood in front of our enemy in our deserted warehouse in Mile End. I didn't even flinch as I rushed forward and plunged the knife straight into the fucker's chest. He was one of the Yakuza. He'd ratted us out to an enemy. He'd deserved to die.

It was my introduction to our way of life.

I was a true Adley now, legitimately part of the firm.

As I'd killed the enemy, my baptism into our notorious crime family's legacy, my mum and sister had breathed their last breath as our Cotswolds cottage fell down around them.

My dad pulled back from me, searching my face. I wouldn't cry. I didn't *want* to cry. I wasn't sad; I was fucking *enraged*. Anger ran thick in my blood. I wanted to find whoever was responsible and kill them. Both the fire brigade and police investigation had said it was an electrical fault—a common issue with such old country cottages. Ours had been over five hundred years old.

It wasn't enough. I didn't care who, but someone needed to pay for my losing my mum and sister. I needed someone to blame. I couldn't take it being an accident.

I needed someone to die ... slowly ... painfully.

"Arthur," my dad said, pulling me back from darkness. "It's only us now. Us and our firm—they're our only family now. You've got Charlie, Vinnie, Eric and Freddie. They're your brothers. Always have been. They'll be with you all your life, just like their dads have been beside me in mine."

Dad put his hand on my shoulder, clutching it tightly. "We've got to keep going, Arthur. No looking back. We've got a firm to run. We can't afford anything to make us weak." Dad got to his feet. I dropped the bag of frozen peas on the table beside me. I wanted to feel my scalding skin. I wanted the fire's scars to remind me of what and *who* I'd lost. Dad looked at the discarded peas and his lips curled in a proud smile— my old man loved any display of strength, especially if it was from me. "Get your coat. I've got a meeting. You're coming."

I followed my dad to the hallway and grabbed my thick black over- coat. We stepped out of our old converted church in Bethnal Green and toward the car that waited for us. The night was freezing cold, my warm breath turning to white smoke as it hit the frigid air. I climbed into the back of the Rolls Royce. My dad sat beside me.

Wordlessly, we pulled out of our drive and onto the roads of our kingdom—East London. I stared out of the window as the streets that we owned passed by. I kept my focus outside, the views moving from battered warehouses with boarded-up windows, terraced council houses and run-down pubs to upscale restaurants and bars, mansions and one-hundred-thousand-pound cars.

Motherfucking Chelsea.

Jack, my dad's personal driver, stopped in front of a mansion in SW3. Jack kept the engine running. Rain had started to pour outside, the heavy drops thundering on the car windows and roof like bombs. Jack got out of the car and opened my dad's door. He opened a black golf umbrella to protect him from the rain. Alfie Adley always had to look pristine. I followed him from the car, and Dad took the umbrella off Jack. "We won't be long," he said to Jack.

We walked to the house, and Dad knocked on the door. A fucking butler of some type answered. Dad pushed past him, knocking him backwards into some no doubt expensive but ugly-as-fuck vase. "I'm here to see George."

"But, sir, wait!" the butler argued. Dad opened the hallway door, and I shut the front door, locking us inside. A man about my dad's age came rushing down a huge central staircase and stopped on a landing.

"Wait here, Arthur. I won't be long," Dad said, his eyes locking on the fucker who was glaring at him with wide and fearful eyes. My dad cut a deadly look to the butler. "Make sure Alfred here doesn't do something stupid like call the Old Bill." Dad cracked his neck, never taking his glare off the butler. "This is a friendly meeting, right, George? No need for things to go south."

"It's okay, James," the man—George, I guessed—on the landing said to the butler, and my father followed him up the stairs. Putting my hands in my pockets, I moved to the wall in the hallway and the pictures that hung there, keeping the butler in my peripheral. I cleaned my glasses on my shirt, rubbing the rain from the lenses so I could bloody see. When I put them back on, I was in front of a picture of a girl about my age. She had dark hair and dark eyes and olive skin. I passed pictures of a brunette woman and George.

Done browsing, I sat on the ornate red sofa in the foyer and looked around the house. Money. Whoever this George prick was, he had a fuck-ton of money.

My eyes moved from the posh artwork and sculptures and went back to the girl in the picture. Then I didn't look away. Just as I wondered who she was, the stairs creaked. My eyes snapped up.

Brown hair.

Brown eyes.

Long legs.

Olive skin.

The girl from the picture froze on the stairs, her eyes widening when she saw me. My eyes dropped to her clothes. She was wearing pyjamas. The white top was sleeveless, and the bottoms were shorts with pink polka dots all over them. Her brown hair fell to her shoulders.

I watched silently as she searched around the foyer, her cheeks blazing red. She came further down the stairs until she was stood on the black-and-white tiled floor of the hallway. "W-who are you?" Her posh accent sailed into my ears. A proper Chelsea girl. No doubt brought up with a silver spoon in her mouth. And what a fucking mouth she had. Full, dark pink lips that seemed to permanently pout. Eric, one of my best friends, called those cock-sucking lips.

In this bird's case, I had to agree.

She folded her arms across her chest but edged closer. "Who are you?" she asked again.

I leaned back against the couch. "Arthur."

"Arthur," she echoed and came closer again. She was only a few feet away. Her skin was lightly tanned and smooth, and her shorts showed off her perfect thighs. Posh birds never really did it for me. But by the twitch of my cock, this one seemed to be the exception. "Arthur ..." she said again, her posh accent wrapping around my name. Suddenly, the sound of raised voices came from upstairs. Her head whipped in that direction.

"Daddy? That's Daddy's voice." She faced me, panicked. "Who's up there with him?"

"My old man."

"Why?"

I shrugged. "Business."

She frowned, then said, "You don't give much away, do you?"

"What's your name?" I asked, ignoring her question.

"Cheska."

"Cheska ... ?"

"Cheska Harlow-Wright." She tilted up her chin—she was proud of her name. My eyes found a picture I'd seen on the wall, one in front of a factory, "Harlow" written on the signage.

All the wealth suddenly made sense.

"Harlow Biscuits." I suddenly knew how they could afford to live in a house like this in the best postcode in Chelsea. There wasn't a home in all of England that wouldn't have had a pack of their biscuits in the cupboard to dunk into cups of tea.

"Yes." She followed my gaze. The picture on the wall was old. An elderly geezer was stood outside the biscuit factory. There was a younger man there too, and a little girl, no more than about four years old, dressed in a bonnet and a red coat. "My mum," she said and moved to the picture. She pointed to the little girl. "When she was little, with my granddad and great-granddad."

I didn't look at the picture. I was too busy looking at her. Cheska the Chelsea girl. "Where is she now?"

Cheska's face fell. When she met my eyes, hers were shining. "She died two years ago." My chest twinged at the sadness in her voice, but I kept my expression straight. My dad taught me from a young age not to show any emotion. To be neutral at all times. To not let any fucker get a read on me. To always be the grey man in the room.

Cheska cautiously sat down beside me. She smelled of roses. When she looked at me, I saw her eyes weren't as dark as I'd thought. They looked green at times, when her head caught the light at a certain angle. She folded her arms over her chest. Her tits were on the small side, but on her, it didn't matter.

"Is your mum at home?" she asked.

"She's dead," I said plainly and glanced to the stairs, then through a set of glass doors to another room where the butler was busying himself cleaning. The raised voices had stopped.

I wondered what Dad had on Cheska's old man. Or what he'd done to deserve my dad's personal attention. My head snapped to the side when I felt a hand on mine. I moved in a flash and gripped Cheska's wrist instinctively, holding it in the air. She gasped, eyes like fucking saucers, and I slowly released her wrist. Cheska's eyes were still huge as she rubbed her skin.

"I just wanted to say sorry," she said. "About your mum." My cheek twitched. I schooled my features and straightened the collar on my coat. "I know what it's like, to be without them," she whispered. Her bottom lip trembled. "How lonely it can be."

I stared at her, chasing away the stabbing sensation in my stomach her words caused. Chelsea Girl had long black lashes that kissed her cheeks when she blinked and freckles scattered over the bridge of her nose. A single small beauty mark sat above her upper lip.

I wanted to taste it on my tongue.

Cheska's breathing came faster, and I saw her nipples harden under her pyjama vest. I smirked as she quickly folded her arms over her tits again. That blush was back on her cheeks. Chelsea Girl was definitely innocent. She looked around my age. But unlike my East End gangster arse, who'd been sucked and fucked the minute I could come, she was still untouched.

As my eyes slid down Chelsea Girl's body, I knew she'd look even better on her knees. Cheska's face blazed like she could read my thoughts.

The sound of a door opening came from upstairs, tearing Cheska's attention from me. I gave her one last look. No doubt this would be the only time I ever saw her. We didn't exactly mix in the same circles. She no doubt went to some rich-as-shit girls' school.

Hushed voices came closer. Dad and Cheska's old man appeared on the landing and walked down the stairs. Cheska's dad's eyes widened when he saw her beside me on the couch, wearing next to nothing. "Cheska. What are you doing up? Get back to bed. It's late."

Cheska jumped to her feet, obeying Daddy's command. "I needed a drink and saw Arthur here." She flicked a nervous glance to me. "We ... we were just talking."

"Get to bloody bed!" her dad shouted again, and Cheska ran, hurrying for the stairs.

Her old man was a dick.

"Night, Cheska," I said loudly. Her dad's face snapped to me and reddened in anger. "It was nice getting to know you." Cheska turned to me, stopping dead on the stairs. I saw her lips twitch and a smile pull on her stunning face.

"Mr Adley, James will see you out," her dad said, gesturing to the butler, who had appeared from the other room. I stared for a few more seconds at Cheska, then met her dad's furious gaze.

"Mr Adley," the butler said. "And Master Adley. This way, please."

Cheska's eyes grew huge as she stared at me and whispered, "Arthur *Adley* ..." Her cheeks paled, and I knew right then that she'd heard of my family, our firm, our fucking notorious last name. There weren't many people in London who didn't know the Adley family. Knew that we were the London reapers. When we came calling, it was because you'd made a deal with the devil. The fucking dark lord himself.

I lifted my chin in pride at the sound of my name from her lips, then her daddy ushered her away out of sight. I fell into step beside my dad as the butler opened the front door, and we stepped into the cold, wet London night. The sounds of black cabs rushing by and pompous twats falling out of pretentious nearby bars filled the air. As I went to climb back into the car, I gave one last glance at the SW3 house. And in the top right window was a hand pressed to the pane, and a pair of brown eyes with hints of green staring back, watching me leave.

CHAPTER ONE

ARTHUR

Marbella, Aged eighteen

"Get the fuck out here, dickheads. The views are fucking spectacular!" Eric winked, then climbed the stairs toward the deck of the yacht, wearing his tight shorts that he claimed showed off his dick to perfection.

The arsehole was such a fucking slut I was surprised it hadn't fallen off with an STD or some shit.

Beside me, Charlie took a sip of his gin and flicked his cigarette ash into the crystal ashtray on the glass coffee table. "If said 'spectacular view' is not a harem of men who've just descended from a CrossFit competition, covered in oil and waiting on their hands and knees, then I'll be sorely disappointed." I smirked at my cousin sitting like a fucking king on an Italian leather throne.

"Artie!" Eric shouted from the back deck. "Get. The. Fuck. Out. Here! We're in bloody Marbella. If we're not pissed and knee-deep in pussy in two hours, I'm going to fucking shoot someone." He wasn't joking. I'd rarely seen anyone enjoy killing quite like Eric. And the psycho did it with his fucking cheesy grin plastered on his face.

I lit a cig, got up from my chair and kicked Charlie's foot. After inhaling a long drag, I said, "Get the fuck out of that seat. You're coming too."

The door opened behind us. "We here?" Freddie asked, rubbing the sleep from his eyes. Out of us all, Freddie was the quietest, the most introverted. But as Eric shouted us again, even he smiled and pulled off his t-shirt, leaving him in his black swimming shorts. He moved past us and climbed the stairs to join Eric up top.

Charlie sighed and stood from his chair. "Just so you know, this is my idea of hell. Marbella in July, how fucking original."

"But at least we've got a bloody megayacht to be here in, you fucking miserable tosser," Eric said, ducking his head into the cabin to check we were coming. He nudged his chin at me. "Artie, get the beers ordered. And keep them coming." I glared at the fucker trying to give *me* an order. "What? We're on holiday. You can take off your gangster-leader hat for a fucking few days and just be one of the fellas. All for one and all that shite." Eric disappeared before I could plough my fist into his pretty face to shut him the fuck up.

Charlie picked up the phone and placed the drinks order with the staff. "Down boy," he said to me afterwards. He reached for a silver tray with our finest blow already sorted into perfect lines on its surface. Taking an ornate glass pipe from beside it, he snorted a line. He offered me the tray. I took a line and inhaled deeply as it hit the back of my throat. "Better?" Charlie asked. I nodded, feeling the coke poisoning my veins and waking me the fuck up. "Then let's go and enjoy the delights of Marbella and our fellow British pieces of shits that visit these shores."

I was making my way to the stairs when the door to the bedrooms opened again and Vinnie came through. His eyes were red and flitting about the living room of the yacht like all he saw were living, breathing demons around him. His hands were shaking, and his teeth scraped along his bottom lip. "Are we here? I'd like to be here now. Don't like the waves too much, Artie. Don't like the waves too bloody much right now. I'm sick of the sway," he said, looking out of the windows at the sea, the muscles in his back twitching.

"We're going over the top, old boy," Charlie said, nodding to the stairs. "A 'spectacular view' awaits us, apparently."

Vinnie's cheek twitched. I moved in front of him until he met my eyes. Fucking blank as always, unreadable, like pits of no emotion. "Have you taken your medicine?"

Vinnie smiled his wide, disturbing joker's smile, his mouth showing a fucked-up type of glee which his eyes didn't reflect. Vinnie owned the smile that struck fear into our enemies. It showcased how fucked in the head my friend really was. "Just taken it, Arthur. I've just taken the magic tablet. It's travelled down my throat and down to my stomach. Yes, yes, the tablet has gone," he said, his psychotic mania seeping out through his incessant talking. His medication did nothing but keep him a bit calmer than normal. It took the edge off his unpredictability, made him slightly easier to manage. But it didn't take away the hallucinations, or the voices in his head.

Vinnie was taller than me by an inch, and fucking ripped from the weights he lifted to blow off steam. His blond hair fell to his shoulders, a wild mess on his head. His blank eyes were bright green, his skin covered in scars and tattoos of the most random things—shapes, animals, and a fucking massive helter-skelter on his back. He'd kill anyone who threatened this firm in a second, hysterically laughing the entire time. He was also a paranoid schizophrenic and had spent a few years in and out of the loony bin, which had done sweet fuck all but make him more deranged and off-kilter. And he was as close to me as a brother. All my friends were. We were the future of the Adley firm, no matter how fucked up we all were.

Charlie, in his Burberry shorts, made his way up the stairs first. Vinnie followed, bouncing and humming all the way like a kid going to Disneyland. I threw my t-shirt off, tossing it to the couch, and tied the waist on my shorts. We had just docked in Marbella an hour ago. We were on my father's fifty-million-pound yacht, and we'd just parked beside the other "moneyed families". No doubt their cash wasn't made in the same way ours was. And they'd fucking hate us for it. One hint of our East End cockney accents and they'd turn their uptight noses up at us.

We didn't give a flying fuck.

I pushed my glasses up my nose and climbed the stairs. The heat of the Spanish sun slammed into me like an iron fist, and I pushed my dark hair back from my forehead. White Mediterranean buildings surrounded us, and tourists sat in restaurants and bars, gaping up at our yacht.

I joined my friends on the rear deck overlooking the restaurants and took a beer from Eric. He spread his arms. "Fucking paradise, boys." I took a swig of my beer and glanced over to the yacht beside us. I didn't see anyone on the back deck, but then I heard the people talking at the front of their boat, overlooking the sea.

"So, where are these spectacular views?" Charlie asked Eric, lighting up another cig.

Eric winced as he met my cousin's waiting gaze. "Well, maybe not spectacular to *you*, Chuck, but definitely to the rest of us." He flicked his eyes to Vinnie, who was circling the back deck like it was a track, and screwed up his nose. "Okay, maybe not to our resident nutjob either since he already has a bird. But to me, Freddie and Artie, what a view it is!"

"Story of my fucking life." Charlie smirked at me. I followed Eric as he headed for the main sun deck at the very front of the yacht.

"The edge gone yet?" I asked Vinnie. He nodded, and I could see by his eyes that his medication had kicked in. His pupils had dilated a bit, and the shaking in his hands had lessened. "Getting calmer by the second, Artie. Getting calmer by the second." He smiled again, his deep dimples making him look a fuck-ton more innocent than he actually was. I put my hand on his shoulder, right over the face of Nosferatu with his sharp vampiric teeth that was tattooed there.

"So, who are we docked next to?" Freddie asked Eric. Freddie was six feet two with dark brown hair and brown eyes. He was slender in build but could fight like a fucking Rottweiler. His old man died a while back, for the firm, shot right through the fucking forehead by a Russian. My dad practically adopted Freddie after that. He'd lived with us in the old church for the past couple of years. He was quiet before his old man's death. Now, compared to the rest of my gobshite mates, he was almost mute.

"Wait until you see," Eric said, waggling his eyebrows. Eric was six four, blond and covered in bright-as-fuck horror-themed clown tattoos. His hair looked like something straight from World War Two—combed over like a good little British solider. Claimed birds got wet for it—we all knew that was mainly referring to Betsy, my cousin and Charlie's little sister. But neither he or Betsy ever talked about that. He also rarely shut his mouth. But that didn't matter when shit hit the fan. He had your back, one hundred percent without question.

As we turned the corner, I saw movement on the yacht beside us. Birds in bikinis, some topless. I couldn't care less. Seen one pair of tits, you'd seen them all. Bored already, I lit another cig and moved to the front of the yacht. I looked out over the ocean.

"Nice tits, sweetheart!" I heard Eric shout behind me. I glanced over to the yacht beside us and saw two girls sunbathing, looking our way—one with dark skin and jet-black hair that fell in spiral curls to her shoulders, and one with light freckled skin and red hair down to her waist.

I went to turn my head again, when someone walked out from below deck and toward the two sunbathers. The hand holding my cig stopped en route to my mouth when I saw her long legs and olive skin. The dark hair that was pulled up on top of her head. She was wearing a white bikini, fucking curves like an hourglass.

As if she was feeling my stare, she looked over, and the minute she did, I recognised those eyes. Those big fucking eyes that were fixed on me and widening by the second. Green-brown eyes that I never fucking forgot ...

Cheska Harlow-Wright ...

The memory smashed into my brain like a crowbar. The memory of her posh accent sank like talons into my eardrums. Chelsea Girl. In all these years, I'd never forgotten this posh-as-shit Chelsea girl.

Cheska stopped dead, the fancy red drink in her hand spilling over the sides. "Cheska!" one of her friends said, wiping the drink off her stomach. But Cheska didn't move. She just kept staring at me.

My eyes dropped to her body, devouring every inch. Chelsea Girl was all grown up. And she was even more fucking gorgeous than she had been back then. I finally took a drag of my cig, eyes never off her, and moved near my friends. Cheska's eyes followed me the whole way, red bursting on her cheeks. I'd thought of this girl often. And here she was, standing right before me, in Marbella.

I stopped next to Charlie, my dick swelling just looking at Chelsea Girl's cock-sucking red lips. My cousin leaned in close. "A friend of yours, old boy?" he asked, nudging his chin at Cheska. I narrowed my eyes at my cousin; Charlie laughed knowingly. I wasn't laughing. I was imagining her underneath me, imagining fucking tearing her apart, pushing three of my fingers into her wet cunt.

Charlie dropped down on the lounger behind us. "Wake me up when something interesting happens." He lay out on the cream lounger and shut his eyes. I smirked at the dark-skinned bird staring at Charlie like he was her next meal. Poor bitch had nothing on her menu that Charlie wanted. Pussy did nothing but offend him. But women always wanted him. He had brown hair and brown eyes, six feet three and cut with muscle. Freddie called him a bird's wet dream. My cousin was also the most ruthless motherfucker I had ever met. No one fucked with Charlie Adley and lived to see the next day. It was why he was my right-hand man and best mate. I trusted him with my life.

"What's your names, ladies?" Eric shouted over to Cheska and her friends. The redhead stuck her middle finger in the air in response. Eric held his hand over his chest. "You wound me, beautiful. You fucking wound me!"

"Then piss off!" she shouted back. Eric laughed, but the bird had no idea she'd just become his next conquest.

I tracked Cheska as she placed her drink down on the table beside her friends. Her eyes kept flicking away from mine before snapping back. I took a swig of my beer. She seemed to breathe faster as I kept my gaze on her. I watched her nipples harden and wanted nothing more than to feel them against my tongue—I wanted to taste all of her. Her tits, her tanned skin, and her posh pussy.

I flicked my cig to the floor when engines roared to my right. Four blokes were riding jet skis toward Cheska's yacht. I narrowed my eyes on the arseholes as they turned off their engines at the side of the yacht, climbed the ladder and walked onto the deck.

A blond pretty boy moved to Cheska and kissed her on the cheek. My blood boiled. I had the sudden need to rip his fucking head off his shoulders. Cheska's eyes stayed locked on mine even as the fucker put his hand on her arse and squeezed. Chelsea Girl had a boyfriend.

To me, he only looked like dead meat.

Then the shitstain looked over at my yacht.

"Who the fuck are these guys?" he asked the girls, his pathetic friends coming to stand behind him like they thought they could be threatening. They had no fucking idea who they were eyeballing.

As if my thoughts were a command, the shitstains before us seemed to suddenly see Eric's ink. His bright tattoos were picture after picture of deranged and psychotic clowns—sharp teeth and claws, mouths sadistic and dripping with blood. Eric's smile turned from dirty for the redhead to fucking crazed in one second, and their smirks melted off their aristocratic faces.

"Happy to introduce ourselves," Eric said, a dark edge to his voice, his cockney accent thickening.

Freddie kicked Charlie's lounger, and my cousin opened his eyes. "You wanted to be woken up when something interesting happened." Freddie pointed to the other yacht's arseholes. "Well, something fucking interesting is happening."

Charlie was beside me in a flash, body vibrating with excitement. "Eye candy or dead meat?"

"The latter," I replied.

"Shame. The bloke on the right is fit. He looks like he could take my kind of rough play."

Eric waved a hand at Freddie beside him. "Freddie Williams." Eric pointed to Vinnie. "Vinnie Edwards." Vinnie ran to the side of the yacht and laughed manically, the muscles bulging in his neck and shoulders. When his laugh faded, a wide, deranged smile stayed on his face as he stood there and stared.

The posh fuckers took a fearful step back, as if my brother would pole-vault over the sea beneath us and land on their deck. "Stay calm," I said to Vinnie so he could hear me. I heard him inhale and exhale, doing what I said, but his smile remained. Good thing about Vinnie, he always listened to me. I was his soulmate's older brother. He'd never cross me in a million years. For Pearl. Everything he did was for, or because of, Pearl.

"I'm Eric Mason." Eric gestured to Charlie. "This is Charlie Adley." Then Eric came to me and hooked his arm around my neck. I put my gaze back on Cheska. "And this is Arthur Adley." Eric gave the pricks on the opposite yacht a mocking bow. "Nice to fucking meet you." His humour dropped. "You might have heard of us."

The twat who had kissed Cheska and opened his fucking trap lost his superior smirk. The blood drained from his face. Of course the arsehole had heard of us. Cheska's mates, who had been lying on loungers, quickly looked at Cheska. She was watching me like a hawk. Her eyelids lowered slightly, and a flush crept up her neck. I wanted to follow that flush with my tongue, and I knew Chelsea Girl would fucking love it.

"Come on," the twat said to his mates, who were practically pissing themselves in fear behind him. Bravado fucking lost. "Let's get a drink below deck." They scurried away like the cowardly rats they were, and Cheska's friends quickly trotted behind them.

"Come on," Eric said to us all. "Let's hit the beach bars. Posh pussy is too much like hard graft. And if I have to look at those twats again, I'm going to end them." He waggled his brows. "Can't have too much fun on day one or the rest of the holiday will be a fucking bust. Best keep the bloodshed until near the end. Go out with a fucking bang."

Freddie laughed and threw his arm around Eric's shoulders, the clown tattoos looking as though they were crawling off his skin.

"Beach bar. Bloody brilliant," Charlie said sarcastically as Eric and Freddie headed off the yacht to the marina. Charlie put his hand on Vinnie's shoulder. "Let's get trolleyed, old boy. Let you scare the fuck out of the tourists for a bit. It'll be fun."

"I like this game. It'll be fun until Pearl wakes up." Vinnie cracked his knuckles and skipped to the back of the yacht. Charlie turned back around to me. I hadn't moved. I was too fixated elsewhere. "If I'm enduring sand in my fucking arse crack, so are you, cousin," he said.

I flicked my chin, wordlessly telling him I'd be right there. When he didn't move, I sent a glance his way. Charlie frowned, then looked toward Cheska, who was still stood on the sun deck of her yacht, still in my line of sight. "Bloody hell," he muttered and disappeared.

I lit up another cig as Cheska kept flitting her eyes to me. I pushed one hand into my shorts pocket. Her green-brown eyes raked over my body, hooking on my tattoos of Big Ben and old London Town on my torso. Her cheeks blazed again, and I felt my dick start to swell. She edged closer to the side of the yacht. I stayed still, watching for what she'd do. Her tits were still only a handful, but they would fit fucking perfectly in my hand. I took another drag of my cig just as Cheska reached the railing.

After a few seconds of staring into the water beneath her, she lifted her head and went to open her mouth, but Twatface appeared behind her. "Ches?"

Her shoulders sagged. I wondered if she wanted this cunt to fuck off as much as I did. I wanted to hear her voice. I wanted to know what she was going to say to me after five years. When Twatface saw me, he fought to look hard by holding his shoulders back and narrowing his eyes at me. He was probably trying not to shit himself.

The minute I smirked at his feeble attempt, he tensed. Panic filled his face. Taking Cheska's hand, he pulled her back. "Come on, Ches. Let's go." Cheska followed him, and I watched her go, letting nicotine fill my lungs.

As Cheska took one last look at me over her shoulder, I flicked my cig overboard and walked from the sun deck to follow my mates. As I hit the pavement on the marina, all my brothers were waiting. I glanced up at Cheska's yacht, and like five years ago, in the top window stood Chelsea Girl, green-brown eyes fixed on me, watching me go.

———

The coke and molly ran thick in my blood. Coloured lights circled the dancefloor, and trance music pounded from the speakers all around us. Some bird in a short blue dress climbed all over me, her over-filled lips kissing my neck as I drank whisky and smoked my joint. I was too fucking wasted to push her off. I rolled my head to the dancefloor, watching people grinding against each other from our table in the VIP room as the slut's hand slipped inside my shorts and ran over my boxers, stroking my dick. Everyone was off their tits on drugs and booze and the freedom that came with their two weeks' holiday in the sun, away from England's grey skies and their fucking mundane lives.

The slut on my lap cupped my dick just as a group of people moved to a table beside us. The green laser lights in the club reflected off my glasses, blurring my sight ... but as I narrowed my gaze, I saw a brunette in a fitted pink dress ... and then she was all I could fucking see. Brown hair down her back, long legs, tight-as-fuck body ... and her focus right on me.

Cheska.

When the lights switched from green to yellow, she became crystal clear. I smirked, only for that smirk to drop when Twatface from the yacht grabbed her face and kissed her. My heartbeat pounded in my ears; the drugs swelled my veins and fucked my brain. Cheska kissed him back, half-arsed. Her eyes were open. They were fixed on me.

"Fuck me," the whore on my lap said. She was a total slapper. And she was gagging for my cock. In truth, she'd seen us in the VIP and wanted to escape the rammed main dancefloor for a night and be around the men who could give her free drinks. But she hadn't stopped touching me since she clapped eyes on me. "Touch me," she said again. I didn't want to touch this rancid bitch. I just couldn't be arsed to fight her off. The drugs were quick and she was here, nothing more to it. I wasn't fucking this slut's hole for all the money in the world ... but now Cheska was here.

And I wanted to see her burn.

Eyes locked on Cheska, whose mouth was getting sloppily fucked by Twatface's tongue, I slid my hand under the slut's dress. Cheska's gaze followed my every move. My attention never moved from her. I pushed the slut's thong aside and slipped a finger inside her. The whore on my lap screamed, her nails digging into my shoulders.

Twatface kissed down Cheska's neck, sucking on her skin, giving her full view of me and what my hand was doing. Cheska's eyes widened, and her cheeks blazed. Her chest lifted up and down, fucking breathless, as I plunged my fingers into the slut's pussy. I couldn't give a fuck about getting this bitch off. But I wanted Cheska to see this whore as *her*. *Her* on my fucking lap, not getting slobbered on by the prick currently trying to eat her neck.

The slut screamed out and her pussy tightened around my fingers as I made her come. The loud music drowned out her screams, but I knew Cheska had heard her by the parting of her lips. The slapper tried to collapse against me, but I pushed her back from me by her forehead, done with having her anywhere near me. "Get the fuck off," I said, not even looking in her direction. I pushed her arse off me, dumping her in the chair, and got to my feet.

I needed a fucking cig.

I crossed the room and pushed outside into the alleyway. I pulled a cig from my pocket and sparked up, inhaling deep. The door opened beside me, and I looked up and saw Chelsea Girl slip through. It slammed shut behind her, making her jump. I put my cig in my mouth and faced her, leaning against the wall. Like she felt the weight of my stare, she turned from the door and faced me.

She inhaled a shuddering breath. "I don't know why I followed you ..." She took a step closer. Fuck, the drugs were good. Ours, of course, so I knew they were pure. But they made this posh bird I first saw years ago look like a fucking angel. "Arthur Adley," she said and smiled. I felt something pull in my chest at my name on her lips.

"Cheska Harlow-Wright," I said, my thick cockney accent sounding common as shit around her fancy double-barrelled name.

"You remember me?"

I closed my eyes, leaned my head back against the wall and took another drag of my cig. "Did you enjoy the show back there?"

I opened my eyes. Chelsea Girl's mouth dropped open and her cheeks blazed bright red. I smirked and waited for her to speak, but the fire door flew open. Freddie was searching for me.

"Artie," he said, all business. High or not, my body immediately went on alert. "Eric's getting into it with a group of loudmouth Welsh pricks," was all he said. "It's gonna be bloody carnage."

I closed my eyes, and my head fell back against the wall. I opened my eyes and flicked my cig to the floor. I moved past Cheska, followed Freddie and headed over to my mates.

Charlie fell into step beside me, tearing himself from some barman he'd clearly been chatting up. "We can't even go a few hours without shedding blood." He smiled at me, teeth shining. "I'm not complaining. Jason there was getting on my nerves anyway. All brawn, not enough brains," he said. "I'm bored as fuck. I could do with breaking a few noses."

"How many?" I asked Freddie, as I saw Eric near the front door, smiling his fucking deadly smile at the blokes around him. I shot a glance to Vinnie, who was bouncing on his feet as he joined us.

"I think it's time to fight," Vinnie said to thin air beside him. "It's time to fight, baby. And I want to fight. I like the smell and taste of blood. I like feeling bones crushing under my hand." Vinnie turned back to me. "We fucking fighting, right, Artie?" he asked, cheeks flushed. "Right, Charlie?"

"No doubt, old boy," Charlie said, rolling back the sleeves of his shirt. "This is Eric we're talking about. He could start a fight with his own bloody shadow."

Vinnie looked beside him. And he smiled, but this wasn't his manic smile. This was a true smile. One he only ever had for *her*. "I promise, treasure," he said again to thin air. "I won't get hurt. I never get hurt. I never want to see you upset."

My sister. Vinnie hallucinated my sister. Had done since she'd died and her death had worsened his issues. Vinnie ran a hand down her imaginary face, caressing nothing but empty space. "You always worry about me, Pearlie-girl. But I'd never leave you, just like you'll never leave me." For all intents and purposes, Vinnie was in a relationship with my sister's ghost and had been for years. It was the only relationship he could probably actually ever have.

"There's nine of them," Freddie said, pulling my focus back to him. "Eric was fingering one of their birds against the club's wall, and her fella saw."

I stopped when we reached Eric. He didn't look away from the beefed-up wankers surrounding him. I put my hands in my pockets and stared at the red-faced twat currently firing daggers at my mate.

"Problem?" I asked, and the twat's eyes swung to me.

"Good. Fucking more of them," one of them said and rolled his hands into fists. I smiled, coldly. Then I stepped forward, and before the cunt even had time to swing his fist, I grabbed his jaw and ploughed my head into his nose. He dropped to the floor, and all fucking hell broke loose. It was a blur of fists and breaking bones as the pricks around us tried to take us on, each one dropping to the ground, not even getting a hit on us—unless it was intended.

Eric lowered his fists and let the main bloke punch him across the face. Eric's head snapped to the side, blood pouring from his lip. He ran his tongue over the blood, then smiled, widening the cut. The guy froze at Eric's reaction. Then Eric was on him. Tackling him to the ground and pummelling his face until the bloke was out cold. I stepped back, pulled out a cig and glared at the fuckers on the ground. I inhaled a drag, letting Eric have his fill of spilled blood, then, resting the cig between my lips, pulled him from the fucked-up prick on the floor.

"Outside," I ordered Eric. He was breathing hard, his knuckles split from all the hits. We passed by the bouncers. I flicked my chin at the mass of groaning twats trying to get up from the floor. "Sort them the fuck out." The bouncers moved to the Welshmen without question. The Adleys fucking ruled this town. Anyone who worked here wouldn't dare question a word I said, not unless they had a death wish. My family had men paid off all over Europe. We ran Spain with our gear.

I pushed through the crowded street, drunken Brits falling over and getting in my fucking way. I pushed a smashed cunt aside when he fell in my path.

"Oi, mate! You got a fucking death wish?" he snapped, trying to get closer to me as he stumbled to his feet.

Charlie walked toward him and nutted the arsehole's forehead, then fell back into step beside me as though nothing had happened. The fucker went down like a sack of potatoes, and his mates rushed around him.

We stopped across the street, and I threw a cig at Eric. The fucker winked and grinned before lighting up. Blood still covered his chin, and the tosser made no move to wipe it away. I looked around my family. All our knuckles were bloodied.

"All that for fingering some slut?" Freddie said to Eric. "She better have been worth it."

Eric raised his hand and put his fingers under Freddie's nose. "You tell me."

Freddie batted his hand away, leaving Eric laughing. I took off my glasses, wiping the spots of blood from the lenses when I heard, "Adley." I turned, and before me was Ollie Lawson. My lip curled just seeing his pretentious fucking face.

I put my glasses back on, took a drag of my cig and blew it out right in his face. Ollie's nostrils flared, but he wouldn't dare do shit against me. His old man owned a few docks around London. A legit business. Import and export. Lawson's old man had offered my dad millions over the years to get ours too. Never with much luck, of course. The Lawsons were smug and smarmy and royal pains in our arses.

Especially this fucker. The sight of his face alone made me want to shatter his skull.

"Lawson!" Eric held out his arms. "No hug for me?"

"You've got blood all over your chin," Lawson said, clearly disgusted. Eric made sure Lawson was watching as he licked at the blood.

"Did I get it all?" Eric asked, knowing he hadn't. Charlie and Freddie laughed. Vinnie whispered into Pearl's ear, and I just fucking glared. I hated this twat. Raised with a silver spoon in his mouth and walked around like he owned our fucking town.

"Anyway, just thought we'd say hello," Lawson said, pointing to his mates. "We're here for a holiday, just like you. A break from the Big Smoke, yeah?" He glanced at each of my mates, but his attention stayed on my cousin. "Charlie, sucked any good cocks lately?"

"Just your old man's," my cousin said. "But that maggot could hardly be classed as a dick."

Ollie's eyes flared. But we all knew he wouldn't raise his fist. Lawson wasn't a fighter. He was nothing. And we didn't waste our energy on nothings.

Then Ollie's eyes drifted over my shoulder and he broke out in a huge grin. "Sorry to cut our little chat short, Artie, but I've got someone I need to see."

Lawson and his mates brushed past us and headed toward the club we'd just been in. I watched them go, only for that fucker to walk right up to Cheska. I tensed, ready to charge at the arsehole for even speaking to her. Then he hugged her; Cheska hugged him right back.

"That's the bird from the yacht beside us," Freddie said. "She knows Lawson?" My nails sliced into my palm as I clenched my fist so hard my bones practically broke. How the fuck did Cheska know Ollie Lawson? Had she fucked him? I felt my anger growing like a fucking demon inside me. That was new. Nothing made me feel much anymore.

I watched them head inside the club, Lawson's arm around Cheska's waist. I curled my hand around the knife in my pocket and fought the urge to follow them. I had just taken a deep breath when my mobile rang in my pocket. I took it out and saw my dad's name.

"Dad," I said, my eyes still fixed on Lawson through the window, at the bar with Cheska. She was smiling at him. She clearly knew him well.

"I need you to pay your Uncle Johnny Bailey a visit."

"What kind of visit?" I asked. My mates gathered around, watching me.

"A thorough one," Dad said.

I nodded at Charlie, and he took out his mobile and called for our transport. "We'll go see him now." I headed away from the club and toward the main road.

"Silly wanker has been giving away presents left, right and centre, and we know he can't afford it," my dad said. That was code, just in case Scotland Yard or some other agency were listening in trying to get something on our firm—that would never happen. We were too fucking careful.

Dad was telling me that Johnny was keeping the blow profits for himself instead of sending them back to London like a good boy. Didn't matter that he'd been in my old man's inner circle for years back in London, running one of the routes here in Marbella for only the last few years. Dad was ruthless. And he wanted me and my boys to send a message to anyone else on foreign shores who tried to steal from the Adley firm.

"I'll call you later," I said and hung up.

By the time we made it to the main road, a blacked-out van was waiting for us. We climbed in and Eric shut the door. My mates looked at me. "You ready for some more fun?" I asked, and each one of them smiled.

We pulled in to a villa far away from anyone and anything. The driver of the van hit the headlights as we travelled down the gravelled roads that led to Johnny's villa and the basement he kept the gear in. I didn't want him knowing we were coming. Wanted to catch that fucker by surprise.

We stopped outside the villa, and I climbed out the passenger side. I walked up the main path to the front door, my men at my back. I didn't knock or ring the bell. I shouldered the door, snapping the lock. My eyes scanned the villa and the staircase that led upstairs. No fucker was here.

"The basement," Charlie said, moving beside me. "I can hear music." I cocked my head to the side and heard it too, drifting up through the kitchen. I nudged my head in that direction. Feeling in my pocket for my knife, I opened the basement door and went down the steps. The music became clearer, and as we descended, so did the view. Table after long table of blow, Johnny's men stuffing it into packets. Then, at the front, smoking a cig and sat like a fucking usurper king on a wingback chair, was Johnny.

His head snapped up. I kept my eyes on him. For a second, I saw real fucking fear flash over his face. Then he schooled his expression and got to his feet. I glanced at my brothers behind me and gave them a short nod—*get the fuck ready to play*.

"Artie, get the fuck over here and give your Uncle Johnny a hug. I didn't know you were coming over to see an old geezer like me." I made my way over to him, watching his men in my peripheral. They were reaching under the tables. No doubt for guns.

I stopped in front of Johnny. His face was red as fuck, and the thieving twat was sweating, drops dripping down his mottled skin and crashing onto the blow-covered floor beneath our feet. He flicked his cig to the ground, then opened his arms. I didn't fucking move. Just stared at the wanker with dead eyes. Johnny swallowed, and his beady eyes moved to my men, who were just waiting for my signal to unleash hell on these cunts.

"Still a moody fucker, I see," he tried to joke. He reached out and pulled me into his embrace. "Artie. No hug for your old uncle?" he said when my arms stayed at my sides.

Placing my mouth near his ear, I said quietly, "Why the fuck would I hug the man who is stealing from his fucking family?" He tensed. Then his arm moved, and I knew he was reaching for the gun I'd seen in his pocket. Pushing the fucker back a step, I twisted his arm around his back, moved behind him and grabbed the prick by his hair.

That movement was all the signal my boys needed. They turned on Johnny's men, who had all reached for their guns. "Watch," I said calmly into Johnny's ear. I pulled on his hair tighter so he had the perfect view of his men that were about to be destroyed before his eyes. Johnny fought my hold, but his weak arse had nothing on me.

A bullet from one of his men flew by Charlie's head. My cousin smiled, then, taking two knives from his pocket, grabbed the fucker by the shirt, sat him down on a nearby wooden chair, and stabbed both knives into his thighs. He removed the blades, ploughed both into his chest, pulled them out again, then plunged them into the fucker's eyes.

Eric charged at a man and rammed him against the basement wall. The wanker dropped the gun, and Eric picked it up and put it in the fucker's mouth. He angled the gun up, then pulled the trigger. His brain redecorated the walls.

Vinnie roared, then ran full force at a man holding a machete. Vinnie slammed him to the floor, then let his fists fly. Vinnie liked to kill with his bare hands. And he was fucking perfect at it, all the time singing "Humpty Dumpty" at the top of his voice: "... couldn't put Humpty together again ..."

Freddie silently slammed a knife into the remaining arsehole's heart, twisting the knife and eyeballing the fucker until blood spilled from his mouth. Freddie spat in his face as he pulled out the knife. The arsehole hit the deck.

"Artie, stop this," Johnny said in my hold as the last of his men dropped to the floor, bathing in their own blood. Vinnie reached into his pocket and pulled out his pliers. He opened the mangled mouth of the man he'd just pulverised and yanked out a tooth. He kept a tooth of everyone he killed in jars back home.

"A tooth for me and Pearl. Not yours anymore." Vinnie held it in the air. "See, Pearl," he said to the ghost of my sister. "They can't hurt our family anymore." He hummed, then stopped and stared at the empty space beside him, his cheeks reddening. "I love you too, treasure." He placed the tooth in the travel tin he carried in his shirt pocket and got to his feet, his eyes snapping in our direction. Johnny stiffened in my arms.

"Artie, listen," Johnny said, his tone hitching higher to maniacal levels. "You're just a kid. You all are. What your old man has you doing here isn't right."

I tutted in his ear. "What's not right is you skimming profits from the firm that's served you well."

"I haven't, I swear—"

I pushed him to the ground and looked around us. There was some rope in the corner. I towered over the fat piece of shit on the ground as the blood of his men crept closer to his sweaty skin. "Get the rope," I said to Freddie. He did. I looked at Eric and Charlie. "Lift him up." I pointed to the metal spindles on the bannister. "Tie his arms to the bottom of the spindles."

Charlie and Eric carried Johnny to the staircase, and Freddie tied his wrists to a couple of the metal spindles. The wall was high, and when they moved back, the fucker just hung there like something out of the Tower of London. As my boys stepped back, wetness appeared on Johnny's trousers.

"Aw, he's pissing himself," Charlie said, wiping his knives off on a white embossed handkerchief he took from his pocket. "Shame he wasn't this scared when he thought it would be a good idea to rob us blind."

"Undo his shirt," I said to Eric.

Vinnie moved behind me, sitting down on the chair Johnny had been sat in earlier. His arms wrapped around the hallucination of my sister, and he was content to hold her and watch the show he knew was coming. I turned back to Johnny; his shirt had been ripped open, his torso bared. Taking my favourite knife from my pocket, the one my old man gave me for my thirteenth birthday, the one I'd used on my first kill, and every kill afterwards, I walked closer to Johnny.

"I'll give it all back." The whites of his eyes shone bright as fear bit at his flesh and bone. I licked along the metal of my blade. I savoured the metallic tinge it left on my tongue. "Artie, listen to me, boy." He smiled at me—it didn't quite reach his eyes. "I've known you since you were born. I'm your Uncle Johnny. I used to pick you up from school." I stopped a foot before him and stared dead into his eyes. Silence filled the basement. "Let me speak to your old man. Get him on the phone. I can work this out with him." He laughed, and it instantly boiled my piss. "You lot are still just kids. You shouldn't be doing this yet. You should be out in the world sowing your oats, not doing your fathers' dirty work."

I fought a smirk. This fucker was there at my first kill. Gave me a slap on the back, a cig and a dram of whisky in congratulations. He didn't care about me being a kid then.

"You stole from the firm." I watched that fucking offensive smile slip from his face. I looked at Eric. "Hold his knees up." Eric moved to Johnny and pushed his knees up like he was sitting on an invisible chair. I moved closer to Johnny, and I nodded to Freddie. He knew what I wanted. He brought over one of chairs from across the room and placed it under Johnny's legs. Eric let go of his legs, and Johnny's feet rested on the seat, knees still bent.

"What are you doing?" he asked, voice shaking. I looked down at his bare stomach. The arsehole had had one too many Sunday roasts. This would be like gutting a pig.

"You said you wanted my old man." I met my "uncle's" wide gaze. "You should do. Dad is a 'kill them quick and get out of Dodge' kind of man." I pointed the knife at his face. "You know this. You stood by his side most of his life." I nodded toward my boys. "Just like my brothers have done with me."

"I fucked up, Artie. I've royally fucked up. Let me make it up to you."

"Charlie?" I said, never taking my eyes off the piece of shit before me. "Would you betray me?"

"Never, cuz," he said plainly.

"Eric?"

"Not in a million years."

"Freddie?"

"Wouldn't ever happen, Art."

"Vinnie?"

"Never, never, never. Not for all the money in the world," he sang. "It would hurt Pearl. I would never hurt my Pearlie."

I cocked my head, looking at the lines on Johnny's face. The pock marks and the burst capillaries. Our firm had done him well. Protected him. Gave him anything he wanted.

"Loyalty." I pressed the tip of my knife into his fat cheek. "All we ask for in return is loyalty." I pressed so hard that blood sprouted and ran down his face like a tear of crimson. "In the Adley firm, our word is our bond. You swore loyalty to my old man." I pulled the knife away. "And you've broken your bond." I put the handle of my knife between my teeth and rolled up my shirt sleeves to my elbows. I took hold of the knife again.

"You were right to want my old man to be your bondsman. He may be ruthless, but he's quick and merciful." A slow grin pulled on my lips. "I am anything but."

"You're insane," Johnny spat, knowing he had no more cards left to play. "You always were a sadistic little fucker." His eyes scanned over my boys. "You all were. All fucking insane." He spat on the ground at my feet. "It's beneath the Adley name, acting like this." His nose screwed up like we were the worst-smelling fuckers in the world. "There's dignity in being London gangsters. I was beside your old man when he created the firm. We lived by a code. We were gentlemen gangsters, not the fucking nutjob murderers you lot have become."

"Nutjob murderers," Charlie said, nodding. "That has a nice ring to it."

"Is this the future of the Adley firm?" he sneered. "You lot?" He shook his head. "I'm better off being dead."

"Glad we finally agree on something," I said and, before he could even believe it, slashed my knife across his stomach, deep and in three directions. Johnny screamed. Blood oozed from the open cuts.

Inside, I grinned at the way he yelled. At the red on his face from the pain. I moved beside him, and his pain-filled gaze followed me. "Ever heard of disembowelment?" Johnny paled. I took that as a yes. I placed my foot on the side of the chair that was supporting his bent legs. "I've just cut your stomach in a way that the minute you drop your legs, your innards will spill from your body and crash onto the floor. You'll die slowly. And it will be painful."

Johnny's breath was coming faster and faster. His body jerked as my foot rocked the chair beneath him.

"No, please," he begged. I never moved my eyes from his stare. He must have realised he was going to die, as he said, "You'll burn in hell one day, Artie."

"You're right," I said. "But that day isn't here yet, and until then ..." I booted the chair from underneath him. The chair skidded across the room, and Johnny screamed as he held both legs in the air using only his strength.

"Bet you wish you'd hit the gym more instead of the pubs, hey, Johnny?" Charlie said, and my boys all stood beside me as we watched his legs lower, his core strength fading, and his slashes rip open.

On a final scream, his effort failed, and his legs fell until his toes scraped against the concrete of the basement floor. In seconds, the slashes I'd made tore open, and out spilled his bowels into a heap on the floor. Johnny's eyes sought me out, and without another word, I walked for the stairs. I heard Freddie taking the pictures my old man would want to distribute to any other of our men who thought about fucking us over. Eric called for clean-up and the retrieval of the blow.

I pushed out into the warm night and slid into the van's back seat. My boys all piled in, and we made our way back to the yacht. I stared out of the window, at Marbella and the drunks falling out of the bars. Johnny was right. I was a sadistic murderer. Because I felt fuck all about killing him. About gutting him like a pig despite knowing him my entire life.

All my emotions had burned in a blazing inferno alongside my sister and mum the night the cottage caught fire and it stripped them of their bones and flesh. I had nothing left. And whatever still lingered liked to kill and cause pain to others. It screamed at me to punish, to seek revenge for my family that died.

"I'm going to get badges made for us." Eric started laughing. As did Freddie. "Club Nutjob Murderers."

"Are we going back clubbing?" Freddie asked. "I've still got at least four hours of drinking and fucking left in me."

I could feel Charlie looking at me. I didn't give a fuck what we did. Clearly my cousin got that message. "Tom," Charlie said to our driver. "Take us to the most debauched club in Marbella. We need to get all kinds of fucked up tonight."

"You've got it," Tom said. I pulled my mobile from my pocket.

GOOD JOB, SON, my old man had texted. Charlie nudged my arm and handed me the picture Freddie had taken of the basement. I was immediately met with blood and carnage and Johnny hanging as if on a stake with his innards hanging out … and fuck, it made me feel good.

CHAPTER TWO

CHESKA

"If you stare at that bloody yacht any more, you'll burn a hole in its side." I looked from Arthur's yacht to Arabella. She was lying on her lounger on the sun deck, head tilted back, her SPF-drenched dark skin shimmering under the blistering Marbella sun.

I took a sip of my mojito, letting the mint and lime cool me down. I saw a few of Arthur's friends on the deck. But he wasn't there. I hadn't seen him since the night in the club. Not long after Ollie Lawson and his friends came, Arthur and his boys had disappeared. I had no idea where to. But they hadn't come back.

My cheeks blazed when I thought back to him looking at me right in the eyes as he fingered the girl on his lap. As her eyes rolled back and she moaned out loud as her orgasm barrelled through her.

A hand waved in front of my face, pulling me back from the other night. From Arthur ... his dark hair, blue eyes and black-rimmed glasses that just did something to me. I couldn't read him. He was as impenetrable as Fort Knox. Even when his gaze had been locked on mine, I couldn't get a bloody read on him. He gave nothing away. It was as if he was soulless. As if he lacked any basic emotion.

Cool.

Calculated.

Deadly.

The hand before my face moved faster. When I shook my head, withdrawing myself from thoughts of Arthur and those eyes that were as unbreakable as a bank safe, it was to see Freya. She smiled, but I could see a tinge of worry in her dark eyes.

She studied me, then put her palm on my forehead as if checking my temperature. I moved her hand away. "Frey," I said, sighing. "I'm fine."

"Just checking you haven't got a fever or anything. Or heat exhaustion." She took a sip of her Chardonnay. Her purple bikini somehow made her Irish features look more pronounced, and made her curves look like something out of a Renaissance painting.

"I'm completely well."

Arabella sat up and moved her Gucci sunglasses from her espresso eyes. Her curls framed her beautiful face. "You do know that yacht belongs to Alfie Adley, don't you?" Her lips were pursed with worry. "That guy you keep staring at is Arthur Adley. *The* Arthur Adley, heir to the Adley firm and their empire of death and destruction."

"I know who he is. I have done since we met at thirteen, remember?"

"Yeah, we remember," Freya said. "But do *you?* Alfie Adley was there to cash in on a debt your father owed. He wasn't there for a night of drinks and billiards."

"I know that," I snapped. Freya and Arabella glanced at each other as though I'd lost my bloody mind. Maybe I had. All I knew was that, over the years, Arthur had become an obsession of mine. And now he was here. In the flesh. Docked next to us. Looking my way with that steely gaze that seemed to make my knees weak and my mind lose all of its senses.

"Daddy made a mistake. He explained it all to me. He made a bad investment." I shrugged. "He sorted it and hasn't had dealings with the Adleys again since."

"Yet, here you are, wanting to fuck Arthur every which way to Sunday." Arabella raised an eyebrow at me, waiting for my response.

The sound of raucous laughter came from the Adley yacht, and I glanced over. Just then, Arthur walked out onto the deck, a large gin glass in his hand. He seemed more often than not to be drinking gin, I'd noticed. It must have been his drink of choice—straight, with ice, no mixer. He was shirtless, wearing navy-blue shorts, his black-rimmed glasses firmly in place.

Christ, he was perfection. His skin was slightly kissed by the sun, and his dark hair looked like onyx under the midday sun's rays.

As if feeling my stare, he looked over, his eyes landing straight on mine. His cousin, Charlie, followed his gaze, his eyes narrowing on me as if I were a problem he wanted to solve. My breathing came faster as Arthur didn't look away from me. Not even when Freddie Williams stood beside him and started talking in his ear.

"Seriously, Cheska," Freya said, and I reluctantly looked at my best friend. "Go fuck your boyfriend or something. Get any thought of Arthur Adley from your head."

Arabella laughed. "Can you imagine taking him home to your daddy? He'd have a damn heart attack."

"Maybe Arthur isn't as bad as you think," I said.

"They're East End gangsters," Freya said. "They're *murderers*! We've all heard the rumours."

"Freya!" I checked none of the Adley boys had heard her. They were sitting around a table, talking, playing cards and drinking. At least most of them were. Arthur was leaning against the glass doors that led inside the yacht. He was silent, as usual. And his eyes were still on me. My thighs clenched together as he lit a cigarette and inhaled a long drag.

Why was that so damn hot?

"What? It's true. Everyone knows about them. They're notorious, Cheska. If Arthur didn't look like that"—her finger moved up and down him—"then you'd be as petrified of him as we are."

"How do you think they got that yacht?" Arabella said. "It wasn't through legitimate businesses like our families. It was through drugs and guns and racketeering." She huffed a disgusted laugh. "It probably doesn't even run on petrol. It'll be fuelled by the blood of the people they've killed."

I rolled my eyes at Arabella's dramatic words. "You've been watching too many crime documentaries. Your imagination is running away with you."

"If you think Arthur Adley doesn't belong on those documentaries, as the *bad* guy, then you belong in Broadmoor loony bin," Freya said. "No one, in all of Europe, has anything on the Adleys. They're criminals of the worst kind—untouchable. You need to keep away. You wouldn't last a day in his world."

"And you have Hugo," Arabella said. "You've been with him for years. His father worked with yours before he died. Now he's cared for by your old man, he'll always be with you. You know you'll marry him just like your daddy wants. And he adores you."

My stomach sank when I thought of Hugo. I loved Hugo—he was sweet and kind and I knew he would be loyal to me. But I didn't *burn* for him. Nothing he did set me alight. But Arabella was right. My daddy wanted us to marry—no, he *expected* us to marry. He never entertained anything else.

"Speaking of ..." Freya nodded in the direction of the living quarters. Hugo and Percy—his best friend—came toward us. Hugo leaned down and pressed a kiss to my lips. It was soft and gentle and loving. I knew, in my gut, that Arthur kissed nothing like that. His kiss would be savage and all-encompassing.

"I'll be back in a few days." Hugo looked across at the Adleys, a hint of worry in his stare. When I followed his gaze, Arthur hadn't even acknowledged Hugo; he was still looking directly at me. "What the fuck is he looking at?" Hugo said. But it wasn't loud enough for Arthur or his friends to hear. Hugo wouldn't dare take them on.

"Barcelona?" Freya asked Hugo, distracting him. Hugo turned to her.

"Yeah. George asked me to close a deal there while we were here. When we get back, we'll take the yacht to Ibiza, yeah?"

"Sounds good," I said. Percy and Hugo left the yacht and took a car toward the airport. Hugo had been working alongside my dad for a couple of years now, during holidays while he finished up sixth form at his boarding school. This summer he started full time. He didn't need university or a degree. He was primed to follow in my father's footsteps in the company—qualifications meant nothing when nepotism was a factor. Hugo was a good man. I knew that. He was the son my father never had.

My father loved me. But I wasn't a son. He'd always wanted a son. His relationship with Hugo was arguably better than his with me.

My eyes drifted to Arthur again, only to see him heading inside the yacht. My eyes were fixed on his tattoo of London on his stomach and chest. He was muscled and toned, but not overly bulky.

He was a living, breathing cocktail of deadly sins.

"Come on," Arabella said. "We're meeting Ollie and everyone tonight for dinner." She laughed and shook her head. "We can watch him moon all over you with Hugo not being there. It's tragic."

I grimaced. I liked Ollie, but not in a romantic way. He clearly liked me, though, and when Hugo wasn't around made no bones about it. Hugo and Ollie had attended sixth form together. It was how we all became friends.

Freya threaded her arm through mine. "Come on, Cheska. Let's have a good night. It'll help you forget the devil on the neighbouring boat."

Devil. That seemed a good title for Arthur. Most people were terrified of him. He was unapproachable, with eyes that could cut you where you stood. And he had the allure of Satan too. A magnet to sin and temptation, stirring wants and desires inside of me that were anything but chaste and holy. And if the rumours were true, he had the evilness of the dark lord too.

We entered the club, Ollie placing a hand on my back as he led us through the packed dancefloor to the VIP section. We sat at our roped-off table, and the waiter brought us bottles of Cristal, Grey Goose, gin and a ton of mixers.

"What can I get you, sweetheart?" Ollie asked.

"Gin," I said and immediately thought of Arthur. Ollie poured me the gin and automatically added tonic.

"So?" he asked. "Did you enjoy dinner?" He leaned in close and ran the tip of his finger down my arm. I shifted in my seat, backing away, hoping he didn't get offended.

"It was nice." I gave him a friendly, hopefully platonic smile. "Hugo would have loved it. It's a shame he couldn't be here."

The grin on Ollie's face fell so hard I was sure it hit the floor beneath us with a deafening thud. He took a long drink of his vodka, then turned to me and said, "He's not good enough for you."

I tensed, blinking in shock at Ollie being so forthcoming. He usually danced around his dislike for Hugo. There was no tiptoeing around this one.

"Ollie," I warned. "Don't. You're my friend. Hugo is my boyfriend. I won't do this with you."

Something akin to darkness appeared in Ollie's eyes. The hairs on my arms and the back of my neck pricked. It seemed to take Ollie a second to pull himself together before he smiled again. "Forgive me," he said, but his words seemed forced and rigid. "You're right. I shouldn't speak about him that way. He's okay, really." Ollie checked something on his phone and let his eyes drift over the club. He suddenly froze. "Twats."

I instinctively followed his gaze. It landed on a couple of the Adley boys, who were at the opposite side of the VIP section in a high-walled private booth. I recognised Charlie as he got up from his seat to let Eric Mason out. Charlie's eyes fell on us. He turned and said something to someone in the booth. My heart slammed in my chest as I wondered if Arthur was in there. If he had another girl on his lap, sucking on his neck, his fingers deep inside her.

"Nick," Ollie said, pulling his best friend's attention away from Freya. Ollie nodded in the direction of the Adleys. Nick followed his gaze, then nodded, some unspoken conversation I wasn't privy to happening between them.

"You don't like the Adleys?" I asked.

Ollie sat back in his chair and moved his arm around the back of mine. "No." I didn't think he would expand on that, as his eyes

narrowed and he drank his vodka, but then he said, "I don't particularly like East End cunts like his scumbag family. They cause my dad's
business no end of problems. They think they're entitled to run all the
docks in London just because of who they are. They're a cancer to
honest enterprises. I've only had to deal with Arthur a few times. And
that's a few times too many." His hand froze in mid-air as he lowered
his drink. "Why? You don't know the Adleys, do you?"

I shook my head, the lie rolling off my tongue. "No. Just heard of
them like everyone else has." I felt Arabella's eyes boring into me from
across the table but didn't look her way for fear Ollie would see
through my deceit.

Ollie exhaled a long breath. "Good." His hand wrapped around my
bicep. "Don't fuck with them," he said, his voice deep and brooking no
argument. Unease rolled through me like a thunderstorm. I tried to
move my arm, but Ollie's eyes only darkened and his grip grew harder.
"I mean it, Cheska. Don't get involved with the Adleys. Especially
Arthur. He's not right in the head."

Ollie finally released his grip. My arm throbbed, and even in the
dimly lit nightclub, I could see the red marks from his fingers. I was in
no doubt that they would bruise.

My eyes widened in shock. Ollie quickly plastered on a soft smile. I
flinched as he gently rubbed his hand over my bruising skin. "I just
don't want you getting mixed up with the wrong crowd, Cheska." His
voice was like silk, but underneath that silk I now knew hid jagged,
sharp blades. "I care for you." Ice ran down my spine as he leaned
closer. "You know that, don't you?" He moved my dark hair from my
shoulder. "I like you ... a lot."

I jumped to my feet. "I'm going to the bathroom." I didn't turn to
see if anyone was following. I rushed through the door and headed
straight for the mirrors. I stared at my reflection. My breathing was
heavy with shock. Ollie ... Ollie Lawson had hurt me. I stared at the
red marks on my skin.

What the hell had just happened?

I needed a cigarette. I rarely smoked, but right now, I needed the
smell and taste to calm me down. Leaving the bathroom, I snuck out
of the fire door that led to a secluded alleyway. Reaching into my

clutch, I pulled out my cigarettes and lighter. I took in a long inhale, letting the nicotine flood my lungs and calm my frayed nerves.

I had barely taken my second drag when the sound of footsteps came from the end of the alley. Something squeezed in my gut, propelling me to push off the wall I was leaning against. My heart kicked into a sprint, and I rushed toward the fire door. I had barely made it three steps before four men moved out of the darkness. My throat tightened in panic, my lungs ceasing to breathe. Hand shaking, I dived for the door handle, but just as I did, the men rushed at me.

My scream was lost to the blockage in my throat, and I was slammed against the wall, a hand slicing across my face. I tried to think, tried to formulate a plan to get away from these men, but my brain wouldn't work. My cheek throbbed and my head ached and I couldn't form any coherent thoughts.

Anxiety welled inside of me like quicksand, swallowing me whole, dousing me in pure terror. You always heard of people being attacked, always assumed that if it was you it ever happened to, you could get away. You would fight, resist and be able to escape. But I was paralysed by fear—muscles locked and eyes wide as I tasted blood in my mouth, my vision blurring as I tried to focus on my attackers.

My ears rang like St Paul's Cathedral's bells, deafening me, closing down my senses. I tried to gasp for breath, for a way to calm my racing heart. But dizziness consumed me. I blinked, managing to focus enough to see a tall man move before me and wrap his hand around my throat. He had acne scars on his face and a deep red scar through his left black eyebrow. Finding a morsel of fight within me, I silently cried out and pushed at his chest.

But he stood stoic. Unmoving. Then he used his grip on my neck to slam me back against the wall. White-hot pain sliced through my shoulders. Then I froze entirely, pushing through the panic and mental fog to realise his free hand was lifting up the hem of my dress.

I acted on instinct, panic stepping aside to allow determination through. "Stop!" I slammed my hands harder against his chest. A granite boulder disguised as a fist rammed into my stomach, knocking the wind from me. I gasped for breath, legs buckling, just as another man lifted my head by my hair to keep me upright.

No, no. no ... please ... !

I tried to scream aloud at the fiery pain ripping through my scalp, but a hand smothered my mouth before any noise could escape my lips. I thrashed as I bit down on the fingers, but it was no use. Nothing was working—I couldn't fight them off. I couldn't fight them off!

Think, think, think!

But I couldn't. Everything was happening too fast. They were too strong, too many of them. I was turned and rammed against the wall. A man moved behind me, pushing my dress up to my waist. Even through my thick head-fog, I heard the telltale sound of a zip being pulled down.

My turbulent panic and hopeless flailing grew to a sudden stop. Like all the oxygen within me had been sucked into a vacuum, rendering me still. Time slowed to half speed, the air around me grew stagnant and heavy, and the looming presence of the man behind me pressed down on me like a quilt of smothering darkness.

My pulse thundered in my ears like a drum-heavy soundtrack ominously counting down to his assault. I managed to move my head a fraction, the rough brick of the wall scraping against my cheek. That was all it took to rip through my paralysis. The clay of the brick gouged into my cheek, jerking my body and mind into motion.

I bit down harder on the hand over my mouth, sinking my teeth into flesh as hard as I could. "You fucking bitch!" the man behind me snarled, yanking his hand away. I took advantage of the moment and stole a much-needed long breath, sucking in the humid, salty Spanish air.

I needed to keep breathing. I just needed to keep breathing. I needed to keep moving, to keep slipping from their grips.

"Stop!" I uselessly begged, trying to kick out my legs, my arms, anything to get them off me. "I said STOP!" I threw back my head, managing to butt the nose of the man behind me. The crunch of broken bone ricocheted off the walls of the alley.

"Fucking spoilt Harlow cunt!" a voice hissed, and two hands wrapped around my throat from behind, cutting off my breath again. His hold was harder this time. I'd pissed him off.

The sticky air kissed my naked behind, my dress still rolled up to my waist, baring me to their eyes. Black spots danced in my vision as the man pushed his fingers against my trachea. I thrashed harder and harder with as much strength as I could muster. But as his grip only grew harsher, I knew this was it. My chances of escape were waning along with my ability to breathe.

As I danced on the verge of consciousness, my arms were forced to either side of me, as if I were bound to a cross. Unyielding hands held me still, but the hands around my neck loosened enough for me to siphon a breath down my burning windpipe.

My eyes welled with tears. "Stop," I rasped out, my throat feeling like it had been shredded by razors. "Please, stop ..." I whispered. But I knew they wouldn't. Then—

"I believe she fucking told you to stop."

I froze. In that moment, the sound of the thick cockney accent was like the voice of God himself in the deserted alleyway.

"Fuck off, prick," one of the men spat.

"No can do."

I managed to move my head to the side, my skin scraping against the rough brick, only to see a familiar head of black hair and piercing blue eyes behind thick-rimmed glasses penetrating through my attackers.

"Arthur," I managed to whisper, tears of relief filling my eyes. His gaze flitted to mine for only a second before it was back on the assailants. Arthur reached into his pocket and pulled out a knife.

The men behind me laughed. "Last chance to fuck off," they said. Their accents were definitely not English or even Spanish. I had no idea where they were from or why they wanted me. "Or you won't make it out of this alley either."

My heart crumbled. They were going to kill me. I fought back nausea and prayed my legs would keep me upright even as my body shook profusely in terror.

Arthur pointed his knife in my direction. "Be good boys and cover up the lady you've stripped down, and I might consider not killing *you*." He spoke with no emotion, his face giving nothing away. "Give her back her modesty, and I might just maim you instead."

"Who the fuck do you think you are?" the leader of the group said.

"Kill him," he instructed his men.

My arms were released as the men holding me rushed at Arthur. I swayed as fear, true and stark, took me in its hold as the three men charged. Arthur didn't move. Didn't even change his stance. He simply waited for the first man to attack and, in a second, slashed his knife across his throat. The man dropped to the floor.

Before the others even had a chance to attack, Arthur stabbed one in the chest, right through his heart, and stabbed the other in his neck, right in his jugular. The men fell like swatted flies around him, the alley floor instantly flooding with red.

The man behind me took his hands off my neck. I sagged against the wall, trying to catch my brain up with all that was happening.

They were dead. Arthur had killed them.

I scrambled back further against the wall. I let my disbelieving eyes seek out Arthur. He hadn't a hair out of place. No droplets of blood were evident on his white shirt. He wasn't out of breath. He was completely unaffected by what he'd just done.

Arthur pointed his knife at the man who had lifted my dress. His head cocked to the side as he studied him like a panther would do his prey—stealthy, cold, controlled.

"Who sent you?" Arthur asked.

My attacker rocked on his feet from side to side, eyes darting around the alley, clearly looking for an escape. There was none. None, unless he managed to get through Arthur.

"No one," he said.

Arthur came closer. "I asked you a simple question. You failed to give me an answer." Arthur reached out and, like a python, grabbed the attacker by his throat. The man lashed out with his fists, but Arthur was too strong for him. "I don't ask questions twice." Looking the attacker dead in the eyes, Arthur pushed his blade, slowly, through the man's shoulder. The man screamed in pain. Arthur seemed unbothered whether people heard the screams or not.

I was as still as statue, frozen in shock. I focused on breathing, my throbbing cheek and neck ignored as I watched the horror show before me. As I watched the boy I had obsessed over for years casually embrace the darkness I had been warned lived within him.

This was the Arthur Adley everyone had heard of. *This* was the boy that had everyone in London terrified.

But this was also the man who had just saved my life.

Arthur pulled the knife from his shoulder and nodded toward the end of the alleyway behind me. "There's some broken glass down there. You're going to go and get a piece."

I frowned in confusion along with the attacker. "What?" he said. "You want me to have a weapon?"

"You have five seconds, or I will kill you where you stand, slowly and painfully." The man ran and picked up a long shard of jagged glass. My stomach fell.

What was Arthur thinking?

"Arthur ..." I whispered, in warning. But Arthur didn't even acknowledge me. His attention was solely fixed on the attacker and the weapon he now yielded.

The man crouched down, ready to attack. Arthur placed one hand in his pocket. I wondered if he was reaching for another weapon, a gun maybe. It quickly became apparent he was simply putting his hand in his pocket in a casual, relaxed manner.

"Open your fly again," Arthur said, and the air in the alleyway grew stagnant with paused breath. He pointed at the attacker with the tip of his knife—a knife that was now dripping with four types of blood— the blood of his slain victims. The attacker did as Arthur said. I turned my head and saw the attacker's cock. He wore no underwear. Bile rose in my throat. He had been going to force himself on me. If Arthur hadn't turned up ...

Arthur stood stoic and strong. He gestured to the glass in the attacker's hand and said, "Now saw off your dick."

I stopped breathing. The attacker's eyes widened. "If you think I'm fucking—"

Arthur's knife sailed through the air and plunged into the man's other shoulder. He screamed and dropped to his knees. Arthur walked toward him, calm as a summer's breeze, and yanked the knife from the man's flesh. He held it at his throat. "You do as I say, and I'll let you live. Don't, and you die. That's your choice."

Arthur stepped back, waiting patiently. With shaking hands, the attacker lifted the shard of glass, staring at it like it was his demise. He brought it to his dick and held it an inch above, eyes flicking from side to side as if he was trying to find an escape and quickly. His breathing was choppy, and tears began building in his eyes. There was no escape. That much was obvious.

Arthur was a towering deadly sentinel, standing silently before his victim, waiting for his instructions to be obeyed. My feet wouldn't move. I needed to leave, to not see this, but I was frozen. It was as though a subconscious dark place inside me wanted to see this depraved act of revenge carried out.

Arthur took a step forward, knife ready to slit the attacker's throat. "Wait. Wait!" the attacker said and, taking hold of his dick, brought the glass shard to press lightly against the flesh. He gritted his teeth and began to saw. I squeezed my eyes shut the second he made the first cut, but I heard the guttural noises that poured from his throat and the sticky sound of glass slicing through flesh.

Panicking, I opened my eyes and focused on Arthur only. I needed to see him to calm me down. He appeared as unaffected as when he'd killed the men growing cold on the ground. When a loud bellow sounded behind me, I looked over to my attacker and fought back nausea on seeing his severed dick lying on the ground. Blood gushed from between his legs, and sweat ran in rivulets down his bright red face.

"Let me go," the attacker pleaded, his voice hoarse from pain.

Arthur nodded once, a succinct silent answer. The man scrambled to his feet, taking his sawn-off appendage with him. He staggered toward Arthur, who stayed unmoving.

Just as he passed Arthur, Arthur threw out his arm in a flash and slit the attacker's throat. A look of pure disbelief shone in the man's eyes for a moment before he dropped to his knees and fell forward, blood dripping from his wounds as he landed beside his friends.

Arthur wiped his knife on the attacker's shirt as the man gargled on blood, then he took his mobile from his pocket and texted someone. He stood, and the realisation of what I'd just witnessed, what had just happened to me, pounded into me like round after round of bullets from a machine gun.

"Come." Arthur came toward me. He wasn't gentle in his approach. He took long strides to where I stood, then lifted me into his arms and walked down the alley to the entrance. I closed my eyes as we passed the bodies lying still and soiled on the ground.

When enough time had passed, I opened my eyes and threaded my arms around Arthur's neck. I felt his strong arms holding me, keeping me close to his chest. I glanced up at his face. He was so ruggedly handsome I could barely stand it.

He had saved me.

He had avenged me.

And he had *killed* for me.

"Thank you," I whispered. Arthur kept his face forward, but I noted a small, quick clenching of his jaw. And if I wasn't mistaken, his arms held me just a little bit tighter.

I heard a car door open and realised we had reached the end of the alleyway. Arthur placed me in the back seat of the car and slid in beside me. I should have been nervous going anywhere with him, but I was the polar opposite. I was safe. I knew I was safe with him.

As we began to pull away, I saw a van stop behind us. Men in black clothes and balaclavas got out and made their way up the alley. "Clean-up", I assumed.

I stared at Arthur, who was texting on his phone, feeling pain build in my wounds. I stared at this boy I had first met at age thirteen. The boy I had thought of more often than was normal. And now he had saved me. I didn't know him. Our brief childhood encounter had been fleeting, yet felt as though it had been seared into my brain with a hot iron.

I was all alone with him for the first time in five years.

I was bruised and battered, but *alive*. Living, breathing, heart beating because of one man. All because of the man everyone told me to avoid.

The beautiful devil who had just killed four men in front of me ... and disturbingly, that didn't diminish my attraction for him one bit. It only made me want to know him more.

Who *was* Arthur Adley?

I needed to find out.

CHAPTER THREE

CHESKA

The car stopped at Arthur's yacht. My mobile vibrated, and I pulled it out of my clutch, which Arthur had retrieved from the alley floor.

FREYA: Where are you? We're worried.

I took a deep breath.

Gone home. Had a headache. I'm going to bed. Have fun. Don't worry about me.

I put my phone in my bag and tried not to feel guilty for omitting the truth about what had happened. But despite my throbbing cheek and my brush with the attackers, I needed to know what Arthur planned to do next. I wanted to speak to him. I wanted to get behind the high walls he had clearly built around him. He was a deep, dark mystery wrapped up in a seductive package, and I was intent on figuring him out.

The driver opened the door beside Arthur and he stepped out. He walked around the boot and opened my door. I climbed out, wincing when my stomach stabbed with pain—the result of the punch I'd taken to my torso. Like in the alleyway, Arthur didn't hesitate; he scooped me into his arms and carried me toward his yacht. Nerves burst in my chest.

Arthur walked onto the back deck and through to the living quarters. I roved my gaze around the area, numbly looking at the cherrywood finishes and Italian furnishings. An older man was waiting, and when I saw his black bag, I realised he was a doctor.

"Not in here," Arthur said to him and carried me through the centre corridor of the boat and into a large master bedroom. He placed me down on a huge bed that was dressed in black bed linen. Arthur stepped back, but from the way he crossed his arms over his chest and remained only a few feet from the bed, it was crystal clear that he wasn't leaving.

The doctor looked at him, appearing slightly unnerved. "Señor? I will examine her now." Arthur nodded his head at the Spanish doctor but stayed where he was. "You can leave the room."

"No," was all Arthur said. Goosebumps broke out on my arms at his curt, cold response.

The doctor looked to me for guidance. "I'm fine with him staying," I said.

The doctor sighed but examined me from head to toe. He hesitated, glancing back to Arthur when he said, "Have you been compromised, señorita?"

It took me a moment to understand his meaning. When it hit home, I shook my head. "No," I said, seeing Arthur's jaw clench again. The doctor stood and started putting his equipment back in his bag.

"Bathe, then place ice on your cheek for the swelling. I will leave pain medication for you to take. There is no lasting or significant damage. You will be fine once the bruising fades."

"Thank you," I said, and the doctor left the room. A man dressed in a dark suit came to lead him away. I looked down at my torn and bloodied dress and felt disgust and the residual embers of fear roll through me.

What would have happened if Arthur hadn't found me?

"Shower is through there." Arthur pointed to an en-suite bathroom. When I struggled to get up from the bed, he held out his hand. Our palms kissed, and my heart doubled its beat and shivers raced through the very marrow of my bones. Arthur helped me off the bed. There was no reason I couldn't go and shower next door on my own yacht. But I didn't want to go back there alone. That thought forced me to remember something, and I felt my stomach cave in.

"They knew my name," I whispered, meeting Arthur's eyes. His hand held me a fraction tighter at that information. I sucked in a stuttered breath. "They called me a spoilt Harlow cunt." I swallowed back the bile that was clawing up my throat. "Arthur ... they knew who I was. They knew I was a Harlow." The fear I had felt from the attack increased tenfold at knowing I was targeted. That they had followed me to the alley. That they had been waiting for the right time to capture me. To hurt me. To take me ...

Arthur stepped closer, so close I smelled the fresh water notes of his aftershave and the spice of what must have been his bodywash. "They won't get you here," he said, and I felt the truth of that statement wash over me like a refreshing summer rainfall. He nudged his chin toward the bathroom. "Get in the shower. Get the smell of those fuckers off your skin."

At his curt attitude, I walked into the bathroom and shut the door. Before I did, I saw Arthur take his phone from his pocket and start calling people. I moved to the shower and turned it on. Steam filled the luxurious space, and I stripped off my dress, avoiding the mirror. When I was naked, I went to move under the spray, but I caught my reflection in my peripheral vision.

I had to see it. Had to see what those monsters had done to me. My stomach rolled—I had red welts from their grips, and my cheek was slightly swollen and sore from the strike to my face. But, bizarrely, what held my focus the most were the finger marks Ollie Lawson had left on my arm. A fissure of unease trickled down my spine as I thought of how he had changed in a second from the kind and attentive friend he had always been to the controlling and aggressive boy he'd morphed into at the club.

And he hated Arthur. Arthur who had just saved me.

My legs were weak as I entered the shower, the hot spray crashing down on my head like holy water piped in from Lourdes. Shock must have still had me in its grasp; my legs buckled and I hit the tiled floor.

Those men knew my name. They had come after me.

Who were they? What did they want with me?

Shivering, I tried to get to my feet, but my pathetic legs wouldn't move, residual shock from the attack rendering them useless. The door to the bathroom suddenly slammed open, and there Arthur stood, backlit by the dim bedroom light, appearing like a fallen angel.

"I can't get up," I whispered, despising the tremble in my voice.

Arthur walked toward me. He didn't look at my naked body once as he picked me up in his arms. "Have you cleaned yourself?" He looked at my half-damp hair and still-dirty skin and must have decided for himself that I hadn't. He removed his glasses and put them on the side of the sink. I couldn't take my eyes from his face, the unobstructed view of his deep blue eyes and long dark lashes.

As if I weighed nothing at all, he carried me under the spray. His white shirt and navy shorts became sodden, and his dark hair went from styled to the side to flat against his forehead. He looked so much younger this way. At times I forgot we were the same age. He always seemed so much older.

Arthur sat me on the stall's ledge and reached for the shampoo on the corner shelf. He poured some into his hand and started washing my long dark hair. I winced when he brushed over a bruise that was forming on my scalp, where the attackers had yanked my hair back. Arthur's hands stopped moving, and he exhaled a long, steady breath. He resumed washing my hair, but this time he was softer, more careful, so gentle in his touch and tenderness that tears welled in my eyes. As I tipped my head back, the tears spilled onto my cheeks, dripping down my neck and melding with the hot water.

I closed my eyes, to try and stop them, to not show any weakness in front of such a strong and formidable man. Arthur pulled away, clearly seeing my tears. I opened my eyes, and when I did, he was staring at me like he never had before. His steel eyes seemed softer somehow, sympathetic. His head tilted to the side, and he placed both hands on my face, careful of my hurt cheek.

With the touch of feather, he smudged the tears from my skin with his thumbs. I swallowed at the heaviness of the moment. The touch of his hands on my face was like a balm to my severed nerves, to the fear that was coursing so thickly in my veins that my entire body ached.

Arthur's white shirt had turned transparent, and through the material I saw his ripped muscles and haunting black tattoos. The London skyline on his torso appeared sinister and gothic—the London of old, Victorian, eerie.

He stayed silently before me as I shed tear after tear, exorcising the images of the attackers, their unwanted touches. When they had run dry, he took the shower head and rinsed off my hair.

He grabbed a flannel from the shelf, covered it with body wash and bent down until he was at my eye level. I held out my arms, and Arthur ran the flannel over my reddened skin. My breathing grew more laboured with every stroke he made. He moved the flannel over my neck and down over my breasts. I was breathless as he skimmed over my flesh, but he never once looked at me with desire. Not in this moment. He was caring for me after an attack. And I was drawn to him all the more for it.

Arthur dragged the flannel down my legs and over my feet. As he stood back up, he hooked his arm around my waist and turned me around. With one arm keeping me steady, he ran the flannel over my back and then down over my backside and the tops of my thighs.

I fought back tears of both sorrow and relief. Sorrow for the attack, but relief that Arthur had saved me. Turning me back to sit on the ledge, Arthur brought the shower head to me and rinsed off the soap.

Who was this man? The man who had just killed four others in front of me, without exertion or guilt. The sadistic man who had forced someone to castrate himself as I watched. And now he was here, caring for me like a saint, when we all knew he was anything but.

Arthur carried me from the shower and wrapped an oversized bath sheet around me. He placed me on the bed, and then ducked back into the bathroom. The door was slightly ajar, blocking Arthur from view. But when I lifted my eyes, I saw his reflection in the fog-free mirror. I saw every inch of him as he tossed off his shirt and shorts. I swallowed as his lightly tanned body came into perfect view. Then he removed his boxers, and I felt my cheeks flush as he moved fully before the mirror, totally bared, running a towel through his dark hair.

My breathing came heavy, and I couldn't tear my eyes away. He was tall and ripped and tattooed and more than well-endowed. Arthur wiped the lenses of his glasses on a cloth and placed them back on his face. Before I could avert my eyes, his gaze found mine in the mirror. I wanted to turn away.

But I couldn't.

I clutched the towel tighter around me and stayed transfixed as Arthur dried himself, never taking his eyes off me, moving the towel over every inch of his skin—skin that was scarred in multiple places. But the scars couldn't take anything away from his rugged beauty.

Drops of water slid down his muscles. I wanted to feel them underneath my hands. I wanted to thread my fingers through his damp hair and feel his full lips against my own. Arthur was nothing like Hugo. In fact, he was the polar opposite in every way. I had never longed for Hugo. I'd never wanted him to possess me, own me and make me forget the very essence of who I was.

Arthur came back through to the bedroom, his towel tied around his waist. From his wardrobe, he pulled out a long t-shirt and a pair of clean boxers. He threw them on the bed beside me. "For you."

"Thank you," I said. He took a pair of black pyjama shorts out for himself, putting them on under his towel.

Arthur tipped his head back and sighed. I wondered what he was thinking. If he was regretting me being here. When he lowered his head, he said, "Get dressed. We need to ice your cheek."

We. The thrill that word inspired was pathetic, but nonetheless real.

I quickly dressed in the clothes he gave me. They smelled of him. Of tobacco and fresh water and whatever laundry detergent the staff on the yacht used.

When I was done, he wrapped his arm around my waist and guided me from his room. His body was hard and strong beside mine, his hand splayed on my stomach to keep me steady.

His closeness left me breathless, light-headed and skin burning.

In the main living room, he helped me down to the couch. He filled a clean tea towel with ice from the freezer and brought it to me. "Thank you." I held the towel to my cheek, hissing at the sting.

Arthur busied himself at the bar, his back muscles flexing with every movement he made. He came back to me with a glass of whisky, and a straight gin with ice for himself. He leaned against the bar and looked out of the bifold doors at the dark sky and glittering lights of Marbella's pretty marina.

"Arthur," I said, needing to hear something from him, *anything*. He barely spoke, and it was driving me insane. He turned to me. "Thank you." He nodded as if what he had done was nothing. As if killing four men wasn't a huge deal, just an everyday part of his life.

Judging by the rumours about his firm, that might have been true.

I took a sip of my whisky, feeling the heat from the spirit coat my throat. It also gave me the courage to say, "You killed those men." Arthur didn't react to my words; they rolled off him as breezily as if I'd mentioned it was warm outside. "You killed them, Arthur ... and what you did to the last man, with the glass ..."

Arthur watched me carefully and said, his voice neutral, "I've done worse, princess."

Princess ...

Despite the endearment, blood drained from my face. "No, I don't believe that ..." Arthur walked over and crouched in front me. His blue eyes searched mine. They were a dark kind of blue, almost navy, a unique colour that suited his dark, mysterious personality. Like the sky at dusk before the darkness came and smothered it with the black of night.

"Believe it, princess." He studied my face, lifting the ice pack back to my cheek. I hissed at the cold, but he held my hand in place regardless. He licked his lips, and I couldn't help but trace the movement with my eyes. He'd licked his lips at my house five years ago, a silly habit of his I'd always remembered. I was as transfixed by it now as I was then.

Arthur took a sip of his gin. "Everything you've heard about me and my men will probably be true." His lip curled a fraction—a flicker of amusement, or maybe pride. "What you've heard about my entire family will also no doubt be true. In fact ..." He tilted his head to the side as he pushed a strand of hair back from my face. I held my breath at the action. "We've done worse than you've imagined." Looking me straight in the eye, he said, "A lot fucking worse."

"You're only eighteen, like me," I said, dumbly, as if that would somehow make him innocent. I shook my head, trying to sort my thoughts into what I wanted to say, what I wanted to know. "I mean, you're too young. And those men tonight … it was easy for you. Killing them." His blank expression only confirmed that to be true. "And the last man. What you made him do to himself …"

Arthur released my hand holding the ice pack and smudged his thumb over my cheek, dragging my skin downwards. The feel of his hand on my face caused my temperature to spike to ungodly degrees. "So innocent," he said, his warm breath ghosting across my cheek. "A true little princess in an ivory tower."

I licked my lips. Arthur's attention snapped to the movement. His addictive scent surrounded me, drowning me, pulling me down to whatever level of hell he resided in. I grew hot, Arthur's clothes suddenly feeling like a blanket of fire.

My gaze dropped to Arthur's body, to the skyline of the gothic London Town tattooed across his chest and abdominals. I lifted my hand to his chest; his nose flared as my fingers brushed over his hard pecs. He put his gin down on the floor beside us and placed his hands on either side of me on the sofa.

He was here, before me, cocooning me with his tall, muscled body, a cage of flesh and bone. I trailed my hand off his pecs and down to his abs. Arthur was as calm as he had been in the alley. I had never known anyone be able to mask their responses and feelings as well as he could. No reaction. Nothing seemed to shake him.

I wanted to see him crack.

I wanted to be the one to mine through whatever invisible shield he wore around him.

"Arthur," I whispered, my hand dipping lower, toward his narrow hips. I saw him harden under his pyjamas. I felt him pressing against my inner thigh as he leaned in even closer. I fought to steady my breathing, wanting to feel every part of him without clothes. Wanting to feel him pushing inside me, his chest pressing against mine as he made me fall apart ...

Then my phone rang, breaking the tension pulsing between us. When it was on its fifth ring, Arthur stood and took my phone from my bag. His eyes flared at the screen, and he handed it to me.

I looked at the screen. Ollie. Ollie Lawson was calling. "Ollie?" I said when I answered. A dark storm broke out over Arthur's features.

It was the first crack in his armour I had witnessed.

"Freya said you're at your yacht," he said. "I'm coming over."

"No!" I turned my head away from Arthur. "I'm already in bed. I'm going to sleep. I have a headache. I'll ... I'll just see you tomorrow or something."

Ollie paused for so long I thought he'd disconnected. Then he said, "But you're okay? You just left the club without telling anyone. I searched for you. I thought you must have gone outside, but the alley was deserted." I turned to Arthur, who was looking out of the glass doors at the marina, a cigarette in his hand.

The alley was already clear? Arthur's men worked fast.

"Ollie. I'm fine. Please, just enjoy your night."

"But you're not hurt? Nothing happened?" A slither of unease sild along my skin at his persistent questions.

"No. Why? Why would you think I'm hurt?"

I heard someone speak to Ollie in the background but couldn't make out the words. "Then fucking check again," he snapped to whoever he was conversing with.

Shaking my head in frustration, I said, "I've got to go, Ollie."

"I'll see you tomorrow," he said after a long, stretched-out pause. His words sounded more of a threat than a caring promise. I hung up and walked to Arthur, confused about Ollie's strange behaviour.

My stomach was still sore as I took steady steps, but the initial pain was easing some after my shower and the pain meds that the doctor had given me.

"You know Ollie Lawson?" Arthur asked casually when I stopped beside him. He kept his eyes on the glittering lights of the marina.

"Yes." I studied Arthur for another reaction. I didn't know why I bothered. I was learning that Arthur gave absolutely nothing away unless he wanted to—I imagined that was almost never. "From school." I felt a sudden chill in the room, so I wrapped my arms around me. "I went to an all-girls boarding school. Private, of course. Hugo was at the boys' side of the school. Ollie went there for sixth form as a day student. I've only known him a couple of years. We have mutual friends."

"Hugo," Arthur said. "Hugo Harrington. Your boyfriend."

I hated hearing the word "boyfriend" from Arthur's lips in relation to Hugo.

"Yes," I said. Arthur drank the rest of his gin in one go. He stubbed his cigarette out on an ashtray and immediately lit up another one.

"Let's get you home, princess," he said, and my stomach fell to the floor. I had bought us some more time with my friends. I wanted to stay with Arthur a while longer. But mostly, I didn't want to go home. I'd been attacked. I wasn't safe on my own. I knew I'd be safe with him.

"What if they find me again tonight?" I said, my frayed nerves seeping into my words.

"I've already got men watching your yacht. They've been on board and done a search. No one is there, and no one is getting to you. I can guarantee you that."

I blinked in surprise. "Thank you," I said, taken aback by his generosity.

Arthur walked back to the sofa and picked up my clutch, then passed me and opened the doors that led to the back deck.

Disappointment accompanying my every step, I followed Arthur off the boat and to mine. I turned to face him. "Thank you, again," I said. He handed me back my clutch.

A cloud of tobacco washed over my face as Arthur exhaled. "Night, princess." He walked back to his yacht without another glance. I jumped on seeing a couple of men in black suits move close by. My heart kicked into a heady, nervous beat, until they nodded at me in greeting and I realised they were Arthur's men who he had ordered to protect me.

Wrapping my arms around myself, I climbed onto my boat and made my way to my bedroom. As I curled up on my bed, I smelled

Arthur's aftershave on my borrowed clothes and closed my eyes, letting it wrap around me. My stomach rolled when I thought back over the events of the night, at the attackers, but more at Arthur killing them so efficiently, so coldly, so brutally.

I didn't know what kind of person it made me, but as I replayed the scene over and over in my head, all I could think was that he'd saved me. He'd killed to save me, not a single ounce of remorse in his dark soul.

I stared down at my hands, the hands that had run over his pecs, his abs and his hips. Despite knowing it was fucked up and wrong, I wanted to feel him like that again. Only this time I didn't want him to hold back. I didn't want him to keep his distance. I wanted him smothering me and making me forget my name. Maybe then I could shake myself of this obsession with him once and for all.

Maybe.

———

The music sailed through the yacht's speakers, and the few glasses of sangria I'd had made me feel loose and free. My eyes travelled to the people dancing on the sun deck, the sun setting on the horizon casting a warm, orange glow. Arabella and Freya came over to me as I leaned against the rail of the yacht.

"Are you feeling okay?" Arabella asked.

I touched my face, letting my fingers graze down my neck. The swelling had reduced a little, but the bruising left an ugly shadow of purple on my cheek and red finger marks around my throat. My foundation and concealer covered them well enough that people couldn't tell. I'd told Arabella and Freya that I had taken a bad fall in my room. I wasn't sure if they believed me, but neither of them had questioned me further. In our circles, lots of questions remained unasked. No one wanted to taint our seemingly perfect lives with a trivial thing like the truth.

I glanced across to the Adley yacht beside us. I hadn't seen Arthur last night or today at all. Hugo returned tomorrow, and we were scheduled to set sail for Ibiza. I looked at the people dancing on the sun deck. Mainly acquaintances of Arabella and Freya, some we knew from our social circles in Chelsea. Although some of our acquaintances were absent.

Ollie Lawson had come to see me yesterday as promised. I had made sure it was off the yacht and in a restaurant with my friends. After the other night, a heavy feeling settled in my gut whenever I thought about Ollie. Something had seemed off about him. Something I could only describe as dark had seemed to linger in his eyes. However, he was his usual charming and attentive self at the restaurant. He had left Marbella now, called back to London by his father. That left tonight. One night without Hugo, without Ollie watching me closely.

The sound of voices from the Adley yacht drew my attention.

"You boring twat!" Eric Mason shouted to someone inside the living quarters as he walked out in shorts and a white linen shirt, his hair swept over to one side as always.

Freddie Williams was on his heels, slapping Eric around the back of the head. "He has business he's got to get done, arsehole," he said. "Or do you want to ring Alfie and tell him his son's fucking off his work so we can go and get pissed instead?"

"Good point," Eric said after pretending to think for a few seconds, and they left the yacht and headed toward the bars of the main strip.

"Ugh. At least they haven't tried to get on board here tonight," Freya said. She stood straighter when Benedict Shaw came over and took her hand, leading her to the makeshift dancefloor without a word.

"She's so cock-whipped," Arabella said, then practically fell to her knees when Cassius Lock came up to her too. She quickly turned her back and downed her margarita. When I smiled and lifted a questioning brow, she flicked her middle finger at me. "Dutch courage, okay? Don't judge me."

"Arabella?" Cassius said. He nudged his head in the direction of the bar inside. "You want to grab a drink?"

Arabella smiled widely at me as Cassius led her inside the yacht. I watched people we knew from home get gradually drunker. People paired off, and the sky grew dark.

"Come on, old boy," a voice said from the Adley yacht. Charlie

Adley and Vinnie Edwards were leaving the boat. Vinnie bounced as he walked, as if he'd been injected with pure adrenaline and his muscles had no choice but to move. Charlie, his arm around Vinnie's shoulders, led him into a waiting car. They sped off, the taillights of the car disappearing into the distance.

I drank the rest of my sangria as the DJ cranked up the music some more. The people on our yacht all gravitated to the dancefloor, pills and shots immediately being passed around. I saw Freya near the bar and Arabella leading Cassius toward her room.

I stared at the people in front of me. Every one of them was wealthy. Every one spoke with received pronunciation like I did. Every one had attended a private school, and not just any—the best England had to offer. We all frequently lunched at the Bluebird in Chelsea—and we were all destined to marry into the same circles. Suitable "society" families.

I was no different.

And it was completely suffocating.

Placing my glass on a nearby table, I left the lights and pounding dance music of the sun deck and made my way to the back of the yacht. The music quietened as I leaned over the back of the boat and stared unseeing at the restaurants behind us.

The familiar smell of cigarette smoke cut through my reverie. Even in the darkness of the dock, I glimpsed the sight of a cigarette's burning end, the orange flicker of tobacco morphing into ashes before it dropped to the ground.

Arthur.

I stood, seeing Arthur's face illuminated as he took another drag. His yacht was in near darkness, barely a light in sight. But I saw the moment he caught me in his peripheral vision. His head cocked to the side, and his blue eyes ran down the length of my dress. It was purple and cut in a deep V to my belly button, the sides of my breasts peeking through the gauzy fabric. It flowed to my feet. My long dark hair was held back off my neck with a few well-placed grips.

I swallowed down my nerves as he drank me in. His hand remained in his pocket, his posture the epitome of calm. I tried to mirror his frame, but inside, my heart was beating as fast as a hummingbird's wings.

The people on this yacht were the furthest thing from Arthur they could possibly be. Arthur may have been richer than sin, but he was brought up in the East End of London. He didn't attend the best schools, or holiday in exotic countries like we all had. He was down-and-dirty Bethnal Green, with the trademark thick cockney accent to match. He had his rivals' blood underneath his fingernails, and fragments of their bones locked away in the cage that was his dark heart.

Yet here I was, following my feet as they left my yacht and took the few short steps to where he stood. Arthur was still smoking, still keeping one hand in his pocket. But he watched me approach like a lion watches a gazelle, the reflection of me flickering on the black-rimmed glasses he always wore. My chest felt as though it was being pressed down upon by a demon as I climbed the steps to the back of his yacht. The rich wooden floor creaked as I straightened and faced the man who had possessed my every thought lately. My dress blew in the warm Spanish breeze, the slits on the skirt exposing my bare legs.

Arthur flicked his cigarette overboard, then turned and walked through the glass doors to the living quarters. I ran my hand over my chest to be sure my heart hadn't leapt free of my ribcage. Every part of me screamed at me to leave, to stop this foolishness. Yet something inside me, something raw and savage and sadistic, forced me to stay. I saw Arthur move to the bar, the only light in the room sneaking in from the bars and restaurants outside.

I glanced over at my yacht. Saw people dancing. Heard them laughing and drinking and having a good time. I should have turned around and left this boat. I should have gone back to Freya and Arabella and had a good time, looking forward to Hugo returning tomorrow and to living my steady, blessed life.

I rubbed my arms, not to stave off the cold but to send blood to my brain, to wake myself up and avoid the temptation trying to lure me in. Because wanting someone like Arthur Adley was only acceptable in my fantasies. Not in real life. And *never* in my social circle.

I closed my eyes, deciding it was time to go. To leave this pathetic obsession with him in the past. It was a stupid secondary-school crush on the bad boy from across town. I took a long deep breath and opened my eyes, set on doing the right thing. But when my vision focused, all my good intentions seeped out of me. Arthur stood in my line of sight, dead centre of the living room, his forbidden deep blue gaze fixed on me. He had a drink in his hand, a cigarette balancing on his bottom lip, and with his defined muscles clearly visible under his shirt, I knew I was staying. He had me in his snare, and I threw all logic away with the Spanish wind and was willingly drawn in.

With trembling hands, I forced myself to tune out the sounds from my yacht and walked through the darkness, over the threshold to Arthur. Turning, I shut the doors behind me, sealing us inside and blocking out the real world. All noise from outside was expelled by the expensive soundproof doors. I was in a vacuum. A vacuum filled with temptation and sin and the forbidden object of my obsession.

Arthur took a drag of his cigarette and pulled it from his mouth, the smoke clouding around us. Apart from when I was smoking them myself, I usually disliked the smell of cigarettes. But not when it came from Arthur. Never then. From him, it smelled like heaven itself.

"You shouldn't be here, princess," Arthur said, his deep voice wrapping around me as tightly as the serpent from the Garden of Eden. He stepped closer to me, and the hairs on the back of my neck stood on end merely at his wickedly addictive presence. My mind tried to warn me to leave, showing me highlights of the night in the alley. Of Arthur cutting down men twice his age in cold blood. Of him ordering my attacker to castrate himself, no expression on his perfect face, no remorse in his corrupt soul.

But he saved you, the newly acquired depraved side of me argued, overriding my brain. *He saved your life.*

Before I could talk myself out of it, I edged forward and stopped right before him. Arthur downed his gin; a half-empty bottle of Bombay Sapphire was on the bar behind him—his brand of choice. He stubbed out his cigarette in an ashtray on the bar. The wash of midnight stubble on his jaw and cheeks only made him look more rugged and severe.

Arthur met my eyes. Then he licked his lips, and I felt my cheeks blaze. "Run," he said, voice thick with warning. Lifting his index finger, he placed it on my jaw. He moved it, light as a feather, down my neck, over the front of my throat and down the centre of my chest between my breasts. My breathing was laboured and my nipples hardened, sending heat flooding between my thighs. "Run, princess. Run far away, back to your ivory castle and the valiant knights that protect you."

I wasn't thinking. I was purely acting on instinct. As his finger lifted from my chest, I caught it in my hand and brought it to my mouth. Following a rebel side of me I didn't even know existed, I took his finger between my teeth and bit down hard.

Arthur's eyes flared, a napalm firestorm igniting in their sapphire depths. He didn't make a sound as my teeth met his flesh. I wasn't a delicate little princess. Right now, I wanted to be anything but perfect or good or someone Arthur didn't want to corrupt.

He acted quickly. In a flash, he pressed his hand to my face, his index finger still in my mouth, and pushed me against a wide breakfast bar. My back hit the marble countertop with a thud. I was numb to anything but Arthur and the godless look in his eyes. His spare fingers were splayed on my cheeks. His eyes were molten as they bored into mine. I bit down harder on his finger until I tasted blood. Arthur hissed, pressing his chest against my breasts, dragging a moan from my lips.

He liked it.

He liked that I caused him pain.

Arthur pulled his finger back from my mouth. It was too dark to see, but I knew there'd be teeth marks embedded into his broken skin. I ran my tongue along my teeth, the tinny taste of blood trickling down my throat.

His blood. Arthur's devilish blood that, to my tongue, tasted like manna from the gods.

Arthur towered above me, his hard, muscled body pressed flush against mine, his ally of darkness wrapping around us. The tip of his nose ran over my cheek. He still held me in his grip, his warm breath lapping at my flushed and wanting skin. He moved back an inch and dragged his thumb over my bottom lip, no doubt smearing my bright red lipstick.

"I'm going to fucking wreck you," he warned softly, darkly, truthfully. My back arched at his depraved promise. My clit throbbed and my muscles ached just waiting for what came next. His thumb smudged over and over my lips until I felt them begin to swell. He pushed his thumb into my mouth and waited. I knew what he wanted, and bit down hard until my teeth broke through flesh. Arthur's jaw clenched and his hips thrust toward me, his cock hardening against my hip.

I swirled my tongue around his thumb as if it were his dick, the mix of his blood and my saliva bursting like vintage Cristal on my taste buds. The muscles in Arthur's neck strained, and he pulled his thumb from my mouth. I barely had time to take a breath before he dragged me across the room by my shoulders to the dining table and slammed me down on top of it. I cried out at the impact of my back hitting wood, but before my voice could even carry into the air, Arthur ripped my dress in two and yanked down my thong.

He tossed it aside and, with a murderous intent in his gaze, pushed my legs apart. I was completely bared to his eyes, a naked offering. His hands ran down my thighs, locking them apart, and he lowered his head and sucked on my clit. I screamed out loud as my back arched off the table, white-hot pleasure ripping through me, devouring me down to my soul. Arthur never let up. He sucked and licked along my clit and slit with a maddening intensity, so intense that I didn't think I could take it. His hands were steel traps keeping my legs wrenched apart, immobilising me. I blinked into the heavy darkness, the lights from the marina glinting off Arthur's dark hair and the frames of his glasses.

Desperately needing to touch him, I reached down and ran my hands through the ebony strands. His hair was like silk between my fingers, and I tried to be gentle. But when Arthur exchanged his relentless tongue for his teeth, he bit down on my clit, and stars burst before my eyes at the addictive cocktail of hedonism and pain.

His fingers bit into my thighs, and I yanked on his hair. A sharp, sex-fuelled grunt slipped from Arthur's lips, evidence of his need sneaking through his impenetrable walls. That sound ... that slip of the shield he seemed to forever wear was like a match to petrol. I pulled on his hair as his tongue slid inside me, pushing, licking, swirling. I moaned, unable to take it, take his tongue and all the things I'd never felt before. Arthur pushed a finger inside me and bit down on my clit again. That was all it took for me to splinter apart.

My skin was a furnace, and I had just reached the height of my orgasm when Arthur stood and pulled his cock from his shorts. My breasts ached to be touched, and I squeezed my nipples as my pussy clenched, holding on to the remnants of pleasure.

My eyes widened when I saw his cock—he was thick and long and bigger than I'd ever had before. Arthur threw his shirt to the floor and stroked his cock before caging me in with his arms and fixing his gaze on mine. His nostrils flared, and just as I reached up to lay my palm on his stubbled cheek, he slammed inside me. My lips parted and I cried out at the intrusion, at the fullness and the slight pain that came with taking someone so big. I was far from a virgin, but I felt as though this man, Arthur Adley, the apparent devil himself, had just torn through my innocence and shredded the memory of all past lovers.

It was him and me and the pulsating darkness. Arthur wasn't soft or slow. He fucked me. *Hard.* He fucked me like the living demon he was rumoured to be—rough and wild and with unmerciful intent.

"Arthur," I whispered. As soon as I spoke, he moved a hand to my throat and wrapped it around my neck so I couldn't speak again. A light sparked in his eyes as he squeezed. I felt all his incredible strength in that single grip. There was a sinful gleam in his gaze as he held me at his mercy, perched precariously between fucking me and killing me if he desired.

He squeezed tighter until I could only breathe a little, but I didn't fear him. I wanted him to push me as far as I could go; I wanted every fucked-up part of this man. If this was the only night I would ever have Arthur, I wanted him in all his raw entirety. I wanted the devilry, I wanted the sadism, and I wanted this man, the man who had made a grown man cut off his own dick, to fuck me with equal amounts of depraved ease.

I arched, tilting my head back, offering him my neck. I wanted him to have it—I wanted him to push me to my limits and fuck me like I was the last pussy he would ever have. A low, feral groan tore from Arthur's mouth, and his free hand took my throat too. He pounded into me harder, as if he was exorcising the good from me.

I would be sore. The way he slammed inside me promised bruises and discomfort, but right now, in this suspended, surreal moment, he filled me like no one before, hard flesh scraping against my G-spot, making me lose my mind.

Arthur moved his face closer to mine, his nose brushing my nose. His eyes were locked on mine as he held my neck like it was his possession, like it was his right to break me if he so wished. Beads of sweat built on his forehead, a lock of his onyx hair falling in front of his eyes. I trailed my hands up his toned bare thighs, needing to touch him. His fingers flexed on my neck as my hands travelled higher, but didn't tighten. My eyes fluttered at the deep feelings accosting my body, but I fought to keep them open. I didn't want to miss a second of being with Arthur, of being taken like this—so brutally, so thoroughly, so perversely.

I felt my channel clench as his thrusts became faster. I was going to come. I ran my hands over the backs of his thighs and to his firm behind, pulling him closer to me. Not believing it was even possible, I felt Arthur push into me deeper, and I cried out at the too-full feeling, at the mix of pain and ecstasy, of being held and controlled.

"I'm going to come," I whispered, his hands on my neck inhibiting the volume of my voice. "Arthur, I'm coming ..." I moaned, and I burst. I broke apart, my body blistering in heat and sensation, the euphoric orgasm taking me in its sharp-clawed hold.

Then Arthur's hands tightened just enough to momentarily stop my breathing. The action only heightened the sensation, sending me soaring, head spinning, coming out of my skin. Then his hold loosened and I began to fall. I plummeted back into my body, breathing deeply, just to be flipped onto my front.

Arthur pushed me onto the table and slammed into me from behind. His hand wrapped around my hair, pulling the grips free, and his chest lay flush against my back. I was unable to move, locked in place, as Arthur fucked me. He did more than fuck me; he consumed me, *owned* me. He wrecked me. He'd told me he would.

No, he'd promised.

And he delivered.

Arthur thrust into me so hard that I felt a second orgasm building.

I couldn't stave it off, I couldn't make it last. Arthur pulled the final ounce of pleasure from me as I lay paralysed beneath him. As my pussy milked his dick, he pulled on my hair and, with a savage growl, came inside me. He pushed into me a few more times, savouring the end of his orgasm. I sucked in a much-needed breath, head spinning with what had just transpired.

Arthur's breathing was heavy, but he kept his hand in my hair, a silent warning to me not to move. I didn't want to. I didn't want to break this moment. I had never been taken like that. Had no idea sex could *be* like that. Any expectation or fantasy I might have had about Arthur had just been obliterated.

How would anyone ever compare to him?

My palms were flat on the table beneath me, my cheek resting on the cold wooden surface. My hands were shaking, too much adrenaline running through my veins. After a few silent minutes, Arthur shifted, and I winced. He slipped out from inside of me, and wetness slipped down my thighs. I closed my eyes and thanked God that I was on the pill. I pushed away any other panic over the fact he had taken me unprotected and tried to stay in the here and now.

Then I felt a soft kiss on the centre of my spine. I froze.

For a second I believed I had dreamed it. Dreamed that the man who had just taken me so savagely was kissing me so softly. So affectionately. It was in such stark contrast to how he had treated me so far.

I held my breath, eyes non-blinking and fixed on the window of the yacht, waiting to see if he would do it again. His breathing was deep, his body heat like a heavy blanket above me. I didn't take a single breath, just waiting, needing, searching ... then he kissed the top of my spine, and I exhaled a shaky breath. Arthur's hand was still in my hair. He pulled the long strands aside and kissed the pulse on my neck. My heart burst into a sprint as goosebumps raced over me.

I risked a glance at him, turning my body just a fraction so I could see his face. His cheeks were flushed. He was devastatingly handsome. Even when I was thirteen, I had found him so. And more so now that I had slept with him.

I swallowed back nerves, not knowing if he would order me from the yacht or coldly move from me, no more affection to be had. But behind the protection of his lenses, I saw deep blue eyes soften a little. Arthur dragged his thumb over my lips just as before.

"I want to ruin you," he said, his deep gravelled voice rolling over my body with the headiness of a summer electric storm. His hard chest was still slick against my back, but he shifted enough that he could lean down to my mouth. And he took it. He kissed my lips, then plunged his tongue inside. His fingers drifted between my legs and pushed inside me. I gasped at the tenderness, the sensitivity from being taken so hard.

Arthur broke from my mouth. "I want to degrade you." I couldn't breathe, my body shuddering as his fingers pushed past my G-spot again. I moaned and saw his eyes flare. "I want to mess you the fuck up." He gripped my cheeks and forced me to meet his eyes. "I want to break you, princess." I froze at his harsh words, but my body sparked to life like a live wire, pulsing with static at his dark desires. Because I wanted it too. My God, I craved his heavy hand. I needed more of what he had just given me. I didn't know what that said about me, but being here, underneath him, I didn't care.

My eyes fluttered shut as his fingers inside me moved faster. "I don't know if I can take any more," I whispered, my core aching.

"You can," he said and pressed against my G-spot until my thighs started to shake. Arthur's teeth scraped along my jaw and over my lips. I fought to breathe as I felt another orgasm building. His chest pinned me down, the muscles cut and defined.

He bit along my neck and down to my breasts. As his mouth wrapped around my nipple, his tongue lashing back and forth, I came. I cried, tears building in my eyes as the orgasm tore through me like a raging fire. It was too much, too much to take after what Arthur had already given me.

My body was wrecked and ruined, exhausted, but so alive as I breathed through the crest of pleasure. My eyelids were heavy, but I felt Arthur move his fingers from inside me and watched him bring them to his lips and suck the evidence of us into his mouth.

And I knew I was done.

I knew that no one could ever compare to him tonight, to Arthur and his wicked presence and the maelstrom of feelings that came with it. Arthur reached to the table and grabbed a cigarette. He lit the end and inhaled, exhaling a cloud of white into the air. I rolled slowly onto my back, letting my eyes rove down his naked body. I wanted to touch him. I wanted to spend an entire night exploring him, no rush, no barriers between us. But I knew it was impossible. This night was all we'd ever get. In no world did we belong together.

Arthur's eyes fixed back on mine. I saw his dick twitch as he moved his gaze down my body before finding my eyes again. He took another drag of his cigarette, then crawled over me as I remained lying back on the table. His face hovered above mine, and he gripped my jaw and opened my mouth. Leaning down, he exhaled, and the smoke from his cigarette entered my lungs. I closed my eyes as the nicotine flooded my body. I tentatively ran my hands up Arthur's arms on either side of my head. His muscles flexed. I studied his body. Scars were scattered up and down his skin. I looked up into his eyes to find him watching me. His lips were slightly parted, and his eyebrows were pulled down, as if he couldn't understand why he was letting me touch him so affectionately.

"Arthur," I tried to say, but he schooled his expression, then took another drag of his cigarette and breathed it into my mouth like before, cutting off my words. He repeated the action until the cigarette was finished and I was utterly spent.

He stubbed it out in the ashtray further up the table. Then he dipped down and kissed me. He kissed me and kissed me until I was starved of air. I didn't care. I could happily die this way. Lips bruised and body depleted.

Arthur finally pulled away. He put his hands under my arms and lifted me from the table to stand before him. My dress hung at my sides, exposing my naked body. I wrapped the dress around me using a torn strand as a tie around my waist.

Arthur pulled on his shorts, leaving the zip and button undone. I could still see the top of his cock and the defined V that only made me crave him more. He moved to the bar and poured himself a gin. When he turned, he held out a glass for me too. I took it and sipped. Arthur was leaning against the bar, watching me.

"We leave tomorrow," I said, needing to slice through the pulsing heavy tension that had built between us.

Arthur sipped at his gin. "Boyfriend coming back, huh?" he said. My stomach dropped at Hugo being brought into this moment. I had a boyfriend. A boyfriend who my father adored. And I'd just cheated on him. I had just fucked Arthur Adley, of the infamous Adley firm.

And I couldn't muster one ounce of regret.

"We're going to Ibiza." I downed the gin, and Arthur casually topped it up. His body was stiff, and his eyes kept darting outside toward my yacht. I guessed he wasn't usually the chatting-after-sex type. Sadness sprouted in my chest. This, whatever the hell it was, was clearly over.

"I'll go." I placed my now-full glass of Bombay Sapphire on the table Arthur had just taken me on. I had just opened the door to leave when I felt Arthur's hand thread through mine. I whipped my head to face him in shock. His eyes were locked on his hand in mine. His jaw clenched and his hand tightened around my fingers. "Arthur?" I whispered, heart thudding.

"Are you staying in London now sixth form is done?" he asked.

I frowned in confusion but wanted so desperately to stay in the moment with him. "I go to Oxford in September. Business Studies."

Arthur lifted his head, and the ghost of a smirk on his lips made my legs weak. "Clever fucker, eh?"

I laughed, and warmth filled my bones as Arthur's hand squeezed mine harder. At the sound of my name being called, I looked over to my yacht. I peered through the window and saw Arabella on the sun deck, clearly searching for me.

This time, I had to go. None of my friends could ever know about this.

Turning back to Arthur, I spotted a pen on the bar. I took the hand that been holding mine and wrote my mobile number across his palm. I was under no illusions. I didn't expect Arthur to call me. And I knew it was the stupidest thing I had ever done.

But, right now, I didn't give a damn.

As I wrote the last digit, I pressed a slow, soft kiss to his fingertips, inhaling his scent and vowing to commit it to memory. I released

Arthur's hand and found him studying me. "Just in case you're ever in Oxford," I said and edged forward. Arthur watched me approach him. I placed my hands on his cheeks, unsure if he would push such affection away. When he didn't move, I pressed a single kiss to his lips. "Goodbye, Arthur Adley." I hurried from his yacht, never once looking back.

I crept onto my yacht and headed straight to my room. I locked myself inside, immediately going into the bathroom. I was breathing hard, the implications of what I'd just done finally hitting home. I switched on the vanity mirror light and looked at my reflection. I looked depraved. My red lipstick was smudged all over my mouth, my mascara had run under my eyes, and I had red marks on my skin from where Arthur had gripped me by my neck, from where he had held me down and fucked me.

A disbelieving laugh slipped from my swollen lips. Arthur had come through on his promise. He had ruined me. He had spoiled me for all others.

And he had well and truly wrecked me.

CHAPTER FOUR

ARTHUR

Aged twenty-three

"Here." Freddie passed me a glass of gin.

I took it from him, and he sat down on the chair opposite me with his whisky. The fire roared beside us. We were all in my converted church, suited and booted and ready for a fucking visit to some of our fathers' business associates.

"What time are the old ones coming?" Charlie asked.

"Midnight," Eric answered and sat beside Charlie on the couch. He ran his hand over his face. "Can you actually imagine ever doing business in the daylight?" Eric said. "I mean, I don't mind this fucking vampire life, but I often wonder what it's like doing business with the sun in the fucking sky, where everyone can see."

"I'm sure we could arrange a nine-to-five job for you," Charlie said. "Office job? Shelf stacker? A bobby in the Old Bill?" Charlie shrugged. "It might be good for you, old boy. Keep you in check."

"Then who'd save your arse on the daily?" Eric said, smiling at my cousin. "Nah, I'll just fucking stick to drug and gun dealing and cold-blooded murder. Seems that's where my talents lie."

"I like killing," Vinnie said casually, his arm over the back of his seat. I knew Pearl was beside him in his head by the way he leaned his body inwards toward her. I often wondered what she looked like in his mind. How she would have looked older. Beautiful, no doubt. "Do we get to kill again soon? I get a fucking hard-on when I get blood on my hands." He smiled at Pearl. "Pearl likes me fucking her after I take some cunt's life. She screams more. Claws my back more. Says it's better for her."

"Thanks, Vin. That's a visual we all fucking needed in our heads," Freddie said dryly and looked at me, shaking his head in disbelief. It used to piss me off that Vinnie spoke about my dead sister that way. But I was used to it now. Let him imagine her alive and well if he wanted. If it kept him from topping himself, what the fuck did I care? I wasn't losing anyone else in my life. I was one death away from insanity at this point. I knew it—they all did.

The door opened and Vera, Ronnie and Betsy strutted into the room. "Look at you miserable fuckers." Vera stopped in front of us, looking at our bored faces. "Who pissed on your bonfires?"

"Hello, sis," Eric said, kissing Vera on the cheek. "Been called to arms by our old men. Waiting for them to get their wrinkly arses in here so we can get going and I can get back to fucking my latest conquest."

"Prostitutes again?" Betsy said, brushing past Eric and sitting next to her brother, Charlie, on the arm of his side of the sofa. "They're the only ones desperate enough to shag you, aren't they? No one would actually fuck you of their own volition."

Eric smiled at Betsy, but there was fuck-all humour there. "That make you a hooker then?" he said, and Betsy's smile slipped into a familiar snarl. "You've ridden this dick plenty to qualify." Eric lounged in his chair like he was the king of the fucking world. "Of your own *volition*."

"You make me sick," she snapped, eyes narrowing.

"Keep telling yourself that, treasure."

"Now now, children," Charlie said to Eric and Betsy. "We don't need to hear any fucking more about your sordid history. Spare us, please. It was hard enough to deal with when it was happening. This constant tug of war you both now engage in is fucking tiring."

"And that's what it is. *History*." Betsy went to the bar and poured herself a large glass of wine. Eric's eyes tracked her the entire way, that same possessive look on his face that he always got around her. Fucking psychos, the two of them. Like Fred and Nancy or some other toxic bollocks. Couldn't be together, couldn't be apart.

Betsy ignored Eric and dropped a kiss on Vinnie's head as she passed, then dropped one on "Pearl's". "Vinnie, Pearl, you both okay?" she asked, like it wasn't fucked up we all just pretended my sister was still here with us.

Vinnie smiled as wide as a fucking clown. "We're good, Bets. Pearl says hello."

"I miss you, Pearlie-girl." The truth of Betsy's statement shone through her face, before she schooled her expression and sat directly opposite Eric, glaring at him as she sipped her wine. Betsy and Pearl had been inseparable as kids. As close to each other and Vera as the fellas were to me. I thought the reason she played along with Vinnie's hallucinations so well was because she couldn't bear to accept that Pearl was truly gone either.

Ronnie grabbed her drink and lit her cigar. She sat down on a chair beside the fire. Vera sat on her lap, wrapping her arms tightly around her girlfriend. "And what's it tonight?" Vera asked. Both she and Ronnie always dressed in suits—waistcoats and pocket watches included. They were fucking good fighters, good shots too, but our old men would never let women into our firm. They were old school and believed women needed to stay at home. It came from the fact that the only woman left out of all our mothers was my grandma. The rest had been killed, killed themselves or fucked off years ago, unable to cope with this life.

It took a certain kind of person to thrive in this fucked-up underworld. Dad didn't believe women were made for the gangster life. One look at these three and anyone could see that was bullshit. But there was no convincing him otherwise. If I was in charge, I'd have them fighting by my side in a second.

"Russians." I downed my gin. "Negotiating the routes for the new shipment of meth we just secured."

"East dock would be best to use for the Reds," Ronnie said, her hand slipping through Vera's long blond hair. She said it helped her think. Ronnie's dark hair was cut short and fell in waves like something from the 1940's. Her dark eyes were lost in thought. She was Jamaican in heritage, but born in London, and a cockney girl through and through. Her and Vera had been together for a few years now. Ronnie had a fucking genius mind for this business shit. But the fact she had a twat made her a no-go to our fathers.

"Artie?" Dad said, coming through the door, Saville Row suit and hat in place. "You lot ready?"

I got to my feet, as did Eric, Charlie, Freddie and Vinnie. The girls raised their glasses at us in goodbye, and we fell into step behind our old men. We got into the van. I sat next to my dad, as always.

"We'll go in. You guys watch the front for the Old Bill," my dad said as we pulled out of the church grounds.

"I should be in the meeting with you," I said. Charlie nodded from the opposite seat.

"These arseholes are old school. Wouldn't take well to you being there just yet. It'll be a quick meeting, then we'll go for food." My dad smirked at my scowling face. "You already gunning for my crown, Artie?"

I shook my head. "No, but these wankers are fucking dodgy. Have been for a while. You should have more back-up in the room than just you lot. I've been hearing about splits in their families, factions breaking apart and wanting other things than the usual shit of drugs and guns." All the old men were looking at me, amused. It just pissed me the fuck off. "We should be sure we're prepared for whatever they might pull. Kill them if we need to."

"Alf, his bloodlust is on another level from even yours," my Uncle Trevor said. He was Dad's brother, Charlie and Betsy's dad.

"Don't I know it," Dad joked, but his smile at me was proud as fuck. I turned and kept my gaze locked on our route to the old ware-house at the east docks. They might think me young, but I studied our "associates". I knew more about the changing underworld than even Dad gave me credit for.

We came to a stop. The Reds were already inside the old warehouse. We all piled out. "Stay out front, fellas. Keep watch," my dad said.

I grabbed his arm. "We should have had soldiers here. We haven't got enough men if something happens. We're too unprotected. We should never be unprotected."

Dad put his hand on my shoulder. "Artie, I've known Alexei and Sergei for years. This is a gentlemen's meeting. That's all. No need for fucking soldiers." He put his hand on my face. "Son, you need to stop being so fucking dire about everything. We might live a fucked-up life, but there's a code to it all. Morals in our own messed-up ways."

"Things change," I warned.

"Artie. Enough."

With that they walked into the warehouse. Me and my boys moved in front of the warehouse doors to stand watch. It was raining; the sky was drizzly and fucking grey, a smoky mist hovering over the ground. The few lampposts scattered around the dock gave off hardly any light in the fog.

I pulled out a cig and sparked it up. I took a long drag, trying to listen to whatever was happening inside. "We're going to get fucking drenched out here," Eric complained, cupping his hands and blowing hot breath into them. "I'm freezing my massive bollocks off."

"The only gangster in London who can be defeated by the cold," Charlie said, smirking at Eric. Eric held up his middle finger.

The sound of raised voices inside suddenly made me tense. I locked eyes with Freddie beside me. His face told me he didn't like the sound of this either. Each of my brothers closed in around me, listening out. Just as my hand moved to the doorknob to get us inside, sounds of gunfire split through the night like fucking blitzkrieg bombs.

I threw the door open and rushed inside, to see our old men taking fire from semi-automatics, blood and flesh ripping from their torsos as the cunts before them pumped lead into their bodies.

Red mist descended over my eyes. I pulled out my gun and started firing. I ran forward, not giving two shits about the Russians firing right at us. Bullet after bullet left my barrel and sliced through Red flesh, ripping into hearts and livers and lungs, dropping the fuckers to the ground. I kept firing. I walked forward, not caring about the bullet that grazed my right bicep. I got as close to these pricks as I could, pressing my barrel to their heads and splattering their brains up the old warehouse walls.

I heard my brothers' guns firing too. Saw Vinnie slicing through the Reds' throats and hearts with his knives, saw Freddie and Eric firing their revolvers at a fast pace. My cousin slit the throat of the final standing man, blood dripping down Charlie's face and neck, crimson coating his hands.

I could hear my breath pumping in my ears. Feel my fucking heart pounding in my chest. I scanned the room, seeing every one of the Russians drowning in their own blood. Like it was in fucking slow motion, I saw my brothers run to their old men, dropping to their knees.

Eric pulled his father into his arms. I watched as he threw his head back and screamed. Uncle Bill's eyes were wide open and his chest housed a fuck-off hole, blood pouring to the ground.

Gone.

Charlie was bent over Uncle Trevor, his forehead pressed against his father's. Charlie's arms shook as Uncle Trevor stared unseeing at the ceiling. Charlie shook him, but there was no life left in his body.

Gone.

Vinnie stood over his dad. His shoulder-length blond hair was slicked with red. His hands and white shirt were coated with his father's blood. "Dad," he said, his voice barely loud enough to break through the ringing in my ears. "Dad! Get up!" he shouted. But when I looked down, Uncle Winston was in the fucking worst state of them all. Half his head was missing; another bullet had shattered his cheek, collapsing his face. "Dad, fucking get up!" Vinnie shouted, his cheeks reddening and his neck bulging with veins.

Vinnie crouched down and lifted Uncle Winston in his arms. "Save him," he said to me. It was the thing to make me fucking slam back into the here and now. "Artie. Save him for me. Please."

"I ... I ..." I couldn't fucking finish off my words. Charlie was suddenly beside me. I looked at my cousin, then followed his blank eyes. My shocked stare locked on Freddie, who was carrying my dad.

"He's still got a pulse!" Freddie said urgently, streams of tears cutting track marks through the blood on his cheeks. "Arthur, he's still fucking alive! Quick!"

Like my heart had been stabbed with a shot of adrenaline, I grabbed my dad and ran for the van. "Get them and let's go!" I shouted. I laid Dad down on the bench seat and didn't even look up as my brothers put their dads' bodies in the back too.

"Fucking drive!" I shouted to the driver and pressed my hand over my dad's chest to try and stop the blood. "Freddie, ring the doc. Tell him he needs to be at the church in the next five minutes or I'll fucking slit his throat." My dad's face was white, the blood draining from his body. I wanted him to open his eyes. I wanted him to speak and say that this shitshow was going to be okay. But he stayed silent. He fucking stayed silent.

I looked up and saw my brothers holding their dads.

"They're gone," Charlie said, his voice sounding like a fucking scream in the van. "They've all fucking gone."

"Artie," Vinnie said, holding his dad to his chest. Half of Uncle Winston's skull was missing. Those Red bastards had taken half his fucking head. "He's going cold. Dad's going cold."

Eric was staring at nothing, lost to his shock and grief. He held his dad in his arms, but didn't have no fucking words.

I didn't know what the fuck to do. They were all waiting for me, looking at me, and I didn't know what the fuck to do!

The van stopped, and the driver opened the door. Another car pulled up. I grabbed my gun, ready to fucking fire, but the doctor stepped out. His eyes went huge when we left the van, our old men in our arms.

"He's still alive," I said to the doc and ran for the front door. I slammed through and rushed my old man to his bedroom, and the doc and the nurse he brought immediately started working on him.

They stripped him of his clothes and washed him down to see the damage. Freddie stood beside me as all my old man's bullet wounds were bared. Hole after hole littered his body from where

those cunts had shot through our entire firm. My dad ... our
uncles ...

A loud, shrill scream ripped through the church. It was one of the
girls. Uncontrollable screams and cries and sobs drifted down the hallway. "I need to operate," the doctor we paid a fuck-ton of money to
said to me.

"Then fucking operate!" I shouted, and Freddie backed me away.

"He needs a hospital. I can't do it here."

I pointed in the doc's face, close to strangling the fucker. "Here. No
fucking hospitals. No fucking police. You'll do it here. And you'll
fucking save him, or I'll kill you myself."

The nurse ran to the car, pushing the scared-as-shit doctor into
motion. The doctor turned and started readying my dad for surgery.
The nurse came running back through, and they got to work on my
old man.

"It's not sanitary," the nurse whispered to the doctor. "This bed
isn't sterile."

The doctor cut me a quick glance. "It doesn't matter. We just have
to bloody save him."

"Artie." Freddie put a hand on my chest. "We need to leave them to
it. They'll work better if we aren't in the room."

My feet ground to a halt as I watched them cut my old man open,
wires and tubes being stuck into him. As much as I wanted to stay, I
let Freddie pull me into the hallway. He guided me toward the living
room and opened the door. It was empty.

He thrust a whisky into my hand. "Drink it. Bloody drink it, Artie!"
I did as Freddie said, but I felt something shifting inside me. Something locking up and turning to fucking steel. Like whatever oxygen I
had in my body was being smothered, leaving only death in its wake.

Death. Everything was fucking *death*.

I didn't know how much whisky I drank. I didn't know how much
time passed, but my brothers finally entered the room. I looked at
Charlie and Vinnie and Eric. Their faces were fucking devastated.
Charlie shook his head at me, and it hit me all over again.

They were dead. All my uncles. They were fucking dead. The
leaders of the Adley firm, gunned down in cold blood by the Russians.

"Uncle Alfie?" Eric asked.

"Getting operated on," Freddie answered for me. Dad was practically Freddie's dad too. Had been for the longest fucking time. I lifted my head and looked at Freddie. His hand shook as he lifted his whisky to his mouth.

I heard footsteps behind us, and the girls walked slowly inside. Vera and Ronnie were managing to hold their shit together. Betsy's face was wet with tears, her skin pale. Her arms were wrapped round herself. Charlie pulled his sister into his arms, keeping her close.

"What now?" Vera asked, and I felt a strange kind of fire igniting inside me. A fucking wildfire that had managed to spread out to the rest of my body before Vera had even stopped speaking.

"Artie?" I whipped my head around to see my grandma in the doorway. She kept her head high, her expression like fucking stone. Grandma was the hardest fucker I'd ever met. Seventy years old but only looked fifty. Grey hair, but styled well. She was dressed in smart black trousers and a white blouse. I shook my head. Her body flinched like she'd just taken a bullet herself. My dad and Uncle Trevor were her sons, but our other uncles were practically her kids too.

Grandma kept her shit together. Then, "I need to see them." She turned and walked down the hallway. As she retreated, my hands started shaking. Not from fear or shock. But from the motherfucking venom that had filled my bones down to the fucking marrow. At the memory of our family dead on the ground, their blood seeping onto the filthy warehouse floor.

Kings taken out like animals.

I felt like I was being remade and reformed, with the fire from hell itself replacing my blood. I felt numb. Felt any fucking humanity I had left burn away to ashes, and I knew the moment I gave my soul to the fucking devil.

Blood.

Betrayal.

Loss.

Death.

Death.

Motherfucking death!

Roaring my rage out loud, I launched my glass across the room. It shattered as it ploughed into the two-hundred-year-old walls. I had to kill them. I had to kill the Russians responsible. All of them. All of the betraying fucks and their families and anyone else who had any fucking part in this massacre.

Lifting my head, I faced my brothers and sisters. "Gather the fucking soldiers," I said to Charlie. "Every single one of them."

"Artie?" Charlie said.

"We kill them." Adrenaline rushed through my veins at the thought of ending our enemies. "We kill them all. Now. Tonight. Not one fucker will survive."

Eric pushed off the wall he'd been leaning against. He nodded, life sparking in his dead eyes. His hands rolled into fists, and a sadistic grin spread on his face. He was in.

"Yeah, we'll kill them," Vinnie said, rubbing his hands together. "We'll fucking kill them all, Artie. All of them. We'll avenge our dads. They'll be happy about this. I know they'll tell me so when we're done."

I looked at Vera, Ronnie and Betsy. "You lot too." The girls looked at each other, questions and shock on their faces. "You wanted in to the fucking firm?" I held out my arms. "Then welcome to the motherfucking firm." Vera and Ronnie smiled cold and bloodthirsty grins. Betsy moved beside them, her chin in the air, and intent in her eyes. "Get all the fucking guns. We're paying the Russians a fucking visit."

I pushed through the door and walked to my father's room. I stopped in the entrance. Grandma was standing in the way, watching the doctor try to save my old man. "They have to die," she said casually, like she was talking about the weather. I heard the sound of a metal hitting metal as the doctor pulled a bullet from my old man and placed it in a metal bowl.

Grandma turned to me and, despite the blood covering me, straightened the collar on my jacket and tightened my tie. "The leadership of this firm has now fallen to you, son." She placed her hand on my cheeks. "You must avenge your father and uncles." I felt the righteousness of those words hit me with total agreement. "We can't be seen as weak." Grandma pushed back some of my hair that was soaked with blood. She'd had blood on her hands for years. It didn't bother her one bit. "The knowledge that the elders of the Adley firm have been killed will already be circulating. That means the wolves will soon be at the door."

"I'll fucking destroy them," I snarled, earning a small, proud smile from my grandma. "No one is taking us out. They will fucking die by my hands if they even dare try."

"They *will* try, Arthur. I'm afraid we are about to turn onto a rocky path. The biggest, most powerful firm in all of London has just been torn down—"

"No, it hasn't," I interrupted, conviction in my voice. "They have no idea what the fuck they've just started. They've opened the gates of hell, and the fucking devil and his demons are now leading the charge."

"Artie?" Charlie called from down the hallway. "The soldiers are here. We're ready." Grandma kissed my forehead, and when she pulled away there was blood staining her cheek. She went back to silently watching my father. I walked down the hall. My family—both men and women—were waiting. I clicked my fingers, and we all left the house, blood and flesh still sticking to our skin and clothes.

We were about to add some more.

As our convoy of cars and vans pulled out of the church and toward the docks and the building that held the Russians, I felt the urge to kill take me over, possess me.

And I let it fucking consume me.

When the vehicles stopped, my brothers and sisters looked to me. We were all in the van that still had the blood of our fathers on the wooden floor. I only had one order for them: "Don't leave any of these cunts alive." I jumped out of the van and saw the Adley soldiers ready and waiting, dressed in suits, all holding semi-automatics and knives.

When I reached the first building that I knew the fucking rats hid out in, I kicked the door open and started fucking firing. The next thirty minutes were a hazy vortex of blood and flesh and bones. Of screams, of killing, of people begging for their lives. No mercy was given. Not to a single one. Their pleas for their lives bounced off my Teflon skin.

Breathless and tasting the blood of my enemies coating my teeth, I walked outside the Russian buildings. The sun was starting to rise over the Big Smoke. I pulled out a cig and sparked up the bloodstained stick. I took in a long drag and turned to the soldiers and my family, who were exhausted but buzzing like electrical wires from their kills. I looked at my sisters; their first kills had given meaning to their usually boring lives. No more shelter for them. They were in this shit now too.

"This isn't over. This is far from fucking over." I paced in front of them. "They'll be coming for our docks. They'll be coming for our routes. They'll be coming for our territory." I stopped and pointed at each member of my family. "They'll be coming for our throats." I smiled coldly, knowing that Russian blood stained my teeth, and shouted, "LET THEM FUCKING COME!" I closed my eyes and took in another drag, then with a fucking grin on my face said, "Let them try and take us Adleys down. We'll see who dies first."

Police sirens wailed in the background. "Go," I said and walked to the van. My family followed me inside. We were silent all the way back, the stench of gunpowder and wet blood clogging the air.

When we stopped outside the church, I walked inside and went straight to my father's room. I stopped dead when I entered. He was lying in his bed, tubes and wires sticking out of him, machines creating a fucked-up halo around his head. He was covered by a white sheet. He already looked dead.

"Coma," my grandma said from behind me. I stared at my dad's sleeping face. He was grey and already had one foot in the grave. Grandma stood beside Dad and brushed his hair back from his face like my mum used to do to me. "The doctor doesn't think he'll ever come out of it. He saved him. But he has no life left in his brain. His body may be alive, but his soul is already below ground."

I let those words wash over me, but I didn't let them strike me. I didn't let them cause me any fucking pain. Nothing would ever cause me fucking pain again. I wouldn't let it.

"Is it done?" Grandma asked. I nodded. She ran a cold flannel over Dad's forehead. "That was one battle in what will be a heavily fought war, Artie," she said, and I knew it to be true. All of London and beyond would be trying to take my father's place in the crime underworld now.

I wasn't going to let that happen. There was a new fucking king in the castle.

I went into the shower, ignoring the blood washing from my skin. When I got out, my fucking skin was itching, and I knew I wouldn't be able to sleep. I threw on some clothes and grabbed my phone and wallet. As I passed by the living room, I saw my brothers and sisters inside.

"Where are you going?" Eric asked.

"Out," I said. Their eyes latched on to me.

Just as I was about to go, Charlie said, "She won't understand what's going to happen." I stopped dead. My muscles tensed, and my anger built so high I thought it would incinerate me on the spot. I turned to my cousin. He was smoking his pipe, but his eyes were glued on me.

"She isn't from this world. The things that will have to be done to keep our firm from being discarded ... she won't get it, Artie." I thought of green-brown eyes and brown hair and the pussy I'd been fucking and licking for five bloody years. The fucking addictive cunt that always drew me back to her, time and time again.

"I'm leaving," I said, my deadly gaze telling Charlie to shut the fuck up. She was my fucking heroin. I wasn't giving her up.

"She'll get hurt," Charlie said, and this time I rounded on him. Charlie didn't flinch as I met him toe to toe, ready to rip his fucking head off if he spoke one more time. I felt my brothers and sisters watching us, but Charlie kept his voice low enough so only I would hear his next words.

"I know you like her, Artie. *Really* fucking like her. We all know this is more than a fuck, despite how you make it seem. We're not stupid." His hand landed on my shoulder. "But you're the Adley boss now. No longer the heir. With that comes a lot more responsibility. With that comes a new target on your head." Charlie stepped back and lifted his whisky into the air. "The king is dead; long live the king."

Despite wanting to rip out his fucking tongue, I knew my cousin wasn't being a prick. I saw the fucking pain in his eyes as he spoke. My father wasn't dead, but even if he ever woke up, he wouldn't be in any state to lead this firm.

It was up to me now.

It was all up to bastard *me*.

My brothers and sisters held their drinks up in the air, all echoing, "Long live the king," and took long sips. Vera smiled at me sadly. I had to leave. I couldn't fucking be here right now, with my uncles' ghosts freshly in the walls and my father a vegetable in his bed.

"I've got something to do." I swiped an unopened bottle of whisky off the bar as I left. I got into the back of the car and got confirmation that my men had cleaned up both death sites and the pigs had nothing on us. Then I sat back and closed my eyes, drinking the whisky as I was driven to the one place I couldn't ever fucking keep away from. Hadn't done for five fucking years.

Oxford.

Her.

The one that kept me coming back for more.

CHAPTER FIVE

CHESKA

I opened the blinds and let the morning sun flood my flat. The minute the sun cut through the glass, I saw it glisten off the large diamond ... the diamond that now sat on the ring finger of my left hand.

My stomach fell just thinking of two nights ago. Hugo down on his knee in the orangery in my father's Chelsea home. My friends and his friends gathered around us, wide smiles and champagne flutes full. The celebrations, the hugs and kisses of congratulation. And the one face that entered my head the minute "Yes" slipped from my lips.

Blue eyes behind thick-framed glasses. The face that would never be mine.

My chest tightened as I thought about being Hugo's wife. About being tied into this life forever. About giving up what I truly loved— no, not what. *Who*.

I sat on the end of my bed and glanced at the clock. I had to get ready for uni. I was now studying for my master's in Business Studies at Oxford. Oxford was my treasured place of solitude away from my father and Hugo. From the life that was slowly suffocating me day by day. I'd decided on my master's so I could stay here a little longer, avoiding the life that awaited me.

And mostly because Oxford was where we met in secret, away from prying eyes. Where, for a few hours every week, I had him in my arms and in my bed. Where I could pretend that he was mine. Where we could pretend that our vastly different worlds didn't keep us apart.

This ring changed everything.

I had to tell Arthur. I didn't know how I would do it. I didn't know how I could say goodbye to him for good. I was pretty sure it would break me.

I made myself get up and shower. I had just slipped on my jeans and jumper when the doorbell rang. Frowning, wondering who would call at such an early hour, I looked at the camera, and my heart stuttered.

Arthur was leaning against the wall. He was wearing a cream Aran jumper and black trousers and was clutching an almost empty bottle of whisky. I buzzed him up, opening the door and standing on the landing to wait for him. I heard his slow, heavy footsteps on the marble steps that led to my top-floor apartment. He never took the lift, always walked up the five flights of stairs.

The minute I saw his dark hair, my chest tightened. He was as beautiful as ever. A lethal, dangerous kind of beauty that stole every ounce of my sanity whenever I looked at him.

But that wave of desire quickly dampened to one of worry when he looked up and I saw complete devastation in his sapphire gaze.

"Arthur," I said, just as he swayed on the top stair and took another gulp of his whisky. He quickly righted himself, then walked toward me, pulling a cigarette from his pocket. He placed one in his mouth, then, stepping closer to me, pushed me back into my flat.

He slammed the door shut behind us and backed me against the wall. He took another cigarette from his packet and placed it between my lips. Lifting his lighter in the small space between us, he drew a flame and lit both our cigarettes. Arthur took a deep drag; I did the same. I blew out the smoke, then ran my hand down his jumper. He never dressed like this, this casual. He always wore suits with waistcoats and handkerchiefs. Pocket watches and expensive shoes.

When I looked up into his eyes, searching their depths, I saw they were red raw, and deep dark circles lay beneath. "Arthur, what's wrong?" I asked. His nostrils flared. I could smell the whisky on his breath and his usual cologne on his clothes. It was the only thing that brought me any comfort at this point.

Something was wrong. Something was very, very wrong.

"Arthur—" My sentence was cut off when Arthur smashed his lips to mine. I moaned as his hand slipped into my hair and he pressed me even further against the wall. I could barely breathe; his entire body weight kept me pinned and unmoving.

My cigarette fell to the floor, and I could smell the tobacco burning on the wooden floorboards. Arthur must have dropped his too, as his other hand took hold of my jaw and he kept me exactly where he wanted me. He kissed me. He devoured my mouth, leaving me a weak, shaking mess against him.

Spinning me around, he slammed me to the bed. I inhaled deeply, trying to catch my breath. Arthur was glaring down at me, stubble coating his cheeks. The pupils of his eyes had almost eradicated the blue. I saw the deadly promise in his gaze. The promise that he was about to ruin me again. He did so every time, but every so often things were even more intense. More aggressive. More suited to what he did for a living.

I knew it as Arthur's devil side. The side with little to no morals, a heady amount of darkness in his soul, and absolutely zero control when it came to taking what he wanted—right now, that was me.

He stumbled off the bed to close the blinds. To keep what we did in here to ourselves. Enough light slipped through the thin material of the blinds that I could see every movement of that body I knew so well.

Arthur threw off his jumper and trousers and climbed back on the bed. His cock was already in his hand, and he was stroking the hard length—he hadn't been wearing underwear. I lay back, and Arthur crawled over me. My heart leapt to my throat when he lifted his hand to my face and softly ran his fingers down my cheek. A lump formed in my throat as I looked into his eyes and could have sworn I saw them shimmer.

Arthur didn't do tender. He didn't do soft and loving. I was utterly in love with him and had been for many years. I had no idea if he felt the same. He never gave anything away. Had never once let himself slip up in my presence, no matter how many times we'd been together.

But there was something different about him today. My body was steeped in dread. Whatever it was, it wasn't good. "Arthur," I whispered, capturing his hand and bringing it to my lips. I kissed his palm and heard his quick, stuttered exhale.

But Arthur ripped his hand back and lifted the hem of my jumper. He yanked it over my head, then pulled down my jeans and threw them across the floor. My bra and knickers went next. I lay naked on my bed, Arthur stroking his cock faster and faster, his desperation evidenced by the clenching of his jaw.

"Suck it," he said, his thick East End accent causing my body to respond as always. I crawled to my knees and swirled my tongue around his slit. Arthur tensed as my mouth lapped at his flesh. I glanced up and saw his eyes glued on me as I wrapped my lips around his tip, then took him into my mouth. Arthur's head snapped back and his hand threaded into my hair. He pulled tightly on the strands, and my body thrived on the pain as it always did with him.

He gave me something I had never known I needed. I seemed to give him something too. Arthur guided my head up and down, and I took him as far down my throat as I could. I cupped his balls in my hands; he grunted and thrust harder into my mouth. By now I knew what he liked. And he knew exactly how to get me off.

We were a fucked-up dance of needs and pain and wants. And only we two knew the choreography.

Arthur pulled my head from his dick and threw me onto my back. I hit the mattress with a thud, and he threw my legs over his broad shoulders. I frowned as I saw a bandage on the back of his arm. I didn't have time to think on it too long—Arthur swiped his tongue along my pussy, making my back arch off the bed and taking all thoughts from my mind.

He sucked on my clit until I saw stars. He worked me hard and fast, giving me no reprieve as he made me come. I screamed out in ecstasy, and before I even had a chance to come down from my high, he had flipped me over to my knees and held my hands on the bedframe.

As I was still feeling the throbbing of my orgasm, Arthur slammed inside me. He pounded into me harder and faster than ever before. I gasped at the aggression, at the maddening pace and the feel of him coming loose inside me. It was like he was fucking the demons out of his soul. But then his head fell to my shoulder and he laid a soft kiss there. Goosebumps broke out on my skin. The kiss was such a contrast to the violent thrust of his hips. Then his fingers squeezed mine. I couldn't look away from our joined hands as he weaved his fingers through mine on the headboard.

He was holding my hands.

He was fucking me like a whore but cherishing me with his mouth and gentle touch. I didn't know why, but tears built in my eyes. Arthur never held my hands. He was rarely affectionate. I had always accepted it as just who he was. But I had dreamed of the moment he would show me he cared. That I was more to him than just some posh bird he got his kicks out of by fucking once a week.

I couldn't fight back the orgasm building inside me. I wanted to savour this moment, bask in it some more. I didn't want this to end. Because this *had* to end. I was getting married. This, right now, was it.

Arthur kissed up my neck as he thrust inside me. I didn't know where he began and I ended as I trembled, crying out his name. Then Arthur stilled and I felt his heat flood inside me. My arms and legs were numb in the aftermath, and I could barely breathe.

Arthur rested his forehead on my shoulder again. Only this time, I felt him shaking. At first I thought it was due to exertion, but then I felt the tears trickle down my back. My heart dropped.

He was crying.

I guided our still-joined hands off the headboard and turned my head. Arthur drew his head back, and I saw the track marks of tears on his cheeks. "Arthur," I whispered, hearing my own voice quiver in empathy.

I lowered myself to the bed, bringing Arthur down with me. He let me guide him against me to rest in my arms. A burst of heat washed through me as he laid his head on my stomach. He had never let me hold him like this before. Never let me cherish him and care for him. And he had never done the same to me.

"It's okay," I soothed, feeling Arthur's shoulders shake and his unrelenting tears pool on my stomach. He held me so tightly, as if I might disappear if he didn't keep such fierce hold. A lump formed in my throat, and I knew that I didn't want to hear what had happened to him. Because whatever it was had crippled him. Arthur, who had always been the most unbreakable, formidable man I had ever met, had been destroyed. I ran my hands through his hair, trying to make him feel safe, feel wanted, feel loved.

I wasn't sure how long we lay like that. But Arthur's shaking shoulders calmed, and his tears on my stomach all but dried. He was awake. I knew this because he was drawing lazy, hypnotic circles on my stomach. And he hadn't pulled away. That affected me more than I was willing to admit.

"They've gone," he finally rasped out, his tired voice sounding like broken glass in the silent room. I tensed. "Dad's in a coma, but they don't think he'll ever wake up."

My eyes widened in the darkness, then I inhaled slowly, trying to organise my scattered thoughts. "Who has gone, baby?" I asked tentatively, keeping my voice soft and quiet. I had never called Arthur "baby" before. But I couldn't help it as I held him so protectively in my arms.

"All of them," he said, his finger moving up to my breast. "My uncles, my father ... all the bosses of our firm." My stomach sank as I realised the gravity of that information. His father and his men were notorious. Infamous gangsters, the most feared men in London, in England, and, hell, in most of Europe.

"Gone where?" I asked, stupidly, but needing to hear the actual words from his lips.

"Dead." Arthur held on to my waist as if the admission would take his strength away. I squeezed my eyes shut in sympathy for the pain he must have been in. Then it dawned on me. Arthur was Alfie Adley's son. That meant Arthur was the heir, and thus ...

Arthur leaned over me, his stomach pressing flush against mine. He put his hand on my cheek, and I instinctively leaned into its warmth. I kissed his wrist and heard his almost silent hiss at my touch. Arthur's gaze tracked over every part of my face as though it was the last time he would see it. I could still smell the whisky on him and knew that the only reason he ever would have allowed himself the liberties of shedding tears and touching me so intimately, *lovingly*, was because he was drunk.

"It's my time now to rule over hell." His words cut through me like a knife. "It's my time to embrace the darkness, princess." He dragged his thumb over my bottom lip, the move I always loved best. He'd done that on the yacht in Marbella all those years ago when we'd first been together. Even now it made me crave him, brought me strictly under his command.

"Arthur, don't," I begged, not wanting him to talk this way. It was too disturbing, too sad, too final.

He smiled at me, and it almost stopped my heart.

"My soul isn't mine anymore," he said, leaning down and kissing across my breasts. "It's Satan's. And, tomorrow, I will become the devil on earth."

"Arthur—"

"You were the good thing, princess," he said, cutting me off. "You were *the* one good thing I had been given." *But now that's gone*, I finished for him, knowing that was his meaning. I brought his mouth up to mine and kissed him. I kissed him softly and lovingly, exactly like I had wanted to for years. And if this was truly it, I had nothing to lose. Arthur kissed me back, and I replayed his words in my head—*I will become the devil on earth.*

I didn't believe he could ever be the devil.

I wasn't naïve. I knew he had a darkness in him that I had never reached, that, frankly, was terrifying. But up until now it had been a mere fragment of the boy I had been obsessed with since the age of thirteen. A part of him that I had been exempt from knowing, except in the bedroom. The way he fucked was depraved. The way he kissed me was savage and revealed that he was made of anything but good and light. But he was still mine. That was my Arthur, one I cherished and, over the years, never wanted to lose.

I didn't know what Arthur Adley, boss of the Adley crime syndicate, looked like. I didn't know him as that man in that role. And I knew by his tone that I would never find out.

So I kissed and kissed him until my lips were bruised and he fell asleep in my arms. I stared down at him and wondered what path lay ahead of him. As I stroked his hair, the four-carat engagement ring Hugo had given me less than forty-eight hours ago glared back at me. In that moment, that ring seemed more menacing than Arthur could ever be.

I didn't want it. I didn't want to be Hugo's wife. But I didn't know how to be anything other than Cheska Harlow-Wright, daughter of the Harlow dynasty, and soon to be spouse of Hugo and socialite of Chelsea.

I closed my eyes and tried not to think of my life's bigger questions. I knew this time with Arthur was limited, and I strived to stay in the now. To hold on to this for as long as I could.

His body was warm on top of mine, his heavy weight keeping me calm. I still felt the echo of him inside me, of his tongue and his hands that had imprinted on my skin.

And I prayed the evidence would never fade.

A cool breeze slapped against my skin. I blinked, and the room slowly came into focus. My bedside lamp was on, and the events of the day slowly filtered into my brain.

Arthur ... *Arthur!*

I scrambled to sit up and saw Arthur's naked back. He was sitting on the edge of the bed, spine straight and shoulders tensed. I looked over to my clock; it read nine in the evening. We had fallen asleep and slept the day away.

Remembering how upset Arthur had been, I reached out and ran my fingers down his spine. He tensed, and I pulled my hand back. I felt more than the cold breeze wash over me. Arthur got to his feet and began to dress. I sat up, keeping my duvet wrapped around me.

"Arthur," I whispered, my softly spoken words shattering the stillness.

Arthur wiped his glasses on his jumper, placed them back on his face, then slowly turned around. I immediately wished he hadn't. Gone were the soft eyes that had fallen apart on me last night, trusted me with his need for comfort. In their place were chilling obsidian stones. Cold and darkness were the only things that lurked in their depths.

And, tomorrow, I will become the devil on earth. Those words ran on a loop inside my head. He was no longer drunk, and now he was sober, those words seemed to ring true. I knew every inch of this man's face. I'd committed each mole and scar on his skin to memory. I knew his eyes—the looks, the pensive and the warm, the humorous and the hurt. This stare, this haunting and brutally aggressive stare, was nothing I'd ever witnessed before.

"Arthur," I said, fighting the lump in my throat. "You're upset. Please, I can help—"

"I'm not your problem anymore, princess." He threw me a dark smirk. I lived for his smiles. But this smirk was one I wished I'd never been awarded. It was dismissive. It was patronising. And it made me feel cheap.

Arthur leaned down to the bed, and I wondered what he was going to do. He finally picked up my left hand and nudged his arrogant chin in the direction of the diamond. "I see it finally happened." He tossed away my hand, and it fell to the mattress with a thud. He grabbed his wallet and phone and made his way to the door. Tears built in my eyes, but I wouldn't let them fall.

"Congrats, princess," he said, and I met his eyes. "Seems like the white knight got you after all. Have fun in your fucking ivory tower." He opened the door, and I reached out for his hand. I wrapped my fingers around his, praying he would hold mine back. Arthur stopped in his tracks, but without looking my way, he tossed my hand away and left.

And I knew. I knew that would be the last time I would ever see him. The Arthur I had known had died, and in his place was this cold devil he warned me he would become.

The boy I loved had sold his soul to evil. And even as I walked to my window and watched his driver usher him away, I felt as thought my heart was in that car with him. He may not have wanted it. May have hated the very thought of it. But it was his regardless. Even if I never saw him again, it was his.

I believed it had been since birth, and forever would be.

CHAPTER SIX

CHESKA

Thirteen months later

Hugo pressed a kiss to my cheek and sat down opposite me. He gave me a fleeting smile before he checked his mobile. "Problem?" I asked, as the waitress dropped off my gin and tonic.

"No, just work stuff," he said, but I watched him closer as the waitress placed his IPA before him. He'd been acting sketchy of late, and I didn't know why. We were due to get married in less than a month. My stomach rolled at that fact. It was here. Just around the corner. I was actually marrying Hugo. It had always been on the cards, but having it come to fruition was surreal.

"Hello, children." My dad took his seat in between me and Hugo. "You okay, Ches?" he asked me in his usual tight-lipped way. I loved my dad. I truly did. But it was no secret that he had never been the warm and loving father most people got to experience. My mum had been the affectionate parent. My father was a businessman through and through, and that occupied all of his time. Family had always been an afterthought to him. I knew he loved me. But I wasn't his entire world and never had been.

"Are you ready for the wedding?" Dad asked me. The waitress placed his sandwich and latte on the table before him.

"I pick up the dress next week. Other than that, everything is sorted." I sipped at my soup. "It's my hen do this weekend. Arabella and Freya have it all planned. I have no idea what we're doing."

"Sounds nice," my father said dismissively and patted my hand. He turned to Hugo. "I've just got off the phone to ..." I zoned out as Dad started talking Hugo's ear off about work. I found myself watching the other people at the café. My dad had made it clear that, despite having a master's in business from Oxford and desires to join the Harlow Biscuit empire, it wasn't my place.

I fought off my rising ire and refocused on the couples and families, all smiling and happy as they caught up over lunch. I wondered what it would be like to be them for a moment. To be that excited to see one's parents or siblings. We had money, and I had never wanted for anything. But all the riches in the world couldn't make up for the emotional poverty that came with lack of familial affection.

Playing with the lime in my drink, I suddenly caught sight of a dark-haired man. He was dressed in an impeccable suit and wore black-rimmed glasses. My pounding heart lodged in my throat. I focused harder, trying to make him out, but on closer inspection it wasn't him.

I took a steadying breath and willed myself to calm down. The man sat down beside a woman in a long red dress, kissing her on the cheek and holding her hand.

I rarely gave myself the luxury of thinking of Arthur. Ever since he walked out of my life thirteen months ago, I hadn't once seen him. Hadn't received one single text.

But that didn't mean I hadn't heard of him. Everyone in London and beyond knew of Arthur now. In the thirteen months since he had taken the helm of the Adley firm, he had caused what could only be described as havoc in the criminal underworld.

Murderer. The Bethnal Green Brute. The Devil himself. Or, as he was more widely known, the Dark Lord of London Town—some catchy headline with which one of the trashy tabloids had branded him.

It had stuck.

I remembered the cold, emotionless eyes that had said goodbye to me in Oxford a year ago. How, in the hours he had slept in my arms, he had morphed from a man with darkness in his soul into what was rumoured to be evil incarnate. He had awoken in my flat in Oxford as the infamous cold-blooded gangster he was now known to be. He ruled our city with an iron fist. He left a trail of misery and bodies in his wake. But the police could never catch him. Arthur was untouchable. He was feared.

And, despite it all, my stupid self was still madly in love with him.

"Cheska!" I shook my head as I was pulled out of my reverie by a familiar voice laughing at my daze. I dragged my attention from the man in the suit and looked up to see Ollie Lawson standing at our table, dressed in a light-grey suit. He was smiling, the same wide smile he'd always had for me. "You alright, love? You were away with the fairies just now."

"Sorry," I laughed and stood to kiss him on the cheeks. "How are you? I haven't seen you in a while. Not since Freya's dinner party a few months back."

He gently squeezed my arms. "I'm good. You?" he asked, and I sat back down. Ollie was always over-affectionate toward me. But he was sweet and harmless. That strange act of aggression from him in Marbella years ago was now a distant memory.

"I am, thank you." I gestured to my father and Hugo. "Just catching up with my boys for lunch." Hugo was shifting strangely in his chair, casting annoyed eyes to Ollie. My father smiled at him, but I could see a strange apprehension at his presence. There was no love lost between Hugo and Ollie. There never had been. Ollie was in business with his father now too. Import and export.

From what I could gather from people in our social circles, the department Ollie ran was doing incredibly well, even better than his father's. He certainly dressed the part, and he had a brand-new home in the most expensive apartments in Knightsbridge to show for it. Maybe my father didn't like him because Hugo didn't. My father and fiancé were thick as thieves, so that would make sense. That, or because Ollie was incredibly successful. Nothing pissed off the rich in our circles more than someone else besting them when it came to wealth.

"I heard you're getting hitched in a few weeks?" He nodded at my engagement ring.

"Yes."

"Well, congratulations." Ollie held up his hand to the waitress. "Their lunch is on me. And send over a bottle of your most expensive champagne."

"Ollie, no—"

"I insist," he said, leaning down and kissing the back of my hand.

"Really, you don't have to," Hugo said, smiling, though I could tell by his gritted teeth he felt undermined.

"My treat. Count it as an early wedding present," Ollie said.

"Then thank you," I said, to try and defuse the awkward tension rolling off my father and fiancé.

"No trouble." Ollie smiled widely and winked at me. "I was hoping I'd maybe be able to steal your heart one day, but this one got to you first," he said, pointing at Hugo. "A chance missed." Hugo practically glared at him. "Anyway," Ollie said, looking over his shoulder and waving at two men who had just entered the café. "Business awaits. Enjoy your meal, and congratulations again." He walked away, and I exhaled in relief.

"I fucking hate that guy," Hugo said as the waitress arrived with the champagne.

"New money," my father said. "No class." I rolled my eyes at the two of them acting like pompous arses and thought of Arthur again. For once he had something in common with my father and Hugo. He'd seemed to hate Ollie too.

"Anyway, I was talking about the China contract when we were rudely interrupted by that one," my father said to Hugo, recommencing their conversation.

So, I ate my food and kept quiet. Just as I was expected to do.

———

"At least you haven't got me a flashing cock necklace to wear," I said to Arabella as she sat on the sprawling super-king bed in my room.

"All in good time, sweetie." She waggled her brows and laughed, pouring me another glass of champagne. Freya and Arabella had brought me to a fancy spa in Knightsbridge. Tomorrow more friends would join us for a night on the town.

"We can relax and get sozzled tonight on this stuff, then tomorrow live it up at the Sparrow Room. I've booked us a table—the full works."

The room shimmered as she said where we'd be going tomorrow. Arabella and Freya were already staring at me when I glanced up, clearly awaiting my reaction. "The Sparrow Room," I said, my throat suddenly dry. I downed the rest of my glass, then quickly refilled it. Arabella laughed at my obviously shocked expression.

"You should see your face!" She nudged Freya. "I know you used to have an obsession with the owner, but that was a long time ago."

"Plus," Freya said, acting nonchalant, "who doesn't want to party in the club belonging to the world's most deadly gangster?" She stood on the bed and dramatically spread her arms. "The notorious Dark Lord of London Town!"

Arabella laughed at Frey and pulled her back down to the bed. But I couldn't breathe. I was pretty sure I was having a heart attack. I couldn't go to that club. There was a reason I had never been there or to the three other clubs he owned across London.

The Adley firm no longer kept their business to East London. They had spread out. *Like a cancer*, I once heard my father snipe at the news. They now owned all of London—the north, south, east and west. Their biggest and most successful club was here in Knightsbridge. I got chills every time I passed the Sparrow Room in a taxi, wondering if Arthur was ever in there. I'd heard he was, often. All the more reason for me to keep away.

I knew it was an epic club; enough of our acquaintances raved about it for me to gather that. But what no one knew, or even suspected, was the five-year-long affair I had had with Arthur.

"We have your outfit all picked out for tomorrow, and"—Freya jumped off the bed—"for dinner tonight." She held up a purple silk

Fendi maxi dress and a pair of low-heeled Jimmy Choos. She came over and shooed me from the bed. "A dinner that is booked for twenty-five minutes' time. So hurry!" I grabbed the dress and shoes and went into the bathroom.

As soon as I shut the door, I leaned against it and tried to stem my panic. I would do this dinner tonight, then cry off tomorrow night. Claim it was food poisoning or something. I couldn't step inside that club. I couldn't take seeing Arthur after all this time. And I certainly couldn't take his rejection. Because I knew that would be what met me. He wasn't the man I once knew; that much was clear. And I knew I had only heard the tip of the iceberg of what he and his firm had done to other gangs and crime syndicates over the past thirteen months. There would be more. So much more.

"You'd better be getting a move on, honey! Fifteen minutes now," Freya shouted through the door. That got me moving. I threw on some more makeup, tied my hair back in a low bun and pulled on my dress. I stared at myself in the mirror. I looked pale. I looked nervous.

I moved to the window and opened it a fraction, sucking in the cool air. I stared down the street, right in the direction of the Sparrow Room. It wasn't far from here. Walking distance. If I concentrated hard enough, I would be able to hear the sound of its music. It didn't really get busy until late, but it opened its doors around now for those who wanted an early start.

"Cheska!" Arabella shouted.

"Coming!" I opened the door to my friends.

We dined, and the entire time I tried to stay in the moment, to enjoy all the effort my best friends had put into tonight. I loved them. They were truly like my sisters. *I* was the bad friend. I had been the one to keep a huge part of my life from them for the longest time. I didn't deserve them.

By the time we returned to the room for drinks, Freya and Arabella were legless. I was tipsy but had kept my head straight for fear I would say something about Arthur if alcohol controlled my tongue.

I tossed my bag on the table as the sound of a text came through.

Laughing at Freya trying to somersault onto the bed in her Gucci play-suit, I opened the screen and struggled to make out what I was seeing. It only took a couple of seconds for me to understand. It was a video, with no sound. My hands started shaking as the camera panned out.

"No," I sobbed, when my father and Hugo came into view. They were bloodied and beaten. Only one of my father's eyes remained open. Freya and Arabella came running to me. Freya covered her mouth with her hand when she saw the screen. Arabella held on to my arm.

And we watched.

We watched as my father and Hugo were beaten and hurt. Then a man in a balaclava and dressed in black came forward with a gun. My father fought his restraints, but the man held a gun to his head.

He pulled the trigger.

I screamed as my father's head dropped forward and life drained from his body. Hugo fought too, looking in horror at my father. Hugo turned to face the attacker. He was speaking to him frantically, begging him for something. For mercy, I imagined. But the killer just held the gun to his head and fired a bullet, killing him too.

My legs grew weak and I collapsed onto the floor. Freya and Arabella followed me down, the two of them wrapping their arms around me.

"Dad ... Hugo ..." I cried, replaying the video over and over in my head.

"The police." Freya got to her feet. "We need to call the police." She had just got to the phone when the door to our bedroom was slammed open and three men marched inside. I went to scream when I saw they were dressed in the same black clothes and balaclavas as the men in the video. But they moved before I could.

One grabbed Freya and covered her mouth to stop her calling out. One grabbed Arabella by her hair and dragged her across the carpet to near Freya. He pulled a roll of gaffer tape from his pocket and bound her hands and taped up her mouth. Freya had the same done to her. Then one came for me. I tried to get up and run, but he grabbed me by the waist and punched me across the face. I tasted blood, felt it trickling from my lip and down my neck.

"Bitch," he snarled and kicked my legs from under me. I plunged to the carpeted floor, and my hands and mouth were taped too.

They lined us up beside the bed, then one of them pulled out a camera. Tears were flooding down Freya's and Arabella's cheeks. I wouldn't give these men the pleasure of seeing me break. I had to keep my composure. I was pretty sure I was in shock after seeing my father and Hugo killed so brutally. And now they were here.

For me.

"Harlow cunt." The man brought the camera closer to my face. "Your daddy and fiancé pissed off some very bad people." I saw his balaclava shift and knew he was smiling beneath it. "They owed some money to some very powerful men." He kneeled before me. "And they thought they were too good to pay the piper." He nodded at one of the other men, the one standing near Freya. "And now we're recouping their debt."

In a flash, the man struck out and sliced the knife across Freya's throat. I screamed, the gaffer tape stopping any noise from spilling out. Freya's eyes widened, and she looked at me, right in the eye, as the wound cracked open and her blood poured in rivulets down her neck.

I screamed. I screamed and screamed as she fell to the ground, body twitching as she fought to hold on to life. Her eyes stayed on me as the life drained from her ... until her body stopped moving, stopped fighting ... stopped living.

The men laughed, and pure rage built in my chest. Arabella whispered something intelligible beside me, and I met her terrified dark eyes. They squeezed shut as more tears fell. When they opened again, her eyes turned to the man who was slowly approaching her. She didn't struggle. My best friend watched with a hauntingly detached calmness as the man who had bound her with tape kneeled down, then pushed a long knife right through her heart.

I turned my head away as Arabella started to gurgle, and this time I felt all the fight seep from my bones. When I had mustered up some strength, I looked back at Arabella as she lay on the floor, her eyes open but her body dead, her blood pooling beneath her.

They were going to kill me. My father and Hugo fucked up somehow, and now we were all going to die because of it. Arabella and Freya were innocent. I was a Harlow. I was the one they wanted.

"Smile," the man with the camera said, bringing the lens to my face. "Your friends are dead. Daddy and Hugo are dead. That only leaves you." I held my breath as he pulled the knife from Arabella's chest and wiped my friend's blood across the top of my breasts. I waited for him to stab me too, but instead he dragged me up by my arm. "No, no death for you. We have other things planned. Really fucked-up things. Death is too easy a way out."

He hoisted me to my feet. They were bare, my shoes long discarded, and my soles stood on the still-warm blood of Arabella and Freya. I fought back nausea as I was dragged into the corridor, trying to keep my eyes on my friends, praying they weren't gone—but they were. I'd seen the light fade from their eyes. I searched for anyone to help, but the spa was silent. The men dragged me away from the main stairs and lifts and into the emergency exit stairwell. I was struck as I stumbled and tried to pull away. They dealt punches to my stomach, to my face and finally, to my head. My vision spun, and I felt another slap burst my lip open further.

I felt as though I'd blacked out for a while. When I came to, one of the men was speaking into a phone. I couldn't hear what he was saying. I felt dizzy, aches and pains accosting me from my side to my head. I tried to keep my composure, keep conscious. I had to escape. I had to get away from here. I needed to get help. I couldn't let them take me.

But when we burst out of the exit and into an alleyway, I was dragged to the doors of a waiting van. Two of the men got in. One was behind me. I quickly looked at him; the knife he had used on Arabella was tucked into his waistband.

Just as he grabbed my arm to push me inside, I thrust my body against him. He laughed, clearly thinking I'd stumbled again. He certainly didn't suspect me of grabbing his knife and plunging it into his stomach. He keeled over, and I ran. I ran as hard and as fast as I could down the alleyway.

I could see the main road in the distance.

My heart beat faster and faster as I heard footsteps on the cobbled stones, someone giving chase. But I had the main road in my sight; it was my target. It was my salvation. I pulled at the tape around my wrists, working it as I ran. I ripped the tape off my mouth with my hands. I fought and fought as I ran, lifting my arms and yanking them down, managing to get one hand free. I risked a quick look behind me and saw the other two men hot on my heels.

But the end of the alley was just a few feet away. As I burst onto the bright main street, a hint of relief hit me. But I didn't let my guard down. I ran for the taxi rank near the front of the spa. People stared at me as I passed. I ignored them. I had to get to the safety of a taxi. I knew of only one person who could help me. The one person I needed to see right now more than God.

The rank was empty of people, and I dived into the back of the first cab. "Drive!" I shouted to the cabbie. His eyes widened in the rearview mirror.

"Bloody hell, love. You okay?"

"Please!" I begged, feeling the delayed shock starting to claw at my throat, anxiety trying to smother me with its heavy body. "Please, just drive." I looked behind me and couldn't see the men anywhere. It would be too conspicuous for them to be seen in public dressed as they were. But it didn't mean they weren't tracking me somehow.

"Where to, love?" the cabbie said and pulled out into the main road.

"The ..." I hitched a breath. "The Sparrow Room." I knew it was only up the road, but I needed time to catch my breath. I couldn't have made it to the club on foot. My energy was depleted, and I didn't feel well.

"They're not going to let you in looking like that, sweetheart. It's as posh as Buckingham Palace."

"I know him," I murmured and sat back on the leather seat, feeling the wounds that had been inflicted on me begin to throb and sting. My entire body seemed to pulse, and I thought I could smell blood. I pushed the images of Freya and Arabella from my head, of Dad and Hugo being shot on the seats to which they were tied. I wasn't safe yet. I just had to get to Arthur, and then I'd be safe. He would help me. Even if he didn't want me anymore, he would keep me safe.

I pulled my hair from its low bun and tried my best to hide my face. The taxi stopped. The entrance to the Sparrow Club was to my left. It was a huge building with heavy-set bouncers guarding the door. I just had to get inside.

"I can't pay you," I whispered to the cabbie when I caught him staring at me.

"It's on the house, darling," he said and unlocked the doors for me. The unexpected kindness almost made me weep, but I kept it together. I just had to keep it together for a little bit longer. "They're not going to let you in," the cabbie said again.

I watched a bouncer remove the rope to let people inside and knew that's how I'd get in. I could make a run for it when the ropes were pulled back. Then I just had to find Arthur's office. I prayed he was there.

The bouncer closed the rope again, and I waited. I kept my hand braced on the door handle of the taxi. When the bigger bouncer controlling the rope moved to open it again, I threw the door open and ran without pause.

I ran as fast as I could past the rope and straight through into the entrance. "Oi!" I heard a bouncer shout behind me, but I kept running. I couldn't stop yet. I ran past the cloakroom and till, following the pounding dance music until I entered the main body of the club. It was packed and dark and wall-to-wall with dancing people. I slipped into the throng, knowing the bouncers would be searching the entire club for me.

I searched around me, trying to find my bearings. The three-floored interior looked like a theatre or opera house, but with dancers and a DJ on the main stage. There were go-go dancers in cages, and the bars teemed with people buying drinks. But then I saw someone in a suit enter a back door near the stage. A bouncer opened the door, and as the light shone on the man in the suit's face, recognition hit. Charlie. It was Charlie Adley.

Hope carried me forward. I pushed through the dancers and tried to think how to get into the door. But a higher power must have figured I was owed a boon—a fight broke out next to the bouncer, and he was drawn into the fray, leaving the door on its latch.

I ran again, using the last of my energy to get through the door. I shut it behind me, hearing the lock click into place, and winced at the bright fluorescent light. My side started to throb with more intensity, and as I looked down, I noticed blood seeping from my side. I'd been stabbed? I didn't remember being stabbed. Had it happened in the stairwell when they had beaten me? I thought I had blacked out ...

Feeling light-headed, I rushed down the corridor. I passed a store-room door, but there were no offices. I climbed a set of stairs at the end of the hallway, praying I would make it to the top before collaps-ing. Muffled voices came from behind one of the doors. I climbed the steps, trying to ignore the pain slicing through my ribs, the swelling of my lips and the energy that seemed to be draining more and more by the second.

When I reached the top of the stairs, I saw Arthur's name on one of the doors and headed in that direction. The voices grew louder as I approached. My hand fell on the doorknob and I turned it, managing to throw the door open. There was a flurry of activity around me, but I didn't pay it any attention. All I saw was the man behind the desk. A man in a designer suit, with dark hair and bright blue eyes shining behind black-framed glasses.

And despite everything, I felt relief flood me, bringing me light. In this moment, seeing Arthur was as powerful as seeing Christ himself.

I reached my hand toward him and whispered, "Arthur ... I've found you ... I've finally found you ..."

Then I closed my eyes and succumbed to the dark.

CHAPTER SEVEN

ARTHUR

I shot up from my seat and moved around my desk, pushing it the fuck out of my way. Charlie, Eric, Vinnie and Freddie had their guns out and targeted on Cheska the minute she bust through the door. I bent down, rolled her over and saw blood pouring onto her dress. She was knocked out, her lip split and her cheek bruised, but fuck, even in this state she was fucking beautiful. But her injuries ... her fucking injuries ...

Fire flared inside me. Someone had hurt her. Someone had fucking hit her. I ripped the dress in two to find a stab wound in her side. "Ring the doctor. Have him come to my house," I ordered Charlie and lifted Cheska into my arms.

I had fucking Cheska Harlow-Wright in my arms again.

I hadn't seen her in over a year, and now she was in my mother-fucking arms, bleeding out and beaten to a bastard pulp. "Call the fucking driver to the back exit," I instructed Eric as I burst into the corridor and raced down the stairs. I heard footsteps following behind me.

"Cheska? This is the bird you were fucking all that time?" Eric asked. I ignored him and rushed to the back exit, kicking it open with my foot. The car was already there. I climbed inside and held her in my arms.

"Home. And fucking get us there quick!" I ordered, and the driver skidded out onto the main road. I pushed back dark brown hair from Cheska's face and studied her cuts and bruises. A strange, fucked-up kind of ache ripped at my chest as I saw her swelling lip and the wound at her side. My sternum ached like I was feeling something. Like I fucking cared. But I'd stopped caring about everything a long time ago. All I felt these days was rage and revenge and the need to tear down any fucker that got in my way.

I pressed my hand against her side to try and stop the bleeding. Her blood was hot against my hand, and her breathing was steady but hollow. Cheska didn't wake up as I touched her. She was fucking out for the count.

I'd seen enough stab wounds in my time to know it wasn't deep, but she was losing blood; that much was clear.

"Faster," I said to the driver. I pressed down harder on her wound and felt something pull in my gut. My jaw clenched as it hit me again, like a fucking crowbar to my stomach.

Cheska. Bloody Cheska Harlow-Wright. She'd always been able to do this shit to me. Her stunning face, her body that I always fucking craved, and those dual-coloured eyes that drew me the fuck in.

"Princess, what the fuck?" I said against her cheek and held her tighter. Her tits were on show since I'd ripped her dress from her. She hadn't been wearing a bra. I glanced at the driver. His attention was on the road, but a wave of possessiveness took me over. I didn't want any fucker to see her like this. Only me. Only I ever looked at her tits and body this way.

I slipped off my jacket and wrapped it around her. A breath lodged in my throat at the sight of her in my jacket. She was slim, and my jacket bloody drowned her. But I liked the sight of her in it. Fuck, I could smell my cologne mixing with her perfume, and I held her fucking tighter.

Blood soaked into my shirt as she lay flush against me, but I didn't fucking care. I tapped my foot on the floor. My bastard skin itched with the need to get her to safety.

I just needed to get her to my motherfucking house.

The minute we turned from the main road to the church grounds, I let myself breathe. When we stopped at the house, I launched the fuck out of the car and ran for the front door. The doctor was waiting. He knew not to fuck me about, and I paid him a fuck-ton of money to be at my beck and call.

"My bedroom," I ordered and rushed her inside. I laid Cheska on my bed and reluctantly moved out of the doctor's way. But I kept her fucking hand in mine. Kept my fingers wrapped around hers. I couldn't fucking take my eyes off her, lying there on the bed.

My fucking bed.

Dark hair.

Green-brown eyes that always saw me and ... *"Arthur ... I've found you ... I've finally found you ..."*

Her voice. Her raspy posh voice as she staggered into my office, and the fucking state of her as she fell to the ground.

Cheska.

Cheska, who I had left in Oxford just over a year ago never to fucking see again. The doctor started cleaning her up, and I needed a drink. I needed a fucking large drink and a drag of my cig.

I released her hand and pushed out of the room. I stared at my hand as I walked down the hallway. It was still warm. Even losing blood, she'd warmed my fucking hand. I went straight to the bar and poured myself a huge whisky and downed half the glass. Memories fucking assaulted me. Memories that I both tried to forget and needed to fuel me.

I'd gone to her the day they'd all been killed. The day Dad got shot by the fucking Russians. My eyes drifted in the direction of my old man's bedroom, where he still lay. Still in a fucking coma, body atrophied and paralysed. No sign of ever coming out of it.

Cheska.

Fucking Cheska Harlow-Wright.

I heard my front door open and knew who it would be. A few seconds later, Eric, Charlie, Vinnie and Freddie came inside. They were all looking at me, waiting for something.

"WHAT?" I roared, not about to deal with their shit. I was on a fucking knife's edge. I was feeling too much. I chose not to feel anything but the hate-fuelled fire inside me these days. She was fucking with my mind. Cheska being here and hurt and fucking seeking me out after a year apart was fucking with my head.

"Firstly, calm your tits, psycho," Eric said, crossing his arms across his chest. "And secondly, your old bird stumbles into the club, beaten and stabbed, and you ask 'what?'"

I pulled out my cigs and sparked one up. I took a deep inhale, the nicotine hitting my veins and giving me a second of fucking reprieve.

"She burst into the club, ran right through the fucking bouncers and into the dance floor." Charlie poured himself a brandy beside me. "Not bad for a bird who'd been stabbed." He smirked at me. "Tenacious little thing, isn't she?"

"She came for you," Vinnie said, speaking directly as always. "She came looking for you, Artie." He tapped the side of his eyes. "Her eyes. Her eyes changed when they saw you. Like Pearl's do when she looks at me." Vinnie slipped his hands into his pockets and started whistling "Ring a Ring o' Roses", his eyes now on the landscape painting of some country house on the wall.

"Isn't she getting married soon or something? I've seen their mugs all over the society pages," Freddie asked, sitting down in an armchair.

"You scan the fucking society pages?" Eric said to Freddie, hiding a smile with his hand.

"Most of the fuckers who owe us money are on those pages, dickhead. I keep track of them so they don't try and dodge town. Those pages seem to know more about the richies than even their own families do."

"Oh, I didn't know you were all here," Betsy said, coming into the room. "I thought you were at the club tonight." She frowned as she looked at us all, then straightened her shoulders. "What's happened?"

Charlie tipped his head in my direction. "Cheska Harlow-Wright."

What else could rock our fearless leader like this?" Betsy's eyes widened, and I knew the fucker had been speaking about me to his sister. Between that and the smart-arsed comments, I was about five seconds away from knocking off his head.

"*The* Cheska?" Betsy asked.

"The very one." Charlie smirked as I shot him a death stare. My cousin and friends were the only people on the fucking planet who didn't piss themselves in my presence.

"*The* Cheska. What the fuck is that meant to mean?" I snapped, getting more fucked off at my family by the second.

"Nothing," Betsy said, shrugging, and got herself a drink too. I lit another cig and leaned against the fireplace, watching the flames dance up the chimney. I pictured Cheska as a kid at her dad's house. Then at eighteen in her bikini on the yacht. Her pressed against me, then spread out on the dining table on our yacht as I fucked her, as I ploughed into her, needing to chase her away. Instead, afterwards, she only wanted me more.

Then years. Fucking years of taking her in every way imaginable. She liked it rough like I needed. Clawed and fought me and made me fucking addicted.

The room was quiet, and I couldn't stand it. I knew they were all watching me. "What?" I shouted, turning with my arms out. "What's with all the fucking silence?"

It was Betsy who spoke, unaffected by my outburst. "Just haven't seen you like this since ..." She trailed off, and we all knew what she meant. The night after I got back from Oxford, after our dads were done and I had to take the helm. The night I siphoned off any feelings and emotions I had for Cheska and became what I had to in order for this family to survive.

We'd fucking gone to war that night. And we'd been fighting on the front line ever since. "She means something to you," Betsy added, clearly choosing her words carefully. "If you're being honest with yourself, she always has."

"I *fucked* her! That's all," I spat, and flicked my cig into the fire, done with this conversation and this dissection of my fucking life. I marched out of the room and straight into my bedroom. When I entered, the doctor was just moving his stuff. A bag of blood was being transfused into Cheska's arm. But she was cleaned up, my sheet and duvet pulled up to her shoulders.

"She's lost blood, but not as much as I'd feared." He gestured to her face. Her fucking beaten face. My hands fisted at my sides. No one as perfect as her should ever look like this.

"I cleaned up her face, but they were surface injuries. I gave her an antibiotic injection and left medicine for her to take when she wakes—both for pain and to prevent infection. She's to take them until the course has finished." He pointed at the tablets on the bedside table. He went to walk past me. "She should wake after she's rested. She got off relatively unscathed, considering what I imagine she went through tonight to even get in this state."

"And her memory?" I asked. I needed to know what had fucking happened to her. I needed to know who the fuck had done this to her so I could kill the cunts.

"Should be unaffected. That's physically, of course. That's not taking trauma into consideration. That could be a potential problem for her." The doctor left when I stayed silent, not asking him anything else. He shut the door behind him, and I stared down at Cheska.

My teeth ached from gritting them so hard. I thought back to the last day I went to her in Oxford. When I was fucked off my face on whisky and just needed her. Out of everyone, I fucking chose to turn to her. And not just to fuck, but to just be somewhere else that wasn't this church or with my family, or with my old man lying in a bed that he would be in for months and months to come. And because I'd liked the feel of her in my fucking arms. In that moment, that fucked-up dark moment, she was the only one I'd wanted.

I shook my head when flashes of memory showed me crying on her like a pussy. Showed me that fucking ring on her finger, that bright diamond catching my drunken eye. She'd got engaged a couple of days before that night. One look at that motherfucking ring and I'd snapped. I'd needed her, needed to fucking own her, and here was another prick's ring on her finger. A finger that had just been wrapped in my hair, holding my fucking face and wrapped around my dick.

I walked closer to the bed and saw her hand still wore that fucking ring.

She was getting married soon. Freddie'd told me that a while back, like I didn't fucking know. I knew every detail. Married at St Paul's Cathedral, then on to the Ritz afterwards. I fucking knew. I knew everything about this bird. She bloody clawed at my head daily, had done since the first time I met her.

Like fucking witchcraft.

I couldn't go down that fucked-up road again. Cheska was pure kryptonite. She was the fucking gatekeeper of shit I needed to keep firmly locked away.

I needed to leave. I needed to send Betsy in here to keep watch over her and take care of her when she woke up. I had work to do, family business shit to deal with, and this bird had no place in my life anymore.

But then my feet fucking led me forward, and I dragged the armchair from the corner of my room to beside the bed, like I was being pulled by some invisible rope to her side.

I lit up a cig and stared at her face. Even bruised and battered, she was a fucking ten. But she didn't belong in this world I lived in. Never fucking had. Didn't stop me from taking her though. I'd fucking stolen her from the light and made her mine in the darkness.

I thought it would be just one time, an inevitable fuck we both knew we had to get out of our systems. But one taste of Cheska Harlow-Wright wasn't enough. Even at eighteen, after my soul had only been fractured, not shattered apart—irreparable and written off. After fucking her in Marbella, I only craved her more. I was meant to get her pussy once and walk away. She wasn't meant to ensnare me. I wasn't meant to get addicted.

I came back to London with her bloody mobile number still stained on my palm. A week later I was knee-deep in her cunt again, and I stayed there for five fucking years.

Until that night.

Until the night everything changed and I had to throw her out of the way of the fucking demons that had taken hold of my ankles and were pulling me down to hell.

But she found me anyway. Thirteen months later, she found me, far from where she should be. An angel seeking out the devil for help. Exactly what kind of help? I didn't fucking know.

So I'd wait in this fucking chair until I found out.

I woke up to the sound of coughing. I opened my eyes and saw Cheska wince in pain. Her eyes slowly blinked open. I turned off the main light and put on a lamp so the room wouldn't be too bright. And I waited. When Cheska's eyes opened, I watched as confusion wrapped around her. She glanced in my direction, and recognition flashed across her face. Even though she was pale, her cheeks flushed red.

"Arthur," she whispered, her voice weak.

"Princess," I said. Her eyes softened at that name.

"What—?" she went to say, then froze, seeming to remember whatever the fuck had happened to her. Her hands started shaking on the bed, then her eyes filled with tears. Her trembling hand covered her mouth, and she flinched, her fingers feeling along her swollen lips.

"They killed them," she said, voice wracked with pain, and my body tensed. Cheska looked at me, her gaze fucking tortured. "Someone killed my friends in front of me, Arthur. Freya and Arabella. They slit Frey's throat and stabbed Arabella right through the heart." A sob ripped from her throat. I couldn't fucking stand it. Couldn't stand that horrified sound or the tears in her sad eyes.

I moved off the chair and sat on the mattress beside her. She looked up at my face, hands shaking as she clutched at the duvet. "Hugo, Dad ... they're gone too."

"Dead?"

She nodded. "Shot." She started crying, fucking broke, and I got her a glass of water from the bedside table. When her hands were shaking too bloody much for her to hold it, I brought it to her mouth. I held the back of her head and made sure she took a sip.

Cheska pulled the glass away but took hold of my wrist before I could move away. Her fingers were weak as piss around me, but fuck did it make something pull in my bastard gut. "They sent a video to my phone," she said. She swallowed like she had a lump wedged in her throat. "Of them killing Dad and Hugo." She sucked in a jagged breath.

Her eyes zoned the fuck out, her thoughts no doubt taking her back to earlier tonight. "Then they came to the spa we were at and captured us. They killed Freya and Arabella in the bedroom but said they were taking me somewhere else. They had other plans for me." She refocused on me and held my wrist tighter. "Something slow and painful." Rage consumed me.

Slow and painful ...

When I got my hands on the pricks that had done this to her, I'd make sure their deaths were fucking drawn out and agonised.

I could feel my blood start to boil too fucking high, to the point where someone, somewhere, needed to die by my hands for me to calm down. I placed the half-full glass down with my free hand.

"Arthur, they tried to drag me to a van in an alley, but ... but I managed to get away." She sobbed and moved her hold from my wrist to my hand. Her fingers wrapped around mine, and I felt a fucking shock of electricity shoot through me like I'd just been stabbed with a cattle prod.

I went to pull back my hand, needing to keep my fucking distance from her. But she held on tighter. Fucking witchcraft. This bird was the only one in the bloody world that fucked my head up this well. I didn't hold hands. Only with her. When her fucking witch's spell had wrapped around me.

"They said Dad and Hugo owed a debt to dangerous people but never paid up. So, they took payment with their lives. With my best friends' lives."

Cheska eventually stopped crying, shock clearly settling in. Her grip on my hand tightened. "They'll be coming for me. They want me as payment. Arthur ... they'll come back for me. They're not done."

Her words, mixed with the sheer fucking terror in her hoarse voice, made me want to snap some arsehole's neck. As she'd spoken every bloody word, I'd felt the fire inside of me scald my fucking flesh until the only remedy would be someone's blood coating my hands.

She was shaking, and her pupils were blown in fear. "Arthur," she whispered, and then pressed her cheek against the back of my hand, almost bringing me to my fucking knees. "Everyone has gone. All my family, my friends ... they've all gone. I'm completely alone ..." Her broken lip dragged along my skin, opening the cut and staining my skin with her blood. "I'm so scared."

Ignoring the fact that she was hurt, I yanked her closer until her face hovered in front of mine. I gripped her jaw and made sure her eyes were fucking right on me. "They're not getting anywhere near you," I growled; Cheska exhaled in relief.

And I saw what else was in her stare. I knew that fucking look. I knew exactly how Cheska felt toward me. For such a smart bird, she was fucking thick when it came to me. Reckless. She was like a kid putting her hand into a roaring bonfire when she'd been told one too many times to back off or she'd be burned. But here she was, hand in the inferno once again.

"No one will dare fuck with you now you're under my protection," I promised.

"Arthur," she whispered, that posh accent washing over me the same way it always fucking did. Like opium or some shit. Calming me right the hell down. I had no fucking clue how she managed to do it, but she was the only thing in my life that had ever had that effect on me.

She was fucking dangerous.

I pushed her hair back from her face. She smelled of antiseptic, but underneath was all her, that familiar smell that used to stick to my skin for weeks after I'd paid a midnight visit to Oxford and fucked her. The scent that almost me drove me insane for days afterwards until I was back between her legs again. That rose perfume she always wore.

"You have no idea who these fucks were?" I asked, about two seconds from climbing onto the bed and fucking her again. She was alive, and the devil had sent her here, all for me to possess. A gift for doing his work to perfection.

It had been too fucking long. I needed to feel her under me, clawing at my back and raking at my hair. Telling me to fuck her harder —then I'd know she was still fucking alive. I didn't care if she was bruised and beaten; the dark part inside me just needed to be inside her to know she was good. That these balaclava-wearing twats hadn't ruined her. Hurt her, killed her.

The daft cunts had no idea they'd just put a fucking Adley bounty on their heads.

"None," she said, ripping me from my head, bringing me back down to earth. She stared off at nothing. "I didn't even know the business was in trouble, that my dad was dealing with dangerous people again." I knew the "again" came from the fact Cheska's old man had dealt with mine in the past. A loan. That was how we'd met. Dear old Daddy had taken a loan from my old man, and he was late with the repayment. So, Alfie Adley paid Mr Wright a visit, and I'd crashed into his fucking daughter with the force of an asteroid colliding with Earth. Cheska's dad took his little virginal princess and placed her directly in my line of sight. Made a fucked-up East End boy take notice of her forbidden posh-as-fuck arse. The future dark lord finding his innocent little goddess, biding his time until he stole her right from under Daddy's neglectful gaze and brought her to the dark side.

Now Daddy was gone. So was her bellend of a betrothed. She was fucking adrift, no home, no family ...

"You said they sent a video to your phone?" I said, needing to step the fuck back from her. The bruises on her face and body were getting darker, and I could see by her heavy eyelids that she was getting tired. I needed to back the fuck off. I needed to calm the hell down. I needed to think. I couldn't ever fucking think around Cheska.

"I don't have my phone. It'll still be at the spa. Everything happened so quickly that I was unable to retrieve it."

"We can hack into your number and messages. Just need your number." Ronnie was a fucking genius at that kind of shit.

Cheska's eyes grew even more heavy. "Sleep," I said. I made myself hold back from kissing her wrecked mouth. Cheska closed her eyes, and her body started losing tension. I eventually let go of her hand. I saw that fucking ring again and wanted to rip it off her finger. Hugo the posh cunt was dead. He had no claim on her anymore.

I got off the bed, needing to clear my fucking head. As I stood, Cheska's eyes rolled open and she looked down at her hand, empty now that I'd pulled mine away. "What's your mobile number?" I asked, that fucking devastated expression on her face hitting me too bloody hard in the chest.

"The same one as always." Cheska stared at me, and the look she was throwing my way made my chest tighten. "I didn't want to change it." She took a deep breath, favouring her side when she did. "Just in case ..."

Just in case I ever called her again, needed her again. She'd been waiting. This fucking bird had been waiting for me to come back to her.

What she didn't realise is that I ran this town. I didn't need to call her to check in on her. I could have found out what she was up to on any given day and she'd know nothing about it.

"Sleep, princess," I said and watched her close her eyes. No one would dare enter this fucking house unless they had a death wish. She was safe here. And until I found out who had come for her, she wasn't setting foot out my front door.

I waited until her breathing evened out, standing at the end of her bed like some demon ready to snatch her soul and drag her to my lair in hell. When she was out, I made my way back to the living room, replaying everything she'd told me in my head. Ronnie and Vera were at the church now too. Good. It was time for a fucking family meeting.

They watched me in silence as I entered the room and poured myself a gin. I downed a glass, then refilled it to the brim. I turned to them, leaning against the bar's counter. "Her old man and fiancé were murdered tonight, along with her two best mates. The attackers tried to kidnap Cheska too, but she got away. Came to find me. That's why she turned up at the club."

"Fuck," Freddie said, shaking his head, and Ronnie got to her feet. If there was one thing that lit a fire under Ronnie's arse it was women being attacked. Even more so if it was by blokes.

"What do you need?" she said, anxious to channel her anger into work.

I had just the job for her. "They sent her a video of her old man and numpty of a fiancé being shot and killed. I want to see that fucking video."

"Number?"

I rattled off the mobile number, not even giving Charlie the time of day, feeling the knowing stare he gave me as I recited the digits off the top of my head. Ronnie left to go to the office and get me what I wanted.

"And the posh bird?" Vera asked, an edge of curiosity to her raspy voice.

"She's staying here."

"The police could deal with this, Art," Eric said. "She's a rich one. Someone they actually give a shit about looking after. They'll be all over her arse with protection. Let the pigs deal with it. We've got enough going on."

"I SAID SHE'S FUCKING STAYING HERE!" I shouted, and Eric held up his hands as my voice echoed around the room.

"Alright, Artie. Simmer the fuck down. I was just saying." The fucking smug smirk on his face told me he knew exactly what he was doing by pushing me. Prick. Betsy covered a small smile with her hand. It was probably the first time in ages she'd actually smiled at Eric and not sent him daggers.

Freddie was playing on his phone. He met my eyes. "It's just hit the news, Artie." He turned his phone so I could see the screen. "They've reported the deaths of the dad and fiancé. Coppers were sent the video of them being shot by an anonymous number. They've reported the deaths of her best mates too." Freddie read the article. "Suspecting Cheska has been kidnapped. No leads. The CCTV all around that part of the city had briefly been cut."

"They won't get her here. They won't even know to come looking. She's not going anywhere while those cunts are still out hunting her."

"She's staying with you then?" Betsy asked, and I saw that fucking spark of something in her eyes. Something like hope. "In your bedroom?"

"It's not like that," I said, knocking back another glass of Bombay Sapphire and feeling it flooding my stomach. I turned to the bar and fought back the image of Cheska pinned to the mattress beneath me, screaming out my name as I wrapped my hand around her throat and sank my dick inside her wet pussy. "She doesn't fucking belong in this world." Something caved in my chest as I said that. I looked up at the mirror on the wall and saw myself looking back. But as I stared, all I saw around me was a black shadow and every inch of me covered in blood—not my own.

Never my fucking own.

"Wouldn't you say that's up to her?" Betsy pushed. I tore my eyes from my bloodied reflection and pointed at my cousin. She just stared back at me blankly, un-fucking-afraid, as per usual.

"Don't," I warned, my voice thick with command. Command to stay the fuck out of my business and back the hell off.

"Just saying," Betsy said, rising from her seat to move beside me at the bar. She poured herself a port and faced me. "You've never cared about excluding women from the Adley fold. Our fathers weren't even cold before you welcomed me, Vera and Ronnie into the firm, guns in hand and, hours later, Russian blood under our fingernails."

"It has nothing to do with her being a fucking bird," I snapped.

"No." Charlie moved beside his sister. "It has to do with the fact that Ms Harlow-Wright is *your* bird. Isn't that right, Artie?" I glared at my best friend. He wasn't taking the piss. I knew Charlie as well as I knew myself. I knew he was concerned for me, had been for a while now. He'd barely left my side in the past thirteen months, since I'd taken the gaffer's role in this fucked-up family. He walked beside me, step by unholy step, as I fell deeper into the fucking abyss. And he never complained once. But I knew he was scared I'd be lost to the depravity of it all—the killing, the blood, the underworld that I ruled with a fucking iron fist.

I faced Betsy, ignoring Charlie. "You're in charge of Cheska. You'll watch out for her while she's here. Stay with her and protect her."

"It'll be my pleasure," Betsy said, then went to sit beside Vera on the settee.

"Your colours match," Vinnie said when the room got silent. Vinnie lived with me now. His old man had watched out for him when he was alive—we all got that Vinnie couldn't be left alone. He needed to be watched. Given too much of a wide berth, the fucker would be out like Jack the Ripper, murdering Londoners for fun in the most fucked-up ways. Plus, he'd told me Pearl was clearer to him in the church. It was the first hint he'd ever given me that he knew Pearl was a hallucination and not actually my sister, all grown up and standing beside him, flesh and blood.

"What you on about, mate?" Eric asked, frowning at Vinnie.

Vinnie's eyes were pinned on me. His hand was beside him on the couch, open like he was holding someone's hand. "All around you is black." Vinnie shook his head, his shoulder-length blond hair covering some of his face. "It never used to be. It used to be red too." His hand tightened around thin air. "It was because of you that the blackness first came," he told what I assumed was his hallucination of Pearl. "When you and your mum burned. Some of the red went and was taken over by black." Vinnie lifted the invisible hand to his mouth and kissed it. He faced me again. "When your old man died, more and more red was replaced by black. Month by month, I watched it turn more and more black until I thought there was no red left."

"But?" I asked, feeling like I was going insane too, actually listening to what Vin had to say.

"There's a bit left. But I only realised it when you held Cheska. She made your red light flare." My chest fucking tightened. Darkness. I always knew it had come for me, had taken me under ... Vinnie saw it clear as day.

That bit of red that remained was all Cheska Harlow-Wright.

"Hers is mostly red," Vinnie said. He smiled, and it looked like the smile of the Rottweilers we kept at our docks to guard the place. "But there's a thin line of black around her too. The darkness has infected her. She might not know it yet ... but she will."

Me. I was that bastard darkness. I was the one who had infected her. Tarnished her innocence.

"Fuck, Vin, you're going to kill us all one day, right?" Eric sat forward on his chair. "We'll wake up one night with you at the end of our beds about to stab us. You're fucking barking, mate."

"Eric," Charlie warned.

Eric smiled at Charlie, and I knew the fucker wasn't finished. "You haven't got paranoid schizophrenia at all, have you? You're a fucking medium or some shit. Talking to the dead all day every day, and that's what sent you to the nuthouse." Eric flicked his thumb at Vinnie. "We could make some serious money off this fucker." Eric winked at Vinnie;

Vinnie smiled back. It was a fucked-up sight, these two sadistic clowns grinning at each other. Normally only their victims got to see those crazy smiles.

"I talk to them," Vinnie said, and we all stared at him. He shrugged. "Our old men. I talk to them all the time." He looked at me. "Even Alfie. He comes to me too."

My jaw clenched. I got the context. He was telling me that my old man was as good as dead. But I refused to fucking believe that. I refused to let him go. He'd wake up. I knew he'd wake up. Some fucking day.

Eric's smile fell. His face had paled at the mention of our old men. He opened his mouth to say something, when Ronnie came back into the room. She pressed something on her tablet and the TV above the fire came to life. Seconds later we were watching men dressed in black silently killing Cheska's dad and fiancé.

When the screen cut to black, Ronnie said, "No sound. No trace. Whoever these guys are, they're good. Really fucking good." Ronnie glanced to Vera, and Vera immediately got to her feet.

She wrapped her arm around Ronnie. "What is it, babe?"

Ronnie rewound the video, then stopped on a particular part. She zoomed in on one of the men's hands. I squinted to see what we were looking at, and I saw the sliver of skin between his leather glove and the end of his jacket. Ronnie was watching me, waiting for me to see it.

"My traffickers." She rubbed the mark on her shoulder. The same one this fucker wore on his wrist. Fire built at my feet and started to rise. I felt it incinerate my bones until it was everywhere. Until it was all I fucking *was*. The darkness, the fire, the evil that lived inside me, taking full control.

"What the fuck?" Vera snapped. "They've appeared again?"

"Been a while," Charlie said, running his hand over his stubble. "What do they want with the Harlows?"

I was burning. I was fucking boiling, ready to explode. "They're not getting near Cheska," I snarled. "Where are they?" I said to Ronnie.

Her shoulders fell. "No address. No trace. Same as fucking always."

"Cunts!" I shouted and threw my glass into the fire, watching it roar as the alcohol fuelled the already high flames. "I'm about fucking done with these wankers!"

Freddie jumped to his feet, staring at his phone. "Fuck's sake!" He turned to me. "We've been motherfucking hit again." I stilled and stared at my brother. He turned his phone to show me the text and the picture of the west dock, the empty shipping containers and the dead guards bleeding out on the ground.

"What the fuck is happening?" I said, grabbing my coat from the back of a chair. I threw it on, and my brothers followed suit. This was the fifth hit on our docks and haulage ships in the past six months. Some fucker was trying to get to me. And it was working. No one fucking took on the Adley firm. And no one challenged me and lived to tell the tale.

"Cowards," I said. "Hiding behind sneaky attacks and killing guards. Face *me*, toe to toe. Cowards. Fucking face *me!*" I opened the barrel of my gun and checked it was full. I clicked it back into place and tucked it into the holster in my coat. "We're going to check it out." I turned to Betsy. "Watch Cheska. Don't let her out of your sight."

"I promise, Artie," she said, and I felt the fire calm a little. Then I walked out of the room, my boys behind me. Whoever was fucking with our gear was going to die. So were the traffickers who'd fucked with Ronnie and now had their eyes on Cheska.

The devil inside wouldn't let me fail.

CHAPTER EIGHT

CHESKA

My legs were stuck. I tried to move them, to run to Freya crawling on the floor a few feet away, but I couldn't reach her. Her eyes widened and she reached for her throat. Blood. So much blood began to pour from her throat, pour from her ears, pour from her eyes.

"No! I cried, feeling my heart crack down the centre into two broken parts.

"Cheska?" I snapped my head to the right and saw Arabella stumbling through a fog. She was searching for me, reaching out her hand for me to take. To guide her home.

"Arabella," I said and reached out my hand. Her fingers had almost met mine when a knife came out of the fog and ploughed right through her chest. Her lips moved in a silent cry for help. But she dropped to the ground.

I screamed as she fell, as Freya's body disappeared in a pool of her own blood. Then the fog cleared. It cleared, and there they all were. Freya, Arabella, Dad and Hugo.

They were gone ... they were dead.

My throat was raw from screaming and my cheeks were sore from tears. I couldn't save them. I couldn't save their lives ...

I heard the humming before I'd even opened my eyes. It would be Freya. She was always singing as she got ready. I smiled, relieved that it had only been a nightmare. My pounding heart calmed as I tried to push the awful dream from my mind. I opened my eyes, only to see an unfamiliar ceiling. The humming was billowing in the air, but it was deeper than Freya's soft voice. It was smoother, and a little more off key.

Confused, I rolled my head to the side and caught sight of a woman I had never seen before. She had long brown hair that fell in loose waves to her shoulders. One side of her hair was pinned back, revealing porcelain skin and bright blue eyes. She was tall and slender, dressed in skinny black jeans with a white shirt tucked into the waistband. She was beautiful.

I frowned, wondering who it could be, then my memory took over and started laying recent events on me like bricks, the weight of which crushed my chest. Dad ... Hugo ... Freya ... Arabella ...

It hadn't been a dream. It hadn't been as simple as a nightmare. It was real. It was all real. A pained sob slipped from my lips. They throbbed as it did. I raised my hand to my mouth and felt that my lips were swollen, and I remembered being hit, being dragged to a van ... running. The Sparrow Club. Arthur. *Arthur ...*

"Arthur," I whispered, my throat like cut glass.

"Shh." The woman brought a glass of water to my mouth. I took the glass and tried to sit up. I had to do something. My friends ... Dad ... Hugo ... "Let me help," she said, her accent hitting me even though my head felt as though it was filled with fog. She was a cockney, like Arthur. She put her hands under my arms and lifted me until I was sitting up. I dropped the glass, soaking the side of the bed, as dizziness made me lose my balance. I held my hand to my head and breathed until the room righted and the wave of nausea ebbed.

"I'm sorry," I said, opening my eyes and letting my hand drop to the damp bed.

"Don't be sorry, darling," the woman said and pulled back the sheets. I looked down; I was dressed in a nightgown. I had no memory of putting it on. I didn't know what was happening. Everything felt too surreal.

As if reading my mind, she said, "I cleaned you up and dressed you after the doctor checked you over this morning."

"This morning?" I asked, confusion rising as I looked around the room. There were old beams everywhere; the roof was angled, the walls white and uneven like many old buildings seemed to be. Vintage furniture decorated the minimal room.

Arthur's house. His famed converted church.

The woman stopped beside me. I searched her face up close. She was so pretty, with a sprinkling of freckles dotted over her nose. "Darling, you've been asleep for about twenty-four hours."

"I have?"

"You were knackered, girl. Your body needed time to rest after what you've been through." She rolled back the sheets and pulled them from the bed. "Are you strong enough to sit on this chair if I help you up? I need to change the sheets."

I moved my feet and, despite the pain in my side, was able to move them off the side of the bed. The woman held my arm and helped me stand. I gasped a little as the pain sliced through my stab wound. When it faded, I let her help me to the chair. It was the chair Arthur had sat in when he came to see me. At least I thought he had been to see me. Maybe I had imagined that too.

"I'm Betsy." The woman gave me a devastatingly beautiful smile. "Betsy Adley." My eyebrows must have risen as she spoke her last name, because she winked and said, "Arthur's cousin."

"Oh." I shook her offered hand. "Cheska."

"Oh, I know who you are." I wasn't sure what that meant or how to read the tone of her words. My head was pounding and I could barely focus. "Here," Betsy said. I looked up to see two tablets and a glass of water in her hand. "Your medicine from the doctor. For the pain." I numbly took them from her, swallowing them down and praying they kicked in quickly.

Betsy stripped the bed and re-dressed it. She kept glancing my way as she did. When she was done, she helped me back to the bed, plumping pillows to place at my back so I could sit upright. I felt as if I was in some kind of awful dream. High waves of emotions kept hitting me like boulders. Sadness, anger, then numbness ... numbness ... I treasured the numbness. I reached out as hard as I could, and I held on to that numbness. Then I thought of Arthur. I glanced down at my hand and thought I could feel his palm against mine. His phantom touch.

My gaze drifted to the door.

"He's not here," she said. I looked at her. "Everyone's out." Betsy handed me a tray that I hadn't noticed on a small coffee table near a grand fireplace. Tomato soup and buttered bread. "I was letting it cool a bit." She laid the tray on my lap. "Try and eat a little. You must be starving."

But my stomach rolled as my mind forced me back to my friends in the spa, to the video of my dad and Hugo. My body jerked and I gasped for breath. I couldn't breathe. I felt like I couldn't breathe!

The bed dipped, and Betsy met my eyes. "Breathe." Betsy took a deep breath, and I followed her action. My racing pulse started to slow and the vice that held my lungs in a grip began to loosen. I breathed in and out, mirroring Betsy until the panic subsided and left only rawness in my chest. "Eat, Cheska. You need your strength."

I stared down at the tomato soup, and all I saw was blood. The crimson blood of Freya, the blood of Arabella ... Dad and Hugo slumped on chairs. "I can't get them all out of my head," I whispered, my eyes glazing and my mind taking me back to that place again. But the deeper I fell into the memories, the more I felt something within me building. Walls. Walls that were stacking on each other at breakneck speed, trying to block the memories out, trying to prevent me from splintering apart.

"I know," Betsy said with understanding. "I've been in a similar position myself." She shrugged. "I mean being there when someone you loved was killed. Right in front of you."

"You have?" I asked, at the same time as feeling was as though I were being anaesthetised. Every breath in my lungs and every pump of blood through my heart took away the sting of the emotions that had been wrecking me, devouring me, slowly killing me.

Shock. It had to be shock. I didn't care. I just didn't want to feel anything right now.

"My step-mum," Betsy said, bringing my focus back to her. She got up and poured me another glass of water from the decanter on the bedside table. I drained the glass again. "Killed a while back by an Adley enemy."

"In front of you?"

"Right in front of me." Betsy barely flinched as she said that. She pushed back my hair, then gathered it in her hand and tied it back into a bun to keep it from my face. "It's all fresh for you. And this kind of event isn't the norm in your life. But, from someone who sees this kind of thing more often, it gets easier. Not what happened to them, but the loss. The ability to move on."

"It does?" I asked. But I was already starting to feel very little. As though the pain was being caged away into a deep part of me for safe-keeping. Secured with a padlock until I was ready to set it free.

But when I thought of Arthur's face, I felt it all. I felt every emotion I had ever experienced with him—love, and happiness and frustration and pain. But mostly need. A burning, consuming, all-encompassing need. Everything inside me was numb, safe behind high walls ... except him.

He was the gatekeeper protecting their door.

Betsy sat down on Arthur's chair and I held onto that need for Arthur. To his safe harbour.

"Eat, darling." I robotically dipped the spoon into the soup and ate. I barely tasted it. The whole time, I felt Betsy watching me. I wasn't sure if it was with suspicion or concern.

When I was finished, she took the tray away, leaving me alone for only a few minutes before she came back in. I heard her talking to someone in the hallway. My heart immediately kicked into a sprint at the thought of it being Arthur. I wanted to see him. I needed to see him. He made me feel safe. Strangely, he had always made me feel safe.

But when Betsy came back in, she was alone. She had a glass of wine in her hand. She sat on Arthur's seat and studied me. "So," she said, after a few strained minutes. "You're her." It wasn't a question, rather a statement of fact.

"Her?" I asked, swallowing the shiver of unease that stirred inside me at the strange comment.

Betsy's lip kicked up at the side. "The one who keeps a morsel of red in Arthur's constant shroud of darkness. At least that's how Vinnie puts it. As out-there as it is, I thought it was pretty fucking poetic."

"I ... I don't understand."

Betsy sipped her red wine. "I know you don't. Because he would never tell you. Because my stubborn, self-sacrificing cousin would never take what he needed or wanted. Instead, he'd allow himself to be consumed by evil, day by day, to spare you, until there's nothing left of him but a soulless ghost of who he once was, filled with only sin and murder and death."

"Arthur?" I asked, trying to decipher the riddles she was speaking in.

The door opened, cutting me off, and I held my breath. But a blond-haired woman came through, closely followed by a stunning Afro-Caribbean woman holding her hand. They were both dressed in black three-piece suits, both wearing high heels. Even through my disappointment, I couldn't help but think how striking they were together.

They stopped at the end of the bed. "Vera," Betsy said, indicating the blonde. "And her girlfriend, Ronnie."

"Hello," I said, wondering who they were and why they had come in to see me.

"Well, you're even prettier in person, and that's with your face being in this sorry state," Vera said.

Ronnie shrugged. "I get why he's so hung up on her," she said to Vera, placing her chin on Vera's shoulder to study me some more.

Vera smirked, then looked at Betsy. "So? What are we thinking?"

"I think by the way she keeps staring at the door and holding her breath every time someone steps through, it looks promising."

"What are you talking about?" An edge of anger crept through my heavy head-fog, igniting the numbness in my heart.

Betsy leaned forward on her chair. Vera crossed her arms over her chest. "Why were you getting married?" Betsy asked.

I tensed and stared at Betsy in shock. "What?" I whispered, refusing to picture Hugo on that chair, pleading for his life, only to get a bullet through his head for the pleasure.

"Why were you getting married?" Vera echoed, and I met her ice-blue eyes that were coldly fixed on mine. Ronnie's expression was blank, but her attention was on me too.

"B-because I loved him." The half-lie felt sinful as it slipped off my tongue.

Betsy sat back in her chair, seeming bored. "You loved him? Hugo Harrington?"

I glanced down at the ring on my finger and felt the energy drain from me, the pretence. I thought back to Hugo, on his knees, asking me to marry him a year ago, and the way my heart and stomach fell because he wasn't who I wanted. Of how only one face came to mind when he did.

Arthur. Always Arthur.

"It was expected of me." I slid the ring off. My finger felt light without it. I hated myself for thinking it, but it felt like a burden falling away. I held the four-carat diamond ring in my hand, the stone projecting spears of light from the lamp beside me onto the bed linen. "My father ... he wouldn't have allowed me to refuse."

I blinked back the tears and the residual ache I felt in my chest at the fact that my father hadn't ever really cared about my happiness. He'd needed the marriage to happen for Hugo to have rights to the business as my father's heir. So that society would see us as a worthy match. He'd wanted all his ducks in a neat little row.

"Did you love him?" Vera asked. I looked up at her, shocked at the direct question coming from someone I didn't know. "Hugo. Did you love him? And don't lie. I can't fucking stand liars."

It felt like a betrayal to the newly dead, but I eventually shook my head and whispered, "Not like that, no." I laughed without mirth. "But I think he loved me, if that matters." I sighed. "I'd been with him for years. And it's not like I had anyone else clamouring for my hand."

"You sure about that?" Ronnie asked.

I frowned. "More than."

"Do you love Arthur?" Betsy asked, just as directly as Vera. I whipped my head to her and felt the blood drain from my face. I shook my head, but unlike the truth that fought to escape when I was asked if I loved Hugo, the lie about not loving Arthur was less forthcoming.

A triumphant smile spread across Betsy's mouth. She turned back to Vera and Ronnie, and an unspoken conversation was shared between them. "He doesn't love me," I eventually said, breaking their odd silent communication. That got their attention. "What does it matter if I love him if it isn't reciprocated?" I straightened my shoulders and gathered all the fight I had left inside me. "I was his fuck buddy for five years, that's all. He would fuck me and leave me. He wouldn't let me into his life, tell me anything about it." I laughed, and even to me it sounded bitter. "I was the posh bit of pussy he shagged because he could. Love didn't even enter the equation for him."

"You're fucking blind," Vera said.

I glared at her. "How so?"

She shook her head, laughing to herself.

"I said how am I fucking blind?" I snapped, no longer caring if she was part of the firm and could shoot me where I lay. What the hell did I have left to lose?

"Oh, hello. There she bloody is." Vera looked at Ronnie, eyebrow raised. "What did Vinnie say? She had a thin line of darkness around her too? Looks like we've just tapped into it."

Betsy got up from the chair and sat on the bed bedside me. "Cheska Harlow-Wright. What my sister-in-arms here is trying to tell you is that Arthur, my dear cousin, is hook, line and sinker obsessed with you. And that you, the"—she made air quotes—"'posh bit of pussy' he shagged are the only one in Arthur's entire life who has managed to stir something inside him. The only person who has made his concrete heart crack enough to let in any kind of light."

My breath was held even though my heart pounded like a fist. I couldn't take in what Betsy was saying. She had to be lying ... but why would she lie? "Cheska, if you think my cousin doesn't love you— obsessively, possessively, and somewhat wickedly ..." She smirked. "Then you're not as smart as your many degrees from Oxford would have us believe."

"He left me," I argued, something like fight igniting inside of me, eradicating the numbness that had blanketed me for the past couple of days. "That night, after ..." I looked at the three women around me and realised that it was their fathers who would have died that night.

"When you lost your fathers. After that night, he left me. Coldly. Brutally. I never heard from him again. He tossed me aside like scraps."

Vera laughed again. The patronising sound grated on my nerves. "He *came* to you. In Oxford. We lost all our family's leaders, our fathers. *His* father went into a coma, our gaffer, the head of our firm. The shit hit the fucking fan for us all, and he came to you. The heir to the Adley throne. He left us all here shell-shocked and broken and travelled to Oxford to *you*. And you think you were just a fuck?" Vera leaned over the foot of the bedframe. "You might be a good shag, I can imagine that, doll, but no bird's cunt is so fucking good that a bloke like Arthur would drop all his responsibilities in the middle of a murderous shitshow just to get his end away."

I stared at her, not knowing what to say, my pulse racing so fast I thought it would bring on a heart attack. "But the way he left ..."

Betsy took the ring from my hand. She held it in the air. "He never said, and would never say to us—Arthur is a bloody fortress." She studied the diamond. "But I think it might have had a little something to do with this." My stomach plummeted. I remembered waking up to him holding my hand, eying the ring then tossing my hand back to the mattress like I disgusted him. No, not me. *That*. That bloody tarnished ring.

"It was the start of his ascension." Ronnie sat on the end of the bed and leaned against the bedframe, casual in my company, like we'd been friends for years. "His ascension to *Dark Lord of London*." She spoke that tabloid-given title with a tired roll of her eyes. "He came home that night changed. Whatever light he'd had left inside of him been stubbed the fuck out."

"You," Vera said, sitting opposite her girlfriend on the bed, the heel from her stiletto boot almost piercing the duvet. "That night he lost our dads, his dad, and ... *you*."

"You're not some posh bird he fucked for a few years, Cheska. You're the only one he ever let in, as little as that might have been. It was more of his soul than he gave to anyone else. You're his bloody saviour," Betsy said.

"From what?" I whispered, unable to process it all.

"From himself. From the darkness that's almost completely

devoured him," Ronnie said. "That will take him under until he's got nothing left inside him, no humanity, no fucking life."

"Everyone is terrified of Arthur, and that's why no one fucks with our firm. You can't beat a man who doesn't fear death," Vera said.

"And as much as that serves us well as a crime family, we love our cousin more than our place on the top of the fucked-up London underworld," Betsy said. "If he keeps living this way, he will die alone, never knowing love and constantly haunted by the ghosts of all the people who fell by his hand." Betsy sighed. "Just like his father." She sipped at her wine. "As much as I adored my Uncle Alfie, in reality, he died years ago. He died when my aunt and cousin burned in the house fire. And instead of loving Arthur harder, he moulded him into a man who could never be fucked with. Who would make the most formidable crime boss in London. He made his son impenetrable. Unfeeling. He made him fucking lethal."

"And a geezer who couldn't express his feelings. Uncle Alfie feared it would make Artie weak if he did." Vera reached across and held Ronnie's hand. "Love, Ches. Arthur was raised to think love was a fast track to ruin." She smirked, but it was laced with sadness. "The strong and formidable Arthur Adley, who kills without remorse, runs far, far away at the first sight of love. Ironic, no? I'd say it's the only thing in life that actually terrifies him."

"Then along comes you," Ronnie said. "Rich, posh, and poles apart from his way of life." She shrugged. "I'm sure it was easy to convince himself that you two would never last, would never really *start*."

She pointed at the ring. "And the one night he lets his walls down and admits he needs you by leaving us all behind to seek you out, he wakes up to *that*." I remembered him crying, feeling the tears on my stomach and his arms tight around my waist as he told me they'd all been taken away. Then I recalled his cold, dead eyes as he left my flat without ever looking back.

I'd seen what they were describing. I'd seen the crack he'd opened in his thick armour. For a few cherished hours, I'd seen the man underneath, the man kept hidden behind an iron cage. And instead of caressing him, I'd plunged my sword into the fracture and pierced the fragile body inside, watching as he bled out.

"He's keeping away from you," Betsy said. I could barely see her through my blurred vision. "He's put me in charge of you."

"He'll keep you safe, but he's going to keep you at arm's length," Vera said.

"I don't want him to," I said, feeling a new kind of purpose pushing through me. One with Arthur as the goal. I would erase the hurt the unwanted ring had caused. I would heal, not widen, the crack in his armour.

"Doesn't matter." Vera tipped her head to the side. "He's fucked up, you know?" She smiled, and I knew it wasn't in pity toward Arthur. It was with pride. "He kills. A lot. He's a fucking death-delivering master."

"I know." I thought back to the men in Marbella when we were eighteen. How he'd cut them down easily and made the fourth guy cut off his own dick.

"And it doesn't faze you?" Vera asked.

I tried to find hatred in my heart for what and who Arthur was. But I had always known. I had always known about his family, about what he had done. I'd witnessed it and still gone back for more. And I couldn't find it within me to hate something that had saved my life.

Twice.

He had now saved me twice.

The world was fucked up. Maybe it took being equally as disturbed to truly thrive. In this moment, with mostly numbness and bitterness running through my veins, it didn't bother me at all.

"Not like it should," I finally replied. The women all looked at each other. I saw something like relief, and maybe a hint of excitement, spark in their stares. It made me feel something. It made some cavernous part of me fill with something unknown. But mostly, I let the fact that they were saying Arthur loved me sink into my bones, eradicating the aches.

I couldn't believe it. A part of me wanted to question them, believe they were winding me up, teasing me somehow, trying to get me to flee Arthur's home. But I could tell by their open faces that they weren't. They adored Arthur; anyone could see that. But they were scared for him too. Scared that this life they all loved was swallowing him, drawing him down to a level of hell from which he could never return.

"It won't be easy," Betsy said. I wasn't sure if it was to me, to Vera and Ronnie, or to all of us. Her gaze was lost to the fire raging in the hearth. "He'll fight it. He'll test her. Push her to the limits to see what she can take." Betsy blinked, bringing herself back to the here and now. "He will challenge you if you try to show him your love. He'll resist, because it's all he knows how to do. He'll try to sabotage it. A future he was told he could never have, *warned not* to have."

"That's not a pass for him acting like a complete twat, of course," Ronnie said, lip curling into a smirk. "Don't let the arrogant fucker get away with anything that pisses you off. Don't allow him to treat you like shit." I found myself smiling at her. She winked. "Push him back. *Challenge* him back. Give him a taste of his own medicine."

I tried to imagine a world where Arthur could love me and I could love him freely. I hadn't ever let myself believe it outside of my deepest fantasies, so it was a difficult concept to grasp. But these women were telling me it was possible. That he wanted me as much as I wanted him. That it was there for the taking, if only I could wade through his darkness to find him.

The flicker of light that apparently still remained.

I was drowning in grief. Crushing waves of sadness were swallowing me whole, dragging me down to the depths. But the possibility of having Arthur—loving him and him loving me in return—was akin to having his hand delving into the choppy, rough sea and pulling my head above water.

I thought of my life now. The strange and unfamiliar path that now lay before me, the one now built from blood and the deaths of those I loved. Unease shuddered through me ... but not when I thought of Arthur walking beside me. Holding my hand.

With him in my grip, I was calm.

"I love him," I said again, stronger this time, with more conviction. "I have always loved him. No one else. Only him." I laughed, not caring that the cut on my lip burned as I did. I had harboured that confession for too many years, never confessing it to a soul. But I was confessing it now, as honestly as a Catholic pilgrim emptying their soul to their priest.

It seemed fitting that confession would be made in a converted church, and ironically about a man who was aptly likened to the devil himself.

"Good," Vera said, and I caught her fleeting smile. Maybe she wasn't as difficult as she made herself out to be.

"Now, on to other business." Ronnie pulled a piece of paper from her pocket and laid a picture before me. It took me a few minutes to refocus from the ember of hope that had sparked in my broken heart. The picture featured a mark of some kind, a brand on someone's skin. It was circular with a V-type shape inside. "Do you recognise it?"

"No," I said, frowning. "Should I?"

"It was on your attackers," Betsy said, then carefully looked to Ronnie.

Ronnie sat up and took off her jacket and waistcoat. She undid her tie and the top few buttons of her shirt and pulled her shirt aside. Her dark skin was smooth and beautifully rich in colour, apart from a small brand in the centre of her shoulder blade. I leaned in to look closer, and I stilled. It was the brand in the picture. The one the attackers wore.

"You used to work for them?" I said, feeling instant fear sink in deep.

Ronnie snapped her head around, and her dark eyes turned ice cold. "I didn't work for them, Ches. I was *taken* by them."

"What?"

The room was silent and thick with tension as Ronnie dressed, right down to her jacket. She sat back on the bed. "It's a story for another time, but I was kidnapped by them." Vera took Ronnie's hand. Ronnie squeezed her fingers tightly. Apart from that telling move, Ronnie was unreadable, appearing unshaken. "I was trafficked, Ches. I was whored out and made a slave." Bile rose in my throat. Ronnie took a deep breath. "The Adleys saved me. Brought me into their fold." She gestured to the picture of the unique brand. "I've been looking for these cunts ever since." She lifted her eyes to mine, promise in her gaze. "And when I find them, I'll murder them. Every last one of them."

"They're untraceable," Vera explained. "Rarely leave any sign of themselves behind. No one knows who they are. We're close to many crime families and organisations around London, shit, all over the UK. No one knows them."

"Your video was the first bit of evidence we've had on them in years," Betsy said. "We were hoping you could shed some light on them."

I shook my head. "I have no idea who they are." I paused when something came to mind. "My father. The men mentioned to me that my father and Hugo owed them money. That they hadn't paid them for some kind of loan." Another thought occurred to me. "Harlow Biscuits? Who's running that right now? Are people looking for me? The police?"

"The board has stepped in at your family's business. They have it covered for now. But you're officially a missing person." Vera smiled widely as she said, "We've sent the little piggies on a hunt to lead them far, far away from us. That buys us some time to work out exactly who we're dealing with."

"Arthur won't stop until he finds them. They've fucked with what's his. So they're all going to die. That's the law of his fucking land."

"His ..." I said, liking the way that sounded as it rolled off my tongue. I liked it far too much.

"Whether he admits it or not, you're his," Betsy said, pure mischief in her expression. "He's been sleeping on it, Ches. I'd say it's time to wake him the fuck up."

A thought quickly came to mind. "My father's computers. His work email. His phone. His home laptop. Maybe those can help you. Hugo's too. They had to communicate with someone over all this. There must be something somewhere that can give you a lead."

"Good thinking, darl." Ronnie pulled out her phone. "I'll get them brought to me."

As Ronnie typed on her phone, I watched her, wondering what she had been through. As I did, the reality of what had been going to happen to me sank in. "They were going to traffic me," I said out loud, a cold chill wrapping around me. "That was the payment they were talking about, wasn't it? They wouldn't kill me, because they were going to sell me? Recoup the money my father and fiancé racked up?"

"You would have been a high-price ticket too," Ronnie said, as if she were talking about general groceries. "I've seen enough auctions to know. They'll be so pissed off that you got away."

"Then they *will* want me back," I realised. If they could have sold me for a lot of money, that meant I was an asset they wouldn't stand losing.

A hand threaded through mine and immediately chased away an echo of the chill. "You're an Adley now. No one will get you," Betsy said, her touch exactly what I needed.

"An Adley," I repeated. Betsy had said it with such surety, such conviction, that it made me believe it. Made me crave it. Made me want to be worthy of it.

"Where's Arthur?" I asked.

Betsy smiled knowingly. "He's out on business for the next several days. But he should be back for the weekend. That'll give you plenty of time to rest and heal. The doctor said you should be feeling a lot better by then. Almost back to normal, I'd say."

"Saturday night," Vera said, her announcement confusing me. She got off the bed. "Let's see if our Chelsea princess can manage to convince the 'lord' that she can come with us on our little night out."

"Where?" I asked.

"You'll see," Ronnie said, clearly confident Arthur would cave and bring me to whatever they were referring to.

As the couple left the room, Vera called over her shoulder, "Let's just hope that you didn't lie when we asked if Arthur's line of work fazed you or not."

That could only mean one thing awaited us on Saturday. The one thing Arthur seemed to bring to London Town in abundance: death.

CHAPTER NINE

ARTHUR

I threw my coat on the rack and walked down the hallway. I cracked open the door to my old man's room. His nurse was changing his nutrient bags. "No change, sir," she said, acknowledging me, and I nodded. I glanced at my dad's face. Still pale. Still thin. Still in a motherfucking coma.

I shut the door behind me and headed to the guest room. I intended on walking past my own bedroom door. In fact, I'd promised myself I'd keep my bloody head down and just fucking ignore it. Instead, I stopped right in front of it and turned the knob. It was after two in the morning. It was pitch black outside and I was knackered. But not knackered enough to fight the fucking pull that yanked me inside that room.

I opened the door. The lights were off, but the light from the blazing fire was enough for me to see her. I tried to stay in the doorway, to see her from afar, but she turned in her sleep, rolling in my direction, and I found myself walking inside. I only made it six steps before I stood stock-still.

The bruises on her face were almost gone. The swelling on her lips had reduced to make them normal size, and the cuts on her body were barely there.

She looked like the Cheska I'd always known. My prim and proper Chelsea girl. The one I sank inside week after week. It was never enough. Never fucking enough.

I stared at the open door behind me. *Leave, you fucking prick,* I said silently to myself. But I didn't. The sadistic cunt that I was sat in the armchair and just fucking listened to her breathe. Watched her chest rise and fall. And tried not to imagine what would have happened to Cheska if the traffickers had got her. Where the fuck would she be now? Where the fuck would they have taken her?

My fists were clenched so tightly that my bones ached. There was nothing. Nothing that Ronnie's research had flagged up so far. Nothing that my acquaintances had heard. It was a motherfucking stealth job. No one knew jack shit.

And that was just pissing me the fuck off.

I was a man that needed answers. When it came to Cheska Harlow-Wright, I had none. She had always fucked with my mind. A fucking algebraic equation my tosser of a teacher expected me to work out. Bloody impossible.

Cheska moved, and the duvet slipped down her body. She was dressed in a purple silk nightdress. It made me think of the first time I fucked her in Marbella. She'd been wearing purple that night, looking like a motherfucking goddess as she'd climbed onto my yacht in the pitch black of night.

Thinking of her back then, and seeing her now, it took all my strength not to climb into bed beside her and fuck her like old times. But I forced myself to my feet. I wouldn't do this. I wouldn't get fucking caught up in this again.

But as I went to leave, I saw her hand. That bloody left hand. The crack in my chest that had never fucking closed started to ache, to fucking widen at the sight of that left ring finger without that bloody diamond wrapped around it. It was gone. That shackle to Hugo the shitstain was gone. I couldn't look away. I couldn't look away from that bare finger.

Leave. Right the fuck now, dickhead, I told myself and took my bastard head from the clouds. I was tired. I was just fucking tired. That's all this was.

I left the bedroom and showered off the past few days of making new contracts with dealers and chasing leads on who the fuck thought it would be a good idea to fuck with my docks. Nothing. Just like what we were finding on the cunts that tried to take Cheska.

A pile of sweet fuck all. And it was doing my nut in.

I wiped through the steam on the bathroom mirror and stared at my reflection. I had to keep my fucking head in the game. I would find the pricks who took Cheska, and then let her go. The bird had filled my head too many times over the past few days. Betsy was checking in too fucking much, giving me updates.

The porcelain of the sink creaked. When I looked down, my hands were clenched on the lip, almost cracking it in two. I moved my hands and ran them down my face. I slipped on my glasses and lay on the bed, staring at the ceiling. I couldn't let myself do this. I had my family to protect. A fuck-ton of people to keep from our doors.

Cheska was a distraction I couldn't afford.

"Who the fuck else is here?" Eric asked as we walked toward the abandoned warehouse just outside Essex. Eric stopped beside a Mercedes. "And what tasteless fucker would take a German car over a British one? Haven't they heard of Bentleys? Aston Martins? Unpatriotic twats."

"Old Sammy said he had one other group he was considering selling the dock to," Charlie said, keeping by my side. "Arthur here said he respected the old geezer too much to strong-arm him into giving it to us." Charlie smiled and nudged me. "Of course, it's fucking game on if Old Sam goes with the other buyer. They'll be wishing they never met us."

A steroid-bloated bloke from Old Sammy's syndicate opened the door to the warehouse. The meeting table was directly in front of us. Old Sammy was sat at the head of the table, and to his left was—

"The fucking Lawsons. Of course it is," Freddie hissed from beside me. Ollie fucking Lawson stood from the table, his right-hand twat, Nick, following his gaffer's lead.

Ollie was all smiles, his veneered teeth offending my eyes. "Here they are, King Arthur and the Knights of the Round Table."

"I'd better be Lancelot in this scenario," Eric said, flanking Freddie. "He was the good-looking fella, right?"

"And what does that make you?" Charlie said to Ollie. "The plebeians beneath us?" Charlie fixed his cufflink, and I saw Ollie's jaw clench. The fucker hated us as much as we hated him.

Almost.

We were oil and water. Our businesses were night and day. We didn't mix.

"Sit, sit," Old Sammy said, gesturing to the chairs on the free side of the table. I pulled out my seat beside Sammy and sat down. That put me directly opposite Lawson.

He glared at me, and it took all I had not to pull out my revolver and pierce a hole in his forehead. But as my father taught me, I didn't react. I didn't give fuck all away. Stayed neutral. He wasn't even worth the wasted bullet.

"What's going on, Sammy?" Charlie asked. "You going legit on us?" Charlie turned to Ollie. "Or are you lot going rogue and selling your soul to the dark side?"

"My business is legit," Ollie said. "In fact, it's doing so well, I need more docks to keep up with demand. Some of us don't need to turn to crime to be successful."

I sparked up a cig and blew the smoke across the table, right in Ollie's face. The prick's nostrils flared. "What do you want for it, Sammy?" I asked. I wanted to get this over and fucking done with. "Cut the bloody theatrics and make your choice—this pathetic cunt or us."

"More drugs to supply to the masses?" Ollie asked, smirking.

A gun fired. Old Sammy's men came crawling from their posts, their own weapons drawn. I flicked my eyes down the table toward

Vinnie, who had fired a shot into the air. He laughed out loud. "Just checking it was stocked with bullets." Vinnie aimed the gun right at Lawson's head. Ollie froze as Vinnie cocked his head, closing one eye as he aimed. Ollie jumped out of his fucking skin when Vinnie slammed his hand on the table and screamed, "BANG!"

Vinnie laughed louder, his sick, taunting laugh directed right at a flinching Ollie. The laugh most of Vin's victims heard right before he tore out their throats. "A-tishoo, a-tishoo," he sang, then pointed his finger at Ollie and Nick, fucking death in his gaze. "They all fall down."

"You're all fucking tapped," Ollie snarled, tapping his head. "Fucked in the head."

"A correct assessment," Freddie said, the look in his eyes just fucking daring Ollie to strike.

Ollie reached into his pocket. I watched him like a hawk. But the pussy wouldn't dare attack us; it wasn't who he was. He just pulled out a piece of paper and placed it on the table before Sammy. "This is what we're prepared to give you. Let me know what you decide."

Ollie flicked his head at Nick, and the two of them walked out of the meeting. When the door was shut, Sammy said, "I was never giving it to that sniffling prick. I owed his father a favour. I always pay my debts. That was the last one—just letting that posh wanker in here for this meeting was payment enough to his old man. Debt done."

"His dad died last year," Eric said.

"Call me old-fashioned, but an outstanding debt is still an outstanding debt." Sammy shook his head, laughing and sucking on his pipe. "The dock's yours." He winked at me. "It's always been for the EastEnders. If you're not born-and-bred cockney, you're not getting shit from me."

I stood and shook Sammy's hand. "Essex, Sammy. Really?"

He shrugged. "The old ball and chain wanted out of the city. Couldn't be arsed to fight her on it. I'm old and don't have the fucking energy anymore."

"The money'll be dropped off tonight," Eric said, shaking Sammy's hand too.

As we turned to leave, Sammy said, "Heavy is the head that wears the crown, Arthur." I stopped and turned to one of my old man's closest friends. He was sat back in his seat, pipe in his mouth. He was staring right at me.

"Luckily, I have a fucking strong neck."

Sammy didn't react, but then he nodded, getting the message to leave it. If anyone else had said that it wouldn't have been without consequence. But this was Old Sammy. He was a fucking East End institution. He was family.

"Plus, haven't you heard?" Eric wrapped his arm around my neck. "The king here has his fucking Round Table to keep him in check. Just ask Lawson."

"That he does," Sammy said and nodded at his man to open the doors. We left, and I climbed in the first car. Charlie got in too. The rest of the boys took their seats in the car behind us.

When we pulled out, en route back to Bethnal Green, Charlie said, "I'm getting people on Lawson. That fucker rubs me the wrong way."

I lit up my cig and took a deep inhale. "He's a fucking pretender. A rich tosser playing with Daddy's money." I took another drag. "The wanker wouldn't know what to do if he really wanted to play outside of the rules and stepped into the underworld. He'd be fucking ripped apart the second he made it through the gates."

"Still, the way he stared at you," Charlie said, looking out of the window, watching the trees blur into one long dark line. "I'm putting men on him. I want to know if he even shits the wrong way. That fucker's not sitting well with me."

I remembered how, in Marbella, he was all over Cheska like a fucking rash. The guy was a bloody creep. But let Charlie tail him. If that fucker stepped even an inch out of line, I wanted know. I rolled down my window and flicked my finished cig onto the road. Cold wind filled the car, and I let it wash over my face.

"You got everything sorted for tomorrow night?" I asked Charlie.

"Done." My cousin smiled. "Should be a good one."

I nodded my head. I couldn't fucking wait. I had pent-up anger I needed to unleash.

And unleash it I fucking would.

———

I sat beside the fire in my old man's old study. There were no windows in the smallish room. Floor-to-ceiling bookshelves covered all four walls. Two library ladders leaned against them on either side of the room. The old desk took up the north side, and two wingback armchairs sat before the large fireplace. A small table sat between the chairs. And on top was my grandfather's old chessboard.

I sat in one of the armchairs. I'd been here for hours. I knew it was dark outside. But I had no fucking idea what time it was. Two in the morning, maybe? I didn't fucking care. I was nocturnal by nature. Late nights were nothing new.

A large gin sat in front of me. Only the lights from the fire and a standing lamp filled the room. This was my old man's favourite room. A place where he could shut out the world and the pressures of leading the family for a fucking minute.

It was my favourite room for that reason too.

I sipped my gin and moved a pawn on the chessboard. I stared at the pieces. My entire fucking life was just one big chess game between me and God.

I wasn't sure who the fuck was winning.

The door slowly opened. I was about to tell whoever it was to fuck off and give me a few fucking hours of peace, but when I saw familiar dark hair and green-brown eyes appear in the doorway, I didn't open my bloody mouth.

Cheska's gaze swept around the room. A flicker of a smile kicked up her lips as she drank in the mass of books. While she was busy observing the study, I was busy looking at her. Her bruises were practically gone, just one place on her cheek where a slight blue tone was apparent on her olive skin.

She wore skinny jeans and a short white t-shirt. There wasn't a scrap of makeup on her face, and she still looked like a fucking model. As if she'd heard that compliment, she turned back to me and squared her shoulders.

"So, this is where you've been hiding?" Her posh fucking Chelsea accent washed over me. Normally I couldn't stand that Queen's English bollocks, but it was perfect coming from her. I lit a cig and just watched her, wondering what she might do, why she was even here. I should have sent her the fuck away, back to my bedroom and out of my sight.

But my mouth chose to stay shut.

She stepped further inside, glancing over her shoulder at me as she turned and closed the door. As it clicked shut, she leaned against the old wood. She met my eyes fucking head-on. Then her gaze scanned down me.

"Arthur Adley without his suit jacket, waistcoat and tie," she said, smiling. "A rare sight." I'd thrown them off the minute I'd got home from Old Sammy's warehouse. I was done with business for tonight. I'd opened a few buttons on my shirt and sat the fuck down in here to drink and smoke and not fucking think.

Trouble found me anyway.

Trouble in the form of a rich bird with long legs and the sweetest fucking cunt I'd ever tasted.

"Impressive collection," Cheska said, walking along the book-shelves. Her hand ran along the spines of the hundreds of old hard-backs. She was edging closer to me, using the books as an excuse to draw in. She stopped at my old man's silver liquor trolley. "May I?" She held up a crystal gin glass. I nodded, taking another long drag of my cig. Cheska poured herself a gin and tonic and moved past me, stop-ping at the free armchair opposite me.

I wasn't fucking inviting her to sit down. I wanted to see if she'd scurry away from my lack of manners or sit the fuck down regardless. Cheska looked me square in the eyes and lowered herself to the seat. My cheek twitched at the challenge in her eyes. Her chin tilted up high, and I wondered if this was what that fucking fancy private school she'd attended taught her.

"You haven't been to see me," she said straight, and took a sip of her gin. She clearly wanted me to see her as a ball-buster who didn't give one shit about my permission to be in here. But the slight tremor in her proper voice gave away her nerves.

"Been busy." I lowered my gin to the table and pulled off my glasses. I cleaned the lenses on my shirt, then slipped them back on my face.

"Busy ..." She nodded. "I'm feeling better now, thanks for asking."

She lifted her legs up to the chair, curling her body over as she leaned closer to the fire. The reflection of the orange and red flames danced on her cheeks, putting fire in her eyes as she glared at me. She clutched her gin in her hands, watching me over the crystal glass's rim.

"What kind of business did you have?" she asked when I said sweet fuck all in response to her snipe.

"Family business," I replied. She nodded, but I saw the flash of rejection in her expression. She inhaled deeply. Her tits pressed against her t-shirt, and it took everything I had to keep my arse on the seat and not overturn the fucking chessboard between us and fuck her on the floor.

Cheska had no fucking idea what I was imagining, how I wanted her pinned against the books she'd just admired as I slammed into her from behind. She gestured toward the chessboard. "You're playing by yourself?"

I finished my cig and flicked it into the fire. "You play?" I cursed my fucking tongue for asking her the question. I'd vowed to keep Chelsea Girl at a distance. We'd find the fuckers who'd hunted her, and she'd run back off to her perfect little life, far away from the dark lord that she'd fucked for a while. I knew how this story played out. Posh and peasant didn't mix.

"God, no." She laughed. The addictive sound filled the room. There were no windows for that laugh to escape through. And I knew that sound would haunt me every time I stepped into this fucking study from now on. "I wouldn't even know where to start." She leaned forward, and the neck of her top showed me her braless tits underneath. The tits that I'd had in my mouth hundreds of times. The nipples that I'd rolled on my tongue and bitten down on to make her scream.

She glanced up at me through her long lashes. She fucking knew what she was doing. But I showed fuck-all reaction. Let her try to pull me in like a bloody siren. I wanted to see how far the posh little princess was willing to go to try and bring me to heel.

She pointed at one of the pieces. "What is this one?"

"A pawn."

Cheska nodded, taking it in. "A lower-valued piece?"

"A soldier," I said. "Not as much power as the others, but it's needed nonetheless."

"Like your soldiers?" she asked. "For your firm?" Clearly Chelsea Girl had been doing her research. No doubt the information came from Betsy. I knew my cousin had taken a shine to Cheska. And I saw the planning and cunning in Betsy's eyes whenever she mentioned Cheska to me. I didn't know what my cousin was up to. But whatever it was wouldn't fucking work.

"Like my soldiers," I confirmed.

Cheska nodded, then moved to the rook. She pointed at the castle piece. "Can only move laterally or forwards and backwards," I explained. She pointed to the horse. I talked her through the pieces until two remained.

"So," she said, "these must be the king and queen. I don't know a lot about chess, but I know that much."

"They're the king and queen."

Cheska sat back in her chair and studied the board. "So all of these ..." She motioned to the pieces. "The entire point of the game is to protect the king?" I nodded my head. "If the king falls, it's check-mate?" I nodded again.

"And let me guess," she said, with a good amount of bite in her voice. "The king has the most power?"

"On the contrary," I said and finished off my gin. I placed down my glass. "That honour belongs to the queen."

Cheska's mouth opened, but no words came out. I picked up the king and studied the ornate ebony piece. The crowned top wearing the cross. "The king is one of the weakest pieces. Needs all the others to protect him, as his skills are limited." I fixed my gaze on Cheska. "He especially needs the queen." I gritted my teeth but let myself say, "She's his most important piece. His protector. His strength."

"She is?" Cheska said, her voice dropping. A blush coated her cheeks and she licked her lips. "And without her?"

"The king is easily captured. Checkmate. Game over."

Cheska nodded. She glanced at the books surrounding us, but I knew she wasn't looking at their titles or covers. She turned back to the chessboard, then picked up her queen. It was ivory, proudly wearing the crown.

Cheska finished off her gin, lowered her glass to the table, then boldly met my eyes. "Then I would say it's in the king's best interests to stop pushing her away."

I let her words sink in. Then I let the torch she'd just brought to my flint ignite. Cheska never broke her gaze from me. She was pushing me. Challenging me. Trying to fuck with me.

This was new.

I smiled. Wide. Her eyes grew round. I leaned forward, resting my elbows on my legs. "The king doesn't take well to mind games," I said and watched Cheska's chest rise and fall harder. "He doesn't waste his time on queens who have fuck-all place in his world." I dropped my ebony king right beside her ivory queen. One light. One dark. Opposing sides. "Queens who pretend they crave the darkness, but in truth want a noble knight on a white horse that will whisk her away to a castle like some fucking fairy tale."

I leaned further over the board. Cheska stayed where she was, her lack of submission making my dick twitch in my trousers. I could smell the shower gel she'd been using—almond or some shit. Something sweet. Something that made me want to lick every inch of her skin.

"The king that the queen is intent on provoking *is* that darkness." Cheska's cheeks burned red, her olive complexion unable to disguise her fucking raw need. "He doesn't live in an ivory castle. He lives amongst the monsters in the haunted forest. There's no daylight in his world, only night. Perpetual fucking night. No moon and no stars in the sky, the landscape nothing but lifeless trees with broken branches and dead rose bushes laced with dagger-like thorns."

I studied Cheska's face, fucking myself up by trying to imagine her in my world. Trying to picture her by my side—a fallen spring queen holding my bloodstained hand. I pushed it from my mind.

It wasn't real. Couldn't ever be fucking real.

"And all around his kingdom were the worst horrors every level of hell could conjure up. Demons and beasts all gunning for the king's evil throne, vultures circling, readying to steal his crown. His throne built on the bones of his enemies, by the victims he had torn apart with his bare, clawed hands." I leaned in closer still. So close that I felt Cheska's breath drift over my face. "The victims he enjoyed killing, enjoyed bringing down, stealing their last breath as he watched them fight for air."

Cheska drew in a ragged breath. "Yet the queen still wants him," she said, and the crack she had smashed into my concrete chest years ago started to throb. I held her stare. Daring her to fucking look away. Telling her silently to run. To fucking jump from the chair and run while she still could.

"The queen knows who and what the dark king is, and she still wants to stand by his side." She dropped her eyes. I inhaled a breath, knowing she would eventually fail my challenge. But her eyes snapped back to mine, swirling with fucking fire. "She has *always* wanted to stand by his side. Even when she didn't know what it meant to be with him, what it entails. When she didn't know it all."

"She doesn't fucking know it all," I snapped, my voice dripping with poison.

I rose from my chair and stepped around the table to hers. I kicked the table holding the chessboard, the pieces clattering to the wooden floor behind me. I caged Cheska in, my hands on the arms of her chair.

"The queen knows shit," I said. "She knows only what she's let herself hear. She pretends she knows what the king has to do to keep hold of his kingdom." I paused and smiled. "What he *likes* to do." I leaned even closer, so close that my nose ran over the tip of hers. "The queen has no fucking idea what she's asking for. She's just a naïve little princess playing at wearing a big girl's crown."

Cheska's expression darkened and, taking me by surprise, she lifted her hand and gripped my jaw. I wasn't easily surprised. And I saw red. I fucking saw red. But instead of wanting rip off her head for daring to touch me, I had to fight back the need to slam her against the wall and fucking destroy her pussy. Fuck her until she screamed and didn't try to fuck with me again.

"This queen is not playing dress-up," she hissed. "She's waiting for the king to stop talking in riddles and fucking expose who he truly is." She smiled, and the cocky sight boiled my piss. Her nails sank into the skin of my jaw, and my cock filled with blood. "She's waiting for the monster she has been warned against to come out to play, not the handsome façade he hides behind."

Cheska brought my face closer to hers, grazing her lips against mine and speaking against my mouth. "She's waiting, has *been* waiting, for the king to show his true colours. Then he'd realise she's not waiting for the valiant knight on his white horse to carry her away to her happily-ever-after. Rather she's waiting for the fucking dragon to appear, to burn any suitor who gets in his way, and claim the queen once and for all. She wants the dragon, Your *Majesty*," she said mockingly. "She wants the fire. She wants the thorns and the razor-sharp branches. She wants the eternal fucking darkness. She wants to sit beside the king on his treasured throne of bones."

Cheska was breathing hard, as if adrenaline was pumping her blood like rapids through her body. I grabbed her wrist and squeezed until her fingers fell from my face. I could tell by the sting those nails left behind that she'd broken the skin and drawn blood. My heart was thundering in my chest, and my blood was lava, fucking scalding and incinerating the walls of my veins.

"You want darkness?" I said to her, pushing her back with my wide chest until she was pinned against the back of the chair, trapped. "Then you'll get darkness. You want the fucking dragon, the fire and blood? Then you'll get the motherfucking dragon. You want the bones, the flesh and the death ... ?" I brushed past her cheek and down her neck, then scraped my teeth against her throat. "Then you'll get fucking death," I said against her scorching skin.

I pulled back, glaring down at Cheska as she lay back against the back of the chair, gripping the arms and looking up at me like I was every inch the dark lord the pathetic bloody papers claimed me to be. "Tomorrow night, you can come with us, and we'll see if you still want all the sadism and depravity you claim your pussy gets soaking wet for."

Her eyes narrowed at my crassness, but as I walked to the door, needing to fucking get away from Cheska and all the fucked-up things my evil soul wanted to hear, she said, "I want the dark lord in the obsidian chariot, black horses carrying us away into hell. Not the white knight. I've already had him, let myself be rescued by him. And he proved worthless."

Cheska stood, swiped a packet of cigs off the fireplace and sparked one up. "I want the king of my dark-hearted nightmares." Cheska looked down, and in her hand were the ivory queen and ebony king. Cheska took another drag of the cig, then stabbed the lit, ashy end into the heart of the ivory queen, a black mark staining the white. I met the challenge in Cheska's eyes with my own, then threw open the door and went to the spare room I'd been staying in while she slept in my bed.

Tomorrow night. Tomorrow night she'd see the true fucking dark king she said she wanted to drag her to hell. Then we'd see if her conviction was as good as her talk.

We'd see if she really wanted to be the queen to stand at my side. Through blood and torture.

Through darkness and hell.

CHAPTER TEN

ARTHUR

I stood at the bar waiting for Betsy and Cheska.

"You sure this is a good idea, mate?" Freddie said beside me.

"She wants to be in this world, then this is her test," Vera answered for me.

"He'll hold back." Charlie smiled cockily at me.

"I won't," I said, eyes pinned on the fucking door. "She wants to see all this shit, how we live. Then she'll see it all. No fucking holds barred."

"Should we prepare a limo to take her ladyship away after she sees the lair?" Eric said. "I can have it on standby at the back door, sick bags at the ready."

"Cheska will be okay," Vinnie said, eyes fucking blown, readying for tonight. Out of all my men, he craved these nights the most. Almost as much as I did. "I've seen it." Vinnie looked up and nodded at the ceiling like the fucking nutter he was. "There's more black around her now. Still some red, but much more black. Everyone is dead. All her family are dead. That always brings more black. And it never goes away."

Something fucking pulled in my gut at that. I stood off the bar, righting my cufflinks, just as the door to the living room opened and Betsy and Cheska stepped inside. I fucking froze on seeing Chelsea Girl. She was dressed in all black. Skinny black leather trousers clung to her fucking legs like a second skin. Legs that seemed to go on for fucking ever. She wore a skintight black top tucked into the high-waisted trousers. Her hair was down and she was wearing makeup. I hadn't seen her wear makeup since she'd collapsed on my nightclub floor. Her sky-high stilettos left her only a few inches shorter than me. They'd make it easier for me to turn her around and sink into her cunt, if she managed to last the night.

Ronnie and Vera got to their feet. The room was quiet. Betsy threw me a smug look and went to stand beside her brother, linking her arm through his.

"Let's go," I said, moving to leave the room.

"One thing first," Ronnie said, and I stopped dead. She turned to Cheska, who was watching her with a suspicious stare. Ronnie's face was steel as she walked toward Cheska and pushed her against the wall. Cheska's back hit the wall with a thud. I gritted my teeth, ready to wrench Ronnie the fuck out the way. I made to move, but Vera shot me a glare. She shook her head, telling me to leave it. I told my cousin with my fucking cold expression that if anything happened to Cheska right now, they'd be sorry.

"You think you're ready for tonight?" Ronnie said. Cheska nodded, chin held high like it had been in the study last night. Never knew a posh bird could have so much fucking fight.

Ronnie smirked, then took hold of Cheska's face and pinned her head back against the wall. With her free hand, Ronnie reached into her pocket and pulled something out. I stepped forward, suspecting it was a blade. But she held the silver metal item up and smiled. "Then you better wear a fucking killer red to go with those heels," she said and twisted the tube in her hand until red lipstick came out.

I rolled my fucking eyes at her theatrics and pushed past them all. I flicked my eyes to Cheska as I passed, only to see her smiling at

Ronnie as she painted her lips scarlet red. Betsy laughed, and my boys followed behind me. We got into cars, and in my peripheral I saw Cheska get into the one at the back with Betsy, Vera and Ronnie.

There would be no attempt to hide her identity at the place we were going. The people there wouldn't give a fuck who she was anyway. And they knew better than to fuck with me. They might be my associates in business, but I had dirt for fucking days on all of them. The place we were going to was my motherfucking domain. No one would dare fuck with any of us Adleys there. And if they did, then it was the perfect place for retribution.

"Ready, old boy?" Charlie asked. I knew he wasn't referring to tonight by the cocky look on his face. It was about Cheska. But I wasn't talking about her right now. She'd see one of our enterprises tonight and fucking leave. Out of my life and back to her world. Then I'd be back to bloody breathing right. Because I wasn't sure I'd taken a full fucking breath since she'd burst back into my life.

The cars stopped at the old warehouse in Mile End. I flicked the collar of my coat up and lit a cig, the freezing cold wrapping around me, then led the way toward the warehouse. To normal people, it was just that— a warehouse, filled with car parts and other mechanical shite. To us and those in my world, it was a gateway to fucking sin.

I threw open the door, then descended the staircase. Adley soldiers opened the steel doors that led to the dungeon.

"Alright, guv," they said as they opened the doors. "Full house tonight." The minute the soundproof doors were open, the sound of fists hitting flesh came barrelling into the East End night. I glanced over my shoulder to see Cheska walking with Betsy, Ronnie and Vera. I flicked my chin at Eric. He nodded back at me, getting my order to keep an eye on her and the women.

Sweat and blood filled the air as we stepped into the warehouse's lair. This was my real fucking club, not the Sparrow Room full of pretentious pricks. This was the club that made me the real money. "Arthur," men greeted as I passed by them. The room was crowded with men and women. All from the crime syndicates that didn't fuck with us. Associates. Acquaintances, and ones I hadn't had an excuse to kill just yet.

Pit after sunken pit was filled with fighters. Bare-knuckle, of course, no fucking pussies in the rings. The seats around the pits swelled with spectators, Caesars looking down on their gladiators.

I led my family through the gathered spectators, as Adley soldiers ran the pits and bets and kept everyone in check. We walked to the back of the warehouse until the real fucking pits came into view. The headliners. The big-money tickets. The ones where the only way out was to be carried out in a fucking coffin.

My men had made sure things were in order and our seats were ready. They were prime viewing, ensuring everyone could see us. See who ran this fucking castle. Who was the real emperor, ruling over them all.

I tossed my coat off and lit a cig, looking down into the main pit to see two men ripping each other apart. One had a smashed jaw and couldn't see from one eye, but the wanker wasn't giving up.

He was close to the coffin.

Betsy and Cheska sat down behind me, a few seats to my right. I looked over at Chelsea Girl. Her eyes were fucking wide as she drank in the room, but she hadn't run yet. As if feeling me watching her, she looked over at me and straightened her shoulders. She then focused on the pit, just as the heavily beaten fighter's neck snapped and he dropped to the floor. The ref gave the signal that it was over and held up the arm of the victor. Cheska swallowed, but other than that made no sign that what she was witnessing was too much.

The wannabe dark queen sucking it up to play in the vicious court.

"Arthur, you fucking twat," a familiar voice said. I turned, taking a drag of my cig, only to see Royal, the president of the Hades Hangmen MC, London chapter. "Long time no see."

"Royal." I looked behind him to see his men watching the fights. My eyes narrowed on the bikers as I noticed someone pretty fucking vital to us was missing. Royal shook my hand and pulled back.

"Where fuck is Rudge?" I asked, not seeing the mouthy tosser anywhere.

"Prick's fucking left us for Texas," Royal said, pushing back his shoulder-length brown hair. He was dressed—as always—in jeans, shit-kicker boots, white t-shirt and his Hangmen cut. The Hangmen were among our closest associates. And Royal was one of the people I knew best outside my family. One of the only people I could tolerate who didn't represent the Adley name. Our history was long, and the fucker currently owed me a favour for bringing back one of the club's kidnapped bitches.

"Texas?" I asked. "What the fuck is in Texas?"

"The Hangmen mother chapter," Royal said, shaking his head. "Arsehole went over there to do a bare-knuckle circuit and never came back. The bloody brown-nose is so far up the mother chapter's president's arse he's practically cleaning his motherfucking teeth."

"He's going to leave us a fighter down," I said.

"No, he ain't." Royal nudged his chin toward his vice president, Jag.

Jag came over and shook my hand. A bloke about my age, maybe younger, came out from behind him. Lithe, tattooed head to toe, with dark eyes that promised fucking death. "Rudge's cousin, Chrome."

"Chrome?" Charlie asked from beside me, shaking hands with the Hangmen and sizing up the new fighter.

"As in Chromium, one of the hardest fucking metals in the world," Jag said. "You thought Rudge was the best bare-knuckle fighter you've ever seen? Wait until you see this little fucker. Makes me glad his cousin has pissed off to Austin. Now we've got an upgrade."

A ref called the next fight, and Royal tapped me on the arm. "That's us." The Hangmen went back to their seats, and Chrome jumped down into the pit. I sat down and watched with vested interest as Chrome killed his opponent in thirty seconds flat, and twenty of those fuckers were just him toying with his prey.

"All I see are pound signs when I look at that fella," Freddie said. "No idea why the fuck anyone would choose Texas over London, but I'm glad Rudge did. I was one stupid joke away from knocking out his teeth myself."

The ref signalled the next fight. Eric got up from his seat and stripped down to his trousers. Cheska's eyes widened and she whispered something to Betsy. Before Betsy could reply, Eric walked up to my cousin.

"Kiss for good luck?" Eric said to Betsy.

Betsy leaned in, and Eric's eyes widened. She stopped before his lips. "Eat shit and die, Mason." She slapped his cheek, the sound loud enough for the spectators to hear.

"Cold-hearted bitch," Eric said, smiling. He pointed at her. "I'm fucking you after I win this." Betsy rolled her eyes, and Eric climbed down to the pit. His sadistically smiling clown tattoos covered every inch of his skin. He was against the Chechen's new fighter. Ten minutes later, Eric was fucking supercharged, with blood on his hands and in his mouth, a dead Chechen eating the sand at his feet.

Vinnie jumped up next. He smiled and leaned down to the hallucination of my sister, the nearby Italians watching him like he was fucking insane. He was. And that's why he'd beat anyone we put in front of him. I never bet against him.

The minute he was in the pit, Vinnie became the animal we knew him to be. The fucker who lived for blood and guts embraced the urge to kill. The only leash he had these days was the ghost of my sister. If she ever left him, there'd be more than me to fucking worry about in London Town.

Vinnie ripped his Manchurian opponent apart, his knives hacking his opponent to smithereens long after he was dead. By the time Vinnie was done, the Manc fighter was just a mangled heap of shredded flesh and bones. Vinnie threw his head back and screamed when the ref finally called the fight.

Vinnie jumped out of the pit, eyes black from adrenaline. "Where now?" he said to me. I tipped my chin at the ref in the next pit. He called Vinnie over, and Vinnie went off to fight again.

I checked on Cheska, who was still as a fucking statue in her seat. My chest pulled. Chelsea Girl wasn't handling the lair well. She caught my eye. Then, with her gaze still locked on mine, she pulled a wad of cash from her bra and handed it to the dealer stood beside us.

"All of it," she said, making sure I heard her fancy fucking voice give the command. "On the Irish." The dealer gave her a betting slip, and Betsy smirked my way. Cheska looked at me again, a fucking challenge in her eyes. I didn't know where this bird had been hiding all these years, but the princess was shaking off her pink dress and owning those fucking leather trousers she'd squeezed her perfect arse into.

Seamus, the head of the Irish mob, came over. Vano, the head of the Romani joined us. These fuckers and the Hangmen were as close I let anyone get to me and my family.

The fights drew on until the middle of the night. When the final ones had been won, my soldiers escorted the last of the fighters and the gamblers out of the warehouse. The only people remaining were us, the Hangmen, the Irish, and Vano's family.

"What's happening?" I heard Cheska ask someone.

Getting up from my seat, I looked over at Chelsea Girl. I shed my jacket and shirt, leaving my torso bare. Her eyes fixed on my chest, then slipped up to my eyes. "We caught some beasts trying to get into my kingdom," I said, knowing only she would get the reference. "And now the king has to rip them apart." Cheska's eyes widened, and I jumped down into the pit.

One of my men pulled out a chain taken from one of our docks. A heavy one, one that helped anchor our haulage boats. The chain fell at my feet, and a bloke was dragged into the pit, a black hessian bag over his head. One of my soldiers kicked away his legs and tossed him to the ground. The prick fell, and then pulled off the bag. He snapped his head back and forth, trying to figure out where he was. Then his eyes latched on to me, and the blood drained from his face.

"Mr Adley." He scurried backwards on his arse like the fucking rat he was. I lit a cig and exhaled the smoke into the air.

"You told the Yakuza where one of my ships would be coming from." The twat on the ground started shaking his head, but one look at his trembling bottom lip told me he was guilty. That and the fucking voice recording of his phone call with Hiro, the leader of the Yakuza, that Ronnie had secured. "And they sank the ship, and all of the gear that was being smuggled inside it and took the deal instead."

I nodded at Ronnie, and she came to the lip of the pit. She pulled out her mobile and played the scumbag's voice for all my witnesses to hear.

"Arthur," the twat said, then smacked his own head like a bloody psycho. "I fucked up. I really fucked up. Please ..." I circled him, smelling the fucking stench of lies and fear slipping off his sweat-laden skin.

I held out my arms. "You were an Adley. Protected by our name." I pointed at his ugly fucking mug. "You should have worn our name with pride. Instead you shat on it. You fucking pissed on everything we are when you sold us out to Hiro and his men." The wanker shook his head, but I didn't want to hear fuck-all else from his mouth. If I had to hear anymore, I'd sew the fucker shut. The fire in my blood was already boiling, the evil inside me salivating for the kill, whispering to me to begin.

I looked at Seamus, Royal, Vano and their men, then finally at Cheska, who was sitting on the edge of her seat. I put my cig between my fingers, spread my arms wide, and said, "This is the Adley Court!" Charlie nodded in approval; he lived for this shit as much as I did. Vinnie bounced on his fucking seat, laughing, waiting for the blood to spill. Freddie watched with a quiet smirk on his face, and Eric clapped his hands in the air. "Where traitors are tried. And they fight for their lives."

I turned and addressed the shitstain on the already blood-drenched sand. "Dennis Short," I said loudly, my voice carrying around the pit and the empty warehouse. "Welcome to the Adley Court. You have been charged with being a traitor." The fucker flinched. "An Adley's word is his bond. A bond you have broken. And I am here to collect."

I stopped right in front of the sniffling wanker and bent down. I pushed the end of my cig against his forehead and watched the fucker cry out. Straightening, I let the anger frothing inside me burst free.

"Mr Adley, please," Dennis the rat begged from his knees.

"Choose your weapon," I said, gesturing to the table filled with weapons.

Dennis whipped his head in that direction. "Arthur, please ..."

"One more fucking word and I'll cut off your tongue," I warned, and at least the fucker was switched on enough to shut his fat trap. "Choose a fucking weapon, then face me." Dennis shook his head. "You turned against us. Now you'll fucking dance with the devil." I pointed at my chest. "Meet the fucking devil." I picked up the chain at my feet. The metal was heavy in my hand, and my dick got hard at the ache in my muscles, at the fact that blood was about to be spilled at my feet.

Dennis ran to the table and picked up a long metal pole. I sparked up another cig, letting the nicotine keep me from just killing this prick outright. He needed to pay. The men around me needed to see that when it came to London, it was *my* fucking town. Everyone else was just a tenant. The minute anyone stepped out of line, they'd be evicted.

The cig hung from my bottom lip as I pushed my hair back from my eyes. The low light of the pit reflected off my glasses. I started swinging the end of the chain in small circles. Dennis's jaw dropped as I began to circle him too.

He held the pole like a fucking lifeline. I lifted my hand and, with my fingers still on the chain, beckoned him to strike. I saw the moment the rat decided to fight. I saw the gritting of his teeth and the tightening of his grip around the pole. He charged at me, pole in the air. When I drew close, he brought it down toward me. I stepped out of the way and, swinging the chain, slammed the heavy metal against his back, smirking when I heard a rib crack.

Dennis dropped to the ground, the pole clattering off the floor. I inhaled on my cig and blew out the smoke. "Get to your fucking feet," I demanded as he rolled around on the floor. Dennis groaned and ignored my command. "I said get to your bloody traitorous feet!" The sound of my raised voice had Dennis scrambling to stand.

I stood stock-still, dropping my arms so the chain hung low. After picking the pole off the floor, he whirled around. I stood completely fucking still as he charged. I didn't even move as he ploughed the pole against my stomach. Dennis blew out a breath as he stumbled across the pit. I turned, the throbbing in my stomach only stoking my flames higher.

"You're insane." He looked around the room at the spectators all getting off on his slow and drawn-out death.

"My turn," I said and, hoisting the chain, slammed the thick links across his face. I heard another crack and knew his jaw had been broken. Dennis screamed and tried to come at me again. But the fucker had lost what little composure he had. He charged, trying to lift the pole to my face, but my chain got to him first, slamming into his stomach, and the pole clattered to the ground. The blow brought him to his knees, saliva and blood mixing as he spat it out on the sand.

My cig was still resting on my lip, so I took a much-needed drag, exhaling the smoke through my nose. Dennis had blood on his face; the chain had bust his lip wide open. "Please," he begged, and his pissant weakness made my skin crawl with disgust.

I swung the chain around in wide circles and walked around him. Dennis shot his hand out, trying to grab the pole and hit me with it. But I was done with his rat face and lying mouth. It was time for the twat to fuck off and die.

Standing right in front of his face, I waited until he met my eyes. I changed the angle of the chain, released it, and watched it wrap around his neck like an iron boa constrictor. Dennis clawed at the chain as it began to choke him, his pale face swelling with red as he fought for breath. As his weak arms were unable to pull the heavy chain away from his throat.

I never turned my gaze away, watching and smoking as the turncoat prick fought to stay alive. He didn't fight long. He reached out toward me, one final move for mercy.

I kicked his fucking hand away, snapping his wrist, and the arsehole toppled over, his eyes retreating behind the glaze only death could bring. I lifted my hand to my mouth, pulled one last drag from my cig, and flicked the ash on his still-warm corpse.

In that moment, I thought of Cheska's ivory queen and the ash stain that had smudged across her pristine chest. I looked up at my family and sought out the only one I needed to see. She was already watching me. She'd lost some colour in her face, but her shoulders were still high, that regal fucking toffee nose still in the air, daring me to bring on more darkness.

I smirked at her challenge. She didn't know fuck all. Because the twat dead at my feet was just the starter course.

I clicked my fingers at one of my soldiers. Still holding Cheska's confused gaze, I moved to the table, picked up a medieval cat o' nine tails and said, "Bring me the next."

CHAPTER ELEVEN

CHESKA

This is Arthur Adley, I silently said to myself as I watched yet another man die at his hands. His very fucked-up and sadistic hands. The sand he stood on was no longer beige but a crimson carpet. Arthur's skin was no longer lightly tanned; no natural colour could be seen under the evidence of his insatiable appetite for death. His tattoo of the Victorian London skyline was now sullied with bits of flesh and bone that he had torn from his victims. Victims who had screamed and cried and pleaded for mercy.

No mercy was ever given. In fact, if they begged to be spared, their death and the pain Arthur inflicted was only drawn out more.

This was him pushing me.

Ronnie, Vera and Betsy had told me it would be the case. Arthur had brought me here to see the very darkest side of him. He wanted me here so I would run away, leave him to his festering wickedness and the evil that had become his safety. Leave him in the sinful cage he locked himself inside.

I kept my eyes on the pit as he struck his fourth "traitor" with a sword to the top of his skull. I forced back the nausea creeping up my throat as the man fell backwards to the ground. Arthur turned, sword in hand. *King Arthur.* I couldn't help but make that comparison as my fucked-up king's blue gaze bored into mine. As he stood, torso exposed, but wearing armour of his victims' lifeblood and lies over his bloodthirsty heart.

And in his murdering hands, he held his very own Excalibur.

Betsy squeezed my knee in support, a silent request to be strong. When we'd entered these pits, I had not been prepared for how the night would end. The blood, the fights, the death.

So much death.

And then there were the "associates". The infamous bikers that rode through London like they were a law unto themselves. The Irish and Romani mafias that everyone had heard of but no one I knew had ever had dealings with. All of them terrifying in their own right, and all of them looking down at Arthur like he really was the dark lord he had been titled.

Royal, the man Betsy told me was the president of the Hangmen, got to his feet. "A fucking show as always, Adley." His men started heading for the exit. "Until next time, mate."

Arthur nodded at each of his "mates" as they left, leaving only the Adleys. But Arthur hadn't moved from the pit. His wild eyes stayed on mine, and I couldn't move. I was a rabbit in his snare, locked in place.

"I take it that's our cue to go," Eric said sarcastically, then pointed in Betsy's face. "You and me have an appointment, treasure."

"Fuck off, Eric," Betsy bit back, but there was a hint of something like excitement in her voice, and she got to her feet, her lips curling up. Eric grabbed her and spun her around. "You're fucking riding my dick the minute we're in that car." He had put his shirt on over his bloodied chest, and red seeped through the expensive material. "It's been too fucking long."

"If you can even call it a dick," Betsy snapped back. But her pupils had dilated, and her skin was flushed. Eric growled, then dragged her from the warehouse.

Just as they reached the door, Betsy shouted back, "Vera, Ronnie,

I'll see you back at the church. Seems like we might be taking the long way home."

I didn't pay any mind to everyone else leaving around me. I was too focused on breathing, on calming my skin, which felt as though it was setting alight as Arthur's chest rose and fell in the pit and the air clogged with tension. I saw the blood on the ground and on his skin.

An Adley soldier dragged the final body from the pit and disappeared out of the warehouse. I tried to find sorrow for the men Arthur had so brutally murdered tonight, but all I saw in their places were my attackers. The men who had killed my father and Hugo. The men who had so easily slit Freya's throat and stabbed Arabella right through her heart.

"Arthur had protected these men, provided for them, given them a place at our family's table," Vera had said as Arthur toyed with the men in the pit like a lion playing with his prey. "The fuckers betrayed him. Fucking Judases, the whole lot of them," she spat, anger lacing her raspy voice.

"They knew what they were signing on for," Ronnie had said as Arthur stabbed a man in the ear. "Their greed and lack of loyalty brought this to them. Stupid fucking tossers. They deserve to die. They knew the contract when they joined the firm. They broke it. They invited their own deaths."

This was the world he lived in, a world I thought existed only in nightmares. In truth, it was at all of our doorsteps, just waiting to catch us off guard and drag us down to their fucked-up level. I had lived a "normal" life, and yet I'd found myself at the mercy of traffickers. Evil waited for any opportunity to sink in its claws. At least in Arthur's cruel kingdom, there was some semblance of code and honour.

I knew something depraved must have burrowed its way into my soul when I realised I yearned to see the men who had murdered my family on the end of Arthur's blood-soiled sword. I craved to see them beg at his feet for mercy and be prescribed pain and agony instead.

I heard a door shut. Casting my eyes around the warehouse, I realised we were all alone. Arthur still hadn't moved. He still stood with a cigarette balancing on his bottom lip, his muscles ripped and shredded from the fights, his skin smothered in cooling blood.

And he was still watching me. He was waiting for what I would do.

This is it, I thought as I got to my feet. The choice. The decision I had to make. Arthur or my old life.

There was no contest.

I walked to the stairs that led down to the pit. Arthur scanned me the entire way down. I saw myself in his glasses as I approached, not even flinching when my stiletto heels landed on the pit's sandy floor and the coppery stench of blood and cigarette smoke permeated the air.

The pit seemed much bigger when I was standing inside it. The table of weapons was beside me. I ran my hand along the weapons, most of which I had never seen before. It was like something from the Grand Inquisitor's torture chamber.

I circled the pit, Arthur tracking my every move.

Finally, I drew to a stop in front of him. Reaching into my pocket, I pulled out the ivory queen piece from his chessboard. I had taken it last night when he had left the study. After he had provoked me and I had provoked him right back, setting off tonight's chain of events. The smudge from the cigarette still stained my queen's chest.

I took the cigarette hanging from Arthur's mouth, put it between my lips and took a long, drawn-out drag. The smoke filled my lungs and I tasted Arthur on my tongue. I blew the smoke into his face. Then I placed the queen at the base of Arthur's throat.

Fixing my gaze on his, I dragged her down through the thick layer of blood on his skin, sullying her remaining cleanliness. Smearing the evidence of death and torture on her smooth, polished surface.

I stopped when I reached the waistband of his trousers. They had dropped low on his hips, the V leading to his prominent cock, a perfect gutter for the blood and sweat that dripped down his body.

Stepping closer, so close that I could feel the blazing heat pulsing from his skin, I tucked the queen into his trouser pocket, his hard cock brushing against my hand as I did. I released the queen, then wrapped my hands around his length through the fine material and gave him a slow, hard stroke before pulling my hand away.

I finished the cigarette, blowing the smoke over Arthur's face one last time before flicking the butt to the floor. Arthur's jaw clenched, then he placed his hand around my throat and pushed me back a few feet until my back slammed against the wall.

His eyes were wild and his nostrils flared. He was breathing hard, pants ripping between his lips, yet the hold on my throat was not tight, just a placeholder, a way to keep me still and obedient as he exerted his dominance. Arthur raised the sword he still held and placed the tip at my throat, above the hand that held me in place.

"Are you scared?" he asked, his voice dropping an octave. The low light in the pit glimmered off the few remaining slivers of clean steel on the sword's blade.

"No," I said, nothing but truth in my response. "You won't hurt me."

"Are you sure about that? I could kill you," he said, pressing the tip harder against my skin. I could feel its sharpness, how easily it could slit my throat, pierce through my flesh.

"You won't," I said, knowing it to be true.

I know it to be true ...

Here stood the most dangerous man in London, his hand around my throat and a sword precariously pressed against my skin. And I knew. I knew with unwavering faith that he would not harm me. It was a revelation, a clear burst of sunshine on a grey and drizzly day.

I was one of the only people who could say with true certainty that Arthur Adley, Dark Lord of London Town, would never ever hurt them.

I swallowed, something shifting inside me at that knowledge, something at a cellular level. Irreversible. An eclipse, his moon casting me in much-needed shadow. It was the acceptance of letting go of my old life and being reborn—my cleansing baptism in hell's raging fire.

It was a heady surge of power charging through my veins.

Arthur's sword nicked my throat, propelling me back into the moment. A tiny trickle of blood ran down my neck and toward my breasts—my communion, my sanguine pledge to join his side. Arthur's eyes were stone, stones rolled in lava and ash and solar flares, as he pushed and pushed me.

"You're so certain," he said, head tilted. His eyes were narrowed as though he was searching for my deception, any doubts in my heart.

There were none. Not a single, solitary one.

Making sure I had his undivided attention, I said, "I am your queen." Arthur stopped breathing. Taking advantage of his pause, I lifted my hand and pressed down on the blade until it was back by his side. He let me take away its threat.

The residue of the recent tragedies faded, and a new feeling was awakened. An opening of a new door in my heart. One that only allowed in Arthur and his family. One that kept me safe, sheltered and in his dangerous embrace. I felt taller, stronger ... changed.

I pressed my palm to his chest, sharing the blood he had just spilled. "I'm your tainted, sullied, and corrupted queen."

"You're not ready for me," he growled, but I caught the hint of yearning in his voice. He was cracking before me, the way the ground fractured during the early pangs of an earthquake. The warning that its devastation was coming. That once its wrath was released, there was no going back to how things were before.

Once Arthur let me into his granite heart, I could never leave it.

"Try me," I taunted, and cupped his cock with my free hand. He was rock hard under his trousers, and he hissed as I squeezed him. I made sure he was looking right at me when I said, "Try your best to destroy me, Arthur. Try your best to break me apart. But I'll still be here when you're exhausted, my claws sunk deeply into your flesh as you drag us both to hell."

"I won't let you go," he warned, and shivers ran down my spine at the malevolent honesty of the threat. "You want to rule at my side? Then I'll never let you leave me. If you walk by my side, you can never ever fucking leave."

I was making a binding contract with the devil. *An Adley's word is his bond* ... that's what Arthur had said in the pit. He was waiting for the verbal agreement to be signed. Waiting for me to finally hand over my soul.

"I am your queen. And you are my king. Your dark kingdom is now ours."

I removed my bloodied hand from his chest and drew a cross over my heart with my finger. "Forever."

And that was when he broke. My world shook as Arthur smashed his mouth to mine. He wasn't gentle—but I had never expected him to be. He was savage and cursed with a wickedness that was born from loss at a young age and a father who saw violence and death and the suppression of feelings as a form of bonding.

But I would love him. *All* of him—the wicked and the warm. I always had. I had never wanted him to change, only to let me in.

Arthur's tongue slid along mine and I moaned, grasping his hair. His hands fell to my leathers. He snapped the button, and I heard it drop to the floor. He wrenched the trousers down to my ankles, and I kicked one leg off my feet. Arthur ripped off my knickers and pushed two fingers straight inside me. His lips pulled away from mine and trailed down my neck. He bit down on my skin, and I tossed my head back, my clit pulsing at his roughness.

I pulled on his hair, so hard that he had no choice but to look up. "I love you," I said, and Arthur stilled. His jaw clenched and his hands moved to my waist, holding on to me tightly. My eyes blurred. "I love you, Arthur Adley," I said, softer, and cupped his cheek. His skin was boiling, and my chest caved when he turned his head and kissed my palm. It was the only flicker of tenderness he offered. A fleeting expression of softness before the darkness blanketed us both again.

A second later, he pulled out his cock and lifted me against the wall of the pit. With blood smothering us both, he pushed inside me, slamming into me with a savage grunt.

I cried out, clutching his back as he filled me after these many months without him. I had missed him. I realised just how much. *Nothing* felt like this. No one had ever filled me this way, possessed me this way.

In this moment, I had never been more sure of anything than that Arthur was made for me. As I felt his hands bruising my thighs as he ploughed into me, his wide, muscled body caging me in, I knew I would never go back on my promise. I would never leave his side. There was no longer a choice. I was soldering myself to him.

Melding our souls, splicing our hearts.

I kissed him. As my pussy started to tighten, I kissed him and kissed him as his hips moved faster. His tongue duelled against mine, fucking my mouth just as hard as he was fucking me. "I love you," I murmured against his mouth, seeing his eyes dilate as the words hit his ears like bullets.

Arthur fucked me until my legs were numb. Until I was him and he was me and the blood and flesh of his victims that marred his skin were spread on my skin as well. His victories mine, and his sins my sins too.

Arthur's grunts and groans were feral, and I felt tension in my lower back, the building of the orgasm he was tearing from me. I raked his back with my long fingernails, his blood joining the crimson cock-tail already tattooing his skin. My pussy clenched, and with Arthur's unrelenting rhythm, I came hard, screaming my release into the empty mouth of the warehouse lair.

I closed my eyes, dragging my cheek against the stubble on Arthur's face. His skin was scorching, and I felt burned, on fire, incin-erated as he took me harder and harder until he stilled, and I felt him release inside me. He roared, and every muscle in his body tensed as he made me his—fully, wholly, *finally*.

I sucked in breath after breath, my body clamouring for oxygen, for the chance to recover. Arthur's body sagged against me, pinning me so hard against the wall I knew I'd have scratches from the rough brick of the pit. My hands were still in his hair, tangled and knotted in the midnight strands.

I loved him. I loved Arthur more than life itself. His darkness and his lifestyle meant nothing compared to that. I loved him despite the malice in his soul. I loved him *because* of it. Not everyone was meant for a life of roses and summer days, all pretty petals and fragrant perfumes. Some were meant for a life of winter and thorns.

It didn't mean they couldn't have love.

Arthur kissed up my neck, his tongue darting out to taste the sweat that his fucking had induced. He still held my legs around his waist; his dick was still inside me, twitching and sending aftershocks of pleasure shooting up my spine.

My breathing had calmed by the time his searching lips found my mouth. His glasses were filthy with sweat and blood, and askew, but he still looked perfect to me. Still tasted like heaven as he kissed me until my lips were swollen and sore.

When he pulled away, his blue eyes were glued to mine. I wished I could read his mind. I wished he would tell me what he felt in his heart as he looked at me, unkempt but now his. But I knew not to push him too hard.

We were here. Together. He had let me breach his high, impenetrable walls. I knew it would take time to hammer through the rest. But I wasn't fazed by the task. I was inspired. To know all of this man. To have him love me and let me see his soul.

It was worth it all.

"You wrecked me long ago," I said, my voice echoing off the cavernous walls. I pulled Arthur's glasses from his face. He looked so young without them. The thick black frames were almost his shield, and without them he was bared and vulnerable. I laid a kiss on either side of his eyes as he breathed heavily. Moving my mouth to his ear, I whispered, "It's my turn to wreck you."

He tensed. But when his hands flexed on my thighs, I knew he liked what I had said. And it was true. His family members had told me that he loved me, that I had been the only person to hold any claim on his iron heart. But I didn't just want a claim. I wanted to consume it. I wanted to own it like he owned mine.

I needed his ruination. It was only fair—he already had mine.

Arthur kissed me again, and I could only imagine how we looked, blood and sweat smothered, reeking of sex and sin. I cleaned his glasses on my top, then pushed them back on his face, my lord holding me in his arms.

Without words, he pulled out of me. I gasped at the loss. He placed me on the floor, and my legs shook from exertion. Arthur crouched down and pulled my trousers back up my legs.

I was stunned. He was caring for me. Sweetly. Gently. As if I might break apart at any minute.

When my clothes were in place, he tucked himself back inside his trousers, then turned for the stairs that led out of the pit. Not a single word was spoken. He hadn't told me he loved me. I didn't expect him to. I knew this was just the first step for Arthur. New territory that he had never seen or felt before.

He began to walk out of the pit but suddenly stopped dead. His shoulders hunched, then released. I wondered what was wrong. But then he turned, lit a cigarette and inhaled. His head tipped back and he closed his eyes.

He was perfection. Raw, savage, tattooed and scarred perfection. He released the smoke into a cloud of white, then dropped his head and met my eyes. Leaving the cigarette balancing on his bottom lip—a move that I was increasingly finding irresistible—he slowly lifted his hand. It took me a moment to realise he was offering it to me.

He wanted to hold my hand.

Pulse thundering in my neck, I reached out and let his hand engulf mine. His fingers intertwined with mine, gripping them so tightly it bordered on painful. I didn't care if he broke every finger. He was holding my hand. The simple gesture, for Arthur, was as difficult as moving a mountain. But he was doing it. He was trying.

This was how he was showing me he cared. The one-man island, inviting me to breach his black-sanded shore.

I moved beside him, and together, side by side, we left the warehouse.

His car waited for us outside the now-abandoned building, his driver patiently waiting for his boss. We slipped into the back seats. My arse had barely touched the leather before Arthur yanked me to his side, his arm slinging over my neck, possessively pinning me against him. He lit up another cigarette and wordlessly passed it to me.

I took the cigarette and sank against him, then passed it back. He was still shirtless, his suit jacket and shirt tucked beside him on the back seat. I reached up to where his hand lay over my shoulder and threaded my hand through his. Smoke filled the air as we travelled from Mile End back to Bethnal Green.

He clutched my hand again as we entered the church. We passed some of his family in the living room, and knowing smirks spread over their lips. Pride in my step, I followed him into his bedroom and straight into the shower.

He fucked me against the tiled wall, then again in his bed. *Our* bed. Because I knew I would never be leaving it.

In the aftermath of it all, we still hadn't spoken a word. But conversation wasn't needed. We had an oath, a contract signed in blood and sweat and sex. He had come for me in his chariot and whisked me to his home, to hell.

To be by his side.

Never to leave.

The lady to his lord.

A dark queen to his perpetually and unrepentantly dark king.

CHAPTER TWELVE

CHESKA

Three weeks later

I stepped into the living room, only to find it empty but for Freddie. In the weeks since the night in the pits, I had barely left Arthur's side. Only when he went on business did I stay at the church. Unless he was going to the Sparrow Room; then he took me with him.

I was remaining hidden. The police were still on the hunt for me. Arthur refused to let me out of the church unless it was by his side. My attackers hadn't been found, and we were no closer to finding out who they were.

I didn't want to leave the church anyway. It had become my haven.

Tonight, Gene Mason returned. I had never met him. He was Vera and Eric's younger brother. Arthur hadn't been particularly forthcoming when it came to the boy. Just that he had been away at a private facility. Vera had explained to me that her twenty-year-old brother had many demons, depression being top of that list. His stint in rehab was over with, and I knew Arthur wanted him home anyhow.

The attacks on his ships and transport hadn't ceased, and he was becoming more agitated the more answers evaded him.

Arthur loved his family like nothing I had ever known. He worked night and day to keep them safe. He didn't speak it plainly, but it was obvious in everything he did.

The outside world believed him evil—they couldn't have been more wrong. However, Arthur did nothing to dissuade them of that belief. He claimed it was better that anyone outside his family thought that way.

He still didn't speak much to me either.

He had never told me he loved me. Never even uttered one complimentary murmur my way. But the way he held me in bed, the way he took my hand, the way he kissed me and fucked me and tracked my every move wherever we went, showed me everything I needed to know.

But there were times when I would see frustration and anger on his face; his eyebrows would pull down and a haunted shadow would flicker over his handsome features. There were times when his moods were dark, so dark he practically pulsed with malice. He grew distant. Drank more. Smoked more. There were even times he left me alone, only to find me later that day and fuck me so hard that his grip branded my skin and I felt him inside me long after he had pulled out.

I hadn't yet figured out the reason for these moods. But I trusted in us. I believed that one day he would tell me.

"Cheska," Freddie greeted me, pulling me from my head. He handed me a gin and tonic; he was holding a martini.

"Arthur isn't back yet?" I asked, just for something to say and to push the worry from my chest.

As I had got to know the Adley family, it was apparent that Freddie was the quietest, except for Arthur. He was always kind and approachable, but he was happiest sitting in in everyone's company, only offering chatter every now and again or when he was asked a direct question. "Not yet." Freddie sat down, and I sat in an armchair beside him. It was the first time since I'd arrived it had been only us two. "They should all be back soon. Eric and Vera went for Gene." Freddie checked his watch, then his phone. I settled back against the chair as he typed out a text.

"So?" Freddie said, eyes assessing, as he put his phone down beside him. "How are you?" He smirked. "How are you finding life on the other side of the tracks?"

"Good," I said, and meant it. "Believe it or not, I feel more at home in this converted church than I ever did in Chelsea."

Freddie nodded. "I do know." I knew Freddie had lived here for years. His dad had died quite a few years back. I didn't know the details, but I knew he was practically Arthur's brother.

"You've lived here a while," I said, half statement, half question.

"Yeah," Freddie said, staring down at his martini. "Arthur told you what happened with my old man?"

"Not really."

Freddie smiled, and its warmth made me mirror it. He was clearly thinking of his father. He loved him. He hadn't even spoken about him, yet his face told me this without words.

"He was a proper geezer," Freddie said. "A talker, unlike me. A fucking hard grafter. And a loyal general by Alfie's side." He took a sip of his martini. "He was an adopted cockney. Born in South London, but moved to Bethnal Green when he was a teenager. Fell into working with Alfie when I was a kid. Alfie liked him. My dad got shit done, no questions, and Alfie respected that."

"Sounds like a great man."

Freddie met my eyes. "He was."

"What happened?" I asked, hoping I hadn't overstepped the mark.

"A deal gone wrong." The warmth he'd been exuding faded to an Arctic chill. "There was a rat in the firm, one of the soldiers. Sold us out to a rival. There was a set-up, a deal that had been infiltrated. There was a shoot-out, and my old man was the one who paid the price."

"I'm so sorry. How old were you?"

"Sixteen."

"I'm sorry, Freddie." I reached forward and squeezed his hand. He stared at the hand, then finished his drink when I pulled away.

"Moved in with Alfie that night. Been here ever since."

"He's like your dad too."

Pain or something similar flashed in his eyes. "Yeah."

"Arthur believes he'll wake up," I said, knowing that Freddie's pain was born from Alfie's coma. Arthur never once visited his dad in his room. He checked in with his personal nurse several times a day, but never visited him. Never spoke to him or held his hand.

"He has to," Freddie said, gravel in his voice. "He has to wake up." Freddie got up and went to the bar. My heart broke for him. To lose another father ... My stomach turned. I knew what it was like to lose people you loved. It felt like a weight constantly on your back. It made you breathless when it became too much. Too heavy on some days to even move.

The padlocked emotions I kept caged away inside me rattled. I held my breath and pushed back the grief I had fought so hard not to feel. I wasn't ready to unleash it. I saw Arthur watching me sometimes, closely, as if he was expecting me to break at any moment. But I couldn't. *Wouldn't.* After everything that happened to them all ... I wasn't sure I would ever recover if the iron of the cage doors holding those emotions back were ever to buckle and set them free.

I embraced the now-familiar numbness of evasion and breathed. Freddie was making another martini, I looked at him and swore I felt his weight too. I felt that maybe he too had a padlocked cage of his own.

"You lost your mum too?" I asked.

Freddie's shoulders tensed, but he nodded and turned to me. He hesitated a second, then said, "I was only little when she died. It was just me and my old man until he went too. We were thick as thieves. He was my best mate. He was everything to me."

"I'm sorry," I said again. I had no idea how I could make such loss better. Pain like a dagger sliced through my heart. I was the same. I had lost everyone too. So had Arthur. This was why he and Freddie were so close. They had both taken tremendous losses.

They truly were brothers in every way but blood.

"Well, this is a fucking sad excuse for a party," Charlie said from the doorway. Betsy was linking his arm, smiling at her brother's quip. "Want to talk about how my mum dumped us as babies and ran off with her psychiatrist? Then we can really have a bloody ball." Charlie rolled his eyes and walked further into the room. He leaned down and kissed me on the cheek, as did Betsy.

"We were waiting for you all to arrive, you prick," Freddie said and winked at me.

"So you talk about death? Way to cast a dark cloud in the room."

"That's okay, Chuck," Freddie said. "You brighten any room."

"I know you're just being a sarcastic twat, but I'm taking that compliment anyway."

Charlie made himself a drink then sat down on the sofa beside Betsy. "So?" Charlie said to me. "How's domestic life with my cousin?" There was a playful twinkle in his eyes.

"Good," I said, hoping my recent worry over Arthur's odd behaviour wasn't obvious on my face.

"Good? Well, that's a ringing endorsement for domestic couple-dom." Charlie smirked at me. He must have detected the worry in me after all, as he said, "There's a lot going on at the moment. Business-wise. Attacks. All that fun stuff. Keeps old Artie busy."

"Plus, he has no idea how to actually *have* a relationship that isn't family," Betsy added. She checked her watch as the doorbell rang. She smiled widely. "That must be Jacob." She left the room.

"Jacob?" I asked Charlie.

He batted his hand in front of his face, then proceeded to light his pipe. "Her latest tool to make Eric jealous, no doubt." Charlie sat back in his seat, crossing his legs. "Don't worry. You'll get used to the most fucked-up relationship of all time soon enough. And the games they play just to piss each other off." Just as Charlie stopped speaking, Betsy entered, arm in arm with a tall, red-haired man in a suit. She got to her tiptoes and kissed him his cheek.

"Drink, darling?" she asked him.

"Guinness," he replied in a Scottish accent.

Vinnie came into the room, his arm suspended in the air, clearly around his hallucination of Pearl. Jacob's eyes widened.

Vinnie looked Jacob up and down. "Oh, this'll be fun."

He sat on the love seat and got drinks for him and Pearl, whispering things into her "ear". Jacob was pale as he watched him, and I wondered how Betsy had explained this, tonight, her family. If she had even bothered.

I heard the front door open and close, then the sound of heels on the hallway floor. "Sounds like Grandma," Betsy said, and my heart flipped. Eva Adley. I had heard of the Adley matriarch from Vera and Betsy. They had told me, in no uncertain terms, that Arthur was her favourite. And that she was a battleaxe. And her word on anything regarding the family was law.

I held my breath as a slim, elegant woman appeared in the doorway. She had white-grey hair that was styled into an elegant short bob. She wore tailored black trousers, a fitted white shirt, and a pair of black Louboutins. A long black jacket rested on her shoulders.

"Grandma." Charlie got to his feet and kissed her on the cheek. Betsy and Freddie followed suit.

Vinnie got up and kissed Eva too. Patting his cheek affectionately, she said, "How's my baby girl?" I knew she was referring to Pearl.

"Good, Eva. She's really fucking good." Vinnie took his place beside Pearl again, whispering into her ear.

Eva Adley's eyes found mine, then Jacob's.

"Seems we have a couple of interlopers in the room," she said. But her attention was barely on Jacob. It was firmly on me. It was clear she knew who I was, but I had no idea how she felt about it.

I got to my feet. "Mrs Adley." I held out my hand. "I'm Cheska Harlow-Wright."

She shook my hand, then quickly dropped it. She reached into her handbag and pulled out a cigarette in a thin black holder. Charlie held up his lighter for her. When the cigarette was lit, she inhaled. As she exhaled, she said, "You're the one fucking my grandson?"

I reared back in shock. Her accent was just as thick as those of the rest of the family. A spark of irritation flared in my chest. "I'm more than fucking him," I replied, a hint of steel in my tone.

Eva's eyebrow rose. "Is that so?"

"Regardless of what you think, I love him."

"Love?" Eva laughed, smiling at Freddie when he placed a brandy in her hand. "Love doesn't always work out well for people in our line of work." She walked past me and sat down in a high armchair like an ice queen. She regarded me shrewdly. "And what do you love about my grandson? The power? The money? The fact that he's a bit of rough for you to enjoy then spit out on your fancy SW3 streets."

Betsy winced, then subtly nodded at me in encouragement. "How dare you?" I said curtly. "Yes, I'm a Harlow-Wright." I held my head high. "And I have both power and money of my own. I love Arthur for Arthur."

"Last I heard, your family was in ruin," she said, and I felt the dagger being plunged into my back. "You father and fiancé were killed for being unable to pay back a dodgy loan. Isn't that right?"

The image of my dad and Hugo shot into my head, easily slipping past my defences, but I quickly pushed it away. "I have my own money. Money from my mum's side that my father could never touch. Lots of it. I don't need a penny from Arthur. Ever." I crossed my arms—it was more for my own self-preservation than out of insolence. "And if you knew your grandson, you would know that he is worthy of love. There doesn't have to be any condition attached to it."

"Mm," she said. "There's the blue-blood arrogance shining through." She sipped her brandy and let her cigarette burn down in its holder without taking a single drag. "But tell me, how can you love someone you barely know?"

"I know him."

"You've known him for all of five minutes."

I stepped closer to Eva, fighting back the need to slice my hand across her face. "I met Arthur when I was thirteen years old. Then again at eighteen." Eva's eyes narrowed. Clearly this was news to her. "Then we were together for five years. I've known him longer than you think."

Eva batted her hand. "A secret affair is not proof of anything." She finally took a drag of her cigarette, then said, "He was a bit on the side to you. You were engaged to a posh twit and fucked Artie behind his back. That's the great love affair you're referring to?"

Anger. That was what swept through me. Molten-hot lava, and anger so great my hands shook. It was rabid, so pure in its potency that I used its heat to spit, "In no universe could Arthur ever be just a 'bit on the side.' I loved him then and I love him now. I am here, and I'm not going anywhere. That's something you're just going to have to come to terms with."

The room was silent. Eva glared back at me, but I thought I saw something flicker in her gaze. Something like approval.

"Grandma." I turned to see Arthur filling up the doorway. He was dressed in a grey pinstripe suit, white shirt and black tie. His blue eyes cut to me, and my heart immediately started pounding.

"Artie," Eva said. Arthur moved to his grandma and kissed her cheek. He poured himself a gin, then turned to face me. I couldn't read the expression on his face as he cut across the room, heading straight for me. He stopped before me, put his hand on the back of my head, crushed my mouth to his and kissed me—*ravaged* me. I fell against him, the people in the room melting away as he pushed his tongue against mine.

Arthur pulled away but kept his hand on the back of my neck, keeping me close. "Princess," he said in greeting. He sat down on his usual seat by the fire and pulled me onto his lap, wrapping his arm around my waist. He always did this when we were in this room. Whenever he was with me, he was always touching me in some way, possessing me, never letting me go.

I wrapped my arm around Arthur's neck, feeling ten feet tall. Charlie sat down, fighting a smirk, as did Freddie. Betsy stayed standing beside Jacob, but when our gazes met she winked at me.

"That's the first and last time you'll interrogate Cheska, Grandma. I mean it," Arthur said. Eva flicked her hand at him in dismissal.

I lay back against Arthur's warmth. Against his hard body, smelling the tobacco on his suit, the musk from his aftershave. I looked at his face. Arthur's jaw was clenched, but then he flicked his blue eyes in my direction. I smiled at him. In seconds he was kissing me again, as if he couldn't get enough. Not giving one shit that his grandma was no doubt fuming across the room in disapproval.

He was choosing me ... Arthur was choosing *me*.

The front door opened again, and Vera's and Eric's voices drifted down the hallway. Arthur didn't get up to greet them. He kept his arm around me and drank his gin like the king he was.

Vera came to the living room first. She smiled, but it seemed strained. "Here he is," she said. Behind her was a medium-height, slim boy with curly brown hair that flopped into his eyes. His gaze was lowered. He wore all black, and long black bandages hid his wrists and forearms. My stomach fell. There was only one reason why someone would need such things. One thing he could be trying to hide.

"Gene." Eva got to her feet. She held him, and he reluctantly held her back, looking as though he wanted to be anywhere but in this room with us all right now. When she pulled away, Gene's eyes flitted away from the floor. He had hazel eyes and pale skin. He was skittish, and clearly had little to no confidence. He was shy. But by the small, nervous smiles he cast at everyone, he seemed sweet.

He scanned the room, eyes landing on me. If he was surprised by me, he didn't show it. Charlie stood and headed toward Gene, and Gene's head lifted for the first time and stayed high. His eyes stayed fixed on Charlie.

"Gene," Charlie said, wrapping him in his arms. Gene tucked his head into the crook of Charlie's neck and held him back. His fingers splayed on Charlie's suit jacket, like he was trying to sink his grip into him and never let go. "You okay, kid?"

"Yeah," Gene said, and a lump formed in my throat at how tightly Gene was holding Arthur's cousin. As if Gene was drowning and Charlie was the lifejacket keeping his head above the waves.

Charlie pulled back and tapped Gene's cheek. "We've missed you, kid," he said, and Gene smiled the sweetest of smiles. He seemed so different to the rest of his family. The opposite of his sister and brother. Eric was larger than life and lethal; Vera was opinionated and could cut you down with one scathing look. Gene ... I couldn't help but think he was too innocent for this life. Too precious. He needed to be wrapped in cotton wool and coddled.

"I've missed you too," he all but whispered. Charlie turned to go to the bar. Gene's hazel gaze followed him the entire way.

Eric appeared behind Gene and put his hands on his younger brother's shoulders. "He's back!" Eric said, then lifted his head to the rest of the room. He zeroed in on Betsy ... then the man at her side. His joy at Gene's return dropped, and his face turned murderous.

"Who the fuck is this cunt?" Eric moved Gene aside and stormed farther into the room.

Before Betsy could open her mouth in introduction, Eric slammed his hand on the back of Jacob's neck. "Get the fuck out!" He dragged Jacob from the room.

"Eric!" Betsy shouted after him, anger in her voice as she ran to the living room doorway. She stopped dead as the front door slammed shut. She backed up a few steps, then Eric was suddenly in the room again. He was breathing hard and had rage in his eyes.

He pointed at Betsy's face. "Bring that wankstain around here again and I'll slit his fucking throat. You fucking know I'm not pissing about."

"You're such a prick!" Betsy went to slice her hand across Eric's face, but he caught her wrist in the air before she could. He slammed her to his chest, and Betsy spat in his face. "Get the fuck off me," she said threateningly, under her breath.

Eric laughed in her face, then released her wrist. "Bitch."

"The biggest," Betsy shot back, then walked to her chair, leaving Eric glaring after her, seething. I caught her eye as she sat down, wanting to know if she was okay. Her smug smile told me she was more than okay; the subtle wink she threw me told me she, in fact, felt victorious.

I had no idea what the hell had just happened.

Arthur tapped my arm. I got up and we headed to Gene. Arthur embraced him. "Gene."

Gene gave him a timid hug back. "Artie." Gene's gaze moved to me again, and I smiled at him.

I held out my hand. "Cheska," Arthur said, but with no other introduction.

"Lovely to meet you," I said, and Gene slightly bowed his head.

Eric held Gene's shoulders again and steered him toward a three-seater sofa. Vera and Eric flanked his either side, like guards who had been charged with protecting their fragile twenty-year-old sibling. Gene didn't speak, only nodded or shook his head in response to anything anyone asked him.

Arthur pulled me down to his lap again, playing with a strand of my hair. His fingertips grazed the top of my spine and sent shivers rico-cheting down my back.

Ronnie arrived an hour later. She shook her head at Arthur, and I knew she had been doing something for him. It would have been some-thing to do with the recent attacks on his drugs. And I knew she was still searching for any trace of my attackers, of those who had taken her. I still didn't know the full story. I wasn't sure I wanted to.

The night rolled on, and it wasn't long before Gene asked to go home. He was staying with Eric. He seemed exhausted, circles dark-ening under his eyes. Vera and Ronnie left to settle in Gene too. Charlie and Betsy left shortly afterwards, leaving only a few of us in the room.

"Grandma?" Arthur said. "You need a car?"

"Soon." She got to her feet. "I'm going to spend some time with my son first." She breezed out of the room. Arthur had tensed as she said that, and I turned and studied him. There was no expression on his face. Only the slight tension in his body told me he'd had any kind of reaction to his grandma visiting his father.

"I'm going to bed," Freddie said, then stopped in front of me. "Eva's bark's worse than her bite," he said. "She's just protective of Golden Boy here."

"Fuck off," Arthur said, but I caught the amusement in his gruff tone. Arthur's arm around my waist tightened. "Night." Freddie walked out of the room, leaving only us and Vinnie.

"Pearl wants to know if you want another drink. Said she misses her brother," Vinnie said, and I heard Arthur's breath hitch at the mention of his sister. I frowned and slipped my hand down over his on my waist. I squeezed his hand. That seemed to ignite something in Arthur, and he stood, lifting me off the chair and placing my feet on the floor.

"We're going to bed," he said.

"Night night," Vinnie said, his disturbing smile coming our way. "Don't let the bedbugs bite!"

Arthur pulled me toward his bedroom. The minute the door was shut, he pulled off his jacket and tossed it onto the nearby chair. The strange mood that he had been in for days and days still stuck to him like the smoke from his cigarettes.

Then he turned on me, backing me against the wall. He wanted to fuck me. Fuck me the same way he always had. But I wanted something else. As he stepped toward me, I ducked away from him and walked into the en suite. I closed the door and changed into my purple silk nightgown. I could hear Arthur pacing the bedroom outside.

When I opened the bathroom door, Arthur was sitting on the edge of the bed. Shirt off, only his trousers on, the fly already undone, that defined V leading the way underneath. "Get the fuck here, princess," he said. I saw he was hard underneath his trousers. His face was flushed and his eyes were piercing as they fixed on me.

He drank me in as I approached him. I stopped beside the bed and went to run my hands through his hair. He caught my wrist in his hand and pushed it straight down to his cock. "I don't like to be kept waiting," he said, and I caught the censure in his voice.

I stroked over his trousers, along his length underneath. Arthur growled under his breath. Then I stopped and pulled back my hand. There were questions in his gaze. "You've been acting strangely," I said and, this time, did rake my fingers through his hair. Arthur stilled beneath me. His hands ran up the side of my legs, up to my thighs, skimming over the purple silk to rest on my waist. I felt my nipples harden. "Tell me," I said. His grip tightened in response. "What's wrong?"

"I want to fuck you, that's what's fucking wrong." He yanked me closer. He wrapped his lips around my right nipple through my nightdress, and my eyes rolled back in my head at the feel. Pleasure fractured within me, sending warm currents of light through my body. Arthur moved his head to my other nipple, and I clenched my thighs together, my hands moving from his hair and down to his neck to feel his pulse. It was racing.

He broke away from my breast and pulled down the straps of my nightdress. The silk slipped from my body and pooled on the floor. He pulled me closer again by my waist—aggressively, dominantly. I adored him this way. But this time ... this time ...

"I want you to make love to me," I whispered. Arthur stilled. He didn't look up at me, though I knew he could feel my stare. With my hands on his cheeks, I guided his face to mine. His jaw was tight, eyes void of any emotion.

"I fuck," he said, his hand leaving my waist and dropping between my legs. He pressed his finger against my clit. I stopped his movements with a grip on his wrist, and he told me, "I fuck and you scream, and that's how it is."

"And you *fuck* well," I placated, pulling away his hand from me. "But that doesn't mean you can't make love to me too." I saw a million thoughts run through his mind as his brow furrowed and his eyes narrowed. A million different burdens tormenting him, his many demons trying to dissuade him from meeting my request.

Dropping to my knees, I pulled the waist of his trousers apart and lovingly kissed along his lower stomach. Arthur hissed and his muscles tightened. My kisses were soft and sweet, and I tried to show him how much I cherished him. I ducked lower and lower until my lips kissed the bottom of his length. I looked up and saw him watching me. Watching me like I was an enigma, like he had never seen me before ... like he had no idea what the hell to do with me.

It occurred to me that he would never have made love. Arthur had just told me himself that he fucked. He fucked hard and well, but he had never made love.

I sat back and ran my palms along his thighs. "I love you," I whispered into the quiet room. "I love you, Arthur Adley."

Arthur growled and went to yank me to my feet. I took hold of his hands before he could reach me. He froze. I met his burning and confused gaze and brought a palm to my lips, pressing the softest and sweetest of kisses to the rough skin. I did the same with his other hand. I lowered them to my shoulders and began to pull down his trousers. Arthur was bared to me, and I smiled at his stoic face.

Lowering my head, slow and steady, I brought his length to my lips. Arthur grunted as I swirled my tongue around the tip then took him inside my mouth. His hands left my shoulders and fixed on the side of my head. I expected him to be rough, to thrust inside my mouth and grip my face. But he didn't. He let me take him as I wanted. And when I looked up, he was watching me. Watching me with a lost expression on his face. Gritting his teeth, skin flushed, but so, so out of his depth.

This was as unsure as I believed Arthur could get. My heart shattered for him. Had he only ever believed that sex should be rough and casual? Had he never craved the deep, meaningful connection that I knew existed between soulmates? That I believed could exist between us?

I got to my feet and pressed my hands on his hard chest. Arthur lay back on the bed, allowing me to take charge. I climbed over his muscled body, straddling his thighs, and I kissed him. I kissed him with a tenderness I knew he had never experienced. He kissed me back, and I wanted to cry at this man allowing me to take control.

My tongue slid alongside his, caressing... just feeling and tasting and kissing. I pulled back and searched his face. I smiled, but something dark flashed across Arthur's face and he growled and flipped me onto my back. He caged me in his arms and glared down at me like I was the worst kind of rival. His eyes grew wide under his glasses. They closed, and I could see movement under his eyelids. I knew he was fighting with himself, fighting back the demons that lived within his darkened soul. His muscles were tensed, and I could tell he was struggling to relax, to let go.

To let us just be ...

"I love you," I murmured again, and Arthur's eyes snapped open. I'd noticed that every time I said it, it was as though he couldn't believe it. As though he didn't believe himself worthy ... he didn't believe himself loveable ...

I froze. That was it. That was why he only ever fucked. That was why he never showed a reaction to anything. He stayed hidden behind the safety of the high walls he had erected long ago because he didn't think he was worthy of love.

Arthur's skin was clammy—the only tell that this was affecting him in any way. That this, my words of love and adoration, were breaking through thickened, battle-scarred skin.

"I love you," I said again, and he pulled back, sitting on his heels. He raked his hands through his hair, looking around the room as if he needed an escape, as if he needed to be anywhere but on this bed with me. As if he couldn't stand to be told that he was loved.

I got to my knees and met his eyes. His neck was corded with strain, and the veins in his defined muscles protruded through his skin.

I cupped his face. He tried to pull away, but I held on tightly. He didn't fight me as much as I'd feared. He grasped my wrists as if to throw me away. But instead his hands held me like a lifeline, the way Gene had gripped onto Charlie, as if he would plummet into freezing depths if he didn't keep tight hold of me.

I moved in slowly, kissing along his stubbled cheek until my lips met his. I kissed him. I kissed him softly, showing him the love I felt for him. The love I now knew he had been denied for so long. A love I knew he had no idea what to do with.

I guided him on top of me as I lay back on the bed. He crawled above me, breathing heavily. I held Arthur's face, then let him be the one to kiss me. He inched his face closer to mine, his breath stuttered and unsteady. Then his lips met mine, and he kissed me. He didn't ravish me. He kissed me the way I'd always dreamed he could and someday would.

And once he started, he didn't stop. Arthur kissed my mouth; he kissed my neck and over my breasts. He kissed down my stomach and reached between my thighs. I widened my legs, and he dropped his head and licked along my core. My head rolled back as his tongue licked my clit, then down to my entrance.

"Arthur," I murmured, lost in the pleasure, lost in the gentleness, the softness. I stroked my fingers through his hair and looked down as he took me with his mouth. His hands were on my thighs, only moving to push a finger inside me. His tongue and finger worked me faster and faster until my back arched and I broke apart.

I cried out into the room, the sound echoing off the old beamed ceilings. Arthur crawled above me. His eyes met mine as he slid inside me, as he hooked his arms under mine and filled me, chest to chest. He groaned, and the sound was a symphony in my ears as he thrust inside me at a steady, maddening pace. As I closed my eyes, tears pricked behind my lids.

In all the years that he had come to me in Oxford, in all the nights since the pit, it had never been like this. It had never, ever been like this for me. And I knew it never would be again.

I opened my eyes. He lifted his face from my neck and saw my tears fall. Arthur frowned, then licked at the falling tears as he increased his pace. He drove me slowly insane, gently pushing and pushing me until I tensed, then cried out in ecstasy as I came. I held on to him tightly as I melted against him. Arthur kissed me, then he stilled, groaning into my mouth as I swallowed the sound of his release.

He fell forward, his head tucking into my neck, his lips kissing my damp skin. He stayed inside me, thrusting softly as our pleasure was wrung out. I ran my hands along his back and stroked his hot skin.

Arthur lifted his head, then pulled out of me, bringing me to his chest. His heart was racing as I pressed my ear to his pecs. His breathing was heavy, and I wondered what he was thinking. I knew he wouldn't tell me. At least, I knew I had to give him time to open up to me.

But this, what we had just shared, was a start.

We had just made love. Arthur had just made love to me. I never thought I would ever see the day when he let me in enough to have that.

He thought himself dark. He thought himself untouchable and unloveable. To me he was anything but.

I stared at the beams in the ceiling. His hand was entwined with mine. I felt him light a cigarette then smelled the smoke crawling around us. The white smoke billowed into the air above us, and I watched as it faded into nothing.

My mind drifted to the conversations we had had. When Arthur had pushed me, trying to test me, to see if I would run away. If I would abandon him because of his life, because of what he had done—still did. If I would eventually shy away from the black hole and empty void that lived within him. If I would finally flee from the demons he fought daily and the ones he let take control of his soul.

I wouldn't. Holding him like this made it worth it. It made everything—all the good, the bad and the depraved—worth it.

"There's comfort in darkness," I said, softly, so as not to disturb the aftermath of our first love-making. But Arthur tensed, and his hand tightened in mine. With my free hand I ran lazy circles on the back of his palm. "People are afraid of the dark." I knew he was listening to every word I said by the way he held his breath. "But there's solace to be found in darkness too." I smiled as I saw the midnight sky through the skylight in the old ceiling. The stars and the moon hung just outside, illuminating us where we lay.

"Like that," I said, pointing at the sky. "We wouldn't see the stars without the dark. The moon." I turned my head to Arthur, to the scars on his torso—knife marks from his hard upbringing, from his many violent fights. Some, from the look of things, that had been close to being fatal. I kissed his biggest scar, then looked up at his watching gaze. "I'm not afraid of the dark, Arthur. I never have been."

He stared at me for so long I didn't think he would give me a response. Then, "Good," was all he said as I closed my eyes and felt him wrap around me, darkness and all.

"Come on, princess. Wake up."

I blinked my eyes open. The room was still dark. But in the slither of light from the lamp on the bedside table, I saw Arthur. He was dressed and waiting for me. I realised he mustn't have slept at all when I saw on the clock that only two hours had passed. "Get dressed."

"Where are we going?" I asked, rubbing sleep from my eyes as I kicked my legs off the side of the bed. Arthur's nostrils flared at the sight of my naked body stretching, but he tossed some underwear, black leggings and his hoodie at me. I quickly dressed, smelling his scent on the hoodie as I pulled it over my head. I laughed when I looked down; the hem fell to my knees. Then my heart thudded erratically when I saw an amused smirk on Arthur's mouth.

He so rarely showed signs of joy that any mere hint of it was breathtaking.

I slipped my feet into my trainers and took Arthur's waiting hand. He pulled me from the room and straight out of the house. He unlocked a Range Rover, and I stood in shock—there wasn't a driver in the driver's seat.

"You're driving?"

"Shock horror," he replied dryly. My chest warmed at the hint of good-humoured sarcasm in his response.

I got in the passenger side, fighting my smile as Arthur pulled out onto the East End streets. I stared out at the houses and the closed pubs. It seemed like a different world to where I was from. Same city, completely different lives. But this one was fast becoming my new home.

We arrived at the warehouse that held the underground fight club. I tensed, realising we were going down there again. But when Arthur led me to the steel doors and they opened, it was only us. I frowned, looking at the empty pits, the empty stalls and seats. It had been cleaned, fresh sand in the pit floors. All traces of blood gone, a heady stillness to the air in the underground room. As if nature knew it was a place of depravity, death and violence.

"Why are we here, Arthur?" I asked, squeezing his hand.

He led me to a back room. It was long and narrow, and at the end were some haybale targets. Arthur threw off his jacket; on the side of his chest was a gun in a holder. He came toward me and pulled out the gun. "You have to learn to shoot," he said, and my stomach sank. I looked at the gun in his hand and recoiled. I'd never held a gun in my life.

"Princess," he said, voice laced with reproach. "I have a fucking massive target on my head." Arthur seemed to lower his walls a fraction. "If you're with me, if you stand by my fucking side, then there's going to be a target on you too." He pounded his chest with his palm, voice hardening and rising in volume. "People want to kill me. *Many* people. For revenge, power, drugs, docks, routes—you fucking name it. Wankers from all over want me dead for either what I've done or what I own. They'll come for you." His voice dripped with the inevitable promise of death. "Or at least they'll fucking try."

He gripped my jaw in his hand. "The wolves at my door will now be at yours too." He laughed, but it was humourless. "And they'll want your blood. Because of *me*, they'll want your blood." I went to speak, but he promised, "And I won't let that happen." His voice cracked a fraction, and so did my heart. "I can't fucking let that happen."

It was the closest Arthur had ever come to letting me know how he felt about me. The closest I'd seen to him losing his cool, to his usually expressionless face betraying his feelings. I stepped closer to him. He swallowed. "They'll come for you, princess. They'll come for you because of me."

This was because of tonight. This was *all* because we had made love. Not fucked. Not screwed. But made love.

It had rocked him. It had affected him more than I ever thought possible.

I nuzzled my head into his hand and kissed his palm. Meeting his wild eyes, I said, "They have already come for me, Arthur. The wolves already came. And not because of you." I closed my eyes and chased my threatening grief from my chest again. I couldn't let the sorrow catch up with me just yet. Then I thought of the trafficking, the blood, and the brand that marked the slavers who had tried to take me, but I *couldn't* think of it all yet.

The padlock rattled again, just as it had when I'd been talking to Freddie. Stark fear stole a breath. What would happen when I let it all in? Would it crush me? Would it destroy me? Would it take me to a place that I couldn't return from?

Arthur opened my hand and thrust his gun into my palm. The metal was cold against my skin, and it felt too heavy to hold—not just the weight, but the responsibility, the gravity of what it meant if I ever pulled the trigger that brushed tauntingly against my finger.

My hands were shaking. The padlock rattled harder.

Arthur moved behind me. He straightened his arms, taking mine with them. His body enveloped me and his cheek pressed against mine. He moved my hand into the correct position on the gun. "Unlock the safety," he said, using my hand to do so. "Aim," he added, then held his trigger finger over mine and pulled. "Fire." The boom from the gun was swallowed by the soundproof walls of the fighting pits. The bullet pierced the white paper target that was attached to a bale of hay, the hole going right through the red circle.

My blood roared through my ears, and a cocktail of adrenaline and fear and the addictive feeling of control raced around my body.

"Good," Arthur said. "Again."

I lined up the shot, then fired the gun. The bullet hit the target, and a rush of relieved breath left Arthur's mouth. His cheek was still next to mine, and he leaned in and kissed me. I felt the tenderness of it shiver down my spine.

Arthur released the gun and left me holding it myself. "Again," he ordered and stepped back. As I felt the trigger under my finger, the balaclava-clad face of the man who'd slit Freya's throat came to my head, the memory slipping through the cage's door. Then the man who'd plunged a knife into Arabella's chest followed quickly behind, showing me her eyes widening as the blade sank inch by inch into her still-beating heart. I remembered how she took the blade without crying or begging, how she met death with a steely bravery and an eerily calm façade.

As I aimed the gun, my hand shook harder. Tears built in my eyes, and the bales before me became a hazy beige blur. I fired, having no idea where the bullet landed. No idea if Arthur spoke to me, tried to help me. I felt it then. I felt the padlock snap and the cage door burst open. My heart plummeted toward the well of grief I had tried to keep sealed off. A place of sadness and despair, a hole of quicksand that wanted to drag me down too deep to return from.

I held the gun steady and aimed again. My head filled with Hugo and my father tied to chairs, frantically begging for their lives. The floodgates of my mind wrenched themselves open.

And as if my dad's and Hugo's and my friends' murders weren't enough for my mind and heart to endure, an image of my mum came next. Her soft but bony hand clutched in mine. How weak it was as she tried to hold me tightly and say her goodbyes. My mum, the one person who had ever shown me love—true love—leaving me, cancer stealing her from my side. I saw her laughing and smiling and taking me to the park. Afternoon tea at Harrods and holding my hand as we walked along Bond Street.

Then she disappeared, her body and bright smiling face misting away with the gale-force wind of death.

Gone.

I fired a bullet as I remembered watching her fade in her bed. When her chest rose, fell ... then never moved again. Her hand, already weak in mine, went limp. Hours and hours passed, and I still couldn't let her go. A little girl staring at her mum's pale, still face, wondering why she couldn't get better. Why she couldn't smile at me again. Why she couldn't heal and not leave me alone.

Because I was. After she had left me, I was alone. Maternal love gone, and a distant father's embrace the pitiful replacement.

Mum.

Dad.

Hugo.

Freya.

Arabella.

I fired the gun over and over until the bullets were replaced by empty rounds sending nothing but air and lost dreams into the bales. Tears flooded my cheeks, and all the fight drained from my body. The gun seemed to weigh ten tons in my trembling hands. My arms fell, dropping it to the ground. My legs felt like jelly, and I felt myself collapsing to the sandy ground, but strong arms caught me before I hit the floor.

All I could see was blood. All I could see were my friends tied up and crying to be free. Their terrified eyes as they realised they weren't getting saved. Dad and Hugo as they silently begged their attackers for mercy on the video. Two men who were not exactly affectionate or loving to me, but who I loved because they were mine. My only family ... I saw my mum kiss my head as she said goodbye, as she told me to be a good girl and that she would watch down on me from heaven ...

My family ... all gone.

I didn't realise I was falling apart, wracking sobs tearing from my chest, until Arthur sat on the floor and pulled me into his arms. His hold was like a balm to my torn soul. "They're dead," I said, hearing gunshots in my mind. The sounds that would have engulfed the room as the attackers fired into my dad's and Hugo's heads.

And my best friends ... they died because of me.

"It's my fault," I said, my throat raw from the sadness, from the guilt. "My friends died because of me. They're gone because of me ..." Arthur held me tighter, and despite the emptiness in my heart, I felt safe. As I collapsed and exorcised weeks and weeks of repressed sadness and guilt, he kept me upright in his arms, never letting me fall.

"Arthur," I cried, clutching his arms just for something to ground me. To stabilise the emotions threatening to tear me apart. "They're gone. All I have, everyone ... they're gone." I was twenty-four, soon to be twenty-five. And they had all gone.

Arthur lifted me until I was firmly in his lap, until I was curled into his chest, and I cried for the four lives that had been lost. Four lives that were my family, that I loved. Taken so brutally, so quickly.

And my angel, my mother, taken from me so young.

Arthur's hands moved to my cheeks and lifted my face. His thumbs stroked away the mass of tears from my eyes, and he leaned in, kissing the wetness from my face. We stayed there, him kissing me and caring for me, until my body shook with exertion, my emotions raw and wrought. He kissed each falling droplet away, my tears glistening on his lips. He consumed my sadness; he savoured my pain.

I was breathless, my chest sore from overuse. When my sobs had ebbed and my tears had begun to dry, Arthur met my eyes. "You're not alone, princess."

I stared into his eyes, needing more. Craving more. Arthur's shirt was wet, and I saw the lines of his tattoo through the now transparent material. I knew my cheeks would be red and blotchy, but I didn't care. I was numb yet wracked with sorrow—erratically flitting from one sensation to the other.

"I didn't think it was possible to feel so much loss," I whispered and let Arthur push back strands of tear-dampened hair from my face. I put my hand to my chest. "I didn't think it was possible to feel such emptiness in here." I sucked in a shuddering breath. "In your heart."

Arthur's piercing blue stare captured mine and didn't let go. Gripping my cheeks harder, he repeated, "You're not alone." Each of his words was a salve. A door unlocking that had been bolted shut. Hope bursting into glimmering light.

"I'm not?" I whispered.

Arthur pressed his forehead to mine. His lips grazed along mine. "No."

I grasped his wrists and embraced the warmth his hands brought to my face. "I'm ..." I pulled back so I could see his face. "I think I'm broken," I confessed, feeling the truth of those words ache in my heart. "I'm not sure I'll ever get over this, over losing them." Arthur's hands flexed on my cheeks, and I knew that was his way of telling me he knew how it felt. Of course he did. He had watched those he loved die around him too. "Can you love a broken queen?" I asked, smiling though my face felt numb.

Arthur searched my eyes. "Can you love a broken king?"

I stopped breathing. As he stared at me, I realised he was waiting for my answer. No, he *needed* my answer. Because Arthur, *my* Arthur, had just let me in a fraction more.

He was broken too. This man, this unshakeable and unreadable titan of a man, was broken too.

"I already do," I said, my confessional whisper wrapping around us in the empty room.

Arthur sighed. "Then don't ask questions you already know the answer to."

His gruff response stopped my heart. Arthur's eyes flitted away from mine, only to fix on them again as his veiled admission sank into my soul. He loved me too. It was the closest he'd got to admitting the words aloud.

This broken king loved his broken queen.

I kissed him. Lips sore and cheeks flamed, I kissed him and tried to pour all the love I had inside me into that kiss. I pulled back and looked at the target. Bullet holes riddled the paper. Arthur picked up the gun and handed it to me. "Yours," he said. As I took the gun from him, he wrenched me forward so hard I hit his chest. Eyes burning, he said, "I need you to learn how to use it. You need to master it. Then use it if you ever need to. No hesitation." Arthur's breathing quickened, betraying just how much he needed this from me.

"I promise," I said and was rewarded with a deep kiss.

"Let's go home."

I followed Arthur out of the pits and into his car. He held my hand the entire way home. I sank into the heated seat and watched the early-morning mist rise over London. Market sellers were rousing from their sleep, readying for the morning of trade. I loved this time of morning. The calm before the storm. When it was quiet and still. The deep breath before the exhale of day.

I felt dead on my feet as we entered the church. Emotionally and physically exhausted.

As we passed the living room, Arthur changed track and pulled me inside. Vinnie sat before the fire, staring into the flames. Arthur nodded at his brother and poured me a large whisky. As I took the drink from Arthur and downed half the glass in one, feeling the hot liquid coat my throat, I felt someone watching me.

It was Vinnie. His head tilted to the side as he examined my face, as if he was listening to someone speaking into his ear. I smiled at him, always feeling such sorrow for this man and the demons that plagued him. A man clearly lost in life's intricate maze. I raised the glass to my lips, needing the numbing effects of the alcohol, when Vinnie said, "They don't blame you."

My hand froze around the glass. He nodded at what I presumed was his hallucination of Pearl. Vinnie took a deep breath. "They don't blame you at all."

"Who?" I asked, feeling Arthur move behind me. He curled his arm around my waist and pulled me back into his chest, as if he knew I needed his steady frame to keep me from falling.

"Your mates," he said with as much ease as he talked about anything else. My heart thundered in my chest.

"My mates." Numbness tried to smother me, to protect me from more pain. But I pushed it back. I wanted to hear this. I needed to.

"They know it's not your fault," he said. "They just wanted you to know." Vinnie stared back into the fire as if he hadn't just carved my chest open and offered me something I thought I could never receive—forgiveness from my deceased friends.

A lifeline.

"And my dad?" I asked, knowing Vinnie never really saw the dead but taking the rope he offered anyway. I knew it was his illness, the hallucinations. Yet I so desperately wanted to believe it to be true that I pushed for more. "Hugo?" Arthur gripped me harder at the mention of Hugo. But he didn't need to be jealous. I hadn't loved Hugo in the romantic sense. But I'd loved him as a friend, as my family. I'd never wished him any harm.

Vinnie cocked his head, then looked at me blankly. "I don't hear them." My stomach sank.

"Come on," Arthur said, clearly seeing exhaustion pulling me down to despair. He guided me to our room and took the whisky from my hand and placed it on the bedside table.

He undressed me, but my thoughts were elsewhere. As he removed my clothes and slipped his t-shirt over my head in place of my night-gown, I asked, "Do you ever believe him?" I let my attention drift to the door, and the living room beyond where Vinnie was no doubt still sitting. "That he talks to the dead?" I swallowed the lump in my throat. "That he just spoke to Freya and Arabella? That they ..." I inhaled deeply. "That they don't blame me. That they wanted me to know."

Arthur stripped off his clothes. When he remained in only his boxers, he stepped closer to me. He put his hands through my hair. "I gave up a bloody long time ago trying to figure out what Vinnie was all about. So I say believe whatever the fuck you want, princess."

"But do *you* believe him?" I treaded carefully when I asked, "About Pearl. Do you believe he truly sees her, or is it really just a hallucination born out of mental illness and the stress of loss?"

Arthur's teeth gritted together, and I knew that the deaths of his sister and mum was one demon he had yet to confront. I knew from Betsy that it was the one part of his life he never talked about. Ever. *Couldn't* talk about. Refused to—always had.

"I think Vinnie believes she's real, and that's all that matters to him. Keeps him from going postal. I know he has an illness—it's been verified by a truckload of doctors." Arthur shrugged. "But Eric's always believed Vin sees something else, sees what most people can't. Sees something more."

"He didn't see my dad and Hugo."

"It's not a foolproof gift, if it even is a gift." Arthur handed me the whisky again. I drained the glass, then let him lift me into his bed. He wrapped me in his arms and I shut my eyes, letting the grief I had pushed away for so long try to drown me again.

I had to face it.

But as the waves of grief and guilt crashed over me, I held on tightly to Arthur, trusting him to keep me safe. I held on as I replayed my loved ones' deaths so vividly in my mind. Then I thought of Vinnie's words: *They know it's not your fault … They just wanted you to know …*

Freya and Arabella didn't blame me. I felt that truth in the depths of my heart. I'd felt the truth of it when Vinnie had met my eyes with unwavering faith and told me so, a message to my guilt-ridden soul from their mouths.

Vinnie hadn't known of my breakdown at the warehouse. He hadn't known that I had broken my heart to Arthur and let the pain I'd been fighting for weeks finally consume me. He hadn't known, yet his message was so timely it made the hairs on the back of my neck stand on end.

So, I would believe him. My soul cried out for me to trust in him, to find solace in his words. And as the sun rose and London began to wake, Arthur held me tighter as his queen, safe in his protective arms and in his care.

CHAPTER THIRTEEN

ARTHUR

She was fucking breaking me.

I sat in my car, arriving at the docks thinking about Cheska. That's all I fucking did. Think of her when I wasn't with her; she was haunting me, fucking with me. She was in my bloody head as if she was possessing me. Her green-brown eyes, and the way they fucking cut through me. Like she always knew what I was thinking. Like she could claw at my chest and grip my heart in her hand, squeezing it and ripping down its walls.

I stepped out of the Bentley, the sky grey and overcast, the freezing rain chucking it down in buckets. I didn't care about the downpour as it ran down my face and soaked through my suit. I didn't give a fuck about anything but Cheska and being inside her cunt as she clawed at my back.

I met Freddie in the woods. I stopped in front of the tree and the stupid twat tied to it. I reached into my jacket pocket and pulled out my knife. I closed in on the prick, who was holding his chin high and trying to glare me down.

"He's saying fuck all," Freddie said. This tosser had been caught wiping route information from one of our haulage ships. One of the haulage ships that had been targeted at sea, millions of pounds worth of coke now getting the fishes off their faces in the North Sea.

I didn't have time for this shit. Lashing out, I slit the twat's throat, his blood spurting to the ground, then headed back to the car. "Be at home for seven," I called back at Freddie.

I climbed into the car, and the driver pulled out onto the road. I stared out of the window and felt fucking twitchy, like I couldn't sit still, like I was crawling out of my skin. I felt fucking *undone*.

And I bloody hated it.

Since Cheska. Since Chelsea Girl met me in the pits and threw her crown at my feet. Since she threw her old life the fuck away and joined the fucked-up darkness that only I offered.

I love you ...

Her voice played in my fucking head on loop. Fucking haunted me. Drove me insane.

I never wanted it to stop.

I pressed my thumbs into my eyes, seeing her on her knees as she sucked my cock, as she lay on her back as I fucked her—no, not fucked, *made love*, she said.

I love you ... your broken queen ...

She was like me. Just fucking like me. My chest ached like it had been punched by a heavyweight boxer. My pulse thundered in my neck and wrist, pounding and pounding, never-fucking-ending.

Cheska was fucking up my head. I'd let her in, and she was fucking tearing me down. I couldn't think with her around me, couldn't bastard think without her. All I wanted to do was keep the bird close and fuck her, sink inside her pussy and listen to her scream as she pressed her tits to my chest, then ... *I love you ...*

The car turned into the driveway of the church. Fireworks were already in the sky. Bonfires littered the fields, Guy Fawkes effigies burning on the pyres.

Fucking Bonfire Night. The fifth of November.

And Cheska's birthday.

She'd been quiet since the other night at the pits. She sat alone a lot, lost in thought. I didn't know how the fuck to help her. She'd lost her mates, her old man and the fuckwit that was Hugo Harrington. She wasn't used to death like I was—especially death by murder. Then it had been piled on her like petrol would be poured on bonfires up and down the country tonight.

The car stopped and I got out. I went straight to my bedroom, my feet almost fucking faltering as I passed by my old man's room. Something inside me tried to pull me to him. The part of me that had cracked open when Chelsea Girl had barrelled back into my life, when she'd stood in the pits in her leather trousers and thrown down the gauntlet, dragging her pristine white queen down my bloodied chest and telling me she was mine.

Mine. That she was the fucking dark queen ready to reign at my side.

The crack she'd caused never fucking closed. The more time I spent with her, the more it widened. And with every inch it grew, the fucking pain almost brought me to my knees. It made me fucking hate her, made me want to push her away and stop fucking up my life. But then she'd smile at me, cast those fucking green-brown eyes on me and ... *I love you* ...

And she'd consume me some more. Sinking her talons further into my brain. I didn't let anyone in. Had *never* let anyone in. No more. Never again after Mum and Pearl, but then Cheska ... she came and smashed through my walls, fracturing the fuckers until she slid into the cracks. Until she got under my skin and started tearing me apart, smothering my brain.

I needed her. I fucking *craved* her.

Cheska wasn't in the bedroom. I quickly took a shower, then went looking for her. Charlie, Eric and Vinnie were already in the living room. "Penny for the guy," Eric said, holding out his whisky glass like the tosser he was.

"Black eye okay as a replacement?" I said and got myself a gin.

"So violent," the fucking plank replied.

"So, old boy," Charlie said, sidling up beside me. "How's the traitor?"

"Dead."

Charlie held up his glass in approval. "I'll drink to that."

My eyes were fixed on the doorway, waiting for Cheska. "Where is she?"

"In one of the bedrooms with Betsy." Charlie nudged me, lips twitching. "Calm down, Artie. It's only been five minutes since you last seen her."

"Fuck off."

"Seriously," Eric said, taking a seat next to Vinnie, "who knew the great Arthur Adley, the Dark Lord of London Town himself, could be tamed by a posh bit of pussy."

"Watch it," I warned Eric.

"Pearl approves," Vinnie said, and I felt my body fucking tense. I eyed my mate. The nutter was staring at me like he could see right through to my brain, see how much Cheska was screwing with my head. Vinnie nudged his head to "Pearl". "She said she likes her, even if she is from Chelsea."

I thought of Cheska the other night when Vinnie had told her that her mates were okay. That they didn't blame her. Cheska had asked me if I thought Vinnie could really talk to the fucking dead. I'd never given it much thought before. Now it was all I could fucking think of. I was dreaming of my mum, Pearl, the fire. Dreaming of my old man getting gunned down before me. Dreaming about them sitting around Vinnie, staring right at me.

Like a tap. She'd made the shit I locked away in my head into a fucking tap. One twist and the drip it had been had turned into a full bloody stream. And I couldn't fucking switch it off.

I didn't feel. That wasn't what I did. I was fucking numb. I had to be to live this life, to be the head of this family. To fucking survive. But there was now a fucking Cheska-sized hole in my chest that was bleeding all over the bloody place.

Gene walked into the room; the kid was skittish as fuck. "Gene," I said, taking in his black clothes and the long sleeves he had pulled down over his arms. Sleeves that when pulled back revealed two black bandages that hid a fuck-ton of razor scars.

That's what people who felt too much in this life became. A fucking shell—cutting, drugs and death the only escapes.

"Hi, Artie," he said and sat down on the chair. He stared at his feet, only lifting his eyes to look at Charlie. The kid felt better in my cousin's company. And he should. Charlie would have anyone in this family's back.

"Where the fuck is she?" I said again, needing to see Cheska's fucking face.

Freddie entered the room and laughed. "Bloody hell, Artie. Calm the fuck down. Never I thought I'd see the day when you were controlled by a bird."

I was going to kill them all. One by fucking one.

Five minutes later, I slammed my glass down on the bar and planned on dragging Cheska out of the bedroom, ready or not. That or fucking her over the bed, not giving two shits who was watching. Just as I passed Gene's chair, Betsy, Vera, Ronnie and Cheska came through the doorway.

"Alright, Artie," Betsy said, a knowing smile pulling on her lips. "You look flustered." Betsy pulled Cheska through behind her. My fucking heart almost stopped when she entered in high-waisted jeans and a white top tucked into them. The outfit showed off every inch of her perfect figure, curves for fucking days.

Cheska smiled at me, her brown hair falling down her exposed back. "Get the fuck here," I hissed, and Cheska walked toward me in her knee-high boots. I cupped the back of her head and pulled her into me. I smashed my lips to hers, tasting something sweet on her lips, no doubt some fucking sugary cocktail Betsy would have made her.

A thunderous chorus of bangs came from outside, echoing around the old church. "Fireworks!" Ronnie said, and everyone in the room headed outside.

When they were gone, I slammed Cheska against the wall. "Happy fucking birthday, princess," I said against her mouth, moving my hands straight to her tits as she pushed against me. My lips dropped to her neck.

I fucking cursed the woman. I was addicted. Didn't want her out of my sight. And as I thought of the fuckers who wanted her, who wanted to steal her from me, to sell her and use as a fuck-toy, I saw red. I wanted to tear the twats apart, limb by limb, and hang their bones on my fucking church door to warn any other arsehole off.

"I missed you," Cheska said, putting her hands on my face. I kissed her again. Words didn't come easily to me. I didn't tell her I loved her or fucking missed her. I protected her, fucked her and made her mine in other ways. That's what I could give. All I knew how to fucking give.

"Let's go." She took my hand. I yanked her back and studied her face. I knew that under her makeup she had dark circles under her eyes. She'd lost some weight, and she had been plagued by nightmares since the night in the pits. I narrowed my eyes, trying to read her.

"I'm good, babe," she said, convincing no one, and kissed my lips. "I promise. I'm ..." She sighed, and I felt her fucking slipping away from my grasp. I'd always known it was a fucking pipe dream, her being with me, being okay with this life. "Just let's enjoy tonight." She flashed her pearly white teeth. "Who doesn't love fireworks?"

Cheska put on her coat at the door, and I followed behind. The rain had eased, and colours of light burst all over the London sky, looking like the fucking Blitz. Cheska stopped next to Betsy. I put my hand around her waist and pulled her back to my chest. I sparked up a cig, then placed it in Cheska's mouth. She took it from me, and I lit my own. Cheska's head fell against my chest as she stared up at the sky. But I kept my fucking eyes on her. That ache was back in my chest, but it was hitting me deeper, harder.

Cheska's hand covered my hand and she turned back to me, exhaling a cloud of smoke, and smiled wide. And that ache in my chest became a fucking canyon. I scanned around the church, past the grave-yard and tall headstones, making sure everything was safe.

Charlie caught my gaze and frowned at me. He winked, but I saw the concern on his face.

I was going insane. This ... *Cheska* was making me go insane. It was why my old man had never recovered after my mum died. Never married again, hell, never even had a girlfriend. Sure, he fucked birds, whores, but once my mum was gone, he'd locked up all his feelings and only siphoned off the anger that consumed him on his rivals. That was the path he'd shown me too. If he'd been awake now, he'd have laughed in my face for being so fucking pathetic over a piece of pussy. Told me I was an idiot and to shut this thing with Cheska the fuck down before it made me weak.

Then Cheska turned and took my mouth, and despite it all, I fucking let her in. I tasted her and let her perfume wrap around me. The fireworks finally ended; only random ones from people's gardens were going off now.

"Drinks!" Betsy shouted, then led us all inside. We made our way to the living room, and shots were poured. "Presents!" Betsy called.

Cheska tensed on my knee. "No, you didn't have to—"

Betsy handed her a present, and I heard the long inhale that Cheska took. Betsy must have seen, as she said, "Open it, darling."

Cheska opened the box. She laughed, pulling out a book on cockney rhyming slang. Betsy shrugged. "Just thought it might help you a bit more round these parts. Not many people round here could hold a conversation with the queen." My cousin nodded toward the box again. "There's a pair of Tiffany earrings in there too."

"Thank you," Cheska said, a hitch in her voice. I held her tighter.

Ronnie got up next. She handed her a box. "From me, Vera and Gene." Cheska took off the lid and froze. "Hairpins," Ronnie said, smirking. "Maybe not the ones you're used to receiving. But ones that'll help you better in this family."

I kissed the back of Cheska's neck as she pulled back the tissue paper. Two long silver hairpin blades sat in the box. Cheska lifted them up. "To carry with you," Vera said. "Just in case."

Cheska felt the end of the blade, pulling her hand away when it brought a spot of blood to her finger.

"My present's lessons on how to use them," Eric said from across the room.

"Leech," Vera said.

"We're fucking blokes," he said, indicating the rest of us. "We don't do presents. Unless you want a hooker. I can get one here in five minutes flat."

"Pig." Betsy rolled her eyes.

"I'm good, thank you, Eric," Cheska said, smiling, then lowered her eyes. I saw my family casting glances to each other, wondering what was wrong with her.

"It means a lot to me," she said, voice tight, and I held her closer. She turned to look at me, and I frowned. "I'm okay," she said, reading my fucking mind as always.

I was just about to push her for more answers when my phone rang. Charlie's went off too. Charlie looked at his phone and spat, "Fuck!" He met my eyes. I pulled out my phone and saw the message. My blood boiled in my veins.

"Fuck," I growled and lifted Cheska off my lap.

Ronnie was on her feet in two seconds when she saw the message. "I'm coming." All my family received the message, one by one.

"We're all coming," Betsy said. I glanced at Cheska. "She'll have to come. Gene too. There'll be no one here to watch them. Unless you want me to call in some soldiers."

"They're fucking coming," I said. My family knew I wouldn't trust any fucker but one of these with her, with Gene. We all went for the cars. Cheska gripped my hand as we piled into the back seat of my Bentley.

"What's happened?" she asked, eyes wide.

"A shipping container has been dumped on my newest dock."

"Okay," she said. "A container of what?"

I ran my hand over the stubble on my chin. "Women," I said and saw the question in Cheska's eyes. "Trafficked women."

The colour fell from her face, then she held my hand tighter as we made for the docks. I replayed the message again. The soldiers guarding the docks had all been wiped out. Mikey, one of my generals, had gone to check on the next shipment and saw the gates were wide open, bodies fucking everywhere. He'd found the dumped shipping container, peered through a crack, and seen a fuck-ton of women in cages inside, drugged to the bloody eyeballs and stark naked.

This was Old Sammy's dock. He still owned it. We just paid him a truckload of money to use it. I'd had it for a few fucking weeks. That was it. And already whoever had been fucking with us had targeted it.

Cheska was silent on the way. Her fucking birthday. The pricks had struck on her fucking birthday. As we travelled the roads, quieter because of Bonfire Night, crashes and bangs exploded around us. Cheska leaned against the window, watching the fireworks burst into the sky. But she never let go of my hand.

Finally, we entered the road leading to the dock. I saw the gate as we passed, the hinges blown and the gates hanging wide open. I narrowed my eyes as I stared at my men dead on the ground. Cheska's hand was shaking, and when I cut a glance her way, her eyes closed, blocking out the sight of my soldiers bleeding out on Old Sammy's tarmac.

The car came to a stop and the engine cut out. The car was silent. I released Cheska's hand, needing to get out and deal with this shit, but she held on tight and shifted her arse along the back seat to my side. "I'm coming with you," she said and lifted that fucking chin.

Leaning over, I took her mouth in a bruising kiss, then opened the door. The sound of fireworks echoed off the docks. I made my way to Mikey and saw he'd already had soldiers stationed around, patrolling the perimeter. His eyes fixed on Cheska as I approached him, no doubt wondering who the fuck she was to me. My brothers and sisters fell into step beside me. Vera and Ronnie flanked Cheska, keeping her protected.

The rain started falling, and my attention fell on the red shipping container. "How the fuck did that get here and no fucker saw?" Eric asked and moved closer to the container.

"No one was left to be a witness." Mikey blew on his hands as the fucking cold wrapped around him. He threw his thumb in the direction of the corpses being lined up along the side of the yard—our men, fucking cut down and murdered. "The next shift doesn't come in for a couple of hours. It's skeleton staff until then. They took them all out."

"Cameras?" Charlie asked, and I heard the pissed-off edge to his voice.

"Cameras were cut, then wiped. No fucking trace of anyone."

I felt the telltale signs of my anger start burning in the bottom of my spine. It swept through my bones and cells until I was made of nothing but rage and fire. People were fucking petrified of us. We should have been able to leave all our docks wide open, our gear completely visible, and no fucker would take them for fear of our wrath. That was the fucking reputation I'd built since my old man had been taken down. We were the fucking London Town reapers. You fucked with us and we'd come for your fucking souls. Whoever was doing this was either new to London and or had a fucking death wish.

I took in the dead, the fucking container, and the fact that no fucker, none of the men that I paid, had a fucking clue what the hell was going on.

"Arthur ..." Mikey shut the fuck up when he saw my face.

I held out my arms, gesturing to the entire fucking yard, and shouted, "WHAT THE FUCK IS HAPPENING? And why the *fuck* do we not already have some cunt's head on a fucking spike for fucking with the Adley firm like this?"

Freddie was over by the container with a couple of Mikey's crew, wrenching it open. My breath came out in fast pants, the cold turning it into white smoke. Explosions of colour blew up the fucking sky, drowning out my rage.

"We'll get them," Eric said to me, and I heard the latch on the container door open. "We'll fucking get them, Artie. No one messes with us. They can't fucking hide forever. And when we find them, we'll strike and tear them apart."

One of the men yanked open the container, and the stench from inside barrelled into us like a freight train. "Shit!" Vinnie spat, slinging his arm over his nose and mouth, his shoulders tensed, ready for a fucking battle.

"No," Ronnie whispered, then cut away from the rest of us. "No." She sprinted for the container.

"Baby! Wait!" Vera gave chase, Cheska and Betsy on her heels.

I started storming toward them, just as a fucking explosion came from our left. I whipped my head to the docks, only to see a boat alight on the water, fire fucking blazing. The flames climbed high and the engine exploded, the noise of which was drowned out by the fireworks still flaring up above.

"Fuck!" Charlie shouted, and my chest pulled so tight I thought it might rip the tendons. "What the bloody hell is all this?"

Vera and Betsy were beside us again, guns drawn, ready to fight anyone who used the cover of the blast to come at us.

I heard Ronnie scream, then turned to see Cheska and Ronnie trying to open the nearest cage. I narrowed my eyes and saw the girls inside starting to wake. "They've got the brand," Ronnie said, her voice fucking laced with pain. "Get them out. Get them all out! They've got the brands on their backs."

Cheska dived forward, helping her. Another explosion sounded—another empty container on the west side of the yard burst into flames. Agonised screams cut through the chaos as some of Mikey's crew crawled away from the explosion, trousers and coats on fire. Eric and Vinnie ran to help them.

"Cheska!" I shouted, my voice fucking echoing around the blazing yard. "Get the fuck here!"

"Ronnie!" Vera ran for her girlfriend.

Cheska and Ronnie were dragging a girl from the cage, the bird's limbs limp and weak. Cheska looked back at me but continued trying to drag the trafficked woman out. I started running, overtaking Vera just as something on the side of the container caught my eye.

"CHESKA!" I screamed, seeing the casing of an explosive on the container door.

"No! NO!" Vera spat when she saw what I was fucking glaring at. Cheska grabbed Ronnie's arm and tried to pull her away, knowing something was wrong. But Ronnie wouldn't move. She fought to get Cheska to stay near the girls, to help her open more of the cages.

Like fucking slow motion, the world tripping into half speed, I saw the fire ignite at the back of the container as I reached Cheska. I threw her to the ground, covering her with my body as the fucking thing blew. A thunderous boom took out the dumped container and all the trafficked women inside, the smell of burning flesh immediately lashing around us.

Cheska was still beneath me. I reared back, turning her over. I hadn't been quick enough. She took too much of the fucking blowback. Scratches and cuts covered her skin, dirt from the ground. "Princess," I said, pulling her into my arms. The fire from the burning container singed the back of my coat. I didn't fucking give a shit. "Princess, wake the fuck up!" I snarled and felt my stomach sink. A fucking great big hole burrowed in my chest, caved in my fucking bones as I stared at Cheska's closed eyes.

Emptiness chased everything else out of my body as I pulled her closer to my chest. She was dead. She was fucking dead ...

Someone touched me, and I lashed out, grabbing their fucking hand. I yanked them to me, ready to rip out their throat for coming too close to me and my bird. "Artie, it's Charlie. You need to move from the fire." I stared into my cousin's brown eyes, letting my brain calm the fuck down and back off from slitting his throat.

"She's gone. She's fucking gone!" I roared. The need to destroy whoever did this consumed me, became all I fucking was. I held Cheska tighter. She still felt warm. Still felt perfect in my arms. My Chelsea girl. The only fucking bird who had ever got through the darkness, the blackness plaguing my fucking half-dead heart.

"Artie, move." Charlie took my arm, dragging me to my feet. I held Cheska tighter as I moved toward the cars, my vision blurred with red. I couldn't breathe, every fucking inhale like taking in boiling-hot air.

I looked up and saw Vera holding Ronnie, Ronnie's fucking stunned eyes on Cheska in my arms. I scanned the yard, the fire raging and the bodies on the ground. Freddie and Vinnie running around, dragging men from the flames. Eric, arms around Betsy and Gene. Cheska limp in my motherfucking arms.

All the life fled from my veins and, in that moment, I became death. I became nothing but evil, revenge all I could crave, the bitter, addictive taste of bloodlust filling up my mouth.

A noise travelled to my ears and I looked down. I fucking froze when Cheska's eyelids started to move, when her arms and legs shifted. "Cheska," I rasped, and her eyes finally opened. She blinked, and then those fucking green-browns fell on me.

"Arthur," she said, dazed, but I saw the fog in her mind clearing by the second. Then her eyes widened and she looked back at the container, at the flames clawing higher, the last of the night's fireworks fizzling out in the sky above us.

"The girls," she whispered, kicking out of my hold until her feet hit the ground. "The girls." She tried to get back to the container. But my arm was a fucking iron cage around her stomach. She was back. She was bloody breathing. And I was never letting her fucking go again. "Arthur!" she cried, trying to break from my grip. "The girls!"

"They're dead," Betsy said from behind us. I heard a fucking agonised wail from Ronnie. She was in her girlfriend's arms, sobbing, clutching Vera like there was no bloody tomorrow. "None of them survived the explosion," Betsy said as vans came racing up the road, our soldiers coming to contain this shitshow. To find me fucking evidence of who it was so I could decapitate the fuckers who were attacking us, once and for all. So I could destroy them and tear their organisation apart.

No one fucked with what was mine.

No one fucked with my fucking woman!

"We're leaving." I dragged Cheska, kicking and fighting me, back to the car. I pushed her inside, nudging my chin at Vera to bring Ronnie in our car too. The soldiers piled out of the van, their eyes turning livid as they saw the carnage. I would be speaking to Old Sammy tonight to find out what he knew.

The soldiers looked at me as I stood by my car. "Clean up, but search the grounds for any evidence of who did this. I'll pay any of you who get me leads or any kind of answer a truckload of money." I met each one of them in the eyes. "Someone is trying to fuck with our firm. Now they've fucked with my family, and that's taken this from fucking child's play to an out-and-out fucking war. Keep your ears to the ground and find me the fuckers who thought it would be wise to mess with me."

I got in the car and got on the phone to Charlie. "Get men stationed around our house. No fucker but family gets in and out. We're staying together—tell everyone to get their bags packed and get their arses to the church."

"Got it, Art." Charlie hung up.

Cheska was staring at the flames of the container through the window, her eyes fixed on the one bird they'd managed to pull out. She was already dead, fucking died alone, naked in a cage. I threw my arm around Cheska's neck and pulled her close. I turned her face to me, gripped her cheeks and kissed her shaking lips. Tears fell down her face, and I tasted the salty water on my tongue.

"You're alive," I said, feeling some of the molten anger inside me turn to smoke at the fact that she was here, beside me, fucking *alive*.

"Those girls ..." Cheska said, her breath hitching. She shook her head. She took my hand and fucking squeezed my fingers with all she was made of. "The one we pulled out ..." She closed her eyes, more tears falling. "She looked like Freya. For a minute ..." Her mate. Her mate whose throat had been slit in front of her. "I tried to save her. I *needed* to save her." Cheska looked up and found Ronnie. She reached across the seat and gripped her hand. "Ronnie ..."

"They had the brand," Ronnie said to all of us and no one at the same time. Her dark eyes were like fucking glass, her deep skin paling. Vera held her girlfriend closer, kissing her forehead, but Ronnie was fucking lost to the past. Locked in the days when she'd lived in a fucking cage, been branded just the same as those birds who were now nothing but ash and charred remains.

"I met them at a nightclub," she said, and Cheska tensed. Ronnie met Cheska's eyes. "I snuck in underage. I met them at the bar. They bought me drinks. They offered me a job, saying they didn't care that I was too young." Ronnie's voice was tight and weak, but she was speaking. She was fucking exorcising her past in the Bentley's back seat as it took us back to the one place no one would dare come for us. The one fucking place I could keep us protected.

My fucking family's fortress.

"I was young," Ronnie said. "I said they'd need to speak to my parents." Ronnie swallowed like she was choking back a lump made of stone. "I didn't know my dad had gambling problems. I didn't know he had racked up thousands of pounds in debt with a loan shark." She shook her head. "Only, it wasn't a loan shark. It was a group, an organisation." Ronnie looked at Cheska's focused face. "A pack of demons pretending to be good people."

"What did they do?" Cheska asked.

Vera pulled Ronnie close, and Ronnie continued. "They came to our door. I thought they were there to get permission for me to work for them, so I could help bring in cash to the house. We were poor." Ronnie gazed out of the window. "But we were happy. When my dad opened the door, I knew something was up. His voice started shaking, and my mum could see something was wrong too."

Ronnie's free hand fisted on her thigh. "They were there to offer my old man a deal—all his debt wiped if he handed me over. If they'd let them take me away."

"How old were you?" Cheska asked.

"Seventeen," Ronnie said. "He said no, of course. My mum was screaming and praying to God to save us from their evil. He didn't." Ronnie's voice grew hoarse. "They shot them." The air in the car became charged with hatred and rage. Not just from me, but from Vera, from Ronnie, and by the tightness of her lips, Cheska too. "They brought them to their knees and killed them. Shot them for refusing to sell me."

"Who would do that?" Cheska asked, her greenness to this life showing in spades. "What kind of loved one would sell their child? Their family?"

"I'd say at least half of that container were debt payments made by desperate or dogshite parents," Ronnie said coldly.

"No," Cheska said, but Ronnie nodded.

"Kidnappings, debt payments, runaways, prostitutes. You name it. They make people vulnerable, or prey on the already weak."

Cheska looked at me and saw by my unmoved face that it was true. We stayed the fuck away from that kind of work, but it was fucking thriving in the London underworld. Dealing in sex and human trafficking was a one-way ticket to money. Lots of fucking money.

"Where ..." Cheska straightened her shoulders. "Where did you go? What happened to you?"

"I was sold. Sold at a market—"

"A market?"

"Like cattle," Vera spat, drying Ronnie's cheeks with her hands. "Paraded in a ring for people to buy as slaves—for cleaning, fucking, or whatever they fucking wanted." The famous Adley anger pulsed from Vera's voice. She was pissed at what her girlfriend had gone through.

"Where did they take you?" Cheska asked. "Abroad?"

Ronnie made sure Cheska was looking right at her when she said, "Knightsbridge."

"But ... what?" Cheska whispered.

"I was kept in a cage, in a basement in Knightsbridge. I was fucked and beaten by a couple who had a thing for pain. For years I served them, gave them whatever they wanted from me. Until they went away on business and the person watching their house had a heart attack and died in front of me."

"You ran," Cheska said, pride for Ronnie in her voice.

Ronnie nodded. "I was from the East End. I knew only one family who could help me. Knew only one group of people who could keep me safe and maybe help me bring my captors to justice." Ronnie smirked and looked right at me. I remembered the day she landed on our doorstep, nothing but skin and bone and covered in bruises, but telling us she'd do anything for us if we helped her. "I knew the Old Bill wouldn't help me." She smiled wider. "So, I came to the good guys."

"The good guys," Cheska echoed, and met my eyes. The look she was throwing my way made my fucking lungs burn. She knew. My bird knew because she'd done the fucking same.

"And they helped me. Helped me find the couple and let me get my revenge."

"The couple ... they didn't tell you who sold you to them? The group?"

"It was a front," Vera said. "A fucking labyrinth of cover-ups and dead ends. A well-oiled machine of deception."

"My old man took her on and gave her work in one of our factories," I said, and the colour slowly came back to Ronnie's face, the fucking life. "Rose to intel when he found out she'd been a hacker as a kid. Vera's old man took her under his wing after that."

"She quickly caught my eye." Vera kissed her bird on the lips. "Then I won her over."

Cheska sighed, and it was heavy. "That's what they would have done to me?" she said, the reality and gravity of her situation hitting home. "Those girls, if I hadn't found you, if I hadn't made it to you at your club ..." She turned to me, and the expression on her face, the fucking look she was wearing, carved the fuck out of my soul, wrenched that crack in my chest wide open into a fuck-off gaping canyon. "The good guys," she said, using Ronnie's words. She shifted closer and pressed against me like she could melt us into one fucking person.

"They shot my dad and Hugo like they shot your parents," Cheska said to Ronnie. She pressed her hand to my cheek. "But you saved me, Arthur. You saved me from that awful, heartbreaking life. You saved me from what Ronnie had to endure for too many years." Cheska reached out and took Ronnie's hand. "You are an inspiration."

Ronnie kissed Cheska's hand and then sat back, the fight leaking out of her. Ronnie met my eyes. "They're stepping it up," she said tiredly, referring to the traffickers. Ronnie darted a glance at Cheska, and I held my woman so fucking tight I thought she might not be able to breathe. They wanted Cheska.

They knew she was with me.

I didn't know how, but they fucking knew she was with me.

Vera and Ronnie must have thought the same thing because the looks on their faces were thunderous. They liked Cheska. Fuck, they loved her, and not just because she was mine.

They wouldn't get her. I fucking vowed to myself that they would never get her.

Cheska stayed glued to my side as we pulled up at the church. I held her fucking close as we went inside and sat down in the living room. One by one my family returned home, bringing their bags with them. We were all staying under this fucking roof until the cunts messing with us were caught.

No one spoke as we all sat around the room. Cheska sat on my lap. But it was the hairpin blades in her hands I watched, as she studied the gift Ronnie had given her. Her fingers danced over the steel and over the intricate filigree handle.

"I have braces for you too," Vera said, nodding to the blades in Cheska's hold.

"Braces?" Cheska asked.

"To conceal them." Vera gestured to her sleeves and the bottom of her trousers. "They lie flat so no one will know you have them on you. Giving you time to plan your escape."

Cheska nodded, but her eyes widened. Then I saw something flit across her face. Something I'd never seen on her before—a shadow of fucking black, a spiral of darkness.

Darkness that matched my own.

My phone sounded in my pocket. I pulled it out, expecting to see a message from Mikey telling me the police were bought off and the yard was cleared. Instead, it was a message sent by an encrypted number.

I opened it up as Eric and Charlie talked of what Mikey had found so far and the others listened. Cheska was busy turning her blades over and over in her hands, and I focused on the video that had been sent.

The video was silent and the quality was grainy. It took me a while to realise what I was looking at. But when the camera panned out and I saw a familiar thatched roof and manicured garden with a wooden fence, I knew.

I tensed, every fibre in my body braced to fucking snap. Cheska whipped her head to me, obviously feeling something in me change. My breathing came fast and hard as I watched some fucker in all black walk to the house that held every good childhood memory I ever had. And I watched as the cunt circled the cottage and poured petrol over the walls and the sides.

And I fucking watched as my mum walked out, checking a noise or something that she must have heard. I didn't move a fucking muscle as I watched the cunt charge at her from his cover of darkness and slam her back into the house, locking her inside, barricading the door with a metal bar. My mum hammered on the glass in the door as they backed away. Then she ran to the living room window just as the flames ignited, trapping her inside.

"Babe?" Cheska's soft voice said, but all I had was white noise in my head as the video showed the cottage starting to burn. Showed my mum running from the window when the heat became too much. Showed me her fucking terrified face as she backed away, the flames swallowing the house like it was being devoured by the jaws of hell itself.

The camera shut off and the room was plunged into silence. But my mum's and Pearl's voices were screaming in my head. Screaming for help, for the fucking help that never came as the house was torched, as my little sister, who was no doubt in bed, found my fucking mum in the thick black smoke of the cottage and held her tightly as the place burned and fell around them. As it fucking ripped the life from their lungs.

It wasn't an accident.

Arson.

It was fucking arson.

They were murdered. Mum ... Pearl ... they were fucking murdered. I didn't even feel myself pushing Cheska off my lap. I didn't think *anything* as I gave myself over to fury and started ripping the room apart, bottles from the bar smashing as I wrenched them down, over-turning tables and chairs and slicing them open with my knife.

They'd been murdered. My mum ... my sister ... Some fucker had—

I searched for my phone, finding it on the floor. I replayed the video, and ...

There.

I dropped the fucking phone when I saw it. When the cunt holding the camera went to shut off the video ... That circle. That bastard circle with the weird-as-shit V shape in the middle.

The brand.

I was shaking, shaking from the pure rage consuming me, drowning me in flames, from the fucking crack that Cheska had cleaved in me when she burst through the door of the club. The crack that had let the feelings seep into my blood and poison me with emotions, too many fucking emotions that I shouldn't be feeling, that I didn't want to ever fucking feel.

"Babe, please, you're scaring me." Cheska's voice cut through the noise in my head, all the fucking noise of screaming, of my blood rushing around me in crushing rapids, and I could hear her, Cheska ... Cheska ... Cheska ...

I threw my head back and roared, fucking roared, trying to get this cement from my stomach, the fucking tar in my blood that was sucking the life from me. I needed it all out. I needed the emotions and the feeling to fucking stop so I could take these fuckers out. So I could do my bloody job and not be swallowed up by the pain, the guilt, the fucking ripping apart of my soul.

Hands on my face wrenched me back to the present, to the room, trashed around me, and my family looking at me with concerned faces. Then—

"Babe, shh, it's okay." Cheska. Cheska was in front of me, her hands on my face. "I'm here, it's okay. Let me help ..."

But it wasn't okay. *She* had done this. *She* had fucking rammed back into my life with the force of a crowbar to the knees and fucked it all up. *She* had cut through the darkness that had settled inside me and tried to bring me to the light. I didn't fucking *want* the light. I didn't want the light or the fucking smiles, the kisses or the making love.

It made me weak.

She had made me too *weak*.

I ripped my head back and saw Charlie pick my phone up off the floor and watch the screen. Cheska's hands stayed in the air, where they'd just been on my face. Like I'd burned her. Like I'd scalded her skin.

"Get the fuck off me," I snarled, and Cheska's face blanched. "*You,*" I said, pointing at her. I pounded my hand on my chest. I needed to close the crack. Needed to stop the pain that was seeping out of it, poisoning my brain, my heart. "*You.*"

"What? Please—" She tried to step closer but stopped when I shook my head at her. "What have I done? Arthur ..."

I slapped at my skull, at the throbbing in my brain. That voice, her broken fucking voice made me feel things I didn't fucking want to fucking feel—*couldn't* feel to do my job right. "You're fucking with my head," I snarled and swiped the bottle of vodka that had fallen to the floor but remained intact. I threw the top into the fire and downed half the bottle in one go. Cheska had folded her arms across her chest, in protection, and was moving toward Betsy. "You fucking crawled into my fucking head, cleaved my fucking chest open and broke me!" I yelled. I saw the phone being passed from Eric to Freddie in the background. Charlie's and Eric's faces were fuming with anger as they met my eyes.

Freddie passed the phone to Vinnie. "Artie," he said, and I saw the fucking disbelief on his face, the fucking moment we all found out my mum and sister weren't lost in an accident after all, that they were in fact murdered. Murdered by the same cunts who had got Ronnie, who had killed all of Cheska's family and tried to take her too.

The ones who had dumped a container full of trafficked women on my fucking dock! It was them ... it was the branded cunts who were trying to come for me, for all we'd built.

They wanted Cheska. They fucking wanted my bird!

I searched the room for Cheska, but she'd gone. A fucking weight pressed down on my lungs like a torture device. My dark heart taunted me, ordering me to get on my fucking hands and knees and find her. That it needed her back. My fucking *queen*. The one who controlled the fucked-up chessboard that was my life.

My most important piece.

But I fought it. I fought it all, trying to yank myself back to the numbness I used to live with, the blackness, the fucking void that kept me from having to feel any of this shit, that let me think. Right now, I couldn't fucking think!

"You fucking prick," Betsy spat and got right in my face. My jaw clenched as my cousin went toe to toe with me. "Don't you dare you take this out on Cheska."

"She did this," I growled, the rage still pumping through my veins in waves, incinerating every fibre in my body. "She fucking made me feel, made me like this!"

"Human?" Betsy shot back. "A fucking living being, breathing, thriving—not a walking demon with nothing in his soul but blackness and hate?"

"THEY KILLED MY FUCKING MUM AND SISTER!" I boomed in Betsy's face and looked to the rest of my family. I caught Vinnie's eyes. They were fixed on the floor, and his body was shaking. Fucking shaking with rage.

"They killed her." Vinnie lifted his head and met my eyes. "They killed her, Artie. She didn't tell me they killed her."

"I don't think she knew," Charlie said, placating Vinnie's fucked-up head, his belief that he still saw and talked to my sister. "When the house went up, she wouldn't have known how the fire was started."

Vinnie nodded, grasping onto that lifeline. He studied his tight fists and said, "We need to kill them, Artie." He nodded, like he was assuring himself it was what needed to happen to make this shitshow okay. "They all need to fall down. All fucking fall down."

"Just remember," Betsy said, moving back into my path, ignoring everyone else, "that Cheska lost her entire family too. Not just *you*. She lost them *all*." Betsy laughed without humour. "And she loves you. Right now, I have no fucking idea why." Betsy moved to the door but stopped and, without looking back, said, "Your mum was like my mum too. And Pearl was my best friend, my fucking sister. You chose to deal with this life yourself. You have people who love and support you, but you chose to remain unfeeling when our dads died. You chose to push us all away and shut down, never letting anyone in. And you'll die alone if you keep doing it. Just like our dads did. Because I, for one, am fucking over trying to revive you."

Betsy left, and her words circled my head as I downed the vodka until the bottle was done. I looked up. Most of my brothers were still around me. Gene and Vinnie were the only ones who'd gone somewhere else, Ronnie and Vera too.

"I need them found," I said to Eric, Charlie and Freddie as they sat nursing their own drinks. "I need them fucking gone." My vision was hazy and I heard my voice. It was broken and slurred. The vodka hadn't numbed the pain in my body like I'd planned. It made it pulse deeper, faster, made the crack sink lower, lower and lower until I couldn't fucking stand it.

"We'll get them," Charlie said, and Eric and Freddie nodded their heads. I stared at the fire, seeing the flames of the cottage again. Seeing some cunt push my mum back into the house, locking her inside.

I sat up when the pain in my chest felt like it would fucking end me. "What the fuck is happening to us?" I said to them. "No one can fuck with us. I make sure of it." I stared into the dying fire, the flames being snuffed out under the burned logs. "We're the Adleys. We fucking run this town." I smacked into the side table. "I'm meant to stop this shit from happening to us. But someone is sneaking through. Someone is fucking sneaking *through*. I'm blind. I'm fucking *blind* to them." I took a half-full bottle of whisky and unscrewed the cap. I drank it down. "I can't see them." I looked at Freddie, Eric and Charlie. "I can't fucking see them. They're hiding in my fucking house, and I can't fucking *find* them!"

"We will." Charlie got to his feet. But I didn't want them to come to me. I didn't want anyone fucking near me. I was poison. The crack in my chest was full of fucking poison.

My shoulder smacked off the wall as I stumbled into the hallway. My room. I needed to get into my fucking room. *No*, the study. I needed to get into the study. No windows. No light. Just darkness. I needed to step into the darkness and let it swallow me whole.

I tried to walk. I tried to walk but all I kept seeing was my mum walking outside, wrapping her cardigan around her to stave off the night chill. Then he shoved her. The branded cunt fucking charged at my mum and trapped her inside the house. The fucking house that she loved. The cottage that she felt safe in. She took us there all the time to get us away from this life, a break from the firm and my dad, who only ever lived for this family, this fucked-up life.

And you'll die alone if you keep doing it. Just like our dads did ... Betsy's voice circled my head. *And you'll die alone if you keep doing it. Just like our dads did ...*

I stopped at the door to my left. The door that I never let myself go through. I turned the knob, then stumbled through. The lights were off and his nurse had gone home for the night. My feet were fucking cement blocks on the floor. But I made them move. I took a swig of whisky and let it burn my throat as I closed in on my dad. On the man I hadn't let myself get close to in over a year.

Everything smelled of antiseptic. The machines that surrounded him bleeped and pierced through my skull. I grabbed the footboard and held the fuck on. My eyes were on his covers, on the duvet that hid him from me.

"Look up, you pussy," I said to myself, then forced my eyes up. I turned away when my gaze landed on his face. On his too-thin body that never fucking moved. Not even a finger moved. My hand shook around the neck of the whisky bottle, but I made myself turn back around.

"Kill him," I heard my dad's voice say, the memory barrelling into

my head. I saw the man in my eyes. Saw him on the floor of the pit. Saw my dad stand behind me and put a knife in my hand ...

"Kill him," he said. I stared down at the knife in my hand. I was thirteen. I'd just turned thirteen. Charlie, Eric and Freddie watched me from the top of the pit. The knife felt heavy in my hands.

"Please, kid, don't," the man on the floor said. I looked at his face. He was bloodied and beaten, and he was on his knees.

"Look him in the eyes when you do it," Dad said, his mouth at my ear. "Make sure he dies looking into your *eyes—the future of our firm."*

"What did he do?" I stepped forward, closer to the man.

"He fucked with us. Ratted us out to an enemy. Some of our men died." I felt it then. Felt the anger start to build. Dad said that no one ever messed with us, our family. And if they did, they had to die.

"Arthur," Dad said again. "Kill him."

I walked forward and stood before the man. I could smell the sweat and piss on his clothes. The blood. I lifted the knife as one of our soldiers ripped open the man's shirt. I kept my eyes on his and pushed the knife into his chest, right through his heart. And I never moved my eyes away from him. I never moved my eyes from his as his mouth opened and he started choking on air. As the knife stopped when it reached the handle.

As he toppled over, and my dad put his hands on my shoulders. "Good, Artie. Real fucking good, kid."

I blinked, and the memory disappeared from my head. I remembered feeling it then. I'd felt the darkness start creeping, the doorway opening to something evil, something that reached its talons into my soul and took up home.

That had been the night. That had been the fucking night that Mum and Pearl had burned. When I'd killed that man, that traitor, they were already ash and teeth lost in the cottage's remains.

And you'll die alone if you keep doing it. Just like our dads did ...

Dad's face was grey and sunken, nothing like the man I'd just pictured in my head. Shot by the fucking Russians. Ploughed down and only alive because I paid a fuck-ton of money to keep him this way.

No one ever came to see him.

He had no one outside of us. His mates were long gone. Mum and Pearl were gone. And me? I never came into this room.

... you'll die alone ...

I downed the rest of my whisky, and my head swam with memories. Of Pearl. *Come on, Artie. Play with me. Hide and seek.*

Of Mum. *Come here,* she said, arms out. I walked to her and she pulled me onto the couch. She kissed my head. *Let's watch TV. It won't be long until you won't want to hang around with your old mum anymore.*

I couldn't fucking take it. The pain, all the fucking pain in my chest. I couldn't look at Dad. Couldn't think of the video I'd just seen. I backed out of the room until I was back in the hallway. I couldn't breathe.

I couldn't fucking *breathe!*

But my heart wasn't done fucking torturing me. Instead it showed me Cheska's face as I told her to get off me. That I was like this because of her. I saw the agony in her green-brown eyes. The trembling of her bottom lip. I closed my eyes, back slamming against the hallway wall, and I saw her above me, riding me, head thrown back and lips parted. Saw her walking down to the pit, leather on her legs and fucking hellfire in her stare.

Saw her stand before me and drag the queen down my chest. *I am your queen.*

Your queen ... your queen ... your queen ...

My fucking broken queen.

I scrambled off the floor, pictures slamming to the ground as I used my hands to steady me. I burst through the door to my bedroom. She wasn't there.

My heart started pounding in dread. I had to find her. The fucking ache in my chest only stopped aching when she was with me. When she was next to me, when my mouth was on hers, when I was inside her.

"Cheska!" I said, slamming open doors. My family stared at me when I found only them inside the rooms. I raced down the hallway, the whisky blurring my vision, robbing me of balance.

"Cheska!" I shouted, knocking vases and other crap off shelves as I bounced off the walls. I needed to find her.

I love you ... Her voice played in my head, threatening to bring me to my fucking knees. Her face. Her face when I told her to get off me, her arms wrapped around her waist like I'd stabbed her in the fucking heart.

I may as well have.

I love you, Arthur ...

"CHESKA!" I slammed open the study door. Betsy jumped to her feet. "Get out," I said to my cousin, seeing Cheska sat on the armchair behind her. "Cheska," I said again, the ache in my chest numbing some as I saw the top of her head, her brown hair.

She was still here.

I pushed into the room. Betsy brushed past me. I felt her burning, narrowed eyes on me, but I didn't look at her. This had fuck all to do with her.

The fire was climbing, and as I rounded the chair, there she was. There she fucking was ... my broken queen. Her eyes were fixated on the chessboard between the two armchairs. I stared down at it to see she had moved the pieces, played the game alone. The queen was off the board, the king fucking wide open, ready to be taken down by his enemies.

His most treasured piece had been defeated.

I dropped to my knees. Cheska didn't move. It was like she was paralysed, numbed to anything around her but that motherfucking chessboard.

I looked at Cheska's eyes. They were dead, fucking blank. This time, my gut twisted not because of the fracture in my chest that was sending an army of suffocating feelings raining down on me like bullets, but because of the dead stare on Cheska's face.

I'd never seen her look like this. Not even when she'd collapsed on my office floor in the nightclub. Not even when she'd woken up and the truth of what had happened had hit home again.

I'd destroyed her, like I always knew I would.

Ruined her.

In my mind's eye, I saw her as a kid on her Chelsea home's stairs, the first time I ever met her, all olive skin and huge eyes. I saw her in that fucking bikini on her yacht in Marbella when we were just eighteen. I saw her face when she realised who had docked beside her, the fucking obsessed look in her eyes that had never faded.

Until now.

"Cheska," I said hoarsely, my voice cutting out. I dropped my head, feeling all the fight drain out of me. When I looked up, she was blurred, tears fucking blocking her out of my sight. "They were killed," I said, and when my eyes cleared I saw something like pain flicker across her face.

Cheska stayed looking down at the chessboard, at the vulnerable king and his queen stuck on the sidelines. "They killed them," I said again, and I stopped fighting the fucking feelings that had been battling to get through to me, to fucking take up every inch of my flesh and bones.

"They burned them alive," I said. Cheska winced. My shoulders sagged, and the alcohol swam in my stomach and head. "I don't know how to deal with it," I said, immobilised, fucking exhausted on the floor at her feet.

Still, she stayed silent.

"This ..." I said and looked up. Cheska was watching me, face shattered, fucking broken. "Feeling," I confessed and saw the ice thaw from her expression. Ice that I knew—even in my drunken state—I'd put there.

"Arthur ..."

"I shut it off. I shut it all off, after Mum and Pearl, after Dad ... then after I left you that day in Oxford," I said, letting it all spill out. All the fucking pain that I'd kept trapped inside me, that had soured and fucking rotted my flesh until it was nothing but a deadly virus running inside me, until I was numb to everything but death and rage.

Cheska shifted on the seat but still didn't touch me. I knew she needed more. Needed me to tell her more. I closed my eyes and remembered her falling on the floor of my club. The fucking ache that started the minute she fell back into my life. Thirteen months. I hadn't seen her in thirteen months, hadn't felt a fucking thing in thirteen months but rage and bloodlust and darkness in the wake of our fathers' deaths.

Then I'd seen her face. Her bloodied and beaten face, and the crack in my chest splintered through my protective walls. The feelings started stabbing at me, day by day, minute by minute, the more I was around her.

"You ..." I remembered her pulling the lifeless bird from the container earlier tonight. The fucking fear, deep and gutting fear, when the container exploded and I thought I was too late. I'd thought Cheska was dead beneath me. That she'd gone. And I'd lost it.

Fucking lost it.

I swallowed the thickness in my throat, then met Cheska's gaze. "You made me feel again. After so fucking long. After the blood and the death and all the dark thoughts ..." I squeezed my eyes shut. "You made me fucking *feel.*"

I heard the rustling of clothes and smelled Cheska's perfume suddenly floating around me. Hands touched my face, soft fucking hands holding my cheeks. I wasn't sure if I was imagining it, if the whisky and vodka were creating a hallucination as strong as Vinnie's. I wasn't opening my eyes to have it all disappear. Cheska holding me took the pain away. She brought it crashing down, but she was also chasing it away.

The bringer and destroyer of everything I was.

"Open your eyes," she said, her posh fucking accent sinking deep into my bones. Soothing all the severed and jagged-edged nerves that currently made me. The heat from her palms warmed my freezing body. "Baby, open your eyes."

I did as she said, and there, right before me, on her knees too, was my Chelsea girl. The only one I'd ever fucking wanted. The only one I'd ever let in.

"I don't know how to fucking do this," I said, and Cheska's eyes turned watery. "I don't know how to fucking feel, how to let all the fucked-up in. How—" I touched her face, her soft skin like silk under my calloused fingers. "How the fuck do I do this?" I rasped, the emotion I was terrified of clawing through the broken tone of my voice.

"Arthur." Cheska kissed me. Those fucking soft lips took mine, and the ache faded more and more, and so did the tar in my veins, the throbbing of my head as it replayed the video over and over again, the memory of Cheska on the ground, in my arms, unmoving ...

I grabbed her waist, pulling her closer. I needed her closer. Her hands threaded into my hair.

"Let me in," she said and kissed my neck. "Don't push me away anymore. Please, just let me in. Fully. No turning back."

"I can't," I said, instinctively trying to rebuild my walls. Close up the crack in my chest. "I fucking *can't*."

Cheska pulled back, then meeting my gaze head-on, said, "I love you, Arthur Adley. More than any woman has ever loved a man before." The half-built walls fucking crumbled as those words tumbled from her mouth. The crack morphed into a fuck-off black abyss. "I love you, and I know you love me, even if you can't say the words aloud."

I groaned and clutched my head, needing the fucking pounding to stop. Eyes glazed, I looked up. "They killed them. The branded bastards who tried to take you. They killed my mum and sister. Burned them alive."

"I know," she said, and tears spilled over my eyes and down my fucking cheeks. She wiped at my face, and my head fell against her shoulder. I breathed her in. I fucking breathed her in and felt her fill my lungs. Felt her run through my body like a damn remedy to the poison that had been lying thick in my flesh and blood for far too long.

"I'm here for you. Let me be here for you." Holding my head close to her, embracing me and fucking keeping me breathing, she said, "Let me love you."

"I don't know how," I hushed out. "I have no fucking idea how the fuck to let you in."

"This is a start." She lifted my head. Her hand fell over my heart. "Don't shut this off anymore. If you feel sad, feel sad. If you feel pain, let your body accept that pain. Joy, sadness, grief, guilt, happiness ... love." She smiled, and it just about fucking crushed me.

"No one can push them out forever. Eventually, something or *someone*," she said, with a kiss, "will break through, and so will every emotion you've forced back into a box where it doesn't belong." Cheska kissed my cheeks, then pressed her forehead to mine. "I want to know you, Arthur. *All* of you. Every bit of darkness, every bit of sadness, all of it. The good and the bad, the hard and the soulful."

"I'm sorry," I said, the words feeling foreign on my tongue. "For earlier." I gritted my teeth, not fucking knowing how to do it, how to let her in, apologise, have her truly by my side. "The video ..." I shook my head. "I didn't know how to deal with it. I still don't ..." My voice broke and I dropped my head to Cheska's shoulder. She sat back, arse on the floor, and pulled my head down to her lap. I went. I wrapped my arms around her waist and fucking kept the rubble of the walls pinned down around my heart, kept her there, in my mind and fucking blood, kept her in the marrow of my bones.

Cheska held my head. Dropped kiss after kiss on my face, my hair, anywhere she could reach. For ages we lay there, the flames from the fireplace dancing in my eyes. But in them I saw the cottage burn, my mum and sister inside, unable to escape. I saw Cheska in my arms in the yard.

"I can't lose you," I said, and Cheska stopped breathing. "I can't fucking lose you too."

Cheska exhaled. She held me tighter. "I can't lose you either, baby."

Bit by bit, the ache in my chest crawled out of me, leaving only numbness behind. But it wasn't a bad kind of numbness. It was like a junkie after a comedown, like the heat that filled your veins when the alcohol started to take effect. Cheska kept stroking my hair, and I felt my eyelids pulling down in sleep. I was so fucking tired.

The fight drained from my body, and I didn't push Cheska out. She stayed by my side, stroking my hair. My breathing grew deep, and I exhaled. But just before I drifted off, I opened my eyes and looked right into Cheska's. "You wrecked me, too," I said, then let myself find comfort in the darkness. "When I met you, princess ... you fucking wrecked me too."

Cheska was asleep on the floor. The fire had died down, and only embers were left. The whisky and vodka were still rolling around inside me, but the fucking aftereffects were staring to kick in. I felt rough as fuck, but I took it. I deserved the hangover from hell I knew was coming.

It was still pitch black outside and fucking baltic. I'd only been asleep about two hours, but I'd woken up and knew I had to see it. I hadn't been back there in twelve years. I had to go back ... and I wanted Cheska to be with me.

I crouched down and stared at her face as she slept. I fucking hated myself for what I'd done to her tonight. She'd been hurt, she'd been put through the wringer at the yard, and then I'd shredded her fucking heart, pushed her away in front of my family. Embarrassed her. Made her feel like I didn't want her.

Nothing could be further from the truth.

I breathed deep. My go-to was to block it all out. Put up the walls again and just go back to how it was. But I wouldn't do it. I'd lose her if I did. And I wasn't fucking losing her again.

"Princess." I ran my finger down her face. Cheska stirred but immediately fell back to sleep. I felt a smirk pull on my lips and thought how fucking strange it felt. I never smiled unless it was before a kill. But with her, like this, refusing to wake, it was a different kind of smile. "Princess," I said again, and Cheska's eyes opened and she quickly sat up.

"What?" she said, panicked, wiping the sleep from her eyes. "What's wrong? What's happened?" Her eyes adjusted to the low light in the windowless room and she ran them over me. "Are you okay, baby? Are you hurt?"

I took hold of her jaw and pulled her close to me. I kissed her mouth, sliding my tongue against hers. I wanted to sink inside her. Fuck her in front of the dying fire until she screamed my name.

Something had changed in me. When I'd woken up only twenty minutes ago, Cheska wrapped in my arms and walls fucking down, everything had shifted.

Nothing scared me. Death didn't faze me. But Chelsea Girl, Cheska Harlow-Wright? She fucking terrified me. Because she'd got in. She'd hooked in her claws, and if she wanted to leave—or if she was taken away—there'd be no going back. I'd be fucking done. Destroyed.

Ruined.

I'd showered and brushed my teeth, trying to get the heaviness of the night from my body, the alcohol out of my system. But from the minute my eyes had opened, I'd needed to fucking leave. My gut twisted, telling me where I needed to go. The car was waiting and a van of soldiers were ready to follow us.

I pulled away from Cheska's mouth. She searched my face. "I need you to come with me."

"Where?" she asked but got to her feet. One hundred percent trust. She trusted me without fail. Heat spread through me at the realisation.

I picked up the blanket that I'd put over Cheska when I'd got up. Gripping her hand, I pulled her to my chest, needing her mouth again. I was fucking addicted. Always had been. But now, after tonight, it felt different. It felt like ... *more*.

"You can sleep in the car," I said, and she followed me from the room, still half asleep, her hand clutching mine. I had her trainers waiting for her at the door and wrapped the blanket around her as we stepped into the freezing night air. She pressed closer to my side as we ducked out of the rain and into the Bentley.

We pulled out onto the streets, practically deserted at this hour, and Cheska curled up against me. I could feel her watching me as I scanned for anyone watching us outside, trailing us. My men in the van, and the few I had in other less obvious cars, subtly following behind, would make sure nothing would go wrong.

Finally, seeing everything was all clear, I met her eyes. "Princess," I said and pushed her hair back from her face. I needed to see that fucking perfect face at all times, unobstructed.

"Are you okay?" She swallowed nervously. "Are *we* okay?"

I dropped my forehead to hers, my chest tightening. Because I only had myself to blame. I'd fucked up. I'd been a selfish prick—had been for too many years. I'd been emotionless and cold for far too fucking long. But I was going to try with her. Chelsea Girl was the only one who could ever make me try lowering my guards. No one else. Just her. Always her.

Fucking forever *her*.

"We're good," I said against her mouth, hearing her exhale of relief. "More than."

"We're going to the Cotswolds?" she asked, reading my fucking mind. She knew me. She'd lost people. She knew what I was feeling right now. I nodded and kissed her head as she curled against me. I thought she'd sleep. But she stayed wide awake as we travelled the couple of hours it took to get to my mum's favourite part of the English countryside.

Cheska took my hand, holding me tighter when my body tensed as we drew close to the cottage, and familiar narrow, winding country lanes came into view. The trees created tunnels around us, their branches bare, ice sticking to the bark.

It was still dark as we arrived. I wanted to be back at the church by mid-morning. I wanted the fucking witch hunt to begin immediately. I wanted these cunts, these circle-branded cunts, to be found.

But I needed this moment of calm before the storm.

Cheska sat up and turned my head to her. "I'm with you." I nodded, then let her kiss me. Let her clutch my hand as the driver drove up a private dirt road. I glanced out the window. The Tudor cottage with dormer windows should have been visible over the bushes. But there was nothing, just a mass of stars in the sky above the quiet village, and crows circling up ahead, like they knew murders had taken place here. Like they knew a fucking crime against my family had been carried out and I was here to see the ghost of the reaper who'd collected them.

The Bentley stopped, and Cheska searched outside the window. Wings beat in my stomach, great fucking wings that belonged to a condor or some shit. I saw my men flood the property, guns and knives drawn, checking it was clear. Jim, the head of this regiment, nodded at me as he came back from the shelter of trees.

All was clear.

But I couldn't move. I couldn't bloody *move*. I stared out the window at the ground, the previously torched ground where grass and weeds now grew. The fucking spot where my mum and sister must have screamed and clutched each other as the fire swallowed them whole.

"You ready, baby?" Cheska squeezed my hand. I locked up. My mouth sealed shut and I felt myself shutting the fuck down, drowning the feelings that were trying to suffocate me. They were forcing me into an iron lung, and I wasn't going to do it. Wasn't fucking going to rip open my chest and let the demons take control.

But then Cheska kneeled before me on the car floor and lifted my head to her. "You can do this. You can get out of the car if that's what you want." She kissed the back of my hand.

Staring at her stunning face, I forced my muscles to relax. I forced myself to let the fucking grief sink into me—grief that had been trying to live in me for years, to take its rightful place in my half-dead heart. To consume me until I couldn't fucking breathe.

I closed my eyes. My head throbbed. It had fuck all to do with the hangover I was diving headfirst into. It had to do with the fact that my sister's and mum's screams were locked in the trees around us, their cries still flying in the fucking wind that blew in a gale-force speed around the clearing.

"I can't," I choked out, seeing the cottage so clearly in my mind. Seeing the front door open and Pearl run outside to the wooden swing on the tree. I saw my mum walk out behind her, tea and biscuits on a tray. Then walking to me as I sat on the bench under the window. Sitting beside me. Just fucking being there.

Just being my mum.

My fucking perfect mum, who those fuckers had barricaded inside and torched.

"I'll be with you," Cheska said, and I turned to face her, her green-brown eyes telling me how much she fucking loved me. Me. A fucked-up murderer. But this bird, this posh and stunning bird loved me.

Cheska smiled at me—it was soft and fucking stunning. "Show me the place you loved before the fire," she said, and I turned my head as I heard the fucking phantom echo of Pearl screaming in laughter as I chased her with my water gun. Too young yet for Dad to have put a real one in my hand.

Artie! No! she screamed and dived through the front door so Mum would protect her.

I wanted to show Cheska that place. I wanted her to see that I hadn't always been so fucked up. I hadn't always been plagued with darkness and demons with fucking razors for teeth. I hadn't always been the killer she knew me to be. I had been innocent once. My soul unbattered and clean. My heart not always black and surrounded by my personal Hadrian's Wall.

I gripped Cheska's hand so tight, I worried I'd hurt her. But I opened the door, the frigid wind slapping our faces, and led her from the car. Cheska wrapped the blanket around her to stave off the bitter cold, and I felt the familiar soil underneath my shoes and breathed in the fresh air. There was no smog and pollution in this air, not like in London.

"So peaceful." Cheska leaned her cheek against my arm. "Show me," she said. "Show me why you loved it so much. Why *she* loved it so much." My mum.

This was Cheska fucking meeting my mum.

"This way." I walked with my bird around the few acres we owned. Through the grove of trees and the kitchen garden that Pearl and Mum had planted long ago, now overgrown and wild, the planters rotting and faded in colour. Cheska never let go of my arm. And with every step, I felt the fucking loss of my sister and mum pierce deeper and deeper. Like it should have years ago.

We came back from the path that led to the garden, and I stopped dead at the place where the cottage once sat. My lungs squeezed like someone was crushing them in their fist. My heart thudded faster and faster, as if it would burst from my chest, and my stomach clenched so tight I thought my muscles might rip in two.

Kissing the back of Cheska's hand, I let go of her fingers and took a step forward. My legs felt like lead as I forced them to make it to the centre of where the house once stood. I tipped my head to the night sky and could smell the smoke that would have engulfed the space. Thick, black smoke wiping out the heavy scent of the roses my sister and mum had planted around the borders.

Roses ... Cheska always smelled of roses too.

I opened my eyes and blinked, every move of my eyelids dropping a tear to my cheeks. The wind took them away as quickly as they came. So I fucking shed more. I shed more and more, damn sinful Adley holy water cleansing the air for my mum and sister. Tributes to their lives. Lives taken by our dark underworld, by some branded fuckers who had been secretly tearing apart my family for too many years to count.

I dropped my head and bent down. My hand raked though the patch of mud under my feet. The earth fell through my fingers. Tears ran down from my cheeks and dripped onto the soil, joining the unseen ash of the family members I loved most of all.

Artie. I closed my eyes as I heard my mum calling my name like she was right behind me. I could feel her hand on my shoulder. Smell the strong, expensive perfume Dad used to buy her every Christmas. *I love you, my boy,* she whispered in my ear. *My sweet, sweet boy. I've missed you.*

"I've missed you too, Mum," I whispered back.

And I fucking broke. My shoulders shook as the years and years of grief poured out of me onto the Cotswolds ground. My botched, stitched-up heart was ripping open and bleeding out beneath me, on the very ground that had held my mum and sister's bodies as they burned, as they breathed their last breaths. My hands and knees planted onto the earth, and I shattered apart.

I fought to breathe as I saw that video in my mind. I mentally retraced the steps of the fucker on the screen pouring petrol on the house and trapping my family inside. He'd struck the match and tossed it onto the fuel with no fucking care at all that he was killing my mum. My fucking *mum.* My sister. My annoying little sister who I just wanted, so fucking badly, to annoy me for just one more day.

Arms surrounded me, and I turned my head in to Cheska's chest. "I'm here," she said, her words wrapping the fuck around me and chasing away the smell of fire that I couldn't get from my bastard nose, the smoke that was filling up my lungs and taking away any ability to take in fresh air.

"They died," I said, voice cracking. "They fucking died and I didn't save them."

"*Couldn't* save them," Cheska amended. "You were a child." A child who was busy taking his first life when it all went down.

I sat up and ran my hands down my face. Cheska sat beside me, hand on my back. "They were killed, princess." She nodded, tears slipping down her pale cheeks. "They were fucking *killed.*"

"I know, baby."

I sighed, then my stomach plummeted as I wondered if Mum could see me now. If, wherever she was, she could see me here, finally finding out the truth about her death.

But my fucking heart stopped at that thought.

"You think they've seen what I've become?" I asked. Cheska tried to read my face, and I thought it was because she didn't know which way to take the question. I wasn't sure which fucking interpretation of it I was asking myself.

Was she proud of me, or horrified at what I did for a living, who I was?

Cheska put her hands on my cheeks. "I think she sees you. I think she sees you and smiles and loves you and is so proud it makes her ache to see you again. To be able to touch you and kiss your cheek and tell you how proud she is that you take care of your family the way you do. How you sacrifice your own happiness time and time again so you don't break, so you don't fall.

"But I think it would break her heart to see those things too. To see the burden such heavy duties press down on you. How you push people away so you don't buckle under the weight of loss." Her bottom lip trembled. "How you *have* love, and have found love of the deepest kind but have fought it for so many years that it's made you battle-worn and feeling unworthy of such a gift."

"She'd love you," I said.

Cheska's face crumpled in sadness. "And I'm sure I'd love her. Your sister too."

I nodded, a smile pulling on my lips. Because Pearl would have loved Cheska. She'd told me many times that she wished she'd had a sister instead of me—her annoying big brother.

I stayed kneeling on the ground until the sky started to lighten. Until the pitch black of the sky started to turn royal blue. Taking Cheska's hand, I said, "Let's go home."

"*Is* it my home?" Cheska whispered, showing me how the wounds I'd inflicted last night had cut her deep.

I didn't know if it was feeling my mum around me that pushed me, or whether it was just Cheska. My heart and fucking black soul recognising her as ours and claiming her for all time. But I pulled her face to mine. "Princess ..." I said, feeling my pulse throb in my neck. Feeling heat scald my skin even though it was baltic here outside. Cheska held her breath. "I ..." I squeezed my eyes shut. "I love you."

"Arthur," Cheska cried and crushed her mouth to mine.

So I fucking took her mouth right back.

"What I have is yours, princess," I said, and Cheska folded into my chest. "Everything, it's all fucking yours."

"I just want you." She sighed. "I've always just wanted *you*. Only ever you, Arthur."

The drive back to London was quiet, the winter sky lightening until the sun was out and we pulled up at the church. Cheska had fallen asleep on me, head in my lap. Not wanting to wake her, I carried her into the church. Betsy and Charlie came to the hallway, checking who'd just come inside.

When Betsy saw Cheska in my arms, with her arms hooked around my neck even in sleep, she gave me a relieved smile and went back into her room. Charlie winked at me, choosing not to give me shit about leaving the house when I'd ordered everyone else to stay locked down.

I placed Cheska on the bed, removed her trainers and put her under the covers. I watched her move around, but ultimately sleep took her under again. I threw off my jacket and went into the kitchen. I boiled the kettle and made myself a cup of tea. I was knackered, fucking empty inside, but ... but I felt different. Like I'd just woken up from a decade of being knocked out cold. Like I'd just stepped out of a year-long storm into a fucking summer's day.

I went into the living room to drink my builder's tea and saw Vinnie was sat in his usual place. The fucker hardly ever slept. He was beside the fire as always. I almost left the room, needing to be alone. But I stopped in the doorway when I thought of Cheska. Of the night he told her about her mates, that they didn't blame her for their deaths. I thought of Eric and what he said weeks back ... *You haven't got paranoid schizophrenia at all, have you? You're a fucking medium or some shit. Talking to the dead all day every day ...*

My feet were moving before I was conscious of it. I sat down opposite Vinnie, my fucking mug of tea shaking in my hand. "Artie," Vinnie greeted me, his manic smile spreading on his lips. I had no idea what went on in my brother's head. Wasn't sure how he got through every fucking day. But out of us all, with the hallucination of Pearl by his side, he was probably—ironically—the only one who lived a somewhat normal life.

I thought that, despite the mental illness, he was happy.

"Vin." I downed half my scalding tea. It burned as it went down my throat. Vinnie was staring into the fire, lost in his head as always. But like he could read my fucking mind, he turned to me, and I knew he was waiting for me to speak. His shoulder-length blond hair fell over half his face. My heart pounded like I'd just run a fucking marathon.

I inched forward on my chair, the rhythmic tick-tock of the grand-father clock behind me my soundtrack as I asked, "Are they okay?" My voice was so weak I wasn't sure Vinnie had heard me. That was, until he nodded his head. I nodded back. "Did ..." I stared at my hands. I placed the tea on the table between us and clasped my hands together. I lifted my eyes to Vinnie. "Did they feel pain?"

Vinnie didn't need me to explain who I was talking about. He knew. Somehow, he always fucking knew. "No pain," he said, shaking his head. "It was quick. Like falling asleep."

Relief coursed through me. I exhaled a sigh and got to my feet. I was dog tired and just needed to sleep. I wanted to fucking pull Cheska close to me and close my eyes. As I passed Vinnie, I pressed a hand on his shoulder in thanks.

He grabbed my hand as I went to leave. I looked down at my brother-in-arms, and he said, "She's glad you went back." The hairs on my neck stood on end. "To say goodbye. She was happy to see you there." I nodded, pretty fucking sure I couldn't have bloody spoken if I tried.

Vinnie let go of my hand. "Your mum likes Cheska. She likes her a lot. Said she's happy you let her into your heart ... at last." Chills spread over my skin. Because I could hear Mum saying it. Hear her thick cockney accent saying those exact words, then kissing me on the cheek.

Vinnie went back to staring into the hearth, and I went to my bedroom in a fucking daze. I threw off my clothes, then crawled into bed with my bird. I grabbed her by the waist and pulled her back into my chest. "I love you," she murmured, still mostly asleep.

As her breathing evened out, I replied, "Love you too, princess." I knew I wasn't ever going to be the most romantic person on the bastard planet. I was a fucking East End London gangster; my blood ran with hate and vengeance. I didn't show love to anyone. But maybe ... just fucking maybe ...

I kissed the back of Cheska's neck, hearing her sigh in response.

Maybe I could make an exception for her. Only ever for her.

Always her.

CHAPTER FOURTEEN

CHESKA

"Again," Eric said as I wiped the sweat from my brow.

I sucked in a deep breath, then held my dagger tightly. I rushed at Eric, knocking his arm away to stop him grabbing me, and pressed the tip of my hairpin dagger to his heart.

"Good," Eric said as I stepped back. "Better."

I grabbed my bottle of water from the leaf-strewn churchyard ground. I gulped the cool liquid down and tipped my head back, looking up at the grey sky. It was freezing outside, but I was sweating. Hours of practice out here, amongst the old headstones, with Eric were helping me shed some of the anxiety I had been feeling lately. The pent-up frustration from the guilt that still lingered in my stomach, and the aching sadness of missing my friends, my dad, Hugo.

I faced Eric again as Charlie stepped into the churchyard with us to light a cigarette. He leaned back against the wall of the house and watched me with an amused expression on his face.

Eric took my dagger and turned the tip on his shirtless body. He pressed it to his heart. "Remember, hairpin daggers are most effective at piercing major organs, not slitting throats or tearing flesh." He pressed it into his skin, leaving a dent to show me precisely where I should aim if I ever had to use it. "Heart," he said, then lowered it. "Lungs. Kidney. Liver," he said, moving to each in turn, then he dropped it to his thigh. "Major arteries. Here." Then to his neck. "Here." He pressed the dagger to his temple and smiled. "And if you want to be a proper fucking savage, the temple. Send this fucker straight into the brain. Through the eye works too."

I felt nauseous at the thought. But I had to know. I had to be prepared for anything. I had been helpless last time someone came for me. If it happened again, I'd be prepared. I'd be able, in some way, to fight back.

So, I had taken Eric up on his offer of training me to use the daggers Ronnie, Vera and Gene had given me for my birthday. Arthur had been teaching me how to shoot. But after Dad and Hugo and that night in the pits, guns were still a bit too much for me.

Still, he had taken me to the church's cellar and helped me aim. He insisted I learn regardless, that in this life I needed to at least know how to use one. And my heart warmed when I thought of the reason why.

Because he couldn't bear to lose me.

It had been a few days since our visit to the cottage, and he had barely left my side. As if I were the Holy Grail, and he the head of the Knights Templar. If I wasn't with him, I was with one of his family members. Someone was always at the church with me and Gene. Adley soldiers patrolled the house twenty-four-seven.

It was a fortress.

I would have thought it all too excessive. But I had seen my friends and family killed. Lived every moment of my kidnapping every day. I had now seen the footage of Arthur's mum being attacked and thrown inside her cottage. And I had seen the fear in Arthur's blue eyes. I had seen the worry as the raking of the city for the unseen enemy came up empty. I felt it as he held me close to him at night. As he kissed me and as he sank inside me, haunted gaze locked on mine.

Eric handed me back the dagger.

"I'd be careful to not show Betsy those moves." I motioned to the red dots that remained on his body from the demonstration. "She might be inclined to use them on you the next time you piss her off." Which was more than often. My head ached when I tried to figure them out. They claimed they hated each other, but their heated looks and frequent shags said otherwise.

"She'd try," Eric said, the clown tattoos smiling demonically on his skin as he threw on his t-shirt. "But we'd just end up fucking and dripping in blood—my favourite."

Charlie coughed behind us. "I'm her brother, you twat. Spare me from hearing shit like that."

"It's okay, Chuck. It's not like I'm asking you to watch." Eric walked into the house. "I need to get showered and head to the club. You did good today, Ches."

"Thank you!" I called after him, getting a wave in response.

Charlie shook his head as I walked toward the house. "They need to either actually get together or leave each other alone," he said, referring to Eric and Betsy. "If I have to hear them angry-fucking one more time while we're all stuck in this house, I'm going to slit their throats myself. There's just some things a brother shouldn't have to be subjected to."

I laughed. "If it's any consolation, I think they love each other to death."

"To death," Charlie mused, flicking his finished cigarette into a drain. "I'm afraid that's what might happen one day if they push each other too far." The spark in his brown eyes told me he was joking, but the way they pushed one another at times—it wouldn't be outside the realm of possibility.

"They'll work it out," I said, shrugging. "It took me and Arthur years to get to this point." I felt my face burn. Charlie knew this, of course. He'd been there through it all.

He eyed me, and I wondered what he was thinking. Then he said, "These past few days ..." He stared off over the top of the ancient headstones in the garden. "Before you. Before you came back, I mean. We'd have been razing London to the ground by now. After he'd seen that video, the old Artie would have been drenched in blood and still taking people down minute by minute until he had found out who was to blame. He would have made us even more enemies, and we would have had to double all our firm's protection efforts for the next few years until the people he took out during one of his black-out rages backed the fuck down." Charlie smirked. "Or until they were killed by my cousin too."

My heart fell.

Dark. That was all Arthur's life was before. Just pure darkness. Nothing good.

"But he's thinking this time. Using his men more. Ronnie, Vera, letting them use the skills they've wanted to bring to the firm for a while now." Charlie stepped off the wall and straightened his jacket and tie. "He's being smart about the revenge. He's coming to us all for advice, involving us in the decisions."

Pride surged through me at Charlie's assessment. "Arthur has always led this family well. He is the best gaffer this firm could've asked for. People either love him or are shit-scared of him. And rightly so. He was born to do this. To run this fucking lawless city. But *this* version of him? This *thinking* Arthur, the one who's using his brain ... this is the one everyone should be fucking petrified of. Because Arthur is strong, and violent, and can fight like a bloody pit bull. But the edge he has on everyone else in the crime underworld is that he's fucking clever. He's intelligent. That's the part of my cousin I've been waiting to see come out, to see put into action. But the rage had to go first."

He laughed. "Or at least turned down to a simmer instead of an uncontrollable flame." Charlie nodded at me, true gratitude on his handsome face. "We have you to thank for that, Cheska. With you by his side, he is truly lethal. And in our world, that's the equivalent of winning the bloody lottery."

I shrugged. "I just love him."

"And he loves you." Charlie went to go back inside, but his attention was pulled in the direction of the garden. I followed his gaze to see Gene sitting down against a tree. He lit a cigarette and just stared out at the sky. A look I couldn't decipher flashed over Charlie's face as he watched Eric's younger brother.

"He seems lost," I said, feeling sympathy for the young man. Twenty years old and so, so lost.

"Yeah," was all Charlie said, then he went back inside the house before I could say anything else.

I followed and had just sat down in the living room when Ronnie burst out of her room and toward us. She had bags under her eyes, and her hair was unstyled, her clothes rumpled. She looked like she hadn't slept in days. Her eyes searched the room.

"Arthur?" she asked.

"Here," Arthur said, coming up behind Ronnie. His eyes immediately fixed on mine, and at the heat in his gaze, I wanted nothing more than to disappear into our bedroom with him. Arthur pushed past Ronnie and leaned down and kissed me. He picked me up off the chair as if I weighed nothing and placed me on his lap. I immediately felt at home.

"I've got a trace," Ronnie said. Arthur tensed beneath me. I stared at Ronnie. Charlie, Freddie, Vinnie and Eric had all stopped talking, and their heads swerved her way. Betsy, clearly hearing the commotion in the living room, slipped inside.

"What did you get, babes?" Vera asked Ronnie.

"They're in South London." She waved the piece of paper in her hand. "The video that was sent to you, the encrypted number," she said, so fast I struggled to keep up. "It came from South London."

"Where?" Arthur said darkly, lighting a cigarette.

"I haven't managed to pin it down yet. But I will. I know I will." A manic, sleep-deprived smile spread on Ronnie's pretty face. "This is the first breakthrough I've had on these fuckers. Ever."

Arthur was still unmoving beneath me. Still tense. "Good job, Ron," he said. Vera got up and kissed her girlfriend.

"I'll keep going," Ronnie said, and they left the room.

"South London." Charlie became lost in thought. "None of the usual lot down there seem likely to have the resources to do something on this level."

"They don't," Arthur said. "This isn't someone we know already. No two-bit drug-dealer unit could swing all this. This is someone else. Some*thing* else. The gangs we know of in South London—*all* through

London—are pretenders next to this group. These cunts are a mother-fucking empire. A hidden fucking empire." Arthur inhaled a drag of his cigarette, then exhaled. "Because only another empire could come at us like this." He flicked the ash into the ashtray beside us. "But empires fall. And these fuckers are going to be buried along with anyone else who tries to tear my family down."

I felt Arthur's lips on my shoulder. "Let's go, princess." I recognised that tone in his voice. I stood, and he followed me into the bedroom. He peeled off my clothes and turned on the shower.

Arthur fucked me against the wall, his lips on my mouth, my cheeks, my breasts. He fucked me hard and fast until I screamed out in the foggy, steamy room. Arthur's skin was slick against mine, his head tucked into the crook between my neck and shoulder as he came, his roar echoing around us.

Still inside me, he carried me to the bed and laid us down. He kissed me like he would devour me. His hands slipped over every inch of my skin like he owned it.

He did. He owned me heart and soul.

Breathless, I tore away from his mouth and gasped for air. Arthur, still unwilling to release me, pulled me into his chest, and I caught my breath, watching the sunlight fade in the skylight above.

"Checked in with my contact in your family's business today." I lifted my head and stared into Arthur's eyes. He had slipped his glasses back on and lit cigarettes for us both. He passed one over to me.

"You did?" I asked, taking a drag.

"They've hired a temporary CEO while you're still a missing person." I swallowed and smoked, the tobacco calming me down. "The police are still running around like idiots, falling for our false leads. They still haven't recovered your dad and Fuckface's bodies." I tensed, wondering where they might have been dumped. Arthur and Charlie thought they had probably been burned. No evidence that way.

"And Freya and Arabella?"

"Both have been buried. Funerals were done as soon as their bodies were released by the police. The investigation is still open." Arthur placed his hand under my chin and lifted it up. "There won't be any answers for their families. At least, not until we bury these fuckers and you're able to be seen again."

I swallowed. "What would I tell them?"

"We'll think of something."

I traced the inked London skyline on Arthur's chest, my fingertip ghosting over the top of Big Ben and the Houses of Parliament. "I'm not sure I ever want to be found." I sighed, feeling more than off-kilter at the thought of returning in any way to my old life.

Arthur put his cigarette in his mouth and pulled me up to lie on his chest. My face hovered above his. Leaving his cigarette perched between his lips, he said, "You're too high profile, princess. You're Cheska Harlow-Wright, not some fucking nobody." A shadow crossed over his face. "If you want to be with me, and not have every fucking bobby in the country thinking it was my family that took you, you have to resurface at some point."

"I never want them to think it was you."

Arthur smirked. His body wet and muscled, that cigarette between his lips, made my thighs clench. "They'll think it was Stockholm Syndrome or some shit. That you fell for the fucking Dark Lord of London Town and I corrupted you, dragged you to my lair and made you my dark queen."

"Well," I said. "It's not too far from the truth."

One of Arthur's hands drifted down my back and over my arse. It dipped lower, following the curves of my behind to my pussy, where he sank a finger inside me, and my forehead dropped to his chest. A moan tore from my throat, and I widened my legs as he added more fingers and pushed them in and out of me at a maddening pace.

"Dark queen," he hissed, and I felt him harden against my stomach. I crawled to all fours, his hand slipping out of me as I straddled his legs and sank down on his cock. My head fell back as he filled me to the hilt.

Arthur's hands landed on my breasts. I rode him, rocking back and forth as ash from the cigarette still between his teeth dropped onto his skin. I didn't think he even noticed it as he fucked me, as I rode him, hips jerking faster and faster, and he dropped one of his hands and rubbed his fingers over my clit.

"Arthur," I whispered, my movements becoming stuttered as I felt the telltale tightening of my thighs and the ache in my lower back. Before I could even utter his name again, I shattered, coming hard and fast. My nails sank into his chest, and he stilled, groaning around his cigarette as he came inside me.

I fell against his chest, my ear pressed over his heart—it was racing. Arthur stubbed out his cigarette in the ashtray on the bedside table and wrapped his arms around me. I could hear the faint sounds of his family in the living room. Of Eric leaving, and the quiet murmurs of Ronnie and Vera as they passed by the bedroom door.

I wanted this. Not my old life. I wanted this family, not the stifling Chelsea social scene. The materialism, the focus on money and how much power you could gain amongst the rich.

"I don't want it," I said once I'd caught my breath. Arthur was quiet, listening. "My old life." I lifted up and braced my arms on his hard torso. "I want to be with you. Not in secret. But proudly by your side."

A smile tugged on Arthur's lips and melted my heart. "That'll cause a motherfucking commotion."

"I don't care," I said vehemently. "Let them think what they want. I'm done with caring what anyone but you and this family thinks of me."

"And your family's business?" he said. "Some of the shares will fall to you. Some of the responsibility if you want it." I'd studied business for years at Oxford. And I was good at it. But ...

"I can keep the shares." I didn't want to completely sever the ties to my mum's legacy. "But maybe it's time for the business to be handed over to someone not so invested." I thought of my father and how much the business took up his life. Possessed him, until that was all he cared about—not his family or child. I thought of Hugo, and how I now looked back on our relationship and knew, with absolute certainty, that there had never been any romantic love between us; rather, it had been familial. And he had wanted my hand in marriage to secure his place at Harlow Biscuits. My father would never have let me close to running the show. He had been a good man in some ways but thought very little of women in general, and especially in a place of work. He viewed them as disposable. A means to an end. Looking back, I wasn't even sure he loved my mum at all. I was starting to believe that he loved the business and power her name had brought to him.

It was business that consumed Hugo and Dad—they were cut from the same cloth. And although we knew little about who killed them, we knew why—because they messed up the business somehow and owed a crime syndicate money. They had borrowed money from ruthless men again, and my best friends paid the price for their default.

"The company's sullied to me now," I said. "It's steeped in blood and lies." Arthur pushed back my wet hair from my face. He understood. I could see that written on his face. I traced over Westminster Bridge on his stomach. "But I'm good with stepping away." I caught his eye. "I'm smart, Arthur. I'm good with business. I don't want to live life on the sidelines. I'm not some little woman for you to come home to, barefoot and pregnant. If I'm with you, in this family, I want to help. I want to be a part of what we all do."

"I have businesses," he said, and my pulse beat faster at the playful twitch on his lips. "Many of them." He shrugged. "Most of them are fronts. But I have a few legitimate ones that turn over an okay profit. Enough to keep Scotland Yard off my back and away from my real work."

Excitement flared inside me. Excitement at what life could look like for us. Arthur championed women in his firm. I could be an asset to him. Leave the life of a socialite that I had never been able to stand anyway.

The smile slipped from Arthur's face and his expression darkened. I knew it was because all this, this dream we were creating ... it would be only that until we found whoever was hunting us. The future we wanted, the one we dreamed of, was all up in smoke if they weren't discovered. If they weren't dealt with.

The thought of what Arthur would to do to them when he caught them made me feel sick. Not because of the killing. They'd killed too many people close to us to be exempt from that kind of justice. But because I feared something happening to Arthur. Him being taken from me after we had finally found ourselves in this place.

Together. Happy. In love ...

A cave formed inside my stomach when I pictured him being hurt, or worse.

Arthur sat up. "I have to go out, princess. I've got a meeting." I reluctantly got off him and watched him dress. Nothing in this world looked as good as Arthur Adley in a suit. I dressed too and sat on the bed, watching him collect his things. He walked over to me and took hold of my jaw. "One day, you won't have to stay behind. You can be right by my fucking side." His lip curled into a smirk. "My queen of darkness."

I laughed at the heat in his eyes and kissed him, just as someone knocked on the door. "Yeah?" Arthur said against my lips, not bothering to pull away. I closed my eyes, deepening the kiss, but a soft cough interrupted us.

Arthur pulled away, and Vera and Ronnie came into the room. They had their coats on and overnight bags in their hands. "What's all this?" Arthur asked.

"I have some hacker friends—discreet hacker friends—who owe me a favour," Ronnie said. "I think they can help me get further into all this. Really help us find out who they are—names, businesses. Everything." She gestured to the piece of paper in her hand—the one with the information about the encrypted number she'd managed to get a trace on.

Arthur was silent for a few strained seconds, then said. "Off the grid." He frowned. Then some silent communication passed between Vera, Ronnie and Arthur. Something that looked important danced between them. I wondered if they'd been speaking in private.

Before I could question them on it, Arthur's phone rang. "I'm on my way," he said to the caller. Arthur kissed me and left the room. Vera and Ronnie were on his heels, and the three of them left the house.

It was dark, and the wind whistled outside as it thrashed against the old walls of the church. My mind drifted back to what Arthur had told me about Freya's and Arabella's funerals.

I should have been there.

I pulled out my phone and, for the first time since they died, I searched their names. My blood curdled when I saw report after report of their deaths. All mentioning my name, suspecting I was dead too.

Then I saw an article that covered their funerals. Tears pricked at my eyes when I saw their parents, holding each other up as if they would fall to their knees if left unsupported.

The grief. The pain. It all hit me like a ton of bricks.

Wrapping my oversized cardigan around me, I headed for the churchyard. I needed fresh air. I didn't care if it was cold. I needed to feel the wind on my face, needed to feel nature on my skin, life flourishing all around me.

I closed my eyes the minute my feet left the back doorstep. The night was clear, and stars were a wash of sparkling diamonds in the sky. The crescent moon illuminated the church's old graves; it was straight from the pages of a Grimm Brothers' fairy tale.

I headed toward the rows of headstones, Freya's and Arabella's funerals heavy on my mind. I came to the first one. An angel stood high on a marble plinth. Its cherubic face was cracked from years of batterings from the harsh, mercurial English weather. I ran my hands over the name engraved on the stone, but it was too worn and weather-beaten to make out the letters.

I walked past grave after grave. Some with names that could still be read, mostly people that died centuries ago. Short lives and long lives —people who were very much loved. A lump clogged my throat when I thought of where Arabella and Freya now lay. What their headstones looked like and what was written for their epitaphs.

Taken too soon.

They were. Too young. Too much life running through their veins.

I missed them. I missed them with my whole heart. My eyes misted over, and I was about to turn away when I saw two headstones in the corner of the garden, underneath a large tree that in the summer would be thick with green leaves, its branches cascading like a waterfall over the two white marble graves. They seemed newer than the rest, more cared for.

My feet crunched on the fallen leaves beneath me. My exhales were clouds of white as the cold night embraced me. I reached the graves and stopped dead.

Annie Adley.

Pearl Adley.

I closed my eyes and felt their loss sink into the depths of my bones. The loss of two people very much loved by their family—especially by their son and brother. I kneeled down and batted away the leaves and twigs that had landed on the top of the headstones from the blustering wind.

"Hello." I cleared the debris from the manicured grass around them. "Nice to finally meet you." I felt slightly silly at talking to them this way. But I wanted to with all my heart. "I'm Cheska," I said, keeping my voice quiet. I smiled at Annie's name. "And I am completely and obsessively in love with your son." I fought back the lump in my throat as his face sprang to my mind. "I promise I'll love him for you both. I promise to care for him when he forgets to care for himself, and I promise that I'll always stand by his side." I inhaled the cold air, feeling it burn my lungs but settle frayed nerves inside me.

I had just risen to my feet when I heard the crack of a twig behind me and smelled cigarette smoke. I whipped around, heart racing, only to find Gene standing a few feet away.

He held up his hands, his face paling. "I'm sorry. I was sat by the tree over there." He pointed to the tree I had seen him underneath earlier. "I didn't want to disturb you."

"Gene," I said, hand on my chest, covering my racing heart. At the sound of our voices, one of the soldiers came running around the corner, gun drawn. He stopped, scanning the area. "Everything okay?"

"Yes." I said, and the soldier left again. I walked closer to Gene and sat down on the bench near the Adley graves. Gene hovered nearby, looking unsure of what to do. "Care to join me?"

Gene ducked his head shyly but sat down beside me. The wind whipped around us, but the branches of the tree sheltered us from most of its harshness. I embraced the silence, happy to be outside, taking in fresh air in good company.

"They were good people," Gene said minutes later, nudging his head toward Annie's and Pearl's graves. "I liked them a lot. *Miss* them a lot."

"I've heard they were. I'm sad I never got to meet them."

Gene lowered his head and ran his hand over the sleeve of his long top, pulling it back enough to show the black bandages he wore underneath. I wasn't sure he even realised he was doing it. A nervous habit he had picked up. I studied his face. He bore a resemblance to Eric and Vera, but where they were both blond with vibrant and loud personalities, Gene was all dark hair and timid hazel eyes. He was quiet, introverted ... damaged.

"He's changed," Gene said, his quiet voice almost getting stolen by the wind. I stared at his profile, and his gaze flitted to mine before he stared out over the trees again.

"Arthur?" I asked.

Gene nodded and rubbed his hands together—another nervous gesture. "When I left ..." He trailed off. "A while back." When he had been sectioned. When the family had paid for him to seek help for his inner demons. "He was ..." Gene frowned as if he was seeing Arthur in his memory, searching for the correct description of the man he used to be. "A ghost," he settled on. "He was a ghost. Empty but for the anger that fuelled him. He didn't live. His eyes ..." Gene sighed. "They were dead. Void of any happiness."

"They were?" I said, remembering Arthur's blank stare as he left my flat in Oxford that night after his dad had been shot. How he'd seemed changed. How the man I had known was long gone. He had always been tortured and haunted. But as he left that day, he had been nothing more than a death-fuelled wraith.

"Like recognises like," Gene said and just about obliterated my soul. I wanted to reach out and touch him, comfort him, but I didn't know his boundaries. I didn't know what he would be okay with. His pale face flushed. "I ..." He clenched his jaw. "Until I saw Artie, I didn't think it was possible for people to change that much." There was a heavy dose of hope in his voice, and I realised that it was for himself. That if Arthur could change, be saved ... so might he.

"Are you okay?" I asked, choosing to not push him on those things and give him space.

Gene didn't answer straight away. But then he answered me with a question of his own. "Are you?"

I listened to the cars driving by beyond the high walls of the churchyard. I breathed in the fresh, winter air. "I feel ..." I wrapped my cardigan tighter around me. "I feel like I'm in a strange kind of purgatory." I nodded, knowing I had expressed it correctly. "I have my old life on one hand, a life so far away from this place, from this kind of life." Gene stared at the ground, but the stillness of his body told me he was listening. "Then, on the other hand, I have a chance at this new life, one I want with all my heart, but one that's just out of reach. Out of reach until whoever wants to hurt me—us—is gone."

I smiled to myself despite my fears. "A life with Arthur. A life I never thought he would ever be able to give me, or I could give him." Gene looked at me, and I nearly cried at the way his eyes seemed to yearn for the same thing. "Until then, I'm here. Staying hidden. Keeping safe until it's clear for me to move on and step into my next chapter." I laughed and shook my head. "Did any of that make sense?"

"Yes." Gene sat back on the bench. His curly brown hair flopped in front of his eyes. "I get it completely."

"How do you feel?" I asked. "Being back here?"

Gene pulled down the sleeves of his top until it half covered his palms. "Like you," he said. "Trapped between the past and the future." He tipped his head up at the sky. "My past ..." He tapped at his head, then his heart. "I have thoughts and feelings ... dark, sinking thoughts. Demons. They drag me down. Until I can't breathe."

I wanted to wrap my arms around him and keep him safe. But I stayed still. And I listened. "I've never quite fit in to this family like the rest of them," he rasped, and I could hear the pain in his heavy tone. "I'm not like my brother or sister. Never have been. Never been like Arthur. They were born for this life, ready to join the ranks and serve the family. Me ..." He sighed. "I'm not sure what life I was meant for. None, I think. Living and me ... they don't seem to be well matched."

"Gene." I fought back the urge to hold his hand, my heart breaking at such sorrowful, morbid words. "You *are*. You're meant for this family. There is a place for you here. You just have to find it. It may seem hidden right now. But your place is here, I know it." I inched closer to him. "Your family love you. They just want you to be happy. Whatever path you choose."

"Happy ..." he said, as if the word was something he'd never heard of, something he had never felt, a concept he couldn't grasp.

"No one," I asked, "or nothing helps you feel happy? Makes something inside of you burn? No one helps relieve the sadness?" His eyes darted to me, and I recalled the day I met him. He'd kept his head low, eyes downcast as he faced us all ... until one person came to him. Until one person held him, and Gene had held him back so tightly it was as if he would never let go.

"Charlie," I said knowingly, and Gene froze. His mouth opened and closed. I didn't think he would say anything, but he turned to me, a flicker of life—and maybe hope—sprouting on his face, and—

"Princess?" At the sound of Arthur's voice, Gene closed his mouth and shut down, looking over my shoulder. I followed his gaze and saw Arthur approaching. He glanced to his mum's and sister's graves, then back to me. His expression softened when he understood what I was doing out here. Who I had found.

"Gene," he said. "You okay, kid?"

"I'm good, Artie." He got to his Doc Marten-clad feet, his black skinny jeans clinging to his slim legs. "It was nice speaking to you, Cheska." He smiled, and the sight stole my breath. He was beautiful. I wanted with all my soul for him to be rid of the darkness that kept him captive, and for his light to bring him home. "Welcome to the family."

I watched Gene walk away. Arthur's finger ran down my cheek. "You're freezing." He held out his hand. "Let's go inside." I let him lead me into the house and straight into our bedroom. I sat on the end of the bed, my conversation with Gene circling my head.

"I like him," I said to Arthur as he took off his suit jacket, waistcoat and tie. He undid the top buttons of his shirt, then rolled up his sleeves to his elbows.

"He's a good kid," he said, and I smiled in agreement.

"He's only five years younger than you, but he seems tired, like he's old and weary."

Arthur sat beside me. "He's had a rough life. Was always at war with himself. But hopefully he's getting better. Eric seems to think this time he might make it without relapsing."

I wondered about Gene and how he seemed to light up around Charlie, at the mere mention of Arthur's cousin. Then I thought back to Charlie today, how he'd watched Gene under the tree, his dark eyes unreadable. I kept those thoughts to myself. It was none of my business.

Arthur took my hand and kissed the back of my palm. "I never got chance to give you your birthday present the other night."

I smiled, and Arthur pulled out a box from his trouser pocket. He opened the lid, and inside was a large set of diamond earrings. "My mum's," he said, and my head snapped up.

"Arthur, I can't—"

"I want you to have them." He squeezed my hand. For a second, he seemed nervous. I had never seen Arthur nervous. I hadn't been sure he could even *get* nervous. "Cheska," he said, voice husky. "Fucking take them, princess." He put them in my palm. "I need you to take them."

"Okay." I ran my finger over the vintage diamonds. "They're beautiful," I whispered. Arthur got up and went to the jacket he'd slung over the chair. He pulled out a bigger square box that looked like it housed a bracelet or something similar.

"Arthur," I said as he crouched in front of me and placed it on my lap. "I can't accept this too. It's all too much." Arthur opened the box, and a band of silver stared back at me, thicker in width than most bracelets but no less stunning. "It's gorgeous," I said. But when I looked up, Arthur's expression was guarded. My stomach turned. "What?" I asked. "What's wrong?"

"I had this made for you."

"Okay ..." I said carefully. The air between us had risen in temperature, thickened with tension—one I didn't understand the genesis of. I placed the box beside me on the bed and put my hands on Arthur's face.

He reached for the bracelet and took it from the box. He was silent, shoulders tensed as he placed it on my wrist, clicking the ends together. Once it was fixed together, the joint disappeared, and I realised that it was the type of bracelet that had to be cut off. It was incredibly pretty, but when Arthur exhaled a long, relieved breath, his shoulders sagging, I knew this being on my wrist meant more than mere decoration.

"Arth—"

"I need you to wear this," he said, voice tight. His eyes were wide, almost possessed. "You can't take it off unless it's cut off."

"Okay." I tried to study the bracelet, to see what was so special about it. But it just looked like any other. Gorgeous. But nothing out of the ordinary.

"I had it made for you. By a jeweller I know." He swallowed, then his face grew stern as he met my eyes. "It has a tracker built into it."

The world stopped. Everything stopped. But my heart beat faster and faster, and suddenly the lightweight bracelet around my wrist felt like an anvil.

"What?" I said, my voice shaking in anger, real anger. I turned my wrist over, taking in every curve of the bracelet. I couldn't see evidence of a tracker, but then I had no idea what one even looked like.

I held out my wrist. "Take it off me."

Arthur clenched his jaw, and his cheeks turned red. His eyes narrowed, and the Arthur of old surfaced. "Take it off me!" I said louder, my voice carrying authority around the large room. "*Now*, Arthur. And if you can't, get me someone who can. I don't want a tracker on me."

Arthur got to his feet, positively vibrating. "No," he said stubbornly, and my anger levels rose to match his. "No!" he bit out again, seeing me about to stand and challenge him.

Arthur's hands slid through his hair and he became ... undone. He unravelled before me, the cool exterior he always wore cracking down the centre, and a manic and haunted man was revealed underneath. He paced back and forth in front of me, neck corded and veins protruding from his muscles.

"You have to wear it," he said curtly, but I heard the slight trembling of his voice. The betrayal of his unease. I was mute. I didn't know what to say, seeing him this way. He was always so calm and collected. I didn't understand why he was like this over a tracker. Over a bracelet.

"Arth—"

"You have to fucking wear it!" he snapped, cutting me off again. I watched him pace like a wolf, hands in his hair, then dragging down his face. "Just in case."

I reached out and grabbed his hand. "Arthur," I said sternly. "Stop."

He did. Stock-still. But his eyes were still blown. Still wide as he towered over me.

He launched forward and placed his hands on either side of my head. "*Listen* to me," he said, his eyes searching mine. "You have to be protected. I have to know where you are."

"Did ... did something happen?" I asked, a trickle of fear crawling down my spine.

Arthur laughed a single laugh, but it was without humour. "Did something happen?" He shook his head, then pressed his forehead to mine. "They killed my mum and sister," he said quietly, so quietly it was heartbreaking. His hands were unyielding on my head, keeping me close. "They killed your old man, your wankstain of a fiancé, your two best mates, and they tried to fucking kidnap *you*," Arthur hissed, eyes squeezing shut momentarily. "They fucking wanted to *sell* you. Like those cunts did Ronnie. Like they did the women in the shipping container."

"Baby—"

"It's *them*!" he said, his wild eyes imploring me to listen. To under-stand. "*They're* the ones behind all the attacks on us. They're the ones sneaking around, fucking with us. And I don't know who they are. I don't fucking know who they are!"

Desperately, he smashed his lips to mine. The kiss wasn't gentle. It was raw and savage and unrestrained. When he broke away, my lips felt empty. "I can't have them taking you. If something happens, if they strike again, if they fucking get to us somehow, I need to be able to find you." His hand slid down to the wrist that wore the bracelet. "This makes it so I can find you. If everything goes up in fucking flames, I'll be able to *find* you." His skin drained of colour and his voice broke to half a whisper. "I can't fucking lose you," he said, so sadly it stabbed through my chest. "Princess ... I can't lose you too."

I put my hands on his face too, anger melting to sadness. We stood at the foot of his bed, hands on each other's faces, holding on to one another for dear life.

"Please," Arthur said, and my blood cooled at the sound of someone like Arthur Adley pleading. "I'll fucking beg if you need me to, princess. But ..." His breathing hitched. "Just wear it for me. Please, just fucking wear it so I can fucking sleep." I thought of the headstones in the garden. The ones he could barely acknowledge when he found me on the bench talking to Gene.

"I can't have you buried out there too," he said, reading my mind. "Not you too ... *especially* not fucking you."

"Okay, okay," I said calmly and kissed his cheeks, his wrists and his lips—softly, soothingly, gently. "I'll wear it," I said. And I would. I didn't like the idea of a tracker on me. But then I replayed the attackers tying my hands and gagging my mouth. Remembered being dragged down the stairs of the spa and almost forced into the van. I never wanted that to happen again. But if it ever did, I would have the knowledge that Arthur would find me.

If this was the insurance Arthur needed to feel calm, I would do it for him. "I'll wear it. I promise," I assured, and Arthur started breathing normally. He had dark circles under his eyes, and I knew he hadn't been sleeping. He was exhausted. And strung out. And worried for me. But there also seemed to be something more. Something else.

"Have you found something out?" I searched his face, trying to understand what had triggered all of this.

Arthur closed his eyes and took a deep breath. He stepped back and pulled his hand back from my face. He lit a cigarette, took a calming inhale and rubbed the back of his neck. "Not yet. Just some things don't seem to be adding up." He stopped whatever he was going to say. "I think I'm going fucking mad," he said and took another drag. "Fucking losing it."

"When was the last time you rested? Truly rested. When was the last time you slept?"

"I can't," he said, dropping his gaze to the floor. "They're fucking out there. And I can't fucking find them. I *always* find anyone threatening us. But these fuckers, these snakes, they're buried too deep. And ..." He shook his head and dropped down to the bed. I kneeled on the floor in front of him.

Arthur's eyes fixed on the bracelet, and I felt the calmness bloom around him. The steadiness of his breath when the light glinted off the silver band. "You're scared of these men," I said, seeing through this outburst, this obsessive need for me to have the tracker on.

Arthur laughed, and the mocking sound made my toes curl. But there was despair in it too. "Scared," he said with another cold laugh. He shook his head, staring again at the floor as he finished his cigarette. "I'm not scared of any fucker in this town. They can come at me all they fucking want, guns blaring and shipping containers exploding. They can try and take me out—let them fucking come." I frowned, not understanding the tortured look on his face.

Arthur's nostrils flared and his jaw clenched. Then, on an exhale, he said, "I'm not scared of anything, *including* death." He looked me dead in the eyes. "But I'm fucking terrified of them taking *you*. I fucking can't breathe when I think of the cunts taking *you*, hurting *you* ... killing *you*."

Tears pricked at my eyes and my throat tightened. Arthur put his hand on the back of my neck and pulled me forward, his forehead pressed to mine. "My biggest fear, my only fucking fear in this whole shitshow of a world, is you being taken away from me." His finger ran over the bracelet, and I felt his fear down to my core. Because I feared it too. I didn't want to live in a world where Arthur wasn't by my side.

"I won't ever leave you," I whispered.

Arthur's lip curled into a small smile. "Can I have that written in blood?"

I sat back and, repeating the move I made to him in the pits, crossed my heart with my finger. Arthur pulled me to his mouth and kissed me. He kissed me and kissed me until I was breathless.

"Come on," I said when the tension in the room had ebbed away. "Let's get a cup of tea."

Arthur took my offered hand and led me to the kitchen. He leaned against the countertop as I boiled the kettle and prepared the teapot. As I grabbed two cups from the cupboard, my stomach growled.

I laughed at the sound, and Arthur's eyebrows pulled down. "You haven't eaten?"

The kettle boiled, and I poured the water into the teapot. "I forgot," I said. Arthur moved straight to the fridge.

He looked at the bare shelves. "This is all there is." He frowned at the container. "What the fuck *is* this?" he said, pulling a pomegranate salad from the second shelf.

I smiled, and his eyes flared at my laugh. "It's Betsy's, I think."

He took the lid off the bowl and grabbed a fork from the drawer. "Well now it's fucking yours." I went to fix the tea, but Arthur turned me around. "Fuck the tea, princess. Eat." He scooped pomegranate seeds onto the fork and brought them to my mouth. They burst on my tongue, and I groaned. I hadn't realised how hungry I was.

I licked my lips. "That's good."

Arthur fed me another forkful, and another, until the entire bowl was gone. The infamous dark lord feeding his queen. By the time I had swallowed the last bite, Arthur was hard in his trousers and his pupils were blown.

Growling, he yanked me to his chest and placed his hand possessively on the back of my neck. "You're never leaving me. You understand? You're fucking staying here forever."

I felt my thighs clench at his harsh, unyielding tone. "The tea," I said as he started biting at my lips, unbuttoning my jeans.

"Fuck the tea," he hissed. "You're going to ride my cock." Arthur picked me up, wrapping my legs around his waist, and took us back to our bedroom.

The tea was completely forgotten.

CHAPTER FIFTEEN

ARTHUR

I checked my phone. Ronnie and Vera hadn't called me. They were still with the hackers. No fucker knew apart from me. I wanted as few people as possible to know about what they were doing. Even my family. They thought the girls were at a meeting with the Scousers up north. And I was keeping it that way.

I had just got back from meeting with Old Sammy. The ex-boss still hadn't heard anything about who'd attacked his old dock. They'd come for him too. Torched his betting shop in Millwall. The fucking Hangmen had been hit in Camden. The Irish and the Romani had been attacked too. Anyone who had ties to me. But last night they went for the Italians. There wasn't a damn syndicate in all of London who wasn't now after these pricks.

But *I* wanted at them. *Me*. I wanted to find them and destroy them. They had a fucking bounty on their heads, and only I was going to collect it. The rest of the families could get in fucking line.

I walked into the living room; the rest of my family had just returned from their duties. Cheska and Gene were sat together by the fire. Betsy was with Charlie and Vinnie. Eric and Freddie were talking at the bar.

I'd just opened my mouth to get them all to report when my old man's nurse came flying into the room. "Mr Adley," she said, breathless, and my fucking blood turned to ice at the panicked expression on her face.

"What?" I asked tightly. Every head in the room turned our way.

Cheska was immediately beside me; Freddie came closer too. "He's woken up," the nurse said, and she may as well have fucking slammed a crowbar into my face.

"What?"

"He's woken up. I've removed some of his equipment from him— mainly his breathing tube. I've called for the doctor. He's in and out of consciousness. He's extremely weak." She smiled, and it lit up her entire face. "But he's *awake*."

I didn't move. Bloody couldn't.

I felt a hand lace through mine, then a firm grip on my bicep. I blinked and fucking slammed back to earth. Freddie was in front of me, as shocked as I was. "Artie," he said. "He's fucking awake."

Cheska squeezed my hand, and I looked into her green-brown eyes, seeing them bloody shining. My heart was pounding and my body still didn't want to fucking move.

Charlie started to come over to me, then his phone rang. He frowned as he looked at the caller and answered. His mouth tightened. "We're on our way."

He hung up, and I felt adrenaline kick in as I stared at my cousin. Something was wrong. "What?" I asked, cutting through the raised energy in the room.

"Another attack," Charlie said. "Fucking west dock this time." He shook his head, disbelief in his dark expression.

"FUCK!" I shouted, knowing I had to get to that fucking dock and sort shit out.

Charlie was beside me in a second. "You're not fucking going anywhere." Charlie nudged his chin at Eric, Betsy and Vinnie. "We'll go. You've got to stay and see Uncle Alfie. Freddie too. This isn't getting in the fucking way of something this important."

"I can go—" Freddie tried to say, but I shook my head.

"No, he's your old man too," I said, and Cheska leaned in and kissed my arm. I pointed at Charlie. "You report to me as soon as you find out what's happened. I want to know, the minute you do, exactly what's gone down and who the fuck did this."

"You know it." Charlie kissed me on the head. "He's fucking woke up, mate." He threw me a blinding smile. They all fucking came over and hugged me and Freddie. Then my cousins, Vinnie, and Eric were gone.

Gene got to his feet. "I'm happy for you, Artie," he said. "I'll be in my room. Say hi to Uncle Alfie for me." I nodded my head as the kid passed us, and gripped Cheska's hand tighter.

Freddie left the room, and I fucking froze. My dad had woken up. It had actually happened. I'd kept him on machines all this time, but deep down, I'd believed he was gone. Now he was here. Actually *here*. Fucking back from the dead. The true gaffer of our firm resurrected.

My fucking old man was *alive*.

"Let's go, baby," Cheska said. I nodded numbly at my bird, kissed her, then walked to his bedroom.

I sucked in a breath as I opened the bedroom door. Freddie was already beside his bed, stood back a few feet while the nurse checked him over. Freddie was watching her. My dad's eyes were shut, but when I came closer, I saw his eyelids move, then open, his blue eyes wincing at the low light.

My pulse raced as his disorientated eyes looked around the room, first to Freddie, then they fixed on me. I thought I'd fucking fall over as he stared at me. I remembered the night he was gunned down. I remembered it with perfect fucking clarity—the Russians opening fire on our firm's leaders and shooting them all to hell. And I remembered Freddie finding a pulse in my old man's neck.

And here he was. Fucking alive and breathing and staring right at me.

His mouth moved, and I knew he'd seen me. He knew it was me. He couldn't speak, and I knew that having been in a coma for so long would make him delusional as fuck. But my dad was looking at me, and I knew he fucking knew me.

Cheska let go of my hand. I looked right at her. "Go to him, baby," she said and stood back away from the bed. I glanced over at Freddie, who had turned fucking white. He met my eyes, and I nodded at him to get closer. The nurse stepped back from the bed, and I stood at my old man's side.

His face was drawn, he was skin and bones, but that was Alfie fucking Adley in that bed. The fucking living legend of our firm.

"Alright, Dad," I said, and his dazed eyes focused on me. He didn't move, but I knew his muscles were fucked after being dormant for so long—atrophy. Dad took in a deep breath, and I uncurled my hand from a fist and took hold of his.

We never did this shit. Weren't like that. But right now ... I wanted to hold his fucking hand.

"You remember Freddie," I said, joking, and nodded to where Freddie stood like a fucking statue on Dad's other side.

"Alfie," Freddie said. Dad followed the sound of his voice. He blinked slowly when he saw Freddie, and I knew that was him saying hello.

My arse hit the seat beside the bed, my fucking legs giving out. Dad turned back to me. Just staring at me. The muscles in my face felt tight, but I pulled a smirk onto my lips.

"I didn't think I was going to see you again, old man," I said. Dad breathed in deep. "Thought you'd finally cashed in your chips with the devil."

Dad's lips twitched and he slowly blinked again: no. That crack, that fucking crack in my chest was back, aching and throbbing, a motherfucking boulder in my throat. I looked over at Cheska, who was watching us with a watery smile on her face. "Got a bird," I said to Dad, winking at Chelsea Girl, and his milky gaze moved to her.

"Hello, Mr Adley," she said, stepping a little closer. "Nice to finally meet you."

Dad looked back to me, like he was trying to say something. Just as he did, Freddie's phone beeped with a message. "They've just got to the dock," he said. "Chuck's looking into what happened." Frowning, I checked my phone, wondering why my cousin hadn't called me. I'd told him to. And he always checked in.

I brought up his number and was about to give him a call, when suddenly Freddie grabbed hold of the nurse, who was changing a bag on one of my dad's drips, pulled out his gun, and sent a bullet straight through her skull.

Everything fucking slowed to half speed as I saw the nurse drop to the floor, eyes still wide, and the door to my old man's bedroom burst open. Men in all black with balaclavas on their faces flooded through.

"CHESKA!" I bellowed as one of the men grabbed her, smothering her mouth with his hand. I let go of my dad's hand and shot to my feet. I reached into my jacket for my gun, but some fucker tasered me from behind. I fought the volts pulsing through me, electrocuting me from inside. When he shot me with it again, I fucking dropped to the ground. I fought it, arms and legs moving, fucking crawling to get to Cheska, who was screaming under the cunt's hand and trying to fight free. But two fuckers wrenched me back, tied my hands and held me down on the floor.

"You're dead," I snarled at them, never taking my eyes off Cheska. "You're both fucking *dead.*"

They dragged me to my feet, and I heard the sound of a gun's safety unlocking. I tried to force my legs to gain strength, then my head whipped to Freddie, who was holding a revolver to my old man's head.

Fucking time stopped.

"NO!" I yelled, just as my dad met my eyes, held my fucking gaze, blinking slowly one more time, like he was saying goodbye, and Freddie fired a single shot. Something inside of me shattered along with the loud racket from that bullet. Whatever frayed bit of worn tether had kept me down, grounded, held back from completely losing it and giving myself over to fucking evil, snapped.

There was no surviving this one. The bullet tore through my dad's head, blood pooling on the pillow behind him. "NO!" I thundered again and used all of my strength to fight the fuckers holding me, throwing them to the ground.

The taser shots had taken most of my energy away. But they had

Cheska. They had my fucking bird, and Freddie had just shot my dad. I had moved a few feet, legs dragging on the floor, to Cheska, when one of the cunts scrambled to his knees and tasered me again until my legs fucking buckled. I swerved my head to Freddie.

The fucking traitor that was Freddie. I had suspected someone, but not fucking Freddie.

"Why?" I growled, gritting my teeth as I fought to get back some fucking strength. Cheska screamed another muffled scream, and I set my eyes on the arsehole that had her. She met my gaze, and I tried to tell her with my eyes to hold on.

To just fucking hold on.

"Why?" Freddie said, coming around the bed. I looked at my old man and felt that crack in my chest fucking erupt with lava, the scalding heat that spiked my blood filling me with nothing but red-hot rage. Freddie stopped in front of me, and I imagined what it would be like to wrap my hands around the fucker's throat.

To squeeze and watch the life drain out of him.

He was my brother. He was my motherfucking *brother*.

Freddie got in my face. Fucking taunting me. "For *my* dad."

My head fucking swam as I tried to think, the taser making me sluggish, pushing a thick fog inside my mind. I thought of Freddie's dad, of Frank. I didn't understand. I didn't fucking understand!

"My old man died because of *him*," Freddie said, pointing his gun again at my dad. He must have seen my confusion, because he said, "My old man wasn't a motherfucking *Adley*. He was from Deptford. He was a fucking South London boy through and through. And he infiltrated your fucking scumbag family for years. Fed information back to the real fucking lords of this town. His real family." Freddie smiled at me. "*My* real family."

"And who is your fucking *real* family?" I smiled. It was cold and promised a slow and painful death.

Freddie stood. "You'll get to meet them. Pretty bloody soon, in fact."

"Let them go." I followed the sound of a quiet voice coming from the door to the bedroom, and my face fucking blanched as I saw Gene stood at the door with a gun in his hand. His hand was shaking. The kid's hazel eyes were wide and wild.

"Gene!" Cheska managed to say before they pushed tape over her mouth. Tears fell down her cheeks as her eyes darted to mine, and I saw the fucking terror there. Not for her. Or me. But for Gene. She'd grown to love him.

"Gene!" I called, just as he was rushed at by one of the fuckers at his side. The kid fired off a shot, but the twat attacking him hit his arm away, directing it to the ceiling. Then he knocked the kid out cold with a punch to the face.

Gene buckled and went down. A heap of black on the ground.

"Leave him," I said to Freddie. "Leave him here, and when I finally get to kill you, I'll make it a little less painful."

Freddie smiled, then said to the twat beside Gene, "We're taking him too. Can't have my old family knowing I was involved in any of this shit." He shrugged. "Plus, it'll piss off Eric and Vera." Freddie smiled wider. "And Charlie, of course. I'd pay anything to see that tosser brought down a peg or two. Or better still, six feet in the fucking ground."

"I'M GOING TO FUCKING END YOU!" I roared at Freddie.

Freddie stepped right before me. My brother. For all intents and purposes, this was my fucking *brother*. All those bloody years he'd lived with us. Here. In this fucking house. I could barely breathe as he looked dead into my eyes. Cheska had gone still in her captors' hands. She met my eyes, and I saw understanding in her green-browns. I was getting her out of this. Some fucking how. I was getting her out.

Freddie snapped his fingers in my face, and a red mist fell over my eyes. He leaned in close and, putting his gun back into his suit jacket, said, "You've lost, Artie."

I boiled inside. Raged. Screamed a fucking silent battle cry in his face. But I became the grey man once again. I let the fuckers behind me think they had me. Let the emotion drop from my face like my dad had always taught me. Freddie laughed, and some of the men in the room laughed back, reading my silence for weakness. Inside, I was a volcano, fire and brimstone and fucking excruciating death.

Freddie faced me again. "You're the great chess master, Artie." He leaned forward until he was only an inch from my face. His smile fell, but laughter still danced in his fucking eyes. "Checkmate."

Externally, I didn't move a muscle. But inside ... inside I had stabbed the traitor with a knife in his eye and was gouging out his still-beating heart from his chest while he still had breath left in his body and could feel every strike.

"Take them," Freddie said when I gave him fuck all back, and the men dragged us from the room. Cheska looked back at me, and I gave her a slow nod. *It's going to be okay. I won't let them hurt you. I'll get us out of this. I'm never fucking letting you go.*

I love you, her eyes said, like she was done, like this was our mother-fucking goodbye. Like she was never coming back to me. I fought to fucking breathe, to not explode. I had to think.

I had to fucking *think*.

Some fucker behind me carried Gene out after my girl. The fuckers behind me pushed me to move next.

As we stepped out of the door, two small vans and a car waited for us. I scanned around us, to the churchyard and drive. My men were on the ground, throats slit. Silently, they'd been killed, no fucking warning, no fucking honour. Freddie had been waiting for my family to leave the house—

The text message, I thought. The message he'd got as he sat beside my dad. It wasn't from Charlie. It was to say whoever the fuck these men were, they had killed the soldiers watching my house and were ready to take us. My mind raced. I wondered if there had even been an attack on the west dock, where my family had rushed to. Or had that been a set-up too? Were they fucking ambushed when they got there?

Were they all fucking dead ... ?

"Split them up," Freddie said, ripping me back to the here and now. I swung my head to him, already tasting the scent of his imminent death on my tongue. "Those two in that one," he said, pointing to a van, then to Cheska and Gene. The fuckers put Gene in the van first.

Cheska turned to face me, and I held my chin up, telling her to wait for me. That I'd be coming for her. That no matter what happened, to fucking hold out for me. A weak smile pulled on her face, and she was pushed into the van. The doors shut behind her.

I wanted to charge. To fucking nut the men holding me and send bullets through all their fucking skulls. But I had to think. I had to fucking *think*. I was outnumbered and wouldn't put Cheska and Gene at risk of being killed.

Freddie smirked at me victoriously as he watched me be shoved into the back of the van. The two fuckers that were holding me got in with me too. As the van doors closed, I saw Freddie slip into the back seat of the car.

My phone rang. One of the twats beside me heard it, reached into my pocket and smashed it under his foot. But not before I saw the name: Ronnie.

She'd found me something. Ronnie and Vera had fucking found me something.

The engine started and the van pulled away from the church. My hands were tied behind my back with gaffer tape. Stupid fuckers should have used titanium cuffs or some shit. Because I was getting out. I was getting out, and when I did, I was bringing the wrath of the fucking devil down on their heads.

Reaching up, I went to the waistband of my trousers and to the hidden pocket. Not making a single bit of noise, I pushed the knife I kept hidden on me out of the pocket, flipped it in my hands and started cutting through the tape. The pricks beside me were watching out of the blacked-out windows, no doubt checking for any of my men following us. The driver was sealed off by a blackout partition.

The tape gave way under my blade, and my hands got free. My breathing deepened as I tried to work off the last of the effects of the taser. I flexed the muscles in my legs, testing their strength. It was enough. It was enough to fucking kill these bastards and get the fuck out of this van.

I gripped the knife harder, then, in a fucking flash, slashed the sharp blade across both the fuckers' throats, one at a time, from behind—they never saw me coming. Their eyes widened as they started to thrash. I pulled them to their backs, weighing them both down with my knees on their chests so they were pinned to the van's floor and the driver wouldn't hear anything. Their blood drenched me. I ripped their balaclavas off as they fought for breath. I stared right into their newly bared faces as death came calling. I didn't recognise them. Nothing about them gave me any idea about who the fuck these pricks were.

They were both clutching their throats, pathetically trying to close up the slash. Then I saw their wrists ... I fucking saw it: the brand. That circular brand with the V-type shape in the centre. The brand that had become my fucking trigger. The mark that made me want to eviscerate them, all the fuckers in the fucked-up group.

And Freddie was one of them. He was bloody one of the ones who'd killed my mum and sister, and now he'd killed my dad, once and for all, Alfie Adley nothing but a corpse on the bed he'd been stuck in for too many months. I pushed the thoughts from my head. I didn't have fucking time to think about all that yet and keep my head straight. I had to get out of this fucking van. I had to get back to my family, to my men.

Then the hunt would begin.

The men stopped moving beneath me, and I silently climbed over them and unlatched the van's back doors. Thank fuck it was an older van that didn't have sensors that would alert the driver. I turned the lock, then threw the doors open. I knew the road the minute I saw it —we were still in the East End. Still in my fucking kingdom.

Seeing no cars behind us, I jumped from the van and onto the tarmac. I slammed onto the hard ground, my skin ripping at the contact. I didn't feel it. Not a fucking thing. My heart and any ability to feel anything was driving away with my fucking bird up ahead, heading to Christ knew where. Only the need to kill and seek revenge kept me going. Kept my mind fixed on what I had to do.

And then I was fucking running. When I got behind a nearby building, I looked back at the road and saw the van Cheska and Gene were in and Freddie's car up ahead. They turned left, then disappeared out of sight.

The minute that van fucking disappeared, Cheska in the back, my bird moving too many miles from me, no longer by my bloody side, a deathly calm spread over me. The dark lord had just lost sight of his dark lady, and that turned the world on its axis. The demons inside screamed at me to get her back. Pacing and roaring at me to get our fucking queen back. To raze any fucker who got in our way to the ground.

My feet were already moving, autopilot kicking in. I saw the King's Head pub up ahead and ran. I fucking chewed up pavement until I burst through the door. Every punter in the place turned to look at me. "M-Mr Adley?" the barman stuttered, and I recognised him as someone my old man knew. My dad had used this pub once for meetings years ago.

"Phone," I barked as I reached the bar. The punters moved the fuck out of my way. I didn't give a shit that I was leaving a trail of blood on the floor; I'd send someone to clean it up later. Right now I had tunnel vision. Every bit of energy I could muster was set onto one task—to get Cheska back, and kill the ones who took her from me. They took my fucking bird from me. They had no idea what they had done. What fucking monster they had just woken up.

The barman frantically placed a phone in front of me. I dialled Charlie's number, knowing that if he didn't answer, they were all dead. But my cousin picked up on the first ring. "Charlie," I said when he didn't speak at first.

"Arthur? Fuck, Arthur! Is that you? What the *fuck* is happening?"

"They've got her," I said through my teeth. I fought to keep that fire in my chest burning, fuelling my anger so I didn't fucking drown in rage and drive after them, killing them all before I even had answers. I didn't just want the foot soldiers dead in whatever this syndicate was—I was going for the king. The fucking mad king who thought it a good idea to fuck with what was mine.

"They've got Cheska and Gene," I said. Charlie grew silent. Fucking deadly silent. "Send a car. The King's Head," I ordered and put the phone down. I walked outside to wait in the fucking shadows beside the pub, just breathing, thinking, letting the evil in my veins rest, gain strength for when I needed it most.

A car came five minutes later. I got in the back. "Get me the fuck home."

I pictured Cheska's face, her fucking green-brown eyes as she'd got into the van. The look of goodbye she gave me, eyes saying *I love you*. Goodbye. She was saying goodbye.

My thoughts blurred to show me my dad. My fists balled on my knees as I thought of my fucking dad. My dad, who had looked at me and blinked slowly—saying goodbye to me too.

Goodbye ... goodbye ... I was fucking sick and tired of the fucking goodbyes!

The car turned in to the church. My family's and soldier's cars and vans were everywhere. I jumped from the car before it had even stopped, burst through the front door and rushed to the living room. My family were already there, fucking bloodied and scraped, eyes wide and ready to bring death to those who had fucked with the wrong firm.

Betsy flew at me and wrapped her arms around me. "Shit, Arthur. Are you okay?" She stepped back, checking over my bloodstained clothes. Suddenly, Charlie was in front of me too. He waited for me to speak. He had cuts and bruises on his face, suit ruined and torn.

"Freddie," I said, fighting back the fucking rage that name off my tongue conjured. But it spilled over. In front of my family, it spilled the fuck over everyone. "IT WAS MOTHERFUCKING FREDDIE!" I swiped at the bar, and all the bottles crashed to the floor. I breathed, closing my eyes to rein the rage back in.

"What?" Betsy whispered, paling.

I paced, exorcising the hyped-up demons inside me, skimming off the too-strong energy they were emitting within me. I needed to take the fucking edge off their wrath until I was ready to unleash hell on the people we wanted to die.

"They've got Cheska and Gene." I looked at Eric, who was ready to fucking murder anyone who got in his path. His little brother had been taken, his brother who had already almost died too many fucking times in his tortured life.

"They ambushed us at the dock," Charlie said. "But Mikey had got there first. He knew something was wrong when one of his men hadn't checked in on time. He'd called for back-up, and they had already killed most of the fuckers waiting to take us out."

"Did they keep anyone alive for questioning?" I asked.

"They killed themselves," Betsy said. "When they knew they couldn't beat us all. They killed themselves first."

"Fucking cowards," I snarled.

"What now?" Charlie asked, keeping his shit together, the fucking calm to my raging storm. That was why we worked as well as we did. Why he was my fucking closest friend. He was my *true* fucking brother.

Not bastard, traitorous *Freddie*.

"I need a computer," I said and rushed to the study. I had to focus on how to get her back. Not on the thought of them hurting her, of fucking selling her ... killing her.

My fingers smashed onto the keys, smearing them with blood. I brought up the tracking programme I used to have hidden on my phone, then ...

"Deptford," I said, Cheska's tracker taking me right to the viper's nest. Freddie had mentioned Deptford. The fucker had never been as smart as the rest of us. But I should have seen the signs. I should have seen that he lived in a family he hated. Seen through his act.

I heard the door open and snapped my head up, my body primed to attack. But it was just my cousin. Charlie was fucking white as his feet stopped just inside the study. "Alfie," he said. Eric and Vinnie came in behind him.

"He killed him," I said. "Dad fucking woke up, and Freddie killed him." I kept my emotions tamped down. I fought to keep them subdued until I was able to set them fucking free. Channel them on the cunts that deserved everything that was building inside of me.

"No!" Betsy said from the hallway, clearly having just seen my dad too.

Someone smashed through the front door of the house. I was in the hallway in seconds—we all were. Vera and Ronnie stood there, guns drawn. "What the fuck happened?" Vera asked, eyes darting around the house for signs of trouble.

"Did you get anything?" I asked Ronnie, ignoring Vera. Her dark eyes fell to my blood-covered clothes.

I heard Eric telling Vera what was happening, that they had Gene. That they had Cheska. That my dad was fucking dead. All because of Freddie. Freddie fucking selling us out. A fucking wolf in sheep's clothing living among us all these bastard years.

Checkmate. His smug voice in my head grated on my nerves. *You've lost ...*

"Lawson," Ronnie said, interrupting my dark thoughts. My focus instantly snapped to her. She swallowed like bile was clawing up her throat. "It's Lawson," she said again when I didn't fucking move. "*Ollie* Lawson."

Fire raged through me, incinerating every cell, every fucking fibre in my body. Ronnie's dark eyes never left mine as her words hit me like fucking bullets. A spray of fucking bullets that sank into my organs, shutting every one of them down. Until I was dead. Until I was fucking walking *death*.

"Ollie Lawson," I said, his name from my lips like fucking cancer. I tensed, stopped fucking breathing, and saw that fucker's face in my mind. All this fucking time it was Lawson... Ollie motherfucking Lawson!

I shook, braced to fucking explode with napalm. He was there, all along, right under our fucking noses. Laughing right in our motherfucking faces!

The cunt kept clear of the underworld, like the fucking rat he was. No honour, no fucking code that all we fucked-up criminals lived by in this town. Claimed his family had a true business. A *legit* motherfucking business. Import and export.

Import and *motherfucking* export.

He traded in humans. Trafficked under the guise of a booming mainstream company. Hidden in plain sight, with pathetic brands on their skin and coward hearts in their chests. A fucking criminal cult packed with pussies too afraid to let their fucked-up faces be seen.

I was going to murder them. Motherfucking Ollie Lawson. Freddie fucking Williams. I was going to fucking massacre them all.

Ronnie handed over a thick file. I took it, the wrath inside me building and building until all I could breathe in was death. "Traffickers. All these bastard years existing under everyone's noses. Gradually taking out crime families. Stealing contracts. Stealing kids, selling them across the world, and taking the entire criminal underworld down like fucking thieves in the night."

"Get everyone gathered," I said, my voice sounding fucked up even to my ears. "Every fucking soldier we have. Get them ready for war. Because we're going in tonight to get these cunts. This coward-laced empire falls *tonight*." I flicked through the file, then stopped when I saw something on one of the later pages. I read the information—text messages, transcripts, emails with no IP addresses ... and my blood turned to tar as it tried to push through my fucking demonic heart.

I lifted my eyes. Ronnie was already watching me, waiting for me to see one crucial piece of information. She nodded in confirmation, and as I read it again, just to let the fucking words sink in, a cool blast of calm trickled down my spine.

Deadly, chilling fucking calm.

My family were looking at me, frowning, waiting for me to relay what I'd just seen that made all this worse. Made my reason for killing Lawson deeper.

Even more deserved.

So I fucking told them. I told them every detail of the fucked-up thing Lawson had done.

Cheska.

Fuck, when she found out ...

That motherfucking betrayal only made my darkness sink deeper into my already evil-tarnished soul. They fucked with my queen. They fucked with my family. Now they were going to drown in their own blood.

I rolled the file in my fist, finger bones cracking. My family members' livid expressions were all staring back at me, thirsting for revenge. "Get your fucking weapons ready. They've got Cheska and Gene. They killed my fucking dad." I lit a cig and let the smoke billow around me. "They killed my mum and Pearl." The rage simmered, reserving its full wrath for Lawson, Freddie and their men, and I let the devil inside me completely take the reins. "Tonight, they all fucking *die*."

I met each of my brothers' and sisters' eyes. They were nodding their heads. Vinnie smiled broadly at me, hyped for blood and death.

First, I needed to make some calls. Because it wasn't just me that these fuckers had messed with. The file in my hand was all the proof I needed to get the other families and syndicates on board. Lawson's network was big, brutal, effective. But so was the rest of the London fucking underworld. Separately, we were lethal. Together ... we were fucking death incarnate.

Tonight we needed all of the Lawson syndicate taken out. Not one of those fuckers would be alive when the sun started to rise tomorrow. But we—my family—we were getting the snakes at the top. We were going to destroy the nest.

"Call Royal, Seamus and Vano. Tell them we've got something they want to see. The Italians, Chechens, Chinese and Jews too. Lawson has fucked with too many of us. For far too long. Tonight, we all pay him back in kind." My family's gazes lit with excitement—vengeful excitement. "But Freddie's mine," I said. "Out of every one of those cunts, Freddie Williams is mine."

I pushed past my family to change and wait for my soldiers to rally.

Then I was going to get my fucking girl.

CHAPTER SIXTEEN

CHESKA

Gene woke in the dark van, groaning as he tried to sit up. They had tied his hands with tape too. He managed to sit, and in the hazy low light—the lampposts outside our only source of illumination—his hazel eyes found me. Confusion glittered in their depths, but it soon cleared and his mouth parted when he saw me, my hands bound and my mouth gagged.

"Cheska," he whispered and searched around us, getting his bearings. Then his shy face, the timid and closed expression he always wore, morphed into determination, and for the first time since I'd met him, I saw a flicker of "Adley" looking back at me. A steely and ruthless resolve in his stare.

"They'll find us," he said, making sure to keep his voice low, even though an opaque partition separated us from the driver. He shifted closer to me. "They'll find out what happened and get us out of here." He frowned, then paled. "Arthur?"

"He's alive," I said from behind the tape. I had managed to get its seal off my lips with my tongue, a gap forming at the top that helped me breathe, let me speak to Gene. "He's in another van."

Gene nodded, and I could see him thinking. "He'll tell us what to do," Gene said, confidently. "When we get out of here to wherever they're taking us. He'll get us out."

My eyes fell to the bracelet on my wrist. Arthur and I hadn't told anyone that I was wearing it. If only we had told someone—Charlie, Betsy. They would be able to find us. Then I thought back to Arthur when our eyes met in his father's bedroom. When they met just before I was put into the van ... when the Arthur of old took hold of him. The one I had known for years, the one who never gave me any indication of what he was thinking.

The ruthless man who, despite his aloofness, I fell so deeply in love with.

The van came to a stop, and fear took me in its grasp. These were the men who had come for me at the spa. The ones I had evaded. The ones who had killed my family—and now they were going to make me pay. I knew it, down to the marrow of my bones.

The sound of low voices sailed through the body of the van, then the doors were wrenched open. A frantic and furied Freddie glared down at us, his shoulders relaxing slightly as he laid eyes on me and then Gene.

"Check the fucking roads," he hissed at a man beside him. "He can't have got far."

My heart kicked into a sprint—a hopeful rhythm. Freddie moved out of the way for a second, and I found the van that had held Arthur. And I saw that it was empty ... empty but for two slain men who were being dragged out of the back, blood dripping from their slashed throats and eyes glazed with the recent veil of death.

A manic smile pulled on my lips. I turned to Gene. "He got away," I hushed out, and relief spread on Gene's face. I scanned the van again; the men surrounding the vehicle looked panicked and harried. "He got away," I said again, reassuring myself, as I was dragged from the van and wrenched to my feet.

A laugh escaped me, and I felt the weight of the bracelet around my wrist. The bracelet that would lead Arthur and the family straight to this gang's door.

Freddie whipped his head around to face me, his expression red with rage. I lifted my chin and thought of Vera, Ronnie and Betsy. Of how they held themselves. They would never let anyone see their weakness.

I would not let him see mine.

Freddie stepped close to me, and in my mind I replayed him killing Alfie Adley back at the church. I heard the agonised scream rip from Arthur's throat as his dad's blood spilled onto his pillow. As Freddie so cruelly and smugly told him he had lost.

"He's going to kill you." I heard the menace in my own voice, a part of me rising to the surface that I didn't even know existed. The part that thirsted for this man's head on a platter, that longed to see him choke on his last breath. A part of me that seemed to expand with every second that I stood before him, looking into the eyes of the man who had lied for so many years, who had looked at the man I loved with disdain and contempt. He had dared to think he had bested his foe.

Bested *us*.

The entire Adley family.

"He'll kill you," I promised, then smiled under the tape. "And he'll make you scream."

Quick as a snake, Freddie sliced me across the face with the back of his hand. My cheek throbbed, and the tinny taste of blood burst on my tongue. I stumbled at the force of the hit. But it didn't fill me with dread or fear. Rather, it emboldened me. The stab of pain ricocheting over my face drove me to push Freddie harder. To bring him to the edge, to make him question every noise and movement around him. Make him nervous for the wrath I knew my much-loved lord would soon be bringing to his door.

Freddie must have seen the lack of fear on my face; he raised his hand again, curling it into a fist. I braced my legs for another, harder blow, but a hand grabbed Freddie's wrist.

"Don't you dare fucking touch her again."

I turned my head to the man who held Freddie's hand, the voice that my foggy mind recognised ...

My breath caught in my lungs when I saw him step out from behind Freddie.

"Ollie ..."

Ollie Lawson. My mind raced with reasons he could have been here. I looked around us. It was an abandoned yard of some kind, old offices and outbuildings surrounding us. A broken-down palace. What was he doing here? He needed to leave. These men ... they would kill him.

"Cheska." Ollie gave me the same smile he'd always worn around me. The one that used to upset Hugo so much he would talk about his hatred of Ollie for days afterwards. Ollie flicked his chin at Freddie. "Take the tape off her mouth, then get back."

Freddie's eyes were molten as they fell on me, but he did as Ollie had commanded, dropped the tape to the ground, and walked to the barely standing garage-looking building across the yard.

What was happening? What the *hell* was happening?

Ollie stepped closer to me, my frantically beating heart trying to coax my hazy brain to catch up with what was staring me right in the face. He looked down my body, that heated gaze he always had for me still burning like hot coals. "I've missed you," he said, and I tried harder to understand what the bloody hell was happening.

Then Ollie lifted his hand and ran his fingers over his mouth ... and I saw it. I saw the circular brand on his wrist, the brand that I had come to despise, to associate with death and pain and devastating loss.

The thing that linked Ollie to a devilish operation that had killed so many people, our families ... and trafficked women. So many innocent and helpless women ...

"You?" I asked, my voice a mere whisper.

Ollie's face fell, and he put his hands in his pockets. "You fucked things up for me, sweetheart." He shook his head in disappointment. "I had a plan. I had everything all worked out. A smooth and seamless execution." A dark shadow crossed his face. "But I hadn't considered Adley." He said the name with pure hatred in his tone. "I hadn't counted on you fighting my men on your hen do. Frankly, I hadn't thought you had it in you to get away, pelting down the alley like that."

The spa. He was talking about the spa. I shut down my emotions, held back the tears that threatened to fall, when it fully hit me. It was Ollie, Ollie Lawson, who had ordered the deaths of my dad and Hugo, of Arabella and Freya.

He stepped closer still. "And I didn't expect you to go crawling to Adley. The motherfucking bane of my life." He sucked on his teeth. "That wanker's always getting in my way."

"You killed them," I said, voice weak. "Arabella and Freya were your friends, and you killed them. Ruthlessly."

"They were collateral," he said with such nonchalance that it set me alight. I felt my organs burn and re-form with the hatred and fire that was igniting in me. An internal eclipse smothering any light that lived inside my soul.

Ollie pushed a piece of hair from my face. I wanted to launch at him, kill him for the things he had done, all the sadness and pain he had caused. "I always wanted you, Cheska," he said and yanked my head back. He smirked as a pained moan slipped from my lips, and I had to breathe through the urge to attack him. I felt Gene standing stoically behind me. I had to protect Gene too. I had to stay alive for Arthur.

It felt as though the bracelet pulsed around my wrist, promising me that he was coming. That he would find us here and destroy the men that had brought us all so much pain.

"I had to make a lot of plans to finally get you. For years I craved you. And this time I wasn't going to fail in making you mine." He shook his head and laughed without mirth. "The first time it was Adley who got in my fucking way too. I hadn't counted on that twat being around. Or even caring about you." His hands curled into fists as he spoke of Arthur. "I should have known. The fucking Adleys were always in our way in this city. Thinking they controlled it all. Making everyone in the underworld piss themselves with fear." His expression grew icy. "Well, not fucking *me*. Not my organisation."

Ollie Lawson ... I was still trying to wrap my head around the fact that the enemy, the shadowy force who had caused so much devastation, was Ollie and his family. He'd attended Hugo's school. He had a successful business. They had it *all*. Apparently it wasn't enough—they had delved into the darkness of the underworld to sate their malevolent desires.

They trafficked humans as if they were nothing.

"It was all going to work so well," he said, pulling me back to the moment. The harsh winter wind whipped around us as I listened to the mad man before me. The devil who had tricked the world into thinking he was some kind of benevolent god. But here he was in front of me, showing me his fanged teeth, scales and horns.

"They would attack you, and I would save you. That was the fucking plan—simple, but effective. I would save you, and you would *see* me." I froze, trying to cast my mind back to whatever he could be talking about.

Harlow cunt ...

The way my attackers had spat my name at the spa. The way the men in Marbella, all those years ago, did too. "You?" I said, shock rendering me almost speechless. "You set that up? In Marbella?"

"I did," he said, almost proudly. "But Adley stuck his bastard nose in where it didn't belong." He smiled softly at me. "My old man wasn't happy about that little stunt I pulled. Not when your old man had just come to us for help with his failing business." My heart thudded slowly, as if my chest had become quicksand and was denying it air. "He'd gone to one of our more obvious associates, one of our fronts, and our man led him straight to our door." My blood ran cold. "Our fathers ended up doing quite a lot of business together—"

"You mean you lent him money you knew he could never pay back," I spat.

Ollie shrugged. "It was your father's choice, and the start of a beautiful working relationship." He paused. "Until it wasn't, of course."

"You killed them," I hissed, nausea rolling in my stomach as I saw my dad and Hugo take bullets to their heads in my mind.

Ollie stared at me a second too long to be casual, and then cupped his hands and blew into them as if staving off the chill. "It's bloody cold out here. Shall we take our conversation inside?"

Ollie nudged his head at the men who had taken us from the

church. One grabbed my arm. "Don't fucking hurt her," Ollie warned them, and the man slackened his grip. "Don't want my girl in any pain."

His girl.

He was delusional.

Ollie Lawson was fucking *bonkers*.

My mind reeled with the knowledge that it had been him in Marbella. He had set up an attack just so he could appear like a white knight and "save" me. So that I would see him, notice him ... *want* him.

I had gone for lunch with him the next day. Shivers ran down my spine when I remembered him pushing me to see if I was okay. Constantly asking. He'd been fishing for answers. Trying to piece together what had gone wrong.

And exactly who had got in his way.

I felt even more nauseous as that information circled my head. Then, the revelation that he was a trafficker. His underground organisation, the masses of money it brought in, was built on the loss and vulnerability of humans. People sold into slavery and sex work. I shuddered. Because he wasn't some ugly monster, some wicked man whose very demeanour kept you at bay. He was an ordinary man; his father had been a seemingly ordinary, good man. Self-made ... but they stood on an invisible empire built on broken dreams and victims' unheard cries.

Gene and I were led into the old garage Freddie had disappeared into. It looked as though it had dilapidated offices at the back, but Ollie led us to the opposite side of the building, ordering us to sit on the floor in a larger room that I assumed must have once been a waiting room of sorts.

Old, frayed and faded furniture was dotted about the room. A fire in an empty oil can blazed in the centre, and Ollie moved beside it, holding out his palms to the roaring flames. I watched him like a hawk, covertly edging closer to Gene, needing to keep him safe until Arthur could get to us.

"That's better," Ollie said after a few minutes. He smiled at me as if his men hadn't just kidnapped us, murdered Alfie Adley and left carnage in their wake.

When he was apparently suitably warmed, he pulled an old cushioned chair toward us and sat casually down. Freddie stood in the corner of the room, watching me and Gene like we were nothing, not even worth being alive. I sensed that if he'd had the choice, we would have already been worm food.

"So, you killed my friends and family?" I finally said to Ollie. "Just to get me back for your messed-up plan in Marbella. Another staged 'attack'?" I laughed cruelly at his patheticness. "And what? You were going to swoop in and save me again? I'd fall at your feet and we'd fall madly in love?" Ollie's cheek twitched, and I knew I had pissed him off. "And you killed my father and Hugo in the process?"

Ollie tipped his head to one side. "Your father and Hugo defaulted on their payments." He leaned forward. "Did you know the trouble your old man's company was in? The great and iconic Harlow Biscuits. Did you know it was about to go into administration, and that you, your daddy and fiancé were about to be ruined? They had no money left to their name, not even a bloody penny."

My pulse raced, but I kept my face neutral. I hadn't known. I hadn't known any of it. "Your old man had already given us the deeds to your house. Hugo's fancy fucking flat in Chelsea. They'd already signed over their cars." His eyebrows danced. "Heirlooms."

"You bled them dry. And when they couldn't pay any more money, they paid in blood."

Ollie's jaw clenched, then his nonchalant façade dropped. "Why do you have to ruin EVERY-FUCKING-THING?!" he screamed.

I flinched at his sudden vehemence. The cool persona he wore was shattering and revealing the true evil monster underneath. He got up from his chair and kneeled before me, voice calm and soft once again. "I wanted you by my side. I wanted you to want me back."

"I could *never* want you. You killed my family. My friends. You drained my father and Hugo of their assets, of their dignity," I hissed.

"Dignity?" he said, affronted. "What dignity?"

"You *killed* them. Tied them to chairs and shot them in their heads as they begged you for forgiveness. For mercy. I saw the video. You *sent* it to me. You wanted me to see it so when you saved me, you would look the hero."

Ollie reached out and ran his hands down my face. I tried to pull away, wrenching my head back. He struck out and grabbed my jaw, yanking me close as he sank his nails into my skin. I cried out at the pain, unable to hold it back. Ollie got in my face. "I've wanted to fuck you for so long." I froze, and Gene's breathing changed. He was angry. I wanted to beg him not to try anything. To not get himself hurt.

"You never stood a chance," I said.

Ollie waved his hand at one of his men. The next second, a woman near my age was dragged in. In fact, as I studied her more closely, that wasn't the only similarity. She *looked* like me. Brown hair, same build, same eyes. She could have been my doppelgänger.

She was silent as she was dragged further into the room. I tried to get her to meet my eyes—the same eyes as mine—but she just stared at nothing. No light in her gaze; alive, but no longer living.

She was dressed in a purple silk dress, and my stomach rolled in dread. Ollie walked over to her, running his hands down her bare arms. He cast a look my way, then palmed her breasts.

"Stop," I said, my heart breaking at the girl's non-existent reaction, her lack of expression. How long had he been abusing her this way? Then I realised ...

"You trafficked her," I said, knowing it to be true. "You stole her."

"I *bought* her," he corrected and kissed her on the lips. She didn't react. But that didn't seem to matter to Ollie. He groaned as if she was kissing him in return, loving him back.

I bought her...

I closed my eyes and recalled Ronnie's story. Ollie's family's business had tried to buy Ronnie too. They'd paralysed her father with debts that he would never be able to pay off and tried to take her as payment.

I bought her ...

This woman's parents, her husband ... *someone* ... they had sold her to save themselves. They'd thrown her to the wolves—to the biggest most vicious wolf of all.

Ollie turned until he was facing me, kissing the back of the girl's neck. "You know," he said and slipped the straps of her dress off her shoulders. The dress fell to the floor; she was naked underneath. It was freezing, but she made no complaint, no move to keep herself warm.

"Your looks aren't the only thing you have in common with her," Ollie said, and the anger crashed inside me, bouncing off the walls of my skin like a pinball machine. Ollie dipped his finger between the woman's legs. I turned my head away from the sight.

Ollie laughed, and I heard him step toward me. "Look at me, Cheska," he said softly. I didn't. I kept my head turned away. "I said look at me, *bitch*!" I whipped my head to him, eyes wide at the way he'd just spoken to me. He smiled lovingly. "That's better." He glanced back at the girl, who still stood staring out at nothing. "You have no idea how many of her there's been."

I stopped breathing.

"It takes me months to find them. They have to look *just* right." His eyes took him far away, but then he hurtled back to earth, his fucking stare on me. "They look like you, speak like you." Ollie leaned forward and kissed my forehead. I recoiled at his touch. He didn't seem to notice—or care. "But they're *not* you, Cheska. None of them ever measure up." Ollie got to his feet and walked back to the girl. In one second he'd taken out his knife, and a second later he stabbed her straight through the heart.

The cool demeanour I had been trying to hold on to vanished. I screamed as the girl hit the floor. Her head hit the cement, splitting her skull. Blood poured out. And I saw it, saw the only bit of life I'd seen in her flash across her eyes as she took her last breath. Relief.

She wanted to die.

My gut squeezed. What had happened to her to make her *want* to die? To have no hope left in her broken heart?

"You killed her!" I snarled. "Why did you kill her?"

Ollie wiped his knife on one of his men's coat and put it back in his suit jacket. "Why do I need her when I have you? Now I have the real thing. After all these years, I finally have you. No more pretenders."

"You *don't* have me," I said, the words clear and loud. "You'll *never* have me."

Ollie flew at me, stopping only an inch from my face. Spittle flew from his mouth as he spoke. "And who does? *Adley*. Fucking Arthur Adley." He laughed. "And you think me a demon? He's a fucking monster."

"He doesn't traffic people," I spat. Ollie shook his head, as if he was disappointed in me. No—as if he was sad on my behalf.

Ollie cupped my cheeks. I tried to pull away, but his hold was iron-clad. And I hated it. I hated it because Arthur held me like this. He always held me like this. When he did, I felt wanted. I felt safe. I felt adored.

When Ollie did it, I felt violated.

"You poor, poor, naïve woman," Ollie said, his tone as soft as if he were speaking to a toddler. "You have no idea of the evil that lives inside him. You haven't seen the amount of darkness that lives in his soul. Aren't you afraid of that darkness inside him?"

I made sure I was looking right into Ollie's eyes. "You haven't seen mine yet."

Ollie reared back as if he didn't recognise me. As if whatever version of me he craved had been poisoned by Arthur's influence. Good. I wanted to be ruined in his eyes. The truth was, Ollie didn't know me now. He had never met *this* Cheska. The one who had been robbed of all her family, her friends. And it wasn't by Arthur. It was by *him*. All of this shit was because of *him*.

He'd poisoned me. He'd ruined the girl he used to crave. I was a monster of his own creation.

Ollie got to his feet, and I knew by the disgusted look he threw my way that I had pushed him too far. I didn't care if he wanted to toss me aside. I wanted him to never touch me. I wanted him to die. I glanced at the girl on the floor. He had to die for killing her, hurting her, stealing her from this life.

"She was a piss-poor imitation of you," Ollie said, following my gaze. "Her parents had really fucked up with their loan. Made a deal with me that they couldn't repay." He kicked her, rolling her onto her back. He shrugged. "But she was relatively cheap to buy. Her parent's debts weren't too much to cover." He took his gaze from the girl and, with a smirk tugging on his lips, said, "Unlike you."

It took a while for his words to sink in. For them to register. My heart shuddered at what he was implying. I shook my head, faster and faster the more his hooked lip turned into a triumphant grin.

He didn't mean it. He was fucking with me.

"I wanted you." Ollie sighed. "But my old man thought my need for you was weird. Kept telling me to forget about you. That I was being a creep." He shrugged. "Unfortunately, a few days later my old man had a terrible, terrible helicopter accident and met his untimely end, leaving little old me in charge of our empire, of the organisation that was unthreading the underworld, one stitch at a time."

Cold. All I felt was coldness. Shards of ice sank into my flesh and scraped down each of my bones, making them ache. It was excruciating. "Our business fell to me, and I had a few people I suddenly needed to pay up earlier than planned."

My dad. Hugo.

"You guessed it." He made sure I was listening as he said, "They didn't take too much convincing. We all knew Hugo didn't love you, not like that anyway. He only ever wanted the company. And dear old Dad was in such deep shit that I made him an offer he couldn't refuse."

"You're lying," I hissed, but my voice lacked any kind of strength.

"It was simple really," Ollie said. "To set it all up. You were due to get married—of course that wasn't ever going to happen once the deal was done. But you didn't have to know that."

"You killed them," I said, feeling that ice start to thaw, rage sneaking through.

"Or did we set that video up to make you think that?"

Every part of me stilled.

No ... no, no, no ... He was lying. He *had* to be lying.

Ollie nodded at his men, smiling at me as they left the room. I heard muffled voices outside the room we were in. Then, appearing at the doorway, risen from the dead, was my father and Hugo.

I broke. As I saw their faces, alive and well, I broke apart.

"Cheska," Hugo whispered, and the colour drained from his face. The man holding his arm pushed him into the room. Hugo fell to the floor a few feet from where we sat.

"Cheska, no ..." Gene said beside me. His voice was filled with sorrow for what I was seeing.

My stare moved from Hugo to my father. My father. Who had sold me. Who Ollie said had *sold* me.

"Cheska," Dad said, and his eyes shimmered with tears. He tried to reach for me, but the man holding him brought him to his knees too, right beside Hugo. They looked the same as they always had. Rumpled from being brought here, but the same.

Where had they been living all this time? Had they even felt guilty for what they had done?

"No," I said, refusing to believe the truth that was staring me in the face.

"Cheska," Hugo said, face crumpling. "I'm sorry, I'm so sorry."

"You sold me," I said, but I was looking right at my father. My *father*. The man who was supposed to care for me. Love me. But all he had ever been was cold. After Mum died, there had been no love in my world. For once, I was glad my mum was dead. If she were still alive, this would have killed her.

"Ollie said he was going to take care of you. He said he wouldn't hurt you. That he loved you." My dad swallowed. As if he knew the words he was spilling were utter bollocks. "You always liked Ollie." Dad's head dropped, and in my whole life I had never seen him look broken. He had never been anything but confident and strong. But before me now, he appeared weak, defeated. Finally, I saw the guilt pulsing off him in waves.

"You sold me," I repeated, his look of apology bouncing off me like I was Teflon.

"The debts were too much." Hugo's eyes were like the girl's had been on the floor. Devoid of life. And I knew, looking at my old fiancé, that he was wracked with the guilt he rightly should have felt. Hugo's ambition had always been his Achille's heel.

I'd just never dreamed that I would be the person they sold out to save their own skins.

"You see, Cheska," Ollie said. "I *was* your saviour." Ollie walked to where my dad and Hugo kneeled. "Your own family didn't deserve you." He shook his head at them as though disappointed in them himself. "You were just fortunate that I was the one they bargained with for your life. I, who loved you. I, who could give you the world."

"A world built on nothing but terror," I snapped, but I didn't take my eyes off Dad. *How could he do this to me? His only daughter ...*

Dad lifted his head. "I'm sorry." His apology tried to hook onto my heart. I cast it away. Hugo's blank expression remained lowered. He was a shell. No more than a living corpse.

"Adley's firm is built on terror, but you spread your legs for him easy enough," Ollie hissed, and I saw my dad's face redden. I saw the slight against me inspire a surge of anger inside him.

"Don't you fucking *dare*," my dad snapped at Ollie, the authoritarian I knew rising to the surface. "Don't you fucking dare—" Before my dad even had time to finish his sentence, Ollie pulled out his gun and, this time, fired a bullet straight through my dad's head for real.

Dad immediately slumped to the ground.

"I'm sorry, baby. Please forgive me," Hugo said, then, finding some spark of life, charged at Ollie. He knocked Ollie to the ground, and I screamed. I screamed as blood drained from my dad's body. And I screamed as one of Ollie's men put the barrel of his gun to Hugo's temple and fired. The next second he was on the floor, beside my dad, Ollie rolling out from underneath him.

Tears streamed down my face, and I didn't think I could take any more. I couldn't take any more blood. Any more deception. Any more death. How much could one person take before they broke?

"Cheska," Gene said, clearly seeing my emotional freefall. I looked at him beside me. "Stay strong. You have to stay strong." I closed my eyes and tried to block out my family on the floor, the girl who at first glance looked like me.

Death. So much death.

Ollie dropped to kneel before me. "Shh, sweetheart."

Looking him dead in the eyes, I spat in his face. "Go to fucking hell," I said and, in his presence, felt my heart turn to stone.

Ollie wiped the spit from his face, then grabbed my hair. He yanked me to my feet, my scalp screaming at the pain, and dragged me to a smaller room at the back of the garage. I heard one of Ollie's men dragging Gene behind us. Ollie threw me on the floor. My cheek slammed against the cement.

"You need to watch your mouth, sweetheart."

I rose to my hands. "You killed Arthur's mum and sister, didn't you?" Ollie stopped dead, then turned to face me. "The fire? The cottage?"

"My dad ordered that one. I was a bit young back then to be making murderous decisions." Gene made a choked sound at the confession. Ollie shrugged. "My old man hated Alfie as much as I hate Arthur. I was glad they fucking burned."

"He'll kill you," I said coldly as Ollie went to shut the door. "He'll find me here and *kill* you."

Ollie paused. "He has no idea who the fuck we are," he said, pride on his face. "For years we've existed here in good old London Town, and no one has found us. My old man made sure of it."

"But that was him, your *dad*." I watched the smile fall from Ollie's face. "*You'll* fuck up. You have fucked up. You fucked up the minute you started messing with the Adleys. You've been too messy in your obsessive search for me, in your need for revenge. You're not your dad. He built an empire. He was Xerxes. You're just the heir who will never match up. And you'll see this empire fall."

"Careful, Cheska," Ollie said. "You don't want to join your family on the floor out here." He held the door, his hands turning white, betraying his ire. "Arthur Adley has no idea where we are. You forget, Freddie knows him. Has been with his family his entire life. He can read Arthur like a book. Adley's hot-headed. He's predictable. And if he does find us ..." Ollie shrugged. "Then he'll join his father. It's about time that entire scumbag family ate dirt. They're a blight on our city and need to be destroyed." He pointed at Gene. "And I'm thinking I'll start with you."

Ollie slammed the door, and the room plunged into a heavy silence. I heard Ollie barking orders at his men. My head buzzed with every-thing that had just happened. I held myself high and vowed not to break.

If we got out of this, that could come later. I could succumb to the pain then. Right now, I had to be steel. I had to be strong. Shifting my body, I angled myself so I could feel Gene's hands. I wrapped my fingers around his and held on tightly.

Freddie might have known Arthur. He might have thought he knew everything about him. But he only knew the Arthur of old.

He didn't know that Arthur had given me a tracker, didn't know that he had sent Ronnie and Vera on a mission to find out who this fucked-up "empire" actually belonged to. And more than that, he didn't know the *new* Arthur—the Arthur who had *me*. The man he had become since he had let me into his walled heart.

And Freddie didn't know the love we shared, the bond that existed between us—infallible, unmoving, vengeful toward those who tried to keep us apart.

Ollie Lawson had no idea what was coming. Because if they thought Arthur was evil before this, that he had untapped darkness in his veins ... They had no idea of the monster he would become to get me back.

I stared at the bracelet on my wrist, practically feeling Arthur's reassuring voice whisper in my ear ... *Hold on, princess. I'm coming to get you. You're never leaving me. I'll never let you go* ...

So, I leaned against Gene, took a strengthening breath, and waited for my dark king to storm the enemy castle.

CHAPTER SEVENTEEN

ARTHUR

Charlie joined me outside the dock's main office. He had been working the past few hours on organising the other gangs Lawson's syndicate had fucked with. The minute I had called them all and told them who'd been attacking them, sending them the proof Ronnie had found, they were all in. Ready and fucking willing to bring these fuckers down —tonight.

Tonight would be another motherfucking blitzkrieg raining down on London. Ronnie, Vera and the hackers had managed to find us every cell, the addresses and headquarters of every one of those cock-suckers throughout London. From Ollie Lawson down to the piece of shit that loaded the slaves on boats and delivered the "products" to people's homes.

They were all dying tonight.

Every seasoned gangster in London was prepped and primed to be done with the empire Lawson thought he ran.

"No one goes in until we do. No leaks. Lawson'll run if he thinks we're on to him. I'm not risking that," I said.

"They've got their orders," Charlie said. "They know if anything goes wrong on their end, we won't get them all." Charlie exhaled. "Every fucker we know is ready for these bastards to die."

I flicked my finished cig onto the ground as Eric whistled and all our soldiers gathered around us. Betsy, Ronnie and Vera came out of the office behind me. Dressed in black, guns and knives at the ready. Vinnie stood beside Eric. He was as still as night. He was about to face off with the organisation who had killed Pearl. Who had taken my sister from his arms, his life. He was ready to watch them die. Ready to send them all to fucking hell. We all were.

I turned to Vera. "You get the bobbies sorted?" We had more than enough moles in the police to build a fucking mountain. Vera had put the word out that something big was going down tonight. And if they heard anything untoward, they were to turn their little piggy noses away. They'd been told that our taking the arseholes out would cut trafficking in the city by at least thirty percent, and if that sounded appealing to them, then they'd turn a blind eye tonight when the London underworld went up in fucking flames.

That, and there would be a distraction planted in central London, smack bang in the middle of tourist central. The Irish had told me they'd sort that. Which meant the night was ready for our version of lightning war.

Tonight, the Lawson gang would burn, just like they'd burned my mum and sister. Like they would soon burn in hell.

I faced my soldiers, all dressed in black, each decked out with a fuck-ton of guns, ammo and knives. Lawson had teams of men guarding the abandoned buildings. I wasn't taking any chances. We were to fucking drive into the yard and rain bullets on all the cunts. No theatrics. No fannying about. Just a straight-up fucking shoot-out.

Then I'd find Lawson and Freddie. Find Cheska and Gene.

"You know your orders," I said to my men. "Leave Lawson and Freddie to us," I said, nudging my head toward to my family. "Once all their men are down, secure the perimeter and don't let anyone in their organisation live. You shoot to fucking kill. None of them breathe a single breath when we're done with them." My soldiers nodded, hard as fuck for the lives they were about to take.

Charlie's phone beeped over and over, and he nodded at me. "Everyone is ready. Royal, Seamus, Vano, the Italians ... all of them. Locked and loaded and ready to fucking roll."

"Fall out," I ordered my men, and everyone loaded into the back of the vans. Mikey and Jim, my generals, took up the lead of their units. I climbed into the last van, my family all climbing in beside me. I sat on the bench seat and sparked up another cig. I checked my guns were loaded and all my knives were accounted for. Then I leaned my head back on the wall of the van and felt it pull off the drive.

My family were silent as we made our way to Deptford. The nicotine calmed me, and I fought back the anger that was pushing and pushing to break free.

Not yet. Not fucking yet.

But soon. Soon I would unleash the fucking demons inside me. I'd lay them all at Freddie and Lawson's feet.

"I'll be okay, baby. I promise," Vinnie was saying to his imaginary Pearl. His pupils were blown and he was strapped with guns. He kissed her on the cheek, then put his arm around her. "I won't let anyone hurt us." Vinnie glanced over at me, then back at Pearl. "I'll look after him, I swear."

I took a deep breath, knowing he was talking about me. Eric met my eyes and nodded. He was ready. More than fucking ready to get his brother back. A pair of green-brown eyes entered my head, and I kept them there, suspended in the air. Right in my line of sight. I kept them there as a talisman. As a fucking guide toward my bird locked inside that fucking abandoned garage.

I glanced down at my phone—one of my replacements for the one those Lawson fuckers had smashed. I pulled up the app and saw that Cheska hadn't moved for thirty minutes. From the blueprints we'd managed to get of the garage, she was being kept in some back office.

I didn't even entertain the idea that she had been harmed. I needed to keep the lid on my rage until we were there. Thinking of her in any state but fucking perfect made the rage bleed out and seep into my bones, my flesh, ripping through my enforced calm.

"Eyes fucking forward," I said to my family, who were all looking up at me. "Just like we did with the Russians. We go in there and offer no fucking mercy." They all either nodded their heads, gripped their guns or flicked their knives. "Once the Lawson soldiers have been put the fuck down, we hunt for Ollie and Freddie." My leather-gloved hand tightened around the butt of my gun. "Then take my lead. We'll see what those cunts do first." I pointed at my gun. "We'll take it from there."

The rest of the ride was made in silence. We stopped, and the driver banged his fist on the partition between us and him. Charlie waited for my signal. I checked the tracker again; Chelsea Girl still hadn't moved.

"Light them the fuck up," I said to Charlie, and he sent the cue for the other syndicates scattered around the city to move in and destroy these pricks once and for all.

I threw a new cig into my mouth, balancing it between my lips, then nodded to Eric to kick open the van doors. He did, my soldiers lining up into one long fucking wall of death. Lawson's cunts, surprised by our arrival, came crawling from the abandoned buildings, shots firing.

I cocked my gun, then brought the fucking rain.

Taking my first round of shots as their cue, Adley soldiers opened fire on the mass of Lawson men trying to take us down. I walked forward, my family and soldiers never breaking our line.

We pushed on, one fucking lethal unit. Lawson men started dropping, their scattered defence crumbling under the surprise attack. I sucked on my cig as I ploughed bullet after bullet into the fuckers that had come for my family, Cheska's family, my fucking blood.

Vinnie laughed manically as he pounded holes in heads and hearts. Ronnie screamed bloody revenge, tears streaming down her face as her bullets hit their targets. We pushed and pushed forward, until Eric shouted, "Now!" and gave Mikey and Jim the signal to split off with their men into the other buildings.

Seeing the garage right before us, my family and I brought down the last few stragglers at the front of the old building and stormed inside. I threw my gun over my shoulder and strode toward the door that led to where Cheska and Gene were being held. I stopped at the door and took an inhale of my cig.

Then I closed my eyes and let the rage I'd been holding back for hours fill my muscles and bones, fucking infuse my blood with lava, ready to unleash hell on the cunts behind the door.

I kicked the door open, and right in front of me, sitting on a fucking old armchair, was Ollie Lawson. And around him were heads. Motherfucking heads on spikes. Heads that had been severed from their bodies. I scanned my eyes over them and knew them immediately.

Cheska's old man.

Hugo, and—

My fucking heart stopped dead as my eyes fell on the third head. Brown hair, olive skin, open green-brown eyes, full fucking lips. I was about to explode. About to lose my fucking head and tear this fuckwit apart with my bare hands, when I looked closer.

It wasn't Cheska.

My fucking heart jumped back to life. It wasn't fucking Cheska.

"Be honest," Ollie said, his legs crossed and his hands clasped on his lap. "I almost had you."

The door slammed shut behind us, footsteps charging toward me. I knew who it was without looking. But before Freddie could get to me, Eric smashed the butt of his gun into Freddie's face and grabbed him, pulling his arms behind his back.

"Same fucking move you always do, tosser," Eric snarled. "Should have known you'd be too fucking thick to try something new."

I heard Freddie fighting against Eric. But that fucker wasn't getting out of Eric's hold anytime soon. I flicked my cig at Ollie's feet, unconcerned about my traitorous brother for now. Ollie watched the butt nearly hit his shoes and smiled at me.

I was going to wipe that smirk off his ugly fucking face.

"So?" Ollie sat back in his seat like we were having a casual conversation. "What brings you to my neck of the woods?"

"Where is she?" I growled, playing the fucking game. Freddie could stew a little in Eric's arms until I was ready to end him. I had to deal with this piece of shit first.

"Oh, you mean Cheska?" Ollie got to his feet. He gestured to the heads of her old man and Hugo. "She was feeling a little unwell after seeing these two. After believing they were dead." He paused. "They weren't, in case you didn't know." I did know; it was what I'd told my family back at my church. Ronnie's file had told me they had sold her to Lawson. They had been on their way to the Caribbean to start their lives over. But when Cheska had escaped Lawson's attack at the spa, he'd held them captive until she was found. Clearly, he'd never planned on letting them get abroad.

I let Lawson have his little fucking speech. Let him believe he was running this show. "You see, they sold her to me, Adley. Technically, she's mine. Payment for their debt." He shrugged. "You know the drill. You dabble in loaning money yourself."

"She's fucking *mine*," I said, my voice guttural and deadly.

"Now that's where you're wrong." I waited for him to continue. "You can't have her if you're dead."

The door to the room I knew Cheska and Gene were in slammed open, and two men opened fire. But we had been prepared. We'd read them fucking perfectly. Ollie wasn't the leader his old man had been. He was a sniffling, spoiled little fucker who had no idea what it took to run a successful fucking crime empire.

Vinnie and Vera were already there, firing bullets into their skulls. Brains spilled onto the floor.

Ollie went to draw his gun, but I was there in a second, sending my fist into his ugly mug and slicing through his hamstrings with my knife. He screamed and fell to the floor. I kicked away his gun, circling him where he lay clutching his legs.

Then Cheska and Gene were dragged into the room by the last two of Lawson's men. Ronnie and Betsy checked the other offices, searching for anyone else. But my eyes were fixed on Cheska. On her beautiful fucking face. Her perfect face that had been beaten, blood running down it. The entire room filled with red as a murderous mist descended over my eyes.

They'd touched my girl. This cunt had touched my fucking girl!

"Let them go," I said venomously to the men who held them. Ollie laughed, actually fucking laughed as he lay on the floor.

The men were distracted by their gaffer's laughter. Charlie used that distraction to aim his gun at their heads and send bullets right into their skulls. Cheska choked on a sob as the man behind her fell away and Vera and Ronnie reached her. They cut the tape from Gene's and her hands.

"Arthur," Cheska whispered in relief, then she saw the spikes around Ollie, the heads impaled on the top. As she walked closer to me, she couldn't take her eyes off her dad and Hugo and whoever the fuck the Cheska lookalike was on the end.

Tears filled her eyes and ran down her cheeks. But she didn't sob. She didn't fucking break. Instead I saw darkness fill her eyes. The same darkness that lived in me—what was mine was now hers too.

I took Cheska's hand and pulled her to my side. I smashed my lips to hers, devouring the fucking mouth I loved so much. I didn't want to let her go. I needed to keep her beside me, but I had to deal with the twat on the floor.

I released Cheska, then gestured with my chin for her to step back. Ollie was glaring at me from the ground. The fucker hadn't liked me kissing my bird.

I laughed coldly, then spread out my arms. "This is it?" I shouted around the empty room. "*This* is the great Lawson Empire?" Ollie was watching me, but now there was amusement in his unhinged eyes. It just pissed me the fuck off. I moved near him and booted him in the shin. I heard a crack and knew I'd snapped his bone. I lit a cig, not taking my eyes off the fucker moaning and gripping his ruined leg.

Cheska stood close by, still as a fucking statue, eyes fixed on Lawson. Targeted on Lawson. She wore a look of death in her eyes, and it was making me fucking hard.

"She screamed, you know," Ollie said, pulling my focus from my bird, seemingly not giving a shit that he was about to die by my hand. I circled him, stamping down on his arm as I passed. Another snap came, and Ollie screamed out into the room. But that scream turned into a high-pitched laugh. A fucking psychotic scream.

"As the fire ate up the cottage, she screamed," he said, panting through his pain.

My blood boiled the minute he mentioned the cottage, fucking propelling me forward. I stamped down on the same arm again. The limb dropped lifelessly at his side. I spat on his face. "Keep talking about my mum and I'll fucking make this last all night, cunt. I'll break you piece by piece, tear your flesh off in strips and then add your severed fucking head to one of these spikes."

Lawson smiled, and shifted until he was kneeling on one knee, struggling to find balance. The cunt met me square in the eyes and said, "Who said I was talking about your mum?"

"I'll kill you!" Vinnie roared, but Charlie held him back before he could rip Ollie's tongue from his throat. "You don't talk about my Pearl. You don't ever fucking talk about my Pearl." Vinnie was breathing hard, his face bright red.

I glared at Lawson. He was going to die. Slowly.

I stepped forward, my knife in hand.

But just as I did, my phone beeped with a message, and Ollie's face lit up. "Seems not all my men are dead yet." A wide smile pulled on his lips. I didn't know what the fuck he was talking about. "Well?" he asked. "Aren't you going to look? If it ever came to this, I wanted to be sure that I was here while you saw it."

"I'd rather kill you than watch some fucking video you get hard about sending," I said.

More beeps went off around me, then silence.

A few seconds later, Charlie walked toward me, holding out his phone. His face looked like it'd seen a fucking ghost.

My cousin pressed play on the video. Betsy and Vera kept their eyes trained on Ollie as I watched. But Lawson only had eyes for me. I could feel the weight of his stare as the video started playing.

I watched as some fucker in the usual black clothes and balaclava carried my sister out of the back door of the cottage. The place was burning, my mum inside, but someone had gone in for Pearl. My heart fucking pounded like a canon at seeing my sister alive, but being taken away.

The video cut off. My hands were fucking shaking with rage, when another scene started to play. Of a woman in a suit. A blond woman with Pearl's eyes. A woman in her early twenties ...

My lungs seized up, and I knew what I was seeing. My mind tried to fucking catch up.

Pearl ...

"Annie," Ollie said, speaking my mother's name. He didn't deserve to speak her motherfucking name. I would rip out his dirty fucking tongue if he said it again. "That right there is my sister, Annie Lawson."

Victory spread across his face as his words sank into my head. Ollie's arm hung by his side, his leg was broken, but the fucker still glared at me. "What better way to fuck you all up than to take your beloved little sister and make her one of our own?"

"You lie," I snarled, but I stared down at the woman sitting in a café in some other fucking country—France or Switzerland or some shit by the looks of things. Someone approached her table, and she smiled, shaking their hand. Every part of me froze. Because I knew that fucking smile.

It was Pearl ... They'd fucking taken Pearl!

"Cunt!" I flew at Ollie, but the fucker was prepared. He pulled out a gun and fired a shot, grazing my arm. I didn't feel the pain, I didn't stop coming at him—I just needed this arsehole dead.

As I lifted my hand to smash his face, he said, "Annie runs our European enterprise." I stilled and pictured her in that suit, shaking someone's hand. The video she clearly didn't know was being recorded.

"Trafficking?" Betsy asked, devastation in her voice. "Pearl's involved in trafficking?"

Ollie raised an eyebrow at my cousin. "Annie wouldn't stand for that shit." He looked at me again. "Quite the spitfire, my sister." I was going to kill him. I had to fucking *kill* him. Pearl was my sister, not his. *My* fucking little sister.

"She's more suited to drugs and guns." He smiled again. "Quite similar tastes to you, actually. She knows nothing about the human trafficking side of our business." He shuddered. "Annie can be quite the little sadist if she doesn't like someone—likes to make them pay. And she loves me. Her big brother. I would never tell her about the true nature of our London ventures. Wouldn't want to incur her wrath."

"Where is she?" I snarled.

"Where the *fuck* is she?!" Vinnie screamed behind me, still being held in Charlie's arms.

"Not here," Ollie said, and my mind became a fucking sludgy mess. Pearl was fucking alive, and working for the Lawsons. No, not working for. She *was* a fucking Lawson. A fucking Adley adopted by the Lawsons, wearing our murdered mum's name.

"She doesn't remember a thing about you," Ollie said, and I heard Betsy suck in a sharp breath like she'd been fucking shot. "She doesn't know that the famous Adley family was once hers." He laughed, and the sound of it grated on my nerves. "In fact, she fucking hates you. *Loathes* you ..." Ollie leaned into me. But I was fucking paralysed, the crack in my chest draining of lava and hollowing out to nothing.

My sister hated us. Hated *me*.

"And if anything happens to her dearest big brother—*me*—then she has orders to bring you all down." All I could see in my head was Pearl. Pearl was alive. Sitting at the café, smiling and shaking some wanker's hand.

My little sister was fucking *alive*.

Ollie moved the gun to my forehead. The barrel pressed into my skin, and fire lit in his fucking eyes. Death. He wanted to bring me death.

I saw blackness dance in my vision, Satan himself ready to drag us both down. "Do it," I snarled, eyes fucking lit, pushing against the gun. "FUCKING DO IT!" I shouted, lifting my own gun to his skull. Ollie smiled a wide smile, clicked off the safety of his gun just as I clicked off mine. We were going to die. The fucker would die right the fuck now even if I had to go down into a fucking blazing inferno myself to see it done ...

Then he froze.

His eyes widened.

And Lawson started choking, lips moving. His hand shook and his gun dropped to the ground. I drew my head back as he fell to the floor, only to see Cheska stood behind him, one hairpin blade in her hand, and the other in Ollie Lawson's neck, the blade cutting right through his pulse.

Her green-brown eyes lifted to mine. I fucking breathed, my slam-

LORD OF LONDON TOWN

ming heart wrecking my fucking sternum. Then I was on my feet, crushing my mouth to hers, her hands desperately raking at my back, my neck and my head. "Princess," I croaked, dropping my hands to her body, checking she was okay.

She was alive.

She was fucking alive.

"I love you," she said, pulling back and staring into my eyes, no tears. There were no fucking tears.

I whipped around. Freddie was glaring my way, still in Eric's arms. But I saw the fear in the rat's eyes. His boss was gone, and now it was his time to face the fucking reaper.

"You knew she was alive." I stopped in front of him. "All this time, and you fucking *knew* Pearl was alive. That she was a motherfucking Lawson." I'd never wanted to kill anyone as much as I wanted to kill this fucker. This two-faced mothercunting *rat.*

Freddie smirked. He knew he was on borrowed time. But he used his final minutes to stick the dagger further into my back. "My old man set it up. Knew when your mum and Pearl would be alone. He organised for the Lawsons to torch the place, then took her from the cottage and away from you fuckers. And now she's one of us." His eyes flared. "And she'll kill you. She'll kill all of you when she finds out what you've done." Eric's gaze burned with fury. "If you're the dark lord, then she's hell itself." Freddie nodded his head. "She'll come for you, Artie. Your sister, the one you fucking mourned, missed every day, *hates* you, and will come to kill you. She—"

I grabbed his face and snapped his neck before he could say anything else. I didn't want to hear his fucking voice anymore. Freddie slumped in Eric's arms, and Eric dropped him to the ground like last week's rubbish.

I turned. All my family were looking at me, their eyes fucking wracked with both pain and rage at the news about Pearl.

My sister was alive.

Vinnie was staring at the ground, his head more than fucked. Everyone looked at me for answers.

I had none. I fucking had *none!*

Rage built from the bottom of my feet to my motherfucking skull.

And I roared. I threw my head back and *roared*. My bellow echoed off the walls, the fucking fight draining out of me. She was alive. Pearl was alive, and she hated us. Despised us. Wanted to fucking see us fall—

Arms wrapped around me from behind.

Cheska.

Turning, I met her watery eyes, yanked her close and held her to my chest. "We'll get her back," she said, and then kissed me. She fucking kissed the fuck out of me, and my body calmed back down.

Always the water to my fucking fire.

I held on to my bird, then cupped her bloodied cheeks. "You fucking killed him." I searched her face for any sign of regret, of shock or guilt. Charlie and my family started taking calls in the background, back to fucking business. But it was all white noise as I looked at my woman, my princess, my fucking queen.

"He deserved to die," she said coldly, her eyes flashing with darkness. "For what he's done. For *everything* he's done to us all." My forehead fell against hers, and everything that was displaced inside me fucking clicked together. In that moment, I knew that aura of darkness, the one Vinnie had told me was wrapped around me, had merged with her red. The same. Whatever it was that Vinnie saw around us, we now were the fucking same. No beginning to mine, no end to hers.

"You came for me," she whispered, and I dropped my hand to the bracelet on her wrist, thanking fuck I'd got her it.

"I told you I would," I growled, taking her mouth again. Her tongue tasted like fucking heaven. "You're never leaving me. Never fucking leaving my side. From now the fuck on, you're an Adley, and whatever we do, you'll be right by my bastard side."

Cheska smiled against my mouth and sighed. "I'm an Adley now."

I growled at my surname on her lips, fucking kissed her harder, forced myself to break away, then said to my family, "Let's get the fuck home."

CHAPTER EIGHTEEN

CHESKA

I stepped out of the shower, breathing in the humid, damp air. I wrapped the towel around me and entered the bedroom. It took me a few seconds to realise Arthur was absent and Eva Adley sat on the armchair. I stopped dead and met her hard gaze.

She was dressed impeccably as always, but as I studied her further, I saw a paleness in her cheeks and redness in her eyes. My heart broke for the Adley matriarch. She had just lost her only remaining son at the murderous hands of a boy she'd raised as a much-loved grandchild. A traitor raised to bring her family down from inside.

"Eva," I said in greeting and walked toward her. She remained silent, watching me with stony eyes as I stopped a few feet away from where she sat. "I'm sorry," I said, feeling completely and utterly drained. "About Alfie. About Freddie. I'm so incredibly sorry."

Eva didn't react, didn't flinch. Instead she got to her feet and met me toe to toe. Her eyes ran down the length of me. I braced, waiting for her censure, for her cold dismissal. But when she opened her mouth, she said, "You killed Ollie Lawson." I couldn't speak, so I simply nodded.

Eva brushed by me, but as her hand wrapped around the doorknob she turned to face me. "It's a hard, dangerous and sometimes thankless job being the lady of this firm's gaffer."

I lifted my chin at the challenge in her voice. "I'm ready for it."

Eva's head tilted to the side as she regarded me. "The road ahead is going to be rough. Arthur won't rest until he has Pearl back. Until the rest of the Lawson enterprises are destroyed."

"I know."

Eva glanced to the roaring fire in the fireplace, then met my gaze once more. "Maybe I was wrong about you," she said, and warmth burst in my chest at those words. But then she shrugged, lips pursing. "We'll see." With that, she left our bedroom, closing the door behind her, her flicker of acceptance bringing a small smile to my lips.

I found him at their graves.

The sun had just started to rise over the Adley church, the dawning of a brand-new day. The harsh wind whipped around my damp hair, sending chills over my freshly-scrubbed skin. I had been desperate to wash the stain of last night from my body. But the stain on my mind wouldn't go no matter how much water the shower head had pelted down on me. The events of the night were branded onto my brain just as sure as the brand that Ollie's organisation wore proudly on their wrists.

I was still numb when I thought of Hugo and my dad. I knew I wouldn't always be. But it was as if my body couldn't take any more pain, had met its threshold over the past several weeks. It had rejected the heavy emotions trying to pierce me from within and created an impenetrable armour around my heart. An armour that only lowered for my new family and, of course, the king who held my heart in his firm grip.

My feet crunched on the fallen leaves on the ground. Hearing the noise, Arthur looked back and wordlessly held out his hand. The hand that I used to dream he would want me to grasp. The easy affection he now gave.

He was staring at the graves of his mum and sister, a frown on his face. Eyes glued on the new plot that had been dug for his dad, finally joining his beloved wife after all these years without her. We would bury him tomorrow; we would say our final goodbyes.

I clutched Arthur's hand tightly, giving him the silent support he no doubt needed. I read the epitaph on Pearl's grave, and I took a deep, sobering breath.

We had no idea whose few remains were buried in this small Adley graveyard. Remains found at the site of the cottage. No doubt planted there after Annie Adley and her much-loved cottage had become nothing but dust.

I laid my head on Arthur's arm, feeling the heaviness he held in his heart. "Everyone is in the living room. Vinnie is still in his bedroom. But everyone else is waiting ... for you."

Arthur was tired, his blue eyes worn and wracked with pain. Because although he had found out that his little sister was alive, he had also found out that she had no memory of belonging to this family, of him. And she despised them. If Ollie was correct, Pearl Adley would now be planning war on the brother she didn't even know she had in honour of the one who was a lie.

"Maybe we can put the meeting off until after we've all slept," I said. Arthur was still covered in dried blood. "Our family will understand. We're all at the end of our tethers."

"No. I want this dealt with." He turned to me and gathered me in his arms. "I want this fucking night over and done with." Arthur breathed in the scent of my freshly washed hair, shoulders sagging as if my mere presence calmed him, settled the rage I knew paced inside him, still seeking more revenge.

I wanted to take him to bed, clean him up and just hold him, letting him know that he was loved, that he was adored. But I also knew him. He took his role as the head of this family seriously. He bore the weight of the firm's pressures without complaint. I vowed that from now on, I'd help him share those burdens. I would lighten his load, even if that could only ever be by caring for him after everything was finished. After loose ends were tied up.

When Arthur released me, he lit a cigarette and put his arm around my shoulders, leading us back into the church, which was now patrolled by twice as many Adley soldiers than ever before.

Now that we were all back safe, he wasn't taking any chances.

We entered the living room. All the family but Vinnie and Gene were gathered on the familiar chairs. The fire blazed, and I breathed in the comforting scent of burning logs.

I stayed by Arthur's side as he poured out two gins at the bar, my hand on his lower back. He passed one gin to me, then sat down on his usual armchair, heading up the casual circle that made up his family meetings. Arthur pulled me onto his lap and placed a kiss on the back of my neck.

"We can get Ches her own chair, you know?" Eric said, a smirk on his face. It was the first bit of levity the day had brought.

"She stays right fucking here." Arthur put his arm around my waist and kept my back flush to his chest. I settled against his warmth, his scent of tobacco and musk seeping into my lungs. Arthur opened his mouth to speak, but Gene came through the doorway.

"Gene?" Eric shifted forward in his seat, no more laughter in his tone. "What's wrong? You okay?"

Gene nodded. He pointed at a spare chair—the chair Freddie used to occupy. "Is it alright if I sit?"

I gaped at him. Gene wanted to sit in on the family meeting. He had never sat in one before. He had never made any attempt to be included in the family business. Arthur and the others had always accepted that he had no desire to join the firm. I could tell by the bright eyes and hidden smiles shining Gene's way, they were more than okay with him taking the newly vacant seat.

"You belong here," Arthur said, and Gene sat down, his cheeks reddening under everyone's attention. But Arthur's words seemed to sink into his ears, and he sat straighter on the chair, as if he had finally found a purpose, a path out of the labyrinth he'd confessed to me he felt he lived in.

Gene met my eyes, and I winked at him. His lip curled up in a soft smirk. Then his eyes shyly drifted to Charlie. Charlie, who was already watching Gene, an unreadable expression on his face.

Charlie only tore his gaze away when Arthur spoke to him. Feeling warmth sprout in my chest, I leaned my head on Arthur's shoulder, looking at my battle-worn family with utter love and respect in my heart.

My family. I had a real family now.

As if he sensed my thoughts, Arthur's thumb moved up and down on my stomach, a gesture of comfort, of love.

"All the cells were wiped out. Not one fucker was left," Charlie said. He put his pipe back in his mouth. "Tip-offs were made to the bobbies about the whereabouts of the trafficked girls and where the Lawsons were holding them. As well as a list of addresses of people who have one or more of them in their homes."

Charlie met my eyes. "We've found a holding cell in Ollie's flat where he would keep the girls that looked like you. The ones he kept for his personal use." My stomach fell, my blood cooling to freezing temperatures. "When you're ready, we'll take you there, and the Old Bill will get a tip-off that Cheska Harlow-Wright was kidnapped by Ollie Lawson and has been held at his home all this time." Charlie flicked his hand in the air. "We'll let them find you, create a story for you to stick to, then lay all the blame at Lawson's feet. You can claim he ran when he got in bother with someone, leaving you there. Then you can put all this shite behind you and finally become one of us." Charlie winked at me and smiled.

"She already fucking *is* one of us," Arthur said, no argument in his voice.

"Hear, hear," Betsy said, holding up her drink.

Arthur turned to Eric. "Anything on Freddie?" Eric had got one of the soldiers to keep one of the Lawson men alive. The soldier had stayed behind at the garage when we left and got answers before disposing of him too.

"Just what the rat fucker had told us," Eric said. "His old man infiltrated your old man's circle years ago. He was one of old Lawson's right-hand men, from being a kid. He sent him into our firm to get them intel. When Freddie grew up, he was raised to do the same job. They fed information back to the Lawsons.

"When his old man died, Freddie was crushed, blamed us, and sought out his revenge. For years, he planned with Lawson how they would take us down."

Eric nodded at me. "Lawson's plan to kidnap Cheska was separate to the one meant for us." He shrugged. "But then that all changed." I took a deep breath to keep calm. "They never expected Cheska to come here. Ollie's stupid fucking mind was blown when Cheska turned up at The Sparrow Room after his attack on her had failed—Freddie had told him you hadn't seen each other for over a year, believed that you'd tossed Cheska aside.

"Freddie hadn't planned for shit to go down when it did, but when Ronnie traced the video he'd sent to you about your mum, he knew he was on borrowed time. That we'd soon find out we had a rat in our midst."

Eric gritted his teeth. "When your old man woke up, Freddie knew he could get you alone. Luckily for him, Alfie waking up coincided with the trap he'd left for us at the dock. Suddenly, he had a way to get you, Ches and him alone in the house—Gene being here was just a fortunate opportunity. He realised he could get to you while the rest of us were at the docks dealing with the shitshow they had staged." Eric inhaled. "He killed your old man of his own accord."

Arthur tensed beneath me. I took his hand and brought it to my mouth. I kissed the back of his palm and felt him relax, exhaling slowly through his nose.

Vinnie came barrelling down the hallway and hurtled into the living room, all rage and fury. His eyes were wide and his hair was in more disarray than normal. "She's gone," he said frantically. "Pearl," he said, his hands shaking. "I can't find her. She's fucking gone." The hallucination. The spectre of Pearl that kept him grounded, kept him somewhat sane. "She's fucking gone!" Vinnie stilled. "The video. The bird on the video. She's taken her away from me." He stopped dead, then, hands balling into fists, yelled, "That fucking imposter bitch has taken my Pearl away!"

Charlie got to his feet, palms up. "Calm down, Vinnie," he said, approaching Vinnie as if he were a wild animal. "We'll get her back," he said softly. "I swear to you, we'll bring her back to you." Vinnie breathed out, panting as though he'd been holding his breath for days.

"You promise?" he said to Charlie, holding on to Charlie's words as if they were an anchor to what little sanity he had left.

"Have I ever lied to you before?"

Vinnie shook his head. "No. No, you've never lied to me before."

"Let's get you a cup of tea. Everything's going to be okay." Charlie ushered Vinnie out of the room, leaving deathly silence in their wake.

"Ron?" Arthur said, breaking the tension Vinnie's outburst had brought.

Ronnie took a deep breath, readying to relay the information on Pearl she'd managed to find after we returned home. "It's true. It's all true. Pearl is alive and goes by the name Annie Lawson." Ronnie shook her head. "I don't know why she doesn't remember you, or her real family, but it's clear something happened to make her forget everything." Vera nodded at Ronnie to continue. "For all intents and purposes, Ollie was her big brother." Arthur stilled. "They took her to Switzerland, to get her away from this family. And there she was raised, schooled, still lives. Ollie visited her all the time. Pearl runs their drug business in Switzerland."

"Who the fuck are they?" Arthur asked, his voice rough like cut glass.

"The Sidel Group," Ronnie said. Arthur sucked in a short breath.

"You're fucking kidding me," Eric said.

I looked to Arthur for an explanation. His expression was stone, but his blue gaze burned with fire. "Our biggest rivals in Europe," Arthur said.

"Your sister runs the rival European business?"

"I—we—had never heard of her by name before," Vera said. "They kept her hidden—obviously. But she's the boss of the Sidels now. No doubt about it. Took over when their—*Ollie's*—dad died last year. We have no idea if she knows it was Ollie that killed him. We just know it's her."

Arthur laughed, but there was no humour in it. "My little sister is our rival. She fucking hates us and, according to Lawson, will have a fucking bounty on our heads for his death."

"We'll sort this," Betsy said to Arthur. Eric nodded at Betsy in agreement. "Pearl's safe ... even though she doesn't know us as her family anymore. She's safe over there in Switzerland, and she's alive. At least we can take comfort in that." Betsy downed her drink. "We'll get her back. Somehow, Arthur, we'll bring her back to us. To Vinnie ... to you."

Arthur exhaled, and I could hear exhaustion in his heavy breath. I put my hand on his cheek and turned his face to me. "Let's go to bed. Let's get you cleaned up, and let's get some sleep. We can come back to this another time. We won. We're all safe. Now it's time to rest a little."

"She's right," Vera said, tiredly getting to her feet. "I'm bloody knackered. We all are. I haven't got bags under my eyes, I have fucking suitcases." She took Ronnie's hand, holding on to it like she might never let go. "We're going to get some sleep too."

I got up from the chair and, keeping my hand in his, led Arthur from the living room and straight through our bedroom into our bathroom. I stripped off his clothes. Arthur watched me silently, heat burning in his gaze. I turned on the shower and took off my clothes too. I stepped into the shower with him and began cleaning him of the blood that still clung to his skin. Arthur didn't take his eyes off me the entire time. It was as though he couldn't believe I was here with him. As though he didn't want to close his eyes in case I disappeared.

When the water ran from red to clear, I switched off the shower and gently towelled us both off. I led him to the bed. Standing beside it, I placed my hands on Arthur's face and kissed him. Arthur didn't hesitate in pushing his tongue into my mouth, sliding it against mine. His hands wrapped around me, an iron cage, bringing me to his chest, his hardness pressing against my stomach.

I moaned at the feel of him, and Arthur lowered me to the mattress. My back pressed into the soft duvet, and he broke from my mouth and kissed my neck, forcing the awful events of last night from my mind, instead bringing me nothing but pleasure and heat and love.

He kissed down my stomach and to my hips. I rolled my hips as he widened my legs, wanting him, *needing* him inside me. His blue eyes caught mine as he wrenched my thighs apart and then licked along my pussy. I cried out as he sucked on my clit, as he pushed his fingers inside me and fought for me to forget tonight and just be with him. The man I loved. The one who came for me, the one who'd saved me.

Over and over again.

I had fallen for him at age thirteen, and now I was with him. In his home, a part of his family, standing proudly by his side.

"Arthur ..." I moaned, threading my hands through his hair. Arthur snarled as I pulled on the strands, and he licked me harder and faster until I was a panting mess on the bed, my eyes shutting as my orgasm closed in. Arthur pushed me and pushed me until I cried out, my trembling thighs trying to close around him, the cresting pleasure too much to stand.

Not giving me a moment's reprieve, Arthur crawled above me, his powerful, muscled body smothering mine. Framing my head with his arms, he pushed inside me, filing me so full I almost lost my mind. He thrust into me hard and fast, his gaze never straying from mine.

"I love you," I said, and he groaned, crushing his lips to mine. He kissed me until I couldn't breathe, until I had to rip my mouth away from his lips to suck in much-needed air.

But Arthur's mouth never left my skin, tasting every inch. We were damp from the shower and the rising heat between us. I raked at his back, and he dropped his forehead to mine as he pistoned into me. My eyes rolled back, and the familiar pleasure built and built until all I could smell and feel and taste was Arthur. Until he was inside me, within me, his soul melding with mine.

"Arthur." I came, my breasts pressing against his chest as I held him tightly to me. Arthur groaned, then, slamming into me one last time, he stilled, roaring out his release.

I clung to him. I held on to him as he caught his breath, beads of sweat forming on his dark brow. Arthur kissed me softly, kissed me and kissed me, until he drew back his head and, making sure he held my gaze, rasped, "Love you, princess. Fucking love you."

My heart leapt to my throat on hearing those words slip easily from his lips. On seeing the sincerity on Arthur's beautiful face as he spoke those three words, deep affection in his gravelled voice.

"I love you too," I whispered back, putting my shaking hand on his cheek. Arthur kissed my palm, then rolled onto his back, taking me with him. He wrapped his arm around me as he splayed me over his chest.

After a few minutes, our laboured breathing returned to normal and Arthur lit a cigarette. I looked up at his face, shifting so he could see me and I could see him. I pushed a fallen strand of black hair away from the frames of his glasses. "You came for me."

He held my gaze. "I'd go into fucking hell for you, princess."

Smiling, I traced my finger along his abdominal muscles. "You're the devil, aren't you? Hell is your domain. You could just walk right in."

Arthur's nostrils flared, and I saw the tug of amusement on his lips. "Then you have nothing to worry about," he said. "No one fucks with the devil." He leaned forward and took hold of my jaw. He opened my lips, then blew smoke into my mouth. I closed my eyes and inhaled the nicotine, feeling it rush through my blood.

When I exhaled the smoke and opened my eyes, he said, "And no one, from this day out, will dare fuck with my dark queen again, or I'll bring the wrath of a million bloodthirsty demons to their mother-fucking door." I believed him. I had seen the look on his face when I had been dragged from the back room, hands tied and face beaten. If fury had a physical body, it would have been Arthur in that moment.

Arthur stroked my cheek with his thumb. "You okay, princess?" I knew he was referring to my dad and Hugo. I thought of them. I shook my head, but the emotions I knew were within me were numbed right now, padlocked away in a familiar cage. Held back to keep me from falling apart. "No," I confessed. "But I will be." I smiled at him and kissed his chest, right over his heart. "Now I'm with you, I will be."

Arthur put the cigarette in his mouth and pulled me up his chest so my face hovered before his. It was my favourite move of his. It was as if I weighed nothing at all.

"You killed Lawson." Arthur searched my face. "You fucking killed Lawson."

"He deserved it," I said. Pride flashed across Arthur's concerned expression. I meant it. There wasn't a part of me that regretted taking Ollie's life. He'd had his gun to Arthur's head after ripping a hole through his heart about his sister. And I couldn't stand it. I'd had to act. Ollie had brought so much pain and death to too many people's lives. I couldn't regret ending the life of someone who would only hurt more and more people if he survived.

And *no one* hurt my Arthur.

"My queen," Arthur said, his words singing to my soul. He wrapped his arms around me and crushed me to his chest. "My fucking dark, corrupted queen. The most important piece on my board," he whispered. "The most fucking important piece in my bastard life." My chest burst with warmth, his words healing any severed nerves I had within me, attaching me further to his soul.

A while later, Arthur's breathing evened out. I lifted my head and, smiling, took the still-burning cigarette from between his lips and stubbed it out on the ashtray beside him. Then I laid my head on Arthur's chest and closed my eyes too.

My life had brought me darkness and pain, but I couldn't resent it when that darkness spoke to the darkness inside him. Together we would rise, and together we would live happily in our dark kingdom. We would find Pearl and bring her back to us. Somehow, we would bring her home at last.

Until then, I had him and he had me.

My lord of London Town, and I his lady, who stood by him, proud to embrace the dark.

EPILOGUE

ARTHUR

One month later

We walked into the pits, every fucker staring at us as we passed them. My arm was around Cheska's shoulders, and her head was high as the wankers all gaped. I took a drag of my cig, passing by the bare-knuckle fights and heading toward the killing pits.

Cheska was dressed in all black, those fucking leather trousers she loved showcasing her arse to perfection. I glared at anyone who tried to look at my bird, death in my eyes for anyone who dared get a fucking hard-on at her presence.

When we reached our seats at the main pit, I turned Chelsea Girl to face me and smashed my lips to hers. Cheska groaned into my mouth and ran her hand down my stomach, cupping my cock and making me lose my fucking mind. Growling, I pulled away, promising with my blazing glare that I was going to fuck her later. Right here, in the pits, up against the wall.

"Well, that was a fucking entrance," Royal said, coming behind me and slapping me on the shoulder. I turned and smirked. "Careful, brother, you almost cracked a smile. It was fucking disturbing," he said.

"Your boy ready?" I asked, nudging my chin at Rudge's younger cousin.

"He's pissed off tonight, so I'd throw a few grand on him if you want to be quids in by the end of the night. Always fights better when he's in a fucking mood."

"Five grand on the Hangman," Cheska said to our bookie, clearly hearing what Royal had said. Shaking his head in amusement, Royal went back to his boys, and I took my seat beside Cheska.

I lifted her off her seat and put her on my lap, where she fucking belonged. Her arm looped around my neck, and my arm around her waist told every bastard in these pits, in the entire fucking London underworld, that she was *mine*. That she was my fucking dark queen and none of these twats was to touch a bloody hair on her head, or they'd face my fucking wrath.

"My turn," Eric said when the current champion in the pit smashed through the skull of his opponent, killing him in one blow. Eric got up from his seat. He moved toward the edge of the pit and looked back at Betsy, a grin on his face. "I win this, and tonight, I'm taking you up the arse."

"You fucking wish," she snapped, but she smiled to herself and looked away.

Charlie shook his head at them, then leaned in closer to Gene, resuming whatever conversation they were having. It was the kid's first time here. And he seemed to be taking it better than I'd expected.

We'd waited to come back until Cheska had played the fucking game Charlie had planned for her and been "found" at Lawson's flat. The entire fucking world now knew Lawson for the smarmy cunt he was. Cheska had broken from her family's business, a silent board member only, and then moved her shit in with me at the church.

And she was never fucking leaving.

There'd been nothing from Pearl yet. But we knew her people were on the move. And heading to our fucking town. I'd be ready for her. Ready to remind her who the fuck she was. She was coming back to us —the easy way or the hard.

"Put me in," Vinnie said, standing right in front on of me, top off and fists clenched. His eyes were bloodshot and crazed. Since Pearl had "disappeared" from his side a few weeks ago, he'd lost weight, he was pale.

My brother had lost his motherfucking mind.

I flicked my chin at the second pit behind us, and Vinnie tore off, no doubt to rip some fucker's head off and toss it onto the sand.

Cheska didn't move off me all night, Vera and Ronnie talking to her beside me. Then the pits cleared out, and the real fucking fun began.

I slapped Cheska on the arse, and she got off my lap; I stood, taking off my suit jacket, shirt and tie. The Hangmen, the Irish and the Romani stayed, as always. And my soldiers brought the table of weapons to the pit.

I jumped down onto the sand and cracked my neck from side to side. My soldier brought out the first wanker who had dared to fuck with my firm. The hessian hood was ripped off his head, and he practically shat himself when I stood before him. I sparked up my cig and took a long inhale, letting the smoke fill my lungs.

I swung my arms wide. "Welcome to the Adley Court. You are charged with being a traitor. An Adley's word is his bond." I pointed at his face. "A bond you have broken. And I am here to collect." I spat on the sand in front of the cunt on the floor and flicked my head to the table of weapons. "Choose your weapon." The tosser didn't try to protest or beg for his life. He knew the fucking score.

He grabbed a crowbar and readied to fight. I glanced up to Cheska. "Get the fuck down here, princess." Cheska rose from her seat like the fucking Adley queen she was.

She strutted down the stairs to the pit and stood right at my side. Her rose scent was driving me fucking barmy. Her eyes fixed on mine, and her fucking lips looked too perfect painted bright red. So I took her mouth, my bird moaning into my mouth and grabbing on to my naked chest as I pushed my tongue against hers, smearing her red lipstick.

I pulled back, hard as fuck for her pussy and the kill I was about to take. I wiped the red off my face and smudged my thumb over her lips, before she caught it in her mouth and bit down hard.

Cheska met my eyes as I hissed, her fucking head high, owning both me and everyone in this fucking pit. "Pick one," I said to Cheska, pointing to the table of weapons.

Cheska walked to the table, brown hair swaying on her back and holding my black heart in her fucking hands. She reached for the spear and headed back to me.

Rising to her tiptoes, she kissed me on the mouth. Then, glaring at the traitorous fucker on the ground, she placed the spear in my waiting hand. "Baby?" she said, lip curled in disgust.

"Yeah, princess?"

"Make him scream."

So I did.

―――――

THE END

―――――

PLAYLIST

Take Me Back To London — *Ed Sheeran, Stormzy*
Come With Me Now — *KONGOS*
Bitter Sweet Symphony — *The Verve*
Fire — *Kasabian*
Broken — *Jake Bugg*
Do I Wanna Know — *Arctic Monkeys*
Got No Love — *The Kooks*
Hide and Seek — *Imogen Heap*
Mad World — *Lily Allen*
Devil Side — *Foxes*
Two Fingers — *Jake Bugg*
You're in Love with a Psycho — *Kasabian*
Firestarter — *The Prodigy*
White Flag — *Bishop Briggs*
The Cave — *Mumford & Sons*
The Prayer — *Bloc Party*
Fire — *Kasabian*
Exile (feat. Bon Iver) — *Taylor Swift, Bon Iver*
I'm Kissing You — *bshp*
you broke me first — *Tate McRae*

Arms Around You — *Jamie Grey*

I'm Not Okay — *RHODES*

Supermarket Flowers — *Ed Sheeran*

I Fall Apart — *Post Malone*

Be My Mistake — *The 1975*

Die Alone — *FINNEAS*

Feel Again (Feat. Au/Ra) — *Kina, Au/Ra*

9 Crimes — *Damien Rice*

I'm God — *Clams Casino, Imogen Heap*

Out of the Darkness — *Sleep Thieves*

Ain't No Grave — *Renée Elise Goldsberry*

What He Wrote — *Laura Marling*

Devil Town — *Cavetown*

Sleep On The Floor — *The Lumineers*

Monster — *Mumford & Sons*

Devil's Waitin' — *Black Rebel Motorcycle Club*

Daydream Believer — *Jonny Fears*

Let It Be — *Labrinth*

Scar — *Foxes*

Break In — *Halestorm*

Die A Little — *YUNGBLUD*

Here's to Us — *Halestorm*

Enjoy the Silence — *Lotte Kestner*

Seasons — *NEEDTOBREATHE*

Hometown Glory — *Adele*

ACKNOWLEDGEMENTS

Thank you to my husband, Stephen, for being my biggest supporter.

Roman, my little smooch. You are the absolute light of my life. I'm so blessed to be your mammy. I never thought it was possible to love somebody so much. You're the best thing I have ever done in my life. Everything is for you.

Mam and Dad, thank you for the continued support. Dad, thank you for always being a champion of my writing and helping me whenever I need you.

Samantha, Marc, Taylor, Isaac, Archie, and Elias, love you all.

Liz, thank you for being my super-agent and friend.

Neda and Ardent Prose, I am so happy that I jumped on board with you guys. You've made my life infinitely more organised. You kick PR ass!

To my TILLSTERS, I couldn't ask for better book friends. Thank you for all for everything you do for me. Here's to another step forward in our Dark Romance Revolution! I love how your little dark hearts are drawn to mine—like is drawn to like. My fellow *dark-hearted little nightmares*.

Thank you to all the AMAZING bloggers and Instagrammers that support my career, and the ones who help share my work, make the most unbelievable edits and videos and shout about it from the rooftops. You're appreciated more than you'll ever know. And lastly, thank you to the readers. Without you none of this would be possible. Dark Romance is my passion, the genre that calls to me most. It's not a 'go-to' genre for many people, but you guys get me, and for that I'll forever be grateful. Some people don't understand us, and our undying love for characters with dark hearts and questionable morals... But we have each other, and that's all we'll ever need!

Thank you for taking a walk on the dark side with me. It's a fun place to be once you take the leap.

"An Adley's word is his bond."

AUTHOR BIOGRAPHY

Tillie Cole hails from a small town in the North-East of England. She grew up on a farm with her English mother, Scottish father and older sister and a multitude of rescue animals. As soon as she could, Tillie left her rural roots for the bright lights of the big city.

After graduating from Newcastle University with a BA Hons in Religious Studies, Tillie followed her Professional Rugby player husband around the world for a decade, becoming a teacher in between and thoroughly enjoyed teaching High School students Social Studies before putting pen to paper, and finishing her first novel.

After several years living in Italy, Canada and the USA, Tillie has now settled back in her hometown in England, with her husband and son.

Tillie is both an independent and traditionally published author, and writes many genres including: Contemporary Romance, Dark Romance, Young Adult and New Adult novels.

When she is not writing, Tillie enjoys nothing more than spending time with her little family, curling up on her couch watching movies, drinking far too much coffee, and convincing herself that she really doesn't need that last square of chocolate.

FOLLOW TILLIE

https://www.facebook.com/tilliecoleauthor

Tillie Cole's TILLSTER FB Author Group

https://twitter.com/tillie_cole
Instagram: @authortilliecole

Or drop me an email at: authortilliecole@gmail.com

Or check out my website:
www.tilliecole.com

For all news on upcoming releases, join Tillie's newsletter

Subscribe to my YouTube channel

Printed by Amazon Italia Logistica S.r.l.
Torrazza Piemonte (TO), Italy